A Song I Knew by Heart

A Song I Knew by Heart

a novel

B R E T L O T T

R A N D O M   H O U S E
LARGE PRINT

By the rivers of Babylon we sat and wept
when we remembered Zion.
—PSALM 137

Where can I go from your Spirit?
Where can I flee from your presence?
—PSALM 139

for my home:
Melanie,
Zebulun,
and Jacob

PART I

Treasure

Chapter 1

I STOOD OUTSIDE my son Mahlon and his wife Ruth's bedroom door, in my hands two coffee cups, the pain sharp shards in my old fingers looped through the handles. I had on my pale blue bathrobe and slippers, my hair still in a net. I'd had it done just yesterday morning, before the funeral, and though I wore a net every night, funeral or no, there came to me last night as I slipped it on and settled into bed that somehow this was wrong. That worrying over my hair enough to put it in a net might somehow be a sin, this vanity.

But I put the net on, like every night, because it was what I'd done every night. It was my life, the way I lived it. Who I was.

A widow who lived with her son and daughter-in-law.

Eight years I'd been there with Mahlon and Ruth. Eight years since my husband Eli passed, and our old house out on 116 had revealed itself to be too big to live in. Just too big once Eli was gone, though the space he took up was no more than any other a man might take.

Because it was the love we had for each other filled that house. Love, one for the other. Then he was gone, me left behind to wander through our rooms, the house emptied of love with the last breath my husband gave out.

Now here I was, with coffee for two at Ruth and Mahlon's door. Up and breathing like every morning, but bringing coffee upstairs. Not sitting downstairs to my kitchen table, where until four days ago there'd been three cups poured and waiting, breakfast on the way.

Because now my son Mahlon was gone, too.

I pushed open the door, and there lay Ruth on the bed, beneath the Wedding Ring quilt I made for her and Mahlon. Cold sunlight fell in through the window, the shade left up last night. She was still asleep, inside the sometime blessing I'd known sleep could be, though half her face was in that light, the other in shadow. Her mouth was open, eyebrows knotted, her chin high like she might be singing some cold and sad song in her dreams, a song so sad she had no choice but to keep her eyes closed to it.

A song I knew by heart.

I looked out that window. Morning sun shone down on the frosted rooftops of the houses in this Massachusetts town, where I'd lived for the last fifty-six years. The air was the thick white veil November air will be, white with itself and that light. Through it, and beyond anything I could ever hope to touch, lay the hills beyond town, gray and empty as my heart this morning.

My only child had died. Killed four days before in a trick of light itself: my Mahlon, on his way home from visiting Lonny Thompson up to Sunderland, hit a patch of black ice from a cold snap too early.

Lonny Thompson. My Eli's best friend since their days at the submarine yards out to Portsmouth, New Hampshire, just after the war. Him the reason we'd moved here in the first place, why Eli brought me here once they were out of the service. He'd been like a father to my Mahlon after Eli was gone, and then'd been diagnosed with the cancer last April, Mahlon on his way home from visiting him.

Black ice on the roadway home. No way for

Mahlon to know it was there, his headlights no help at all. Useless as this sun in through their bedroom window.

And it came to me then, a moment as deep as the sorrow I was inside. A moment as unexpected and sharp as the death of my child.

This: the memory of light.

Light, and the way when I was a girl it fell through the pine and live oak I grew up in a thousand miles south of here, the way it fell through palmetto and magnolia and water oak too. Light sifting down through the woods to spread like scattered diamonds on the ground before me as I walked to the creek. Bright broken pieces of light on the pinestraw at my feet so many perfect gifts of warmth.

All this came to me, whole and perfect and real. All of it in just the time it took to look out that window to see those empty hills, the rooftops.

My boy, my Mahlon.

Ruth woke, stirred beneath the quilt. Her eyes blinked open, blue-green eyes so clear and crystalline there was never a doubt in my mind why my Mahlon'd loved her from the minute he met her. You could see in her eyes her good heart, constant and certain. It'd been my Mahlon's blessing to find her, to see that good heart, recognize in those eyes a heart worth holding on to. Twenty-three years they would have been married this next February.

Ruth's eyes shuddered open to this cold room, and I saw the ugly promise of what was left to her, a promise I'd seen fulfilled every day for the last eight years of my own life: her husband was gone, and wouldn't be back.

She blinked, blinked again, squinted at the light, her eyebrows still knotted up, her mouth still open. She quick reached from beneath the quilt to beside her, where, if God loved us all as He said He did, Mahlon should have been.

She still had on the black dress from yesterday. From the funeral. She hadn't taken it off last night.

I knew what she was just then being given, knew the pain of that move, of a hand to the flat quilt, to the pillow gone untouched, to cold sheets. It was a move wouldn't go away, this touching to see if any of what'd happened weren't a dream.

It was what I'd done every night these last eight years: come awake sometime from inside the forgiveness of sleep, and reach for my Eli.

Ruth's hand stopped when she found the empty pillow beside her, on her face the puzzlement that showed she knew it wasn't a dream.

"Bless your heart," I said, and moved toward the bed. Ruth blinked again, her eyes now on me and still with the startled look. Like I was no one she'd ever known.

Then her mouth finally closed, her chin set to trembling, and I knew her now better than I ever would've hoped.

It was grief she'd been given, the black and empty gift God gives you like it was something you were owed. It was grief she'd been given, and grief we shared.

"Naomi," she whispered, the word only sound. She reached that hand from the quilt out to me, sat up in bed, her full in the light now.

Naomi. My name.

Now she was crying, her eyes closed again, her mouth and chin giving in to this morning's discovery. One she'd make brand-new every morning from here to the end.

Still her hand reached for me, her shivering in her black dress. And still that empty whispered word *Naomi* hung before me, its own black dress. One I had to wear whether I wanted it or not.

The name of a woman whose husband had died, who knew the feel of cold sheets. The name now too of a woman whose only child was gone.

The name, I heard in the shattered heart that'd spoken it, of a woman whose life'd been poured out like water on the ground.

Ruth still held her hand out to me, and I whispered again, "Bless your heart," though the words were just as empty as my name. Just sound, air out of me.

I went to the dresser, set the coffee cups on Mahlon's side, next to his nametag from work, and the penholder, the spare change, and half-roll of cherry Lifesavers he dumped out of his pockets at the end of a day. What four days ago was only the clutter of a man's daily life, but was now, I saw, bits of the failed history of my own blood.

I turned to Ruth, up on the edge of the bed now, hands in her lap. Her eyes still closed, her heart let out the broken silver sound of grief I'd heard myself give up too many nights and days, and then I was beside her, and I reached to her. I touched her hair, felt the softness of it, felt the deep chestnut beauty of it. Beauty my son'd known and felt and never would again, and in that cold moment of seeing what had been and would never be again, I took my daughter-in-law in my arms, pulled her close to me. I closed my eyes, felt her arms rise to me, move slowly to me, and we held each other.

Two widows, in each other's arms. Another house emptied of love.

God in His heaven, and nothing right with the world.

And I had to ask again: Why call me Naomi?

NAOMI WAS A TEENAGE GIRL in a flowered cotton dress, a girl who walked summer afternoons barefoot through that broken perfect light of the woods to the creek. She was a girl who walked the pinestraw littered through the woods, a warm and prickly carpet beneath her, a girl born and raised in that South Carolina light, in a small town on a deepwater creek that led to a harbor that led to the great green sea.

And once through those woods, she was a girl who stood at the edge of the marsh that bordered the creek all bathed in unbroken light, colors all around too rich and beautiful and full of the peace of a girl's afternoons to be believed: the greens and browns and reds of the saltmarsh hay and yellowgrass, the shiny solid black of pluff mud at low tide, the soft green and blue of the creek itself. Shattered light banged up off the water those afternoons, the sun on its way down too fast, too fast, even though these were the longest days of the year, days that seemed somehow to stretch long and slow and full of themselves until now, in the afternoon, when the day seemed to hurry itself too fast for how slow and forgetful it'd been all day long.

That was when the girl, this Naomi, watched the water, and the harbor, and the church spires of Charleston across it all reaching up like they might pierce the sky itself; that was when she watched and watched, and then finally here they came: her daddy, and his shrimp boat, the *Mary Sweet,* making the long turn in from the harbor and into the creek, the trawler seines pulled high beside her clean white hull like hands up in praise, she always imagined, this girl standing each afternoon on a small bluff on a deepwater creek in a South Carolina town, all of it loved by this sun, warm down on her, perfect and whole and light.

And once she saw her daddy's boat head into the creek, she waited, waited, and then, when the *Mary Sweet* pulled near even with her, she waved to her daddy high in the cabin, there at the wheel, her daddy always putting on surprise she was there—his mouth open, eyebrows high, head quick turned to her like he hadn't seen her from a half mile out—then letting one sharp hoot from the horn, a signal to her he'd seen her, and to her momma a mile away back to the house that they'd made it in, he'd be home before long.

This was Naomi: a girl blessed with a momma and daddy, a creek to walk to, pine-straw to feel beneath her feet, the pine smell up off it a blessing too, all of it dressed in colors so full there was no need to name them or think on them. Colors it was enough just to look at to have them live in you.

She was a girl, too, blessed once more and forever, though she could not know it those afternoons in summer light so sweet she could taste it on her tongue: once her daddy'd turned his attention to the docks a quarter mile up creek where he'd raft up the *Mary Sweet* to the other trawlers, this Naomi was a girl who turned her own eyes to the stern of the boat, and to the boy in blue jeans and black rubber boots on the deck back there, hands on his hips, his shirt off and skin brown for this peaceful sun, his hair a kind of sun-drenched brown made light for that sun, his eyes squinted near shut for that sunlight too, him watching her.

Eli. The boy who'd sat behind her three years running at Mount Pleasant Academy. The boy she'd been baptized in the ocean with summer before last, a good twenty or thirty kids saved one night at a revival out to Sullivan's Island.

The teenage boy her daddy'd had to hire to do the best he could to replace her older brother, off to the war.

Eli. The boy she loved.

Naomi was a girl who gave him the smallest of waves, the boy, her Eli, giving one back, a hand up from his hip and waving just once and then smiling before heading to the bow to ready the lines he would cast to raft them up.

And though she could not know it then, his was a smile she would carry with her the rest of her days, and though she could not know it too their hands raised to each other was a pact sealed all the way back then, made with no true notion in their hearts they were making it, but making it all the same: *you have my heart.*

Naomi. A girl who turned each afternoon from all this, from the whole of her life laid out before her and ready to be lived, and headed back into those woods toward home, where she and Daddy and Momma, and best of all her Eli, would be having supper soon.

That was Naomi.

RUTH CRIED, AND CRIED. It seemed days, maybe years we two were inside that silver sound she made, the two of us still in each other's arms, nowhere any hint we'd ever let go.

But I knew that moment'd have to come, and come on us soon. We'd have no choice but to let go each other, pull away, take in that next breath. And the next.

My cheek on Ruth's shoulder, I didn't want to open my eyes. I didn't want to see the new world we'd both been born again into this morning, or the same faithless sun that couldn't find its way to melt off a patch of black ice.

Why call me Naomi, I wanted to know. Better to call me empty for all of what God'd given me, then taken away.

I opened my eyes. Here was the same cold sun, the same thin frost on rooftops. Hills still as gray and empty as my heart.

And here was my hand, on Ruth's shoulder and holding tight, lit with that sun. My old woman's hand sharp against her black dress, the wrinkled and spotted skin across my bones as thin as the frost on these rooftops, my knuckles a gnarled row of pain.

My hand. Mine. No choice to it. No way to deny the age upon it, and the pain. But in my hand, the dead white of it on the black of Ruth's dress, I saw what it was I had to do. I saw it.

It was the light I wanted back, and I believed, in the way an old woman believes and cannot know but believes all the same, that I could go back to that light I'd known when I was a girl. To the peace of it, and the warmth.

And then I knew I would leave this place. Where I'd lived the last fifty-six years, this cold Massachusetts town burdened with a light too heavy, too sharp.

My precious baby, my Mahlon, gone. My Eli's passing on brought back this day as new and strange and cold as it was my own first day after. My own black gift, brand-new and as old as the world.

I would leave, and I knew it. Though Naomi was a girl long dead and gone, I knew I could go back to that place. I would return to those colors it was enough just to look at to have them live in you, and to the water, and that light up off it, and that joy.

Then it was me to cry, those silver sounds out of me now, and I closed my eyes, held Ruth even closer.

Why call me Naomi?

Who was she?

I let go Ruth, despite the love I had for her and would always have, and I brought my old woman's hands together in my lap, felt fresh the arthritis in them, and I began to leave, my hands in my lap my first gathering together of me for the long way home.

I looked down from the window, said, "We have to eat something. We have to get up."

Ruth lay back, slowly, as though she had to think on the possibility of the bed beneath her. Like she was taking into account the empty and cold sheets, and found she had no other choice but to give herself up to the empty of it.

I looked at her out the corner of my eye. She was stretched back in her black dress, one arm across her eyes, the palm of that hand open and up to the room. Her other hand lay flat on the untouched pillow beside her, and I saw that the two of us were alone and together in this room with its windows wide with this light, my son and my daughter-in-law's room filled with the everything of a half-roll of cherry Lifesavers, spare change, and the smell of the coffee I'd brought up.

We sat there, neither of us moving, neither of us breathing, it felt, until far into the morning. Shadows outside eased and shifted, made way for new shadows, all of this movement only the empty fruit of that faithless sun.

The world changed.

I stood, though not of my own, but called by the force of whatever mystery the place I'd once called home and would call home again held out to me. I stood, went to that window, and pulled down the blind.

Chapter 2

I LEFT HER THERE, went on downstairs with my one coffee cup, my other hand holding hard the banister. There were things I needed to do.

There were the girls I'd spent most of my days with all these years and how to say good-bye to them. The five of us quilted four mornings a week, spent every Tuesday night together for cards, and now I was at the bottom of the stairs, here in the foyer, and I let loose the banister, slowly moved my fingers, flexed them far as the pain would let me.

Before me was the front door, to my left the kitchen, to the right the front room with all my quilting supplies and the sewing machine set up, the TV in there too. Through that room was my bedroom, through the bedroom my bathroom, the bathroom leading into the kitchen, the kitchen back here to the foyer. One big circle of rooms same as Mahlon and Ruth lived in upstairs, and for a moment I looked into that front room for no other reason than that I wanted to stare square in the eye how big the job of moving would be.

Here was the room, same as ever, cluttered with piles of folded material along two walls, baskets full of cut-up material on the sofa, bags of batting heaped on Eli's old recliner. The sewing table in the center of it all spread with the latest effort we girls were after completing, a red and gold and green Star-fly we'd figured on finishing up by Friday this week.

But that was before what happened four days ago, and now the room, so filled with plans you could hardly make out there was a hardwood floor beneath it all, seemed somebody else's room. Big plans made by someone I didn't even know. Like every year, we were setting up to work a booth out to the Christmas Bazaar on the commons in Deerfield next month. But that was before, a plan made in a world where it seemed work would always get done, and there'd always be someone here to do it.

I would have to say good-bye to them, good-bye to Mary Margaret, and to Phyllis and Carolyn and Hilda. My friends, and I wondered, would they try and talk me into staying? Or would they all understand, all of them women my age whose lives had seen their own miseries enough to believe maybe leaving here was the best anyone could do to find what joy was left?

They all knew sorrow, the same sorrow any woman our age would have no choice but come to know for the years and loved ones they'd tallied up and marked off like so many days on a calendar. Just this summer Phyllis's girl had a miscarriage five months along; Hilda lost her husband three years ago to pancreatic cancer, Carolyn losing hers fifteen years back to nothing other than a night of sleep he didn't wake from.

Mary Margaret, my oldest and dearest friend, lost her parents when she was nine to a train wreck on the New Haven line, her left to two maiden aunts in Greenfield and a house she wasn't allowed to sit down in for fear of marring the Chippendale chairs.

They knew their own lives, their own histories. Yet still they were here, still hanging on to the work of gathering a few days a week to make quilts, all of us together to talk and to

drink coffee and to laugh and to cry. And
sometimes just to sit and be silent, before you
nothing more to think on than the stitch line
you were following around the scrap of material off a dress or a blouse or a tea towel you
never thought you'd give another whit's attention to. They were still here—*we* were still
here—but the notion of carrying on this way,
even with all the help this company of friends
could give, seemed not enough on this day.
Not enough, I saw in the clutter of work to be
done, to keep me here.

I turned from the room, headed to the
kitchen. It was the leaving that mattered, and
that moment of the memory of light I'd seen
and forgotten and found again, today. That was
what mattered.

Air sharp with the smell of coffee left too
long in the pot met me in the kitchen. A smell
I wasn't used to, Mahlon always certain to finish off the pot before heading out the door for
the drive on over to Easthampton, and the
food-distribution house he drove truck for.

Each morning we were all three of us down
here, a room warm and smelling like home for
the fresh coffee and biscuits I made. This was
where each day we three laid out plans long
before daylight, Mahlon smiling over his cup
of coffee and drizzling warm maple syrup over

the biscuits in front of him like he'd done most every day of his life, and it occurred to me only now, once inside a kitchen he'd never visit again, that those biscuits were a kind of lifeline back to South Carolina. The recipe was my momma's, but nothing I ever wrote down, simply a way of making something with my hands I'd learned from the hands of my mother: flour in a bowl I kept under the counter draped over with a tea towel, pulled out and set on the counter once the coffee was on; a pinch of baking powder dropped into it, a little dollop of lard and an egg, a little bit of buttermilk tipped in too. Then I'd work it all together right there in the well of flour, until up came first one and then another until I had six biscuits, each dropped into the old iron skillet I'd already warmed up in the oven, in the bottom of it a little dribble of oil, then all of them slipped into the oven to cook for a while, the bowl of flour covered again with the tea towel and settled back under the counter for the next day.

All of that learned and never learned at all from my momma. My son had eaten of the love of his grandma's hands each morning, and I could not recall his ever asking where I'd learned how to make them, or volunteering such to him of my own.

Now he was gone. Gone, too, the talk of deliveries he'd be making to markets up in Greenfield or sometimes all the way out to Pittsfield, and every Thursday morning to the Super Stop & Shop on upper King Street, where Ruth worked as a cashier. Gone was Ruth filling him in on their rec-league softball game coming up or some doings at the store, and of course me yammering on about the crafts fair over to the commons in Amherst or at the Holyoke Mall or wherever we were getting our quilts ready for. All of that gone.

Those were our mornings, the windows black in winter, gray and lavender in summer, the smell in here of that coffee and the biscuits baking. My Mahlon smiling, winking at Ruth every time he said anything about the Thursday-morning deliveries to her Stop & Shop, and the smile from Ruth he got for it. Then him making fun of one or another of my friends for the petty gossip I passed along: who was seen at State Street Market flirting with Jonathan the butcher; who it was over to the Friendly's on King eating a sundae the size of a breadbox; who bought pre-quilted backing at the piece goods store, and would she be passing it off as the real thing for the Christmas sale?

But this morning I hadn't even thought of

the fact we wouldn't need near as much coffee anymore. It was a habit I'd have to break, my measuring out the five scoops into the filter and enough water for three of us while the two of them got showered and dressed for the day ahead.

And I remembered then what I'd come downstairs to do: count up the things needed doing so I could leave this place, and head for home.

I took the pot from the coffeemaker, went to the sink, poured out that coffee gone too burned to drink. The black-brown of it flooded that white for a moment or two, the smell up to me too thick, too dark, and I turned my head from that smell and color too much the smell and color of death this morning.

And it was only then that the stillness of the kitchen, this house, the whole world around me pressed its full weight upon me. Or maybe it was just then that I felt for this first moment the weight that was always there, had been since the beginning. Since the first breath I'd taken in as a baby, fresh from the warmth and blood and water that meant I was alive, the first breath we none of us could ever remember but that was real and true for the fact we were alive, here and now. The weight of life, pressed down hard on me, and I had to close my eyes, no choice to it.

It was a weight my son Mahlon would never know again, and a weight lifted from my Eli eight long and short years ago, and I envied them the lifting of that weight. I envied them the fact the stillness of this world, and all its empty light and melted frost and air thick and white and cold, was something they would never know again.

And I wondered after Heaven, and if there really were such a thing as I'd banked on my whole life this far. I wondered if Heaven weren't just the joy of not having to face the rest of the heartaches this world held every breath you had to take in. Of having this weight lifted, finally.

I opened my eyes, looked at the ring of brown color there in the bottom of the sink, a kind of halo of burned coffee too real and thin and burned to be argued for or against.

Things to do, I whispered as a kind of instruction to this empty kitchen, and to the world outside the window, and to my hollow heart as well.

Breathe in, I whispered.

I breathed in.

And turned from the sink, headed through the bathroom into my bedroom, where lay my bed, already made, ready for whatever might arrive this day.

There on the hook on the closet door, on its hanger from the dry cleaners, was my own black dress, what I'd worn yesterday. The black dress I could take off at the end of a day.

I went to it, reached to the left breast, where I'd placed it over my heart, and unhooked the gold locket pinned there. Where I'd worn it every day, since a day in 1952.

Breathe in, I whispered again.

I stepped backward to my own bed, settled on the edge of it, and opened my hand.

Here it was: only a locket, no filigree to it, no words engraved. Only a locket, plain as my hand was old.

I opened it, inside what I knew would be there but hadn't the courage to behold yesterday. But the surprise of it still enough to keep me from breathing in all the same.

Two photos, each no bigger than a quarter. Two faces: Eli, from his Navy portrait, and Mahlon, a baby with his eyes closed in sleep.

Things to do, I whispered, and whispered in answer, *Keep this close.*

I breathed in, and closed the locket, felt the gentle snap of it shut in my hand.

From above me came the creak and groan of the floorboards. Ruth was awake, and out of bed, and then the shower cut on up there. I thought of her breathing in just then, too, and knew we two were more than blood kin would ever be.

I looked at the locket, then closed tight my hand around it. No matter the pain.

Chapter 3

THE HOUSE I grew up in sat on the corner
of Whilden and Venning in Mount Pleasant. Two bedrooms, a kitchen only big enough
to turn around in, a front room with a table
and chairs at one end, a sofa and radio at the
other. It was a white-plank house up on a redbrick foundation two feet high, and fronted on
Whilden, the front porch with a roof over it,
out back a smaller porch without one, at the far
rear of the yard a low old live oak. Just far
enough out from under its canopy so that
acorns dropping didn't sound like firecrackers
to those inside was the shed where my brother
slept before he went off to the war.

That was where Eli stayed. A place when my

brother lived there that was nothing I'd ever cared about, just a cot and a barebulb light hung from the rafters, tacked to the walls articles and pictures about the war he'd cut out of the *Charleston Post* and *Life* magazine.

But after Eli'd moved down in April of 1944, the room became a genuine mystery to me, a place I wanted to see more than I ever had before just to catch an idea of how this boy spent his time. But it was a place I wasn't allowed for the fact I was a girl of fifteen and he was a boy of sixteen. Once the radio shows we listened to each night were over—*Amos 'n' Andy, The Shadow,* big-band broadcasts from hotels in New Orleans and Atlanta and sometimes even New York—Eli'd say good night to us all, head back through the dark of a yard shadowed over on even the brightest moonlit nights by the pine and live oak grew everywhere out there. Sometimes, if I was sure Daddy and Momma weren't looking, I'd stand in the kitchen and watch out the window him step off the back porch and into the grass back there, disappearing a second later from the long rectangle of light the open back door cast, and into the dark.

It was a life we were all living, a routine one the same as anyone's life is routine but seems only after it is over as rare and new as the next sunrise you'll see. And the path we two began started on just one of those evenings, an evening like any of the others, but an evening so sure and sharp in my head even now, these many years later, that I can feel the heat and humid air of that August afternoon, breathe in the smell of the food at the table—cheese grits and fried shrimp and boiled crookneck squash—and I can see too the sun in through the kitchen window just above Eli's left shoulder.

He wore a clean white shirt buttoned to the neck, ironed this day and all of them by me, part of the job I had of taking care around the house. Momma took in the laundry of the rich people up and down Bennett Street, washing and wringing and hanging dry sheets and shirts, trousers and slips and skirts and the all of it. Our yard and her days back then were filled with the lives of other people, the lines of clean clothes hanging out to the yard like midday ghosts in the thin breezes off the harbor. But it was money she was making, the regular bits of it my brother sent us from somewhere in Italy not enough, Daddy's hauls only as big as one man and a boy named Eli could take in. My ironing of both Daddy's and Eli's clothes, the sweeping clean the floors, dusting and mopping and readying for dinner was my own way, my own contribution to her, and to Daddy.

And to Eli.

Here he was across from me at my family's table, here in my life, me squinting at him for the sun in through the windows just above his left shoulder. An August evening, hot and humid.

That was when he moved, leaned to his left, and now his head blocked out that sun in through the window. He was a silhouette to me for an instant until my eyes adjusted, and here was his smile.

I said, "Thank you," and he nodded, said, "You're welcome."

And in this nothing moment of words we'd most likely said to each other a thousand times before, in this lack of anything other than the expected and obliged, it all began.

I knew it in that moment, no matter how young I was, no matter how little of the world I understood, no matter how big my ignorance of matters of the heart and the notion of love was. I knew that this was him. This was the one I would marry, whose life I would stake my own on, our lives traceable from this moment of the sun eclipsed by his face, those needed and nothing words the firm foundation of our lives together, the saying of them a moment somehow so full of the two of us that even my daddy and momma must have felt it, for in this moment Momma dropped her fork, a sound so loud in its own surprise that Eli and I looked directly to her sitting beside me.

Here was Momma and Daddy both, him there at the head of the table, the two of them looking at us two, their eyes open wide, astonished and surprised and faced with the end of my childhood, all in this moment.

That is what I saw in them both: my childhood, over.

Daddy blinked, quick cut his eyes to Momma, whose hand went to the table, felt for the fork, her eyes still on us. She looked down, but not before meeting Daddy's eyes a second, and found the fork, picked it up, and settled it across her plate. Her hands, I saw, were red as ever for the work of her life, as red as the blush rising up her neck, growing in her cheeks.

She cleared her throat, said, "Excuse me," as though this might be Sunday dinner with Pastor Stewart. She tried at a smile, and I can recall to this day, here and now, the accomplishment I felt even then, not a minute after I'd fallen in love: I was grown up.

No surprise, then, when across from me came Eli's words, "Would it be all right if Naomi and me went for a walk after dinner, Mr. Reilly?"

I looked at Eli, his brown eyes to Daddy,

waiting. His smile was gone, in its place the serious look of a man who knew what I knew of who we were.

He knew.

Daddy was silent a few seconds, looking at Eli, in his hand his own fork, held tight as a seine line hauled in from down deep. He wasn't going to drop his fork for this turn in their lives.

He pursed his lips, looked a moment at me. "Naomi, run go get your daddy here another glass of buttermilk," he said, and reached to his glass, still half-full, held it out to me.

I knew enough not to ask him what I would have at supper just yesterday evening had he made such a request, a question I knew I would've asked even a minute ago, back before Eli'd blocked the sun, and begun our love: why do you want more, I'd have asked my daddy, when you're not through with what you have?

I only stood, took the glass from his hand. But not before he looked at me a long second, both our hands on the glass, our fingers touching, and I believed I saw in my daddy's eyes a kind of fearful smile, afraid and proud at once.

He let go, and now Momma was rising beside me. Without word we two were into the kitchen, me bent to the icebox and pulling out of it the pitcher, the handle cold and hot at the same time for the blood through me, rising into a blush, I knew, as certain as the one flowered full on my momma's face.

I turned, saw her looking at me, that piecemeal smile still on her, her trying hard both to let it go and to keep it down. "What's wrong, Momma?" I said, as though I wouldn't have an idea.

She said, "Naomi," and the word had been as full that moment as it would be empty from Ruth so many years later.

It was full of herself, I could hear, and full of me, too, and full of the joy and the grief of what a mother can only know: someday the lives of our children are no longer our own, and have to be surrendered willingly and with love and fear in the sad and faithful truth we have not given them all they need to know.

And still, because I was yet a child, I said again, "What's wrong, Momma?"

She shook her head, touched the back of a hand to her eye, and I smiled myself for this, for my momma about to cry, and I filled Daddy's glass to the brim.

"These dishes," she said, and turned to the stove, pulled the sieve from the row of pots and pans hanging on the row of pegs on the wall behind it. She settled the sieve on the coffee can there on the stovetop, lifted the skillet, and poured off the grease into the can. "All I'm ever doing," she said, her eyes to the work of holding that skillet high and tipping it.

I stood watching her, my momma doing her best not to say what she wanted to say, and heard now from the front room Daddy's voice low but in the certain pitch that meant he was telling Eli precisely what he wanted to. Words I could only figure had to do with me, his baby girl, while now and again Eli wedged in *Yessir,* and *Yessir,* and *No sir,* and *Yessir.*

Momma still poured the grease, the thin stream of it into the can like brown molten glass. Here were her hands again, the red of them, and I saw her wrists begin to quiver for the weight of the cast-iron skillet.

I put the glass on the counter, closed the ice-box door, went to my momma just as she finished. I put my hands to hers, lifted the skillet from them, settled it back on the stove. She was looking at me, that same rim of near-tears in her eyes, her hands out in front of her as though I'd robbed her of something important.

And then I put my arms around her, pulled her to me, me nearly as tall as her by then. She seemed to melt at my touch, her shoulders falling, arms gone loose, and then her arms were up and around me, her head on my shoulder. She took in a deep breath and let it out slow, like this was the end of the long day of work and heat and food and care and living it truly was.

No sir, I heard from the front room, then *Yessir.*

ELI AND I STEPPED off the back porch and into the grass, the canopy of live oak a kind of cathedral made all the bigger and quieter and fearful for what we were about to do: walk alone for the first time.

Daddy called out from behind us, "Be back in a half hour, and y'all walk careful. We don't want stories coming back at us from the neighbors."

"Yessir," we both said at the same time, and looked at each other, smiling for saying it together, only to look away just as quickly. Already my mind was on that half hour, the huge empty of all that time, thirty minutes as wide and deep and too big to swim as Charleston Harbor.

We passed Eli's shed, the canopy giving way above us to reveal a blue sky going darker blue and even emptier, then we were out on Venning Street, an oyster-shell road like every other road in town, this one heading east and away from the house. A street just like ours, on

it none of the big houses where Momma's cus-
tomers lived, but people like us in houses like
ours, all of everyone living in them watching
from their front porches and windows, I was
sure. No matter what Daddy wanted, we'd be
a story even before we made it home.

Naomi Reilly and that Robinson boy, Eli, I
could hear from that empty sky above as we
walked, the same words echoed in the tender
shock of sound the crushed oyster shells gave
out with each step we took. *Naomi Reilly and
that Robinson boy, Eli,* I heard from the trees
around us, the airy twists of Spanish moss
down from the branches a language of whispers: *Eli and Naomi, Naomi and Eli. Eli Robinson and Naomi Reilly.*

Naomi and Eli Robinson.

Naomi and Eli.

"Your momma is a good cook," Eli said, and
I took in a breath for the solid sound of his
voice out here, those whispers knocked clear
away.

"Yes," I said, then, "She is."

We walked a few more steps, the air silent
and awful for it, and those names whispered
again around me. *Naomi and Eli. Eli and
Naomi.*

I looked at the road leading out in front of
us. The evening sky and the growing edge of

dark made the shells all the whiter somehow, and made too the silence between us all the quieter, the small crunch of our steps lonely and pointless.

It was my turn. It was supposed to be me to say whatever next words we were going to try and let be the beginning of what might become a conversation.

But what words were they? What could I say?

And in that instant there came up from the trees around us the sudden whirling drone of treefrogs, the sound loud and shiny as it was every night at this moment, as though the frogs—small and pale green and hidden everywhere through the trees—were all of one mind, all tied one to another and waiting for the cue a certain shade of evening sky made.

It was a sound that came every night all summer long, one that cut on and off throughout the night and sometimes even into early morning. A dance of sounds tree to tree to tree, but so much a part of every night sometimes you had to think on it to hear the sound they made.

But here it was, brand-new this night, as perfect and puzzling a sound as the words *Thank you* spoken across the dinner table.

"It's like I never heard them before," I said,

the words out of me before I had time to weigh them, and already I was afraid I sounded like some kid with a crush, making schoolgirl romantic here at twilight.

Eli said, "When I listen to them at night out to the shed, it's like I can hear something else. Like they're all telling each other some story they all know the ending to."

I turned to him. His eyes were to the trees behind me, the huge live oaks that grew beside the road. The sun was down now, his white shirt even whiter, his tan face even richer.

He looked at me. Here were his brown eyes, a brown so deep in this slowly failing light I thought I could see the story of both of us. I thought I could see the story we both knew the ending to already.

He shrugged, looked down, shrugged again. He was smiling, bashful, as embarrassed over his words as I'd been over mine. But there were no other words he could've spoken. Those words right out of his heart were all I needed to hear, and what he needed to speak. What he felt and knew and believed.

It was a story they were speaking, and we both already knew it was a story about us.

Chapter 4

WE WALKED, and we talked, and the light went right on away from us, the tree-frogs kept right on telling their story, and I came to begin to know my husband, though in the hesitant and anxious and nervous way of a boy and girl first finding the words to tell who they are.

He told me of his daddy, how when he died five years ago he'd thought he wouldn't miss him, thought he was man enough even at eleven to make it through.

"But I was wrong," he said, and I looked at him beside me. We were on McCants Street now, headed toward the harbor. He had his hands behind him, his head down, watching each step he took.

His daddy had been a shrimper too, and I knew, like everyone in Mount Pleasant and all of the Lowcountry, he'd been lost at sea in a squall that took him and his boat and his crew of three all in fifteen minutes. That year, Eli's third in the seat behind me at Mount Pleasant Academy, he'd changed from the boy who jabbed a pencil now and again into my shoulder just to hear the laugh his pals would give when I jumped, and into the quiet boy I'd known him since to be.

I told him how I missed my brother, though back when he was here to home I did nothing but complain over him, how he picked on me and ribbed me and made demands on a kid sister—*I ain't listening to Little Orphan Annie! You got no choice but to give me your last piece of bacon! You tell Momma you saw me talking to Lula Beauchamp and I'll make sure there's a palmetto bug in your bed every night from now on!*—so much that it felt like my birthday once he was gone.

Eli smiled at this, his hands still behind his back, and slowly shook his head. A hundred yards or so up ahead lay the dead end of Mc-Cants, the trees on either side of the road stopped, beyond them lavender light that was the water of Charleston Harbor.

"Remember when we got baptized?" he said, and it seemed the words might as well have come from me, for that was what I'd been thinking on too. About the light that evening summer before last.

I wanted to bust out with the words *You read my mind* and make a fuss, but all I heard was the schoolgirl romance again, and the fact I'd seen a dozen movies down to the Riviera in Charleston of a Saturday afternoon where *You read my mind* was a line I didn't believe even hearing it from up on the big screen.

But it was the truth, my thinking about that night we'd been baptized in the ocean out past the dunes on Sullivan's Island in the same instant he was, and instead of remarking on the way our thoughts were already driving toward one, I put it away, held it. A piece of the treasure of our lives together I knew enough to hold close and savor, even all the way back then.

"I remember," I said, and saw that last night of Revival, the tent awning set up on this side of the dunes out back of First Baptist Sullivan's Island, and the white-haired preacher down from Spartanburg who'd set aside this last night for the youth. I'd sat up front with a couple three girlfriends, and we'd all listened sitting on wooden folding chairs set up in rows in the sand. The sky'd grown darker with the sun already set, the heat and the close of all these kids turning the evening into a haze of color and darkness and light and words, all of it coming together to give me a kind of truth that goes beyond trying to capture here in words.

The preacher, his white hair parted on the side and in a white shirt and black tie and black pants, talked about our lives having a path set up in front of us, a path narrow yet walkable all the same, but walkable only by God's grace. It was the same old story I'd heard my whole life long, but on this night I heard something else, a voice that dug sharp and clean into me, a voice from inside me giving the truth like the knife everybody always said it was, but this knife warm, and kind, and forgiving. Still the preacher talked, him nowheres near in the sweat and pitching a fit like I'd seen some pastors before. He only spoke calm words in truth, and when at last he said what I'd known all along too, that same old story—that the grace we needed to walk that narrow path was named Jesus, the same Jesus as every Sunday since I could remember—there'd come to me

the startling fact of it all, the kind of knowledge you can't get by adding numbers in a certain way, or reading a chapter enough times to
memorize it for the test in class.

It was the fact of Jesus I saw, the fact He was
who He said He was, my savior, and now here
were my girlfriends, and here were other kids
from over to school, and here was that kid
who used to sit behind me when we were at
Mount Pleasant Academy, the Robinson boy,
and here was me, all of us standing and moving up toward the preacher, him making the
altar call for all those who wanted their lives to
be lived with meaning, and in truth.

There are no words for this, I am only seeing now, for this truth given to your heart.
There is only hearing it, and responding. Like
love between a man and woman, but so very
much more.

Then we were all walking out from under
the awning, the sky this same lavender as now,
here with the Robinson boy two years later.
We stood at the end of McCants now, before
us the harbor, the lights of Charleston coming
on, the spires across the water reflected in a
quivering way across the lavender water.

"Two by two," Eli said, and I looked at
him. The one I'd already claimed, in me the

revealed knowledge he was the one. Nothing I could have figured from counting numbers, or reading a book.

"Everybody walking two by two down to the beach," he went on. "Following that preacher right down to the water and on in."

I turned, looked again out at the water. I said, "I was afraid. I didn't know what it would be like. Baptized." I shrugged, smiled. "I was afraid when I came up out the water I'd turn into a hankie waver, or handle snakes or whatnot."

He gave a small laugh, and I shrugged again, saw us all walking between the dunes toward that lavender ocean, sea oats on the dunes bending in the evening breeze up off the water, the small cool of the air moving welcome, and frightening too. We were headed for a baptizing, headed for being born again, and I was filled with fear of what exactly this might mean. Of how my life would change, and then we were through the dunes, each of us pausing a moment to take off our shoes and drop them in a pile just where the sand sloped flat and away from the dune, all of us moving barefoot in the warm sand, moving together to our next new lives.

Someone started singing, someone far and

away behind us, back where all the parents followed, all of them through the service standing
off in the dunes and out from under the
awning, so we children could listen, and hear.

> *Blessed assurance, Jesus is mine*
> *Oh what a foretaste of glory divine*

It was a haunted feel the words gave to me,
their rising from all around behind us, ahead of
us the darker sky to the east, above the water.
The white-haired preacher was down to the
water now, the harmless white lace of the foam
around his ankles, then his knees, and now I
heard the kids behind me picking up the song:

> *Heir of salvation, purchase of God,*
> *Born of his spirit, washed in His blood*

Then it was me too to be singing, carrying up
the tune like it was a gift, everything I owned,
a song given out with no music to help it but
the breeze off the water, and the water itself,
and this lavender sky, and I sang:

> *This is my story, this is my song,*
> *Praising my savior all the day long,*
> *This is my story, this is my song,*
> *Praising my savior all the day long.*

Here I was, next in line, the girl who'd walked beside me all the way down here rising up out of the water, lifted by the preacher, it seemed, her mouth open wide for air, her hands together at her chest, her moving toward me and past me back toward the sand, and then the preacher took my hand, us waist deep in the warm water, around my legs the slow swirl of my skirt dancing with the tide.

He turned me so that I stood sideways to him, and now I could see what was happening behind us all, saw the string of kids who'd come to the call trailing off through the surf to the beach, all their faces lost to me for the twilight sky behind them to the west, that sky a dark and sweet orange. Families were up on the beach, a mass of dark figures standing together, somewhere in them my momma and daddy, all of them singing now that same couple of lines again and again, *This is my story, this is my song . . .*

The preacher put a hand to my back, took both my hands with his other hand and brought them to my chest. "Child," he said, "do you accept Christ as your Lord and Savior?"

His eyes were on mine in the dying light, and I saw in them that the truth he'd been talking about and the voice inside me were the same, speaking the same words—*Christ is my savior*—and I nodded, whispered, "Yes."

"Then be baptized in the name of the Father, and of the Son, and of the Holy Spirit," he said, the words slow and solemn, his eyes turned up now to the sky, and I fell back into the warmth of the water, and then I was up again in an instant, the salt water bitter in my eyes as I tried to open them, me fearful still but filled suddenly with a sort of courage to try and see exactly what this next new world would be like.

And then my foot in the sand gave way beneath me. The pastor, one hand still to my back, the other still holding tight to my hands, seemed to tip forward with my weight going down, and the courage and fear and all else I'd been filled with disappeared for the shock of embarrassment, of how in this next second I'd end up back in the water, pulling this good man after me and under, all of this night's news of truth and grace lost on me and everyone watching for the pitiful fact of me falling down.

All of this in an instant, even before I was an inch closer to the water, even before my foot in the sand beneath me had failed fully to catch me.

Then there came another hand at my arm,

there at my elbow, and I felt myself lifted by that hand and the preacher's all at once and all in that instant. I heard the preacher give a small laugh, say, "Now go in grace, child," and heard whoever it was belonged to this other set of hands—the next one in line to get his dunking, I guessed—give a laugh, my hand to my eyes and wiping away the salt water, me laughing too though for the nervous of it, and for the embarrassment.

I moved back along the line of kids, my black skirt and white blouse heavy for the water, and tried to see in the growing dark any smiles or laughs or shaking heads at me and my clumsy coming into the fold. I knew they'd all seen me falter, even everyone up on the beach, that dark cloud of people spread along the sand watching every move every one of us entering God's kingdom made.

But I saw nothing. Only kids, like me, some of them with hands together at their chests and crying, some of them with eyes to the water, some with their arms crossed. All of them alone, and thinking. Just alone with themselves, and with God.

Nobody'd seen.

Then I was up on the beach, and here was Momma holding up a big towel and crying, moving toward me from the crowd, Daddy behind her and smiling at me. He held my shoes up in one hand, his other arm around my momma. "Easy to find which ones was yours, clodhoppers big as these," he said, his voice soft and low, and I couldn't help but smile.

"Now hush," Momma whispered to him, her eyes on me. "Brought this towel just in case," she went on, "so let's take care and dry you off now," her whispered words broken and filled up, all at once.

I looked at him, and Momma. They were the same people they always were. My momma and my daddy. But this night, somehow, the love they were showing me, the same they'd always given, was deeper, carried somehow more fact to it. There was a point to it I was supposed to understand, and now understood. This was a towel to dry me off, these were their hands to hold me, these were their words, to carry me through.

Here was the next new world: the one I'd been blessed, I finally saw, with being in from the very beginning.

Momma's arms were on my shoulder, rubbing soft and careful through the towel, and we'd made our way back toward the dunes.

"But there was nothing to be afraid of," I said to Eli, the lavender on the water before us gone a royal purple by then, the sky above the church spires across the water no different, like the two were one: water, sky. "Haven't started to handling snakes yet, nor waving hankies." I shrugged. "There wasn't anything different. Just I knew my momma and daddy loved me was all."

I'd never talked like this to any boy before, told what was on my heart clear and plain. I'd never.

"I figured the whole world was going to change on me, too," Eli said, his eyes out to the water. "But that was what I was hoping for. That the whole world would change." He looked down, glanced an instant at me, cut his eyes to the water again. "My daddy'd died. My momma was about to go on and marry somebody else, like he'd never lived. Like my daddy'd never even lived."

He took in a breath, a quick and hollow one, and I looked away, like there was something out on the water I wanted to see too.

He said, "I was hoping I'd come up out the water and see the whole world'd changed, and maybe some kind of sense'd come into my momma's head. That maybe the world'd right itself because of me giving up to being born again." He stopped, gave out a short *tss,* a silent whistle of air for the silliness, I figured, of what he'd believed. Of what we'd both believed: the world changed when you were saved.

"But then you nearly took your spill there in front of me," he said, and I turned to him.

He was smiling at me.

"Almost yanked that preacher in with you, too," he said.

He'd seen me nearly fall, when I'd thought always nobody'd noticed. And it was nobody seeing me and my embarrassing entry into Grace that had let me know Grace was there.

But he'd seen me. Eli had seen me.

He was still looking at me, and me at him, and I felt the blood rushing up to my face.

"And it was your nearly pulling him in after you that got me to see nothing was going to change," he said, his words suddenly quieter, that smile gone. "I knew it then, because of you. Wasn't the world was going to change on me, but it was me had to change." He paused. "I knew it just as soon as I put my hands out and took hold of you, helped the preacher up with you."

"That was you?" I said.

He turned once more to the water, him a profile now, dark against that purple sky. "So in a way it was you had a hand in me getting saved." He paused again. "And in me starting to get ahold of the fact that my momma's marrying Mister Gordon Stackhouse didn't mean my daddy was gone."

"I always thought," I began, and stopped. "I figured nobody," I tried again, but there the words stopped, the empty sound of them trailing off into this night.

Because it was then the all of what'd happened two years before came to me, and I discovered how our lives'd already been put together without our even knowing it. Only then did I understand how our lives'd intersected in the twin misunderstandings of how a life could be saved: I'd been afraid the world would be different, and it wasn't. He'd been afraid it would stay the same, and it did.

The way you wanted your life to change, I saw, didn't matter. Grace would come to you in the way it would come, and with it would come a change in you. Here had been God's hand, unseen and unknown in our lives, but holding us as close together as two children at a beachside revival might get.

I looked at him, still a profile to me. There were words I wanted to give to him, words I wanted to try and surrender to him about this discovery, about how God'd already put us together to live our lives changed in an unchanged world. There were words I wanted to get, words just out of reach, a language of God's will as clear yet as foreign as the story those treefrogs sang of the two of us.

"Then they got married," he went on. "And we moved, like they'd told me would happen." He stopped, turned full to me, his white shirt crisp in the twilight on us. I looked up to his eyes, saw by the last breath of light out here that he was looking at me, and he was smiling. "Then Miss Naomi Reilly's daddy calls up Mister Gordon Stackhouse and asks can he spare his stepson for a while to work the boat, seeing as how his boy is off fighting the good fight. Room and board plus five dollars a week." He shrugged. "Wasn't never a second thought. Not because living up to Georgetown was bad, or that God sent me an evil stepdaddy and an annoying little Stackhouse stepbrother. Nope."

He put his hands together in front of him, laced his fingers together like he might be thinking to start on a prayer. He shrugged again, and I could still see the smile.

"It was you," he said. "I saw you nearly fall, and I helped keep you from falling. For that little second it seemed you needed me. And it was good to be needed, when it felt like nobody on God's green earth needed me anymore."

I reached to him then, and though I knew it was wrong, knew a fifteen-year-old girl ought never be so forward, so bold, I put my hands on his, felt him unlace his fingers, felt him take both mine in both of his, and hold my hands.

It was the calluses I felt first, already there for the work he knew. But then I felt the warmth of his hands, and it was that warmth I kept, and have kept, all the days of my life.

"Eli," I said, and it seemed now the right words were taking shape, lining up in my heart to tell him all I wanted to tell him: that I knew he was the one.

"Eli," I said again, and took in a breath, ready to speak.

And heard a car horn start to honking off in the distance, behind us somewheres a couple blocks away. It was a strange sound, there in the silence between us where room'd already been made for words to come. A car horn honking, three long calls in a row, then a pause, then three more.

Then just as far off, just as odd, my name, called out long and hard: "Naomi!"

Daddy.

We both turned to it, heard again "Naomi!" and looked at each other.

"Hasn't been but twenty minutes," I said. "We're not late getting back."

"Don't matter," Eli said, and turned again toward where the word came from. "Sounds like he means business," he said, and now he let go one hand, held tighter to the other, and we were off at a quick walk, headed back up McCants and away from the water, away from the end of this day's light.

We let go each other's hand before we passed the first house back off the water, the porch light there already on, and though I didn't like the empty of my hand and the cool left where his warmth had been, we both of us knew why we couldn't run and hold hands at the same time: somebody'd see us, if they hadn't already, and give back to Daddy the news, and things would go from there. So we'd let go, and we ran.

Here were more houses with porch lights on already, some with lights just cutting on as we passed. Daddy hadn't called or honked again, but people stood on some of the porches, mommas mostly, arms crossed and watching us and wondering, no doubt, what Daddy's carrying on and the sight of us two running was all about. Then we were on Venning again, what'd been a whispered crush of sound as we walked the shell road a few minutes before now a reckless noise, the two of us running.

It was dark now, and as we headed on into

our backyard, past first Eli's shed and then back beneath the live oak and onto the grass, I could see the back door off the kitchen open wide, all that harsh white light spilling out.

I could see too on the concrete steps off the back porch, silhouetted for that light, two shapes sitting there, leaned way forward and rocking slow.

Momma and Daddy.

Daddy had one arm up on Momma's back, their heads in close to each other so that they seemed almost one, Daddy's hand patting Momma's back slowly.

Momma was crying, I heard, in this night air thin glistening slivers of her voice gathered and tossed, gathered and tossed. She was crying, her shoulders moving with the sounds she made, and I thought, *We were only holding hands. We were only holding hands.*

I slowed down then, Eli too, in me a kind of fear already welling up, taking root with each loud breath I took in and gave out, trying to gain air for having run here. Something was wrong, I knew, something bigger than our holding hands. Something big. Something huge.

Here we were, almost to the square of light that open door made on the grass, and for some reason I glanced away from my momma and daddy to that kitchen window, and in that same glance so many things fell into form before me, for it was in that moment I saw through the kitchen window the officer, saw him looking out at me, his hat off but the unmistakable green of his jacket, the epaulets and gold bars there, and the khaki shirt, the thin khaki tie knotted at his neck, him looking at me; and I saw in there beside him, crowded into that small kitchen, Pastor Stewart in his white shirt and black suit, his tie even thinner than the officer's, clutched in his hands the brim of his black hat. He was looking at me too, hanging back in the doorway like he had an idea to come on out but was waiting for some signal from me.

And I saw in this same instant, saw all of this in that same instant, Momma's arm move out from inside her silhouette, and saw caught in the light her hand, in it the shivering piece of pale yellow paper. I saw it shiver and shiver with those glistening slivers of her voice gathered and tossed.

I stopped, felt the air leave me.

Daddy looked up then. I couldn't see his face, couldn't see him for the light behind him, couldn't see Momma's face, either. All I could see was her hand, and that paper shivering, all of it carried on the sound of her crying.

"They took him," Daddy whispered up at me. "They took my dear sweet boy," he whispered, and now I stepped into the square of light, my legs no longer mine, my eyes somebody else's eyes, somebody else's life.

"My boy," Daddy whispered, and now I fell to my knees at their feet, lay my head on their legs and laps, the same slivers of sound as my momma's making their way up my throat, cutting and scraping their way up.

Daddy touched at my hair, seemed to want to speak, though I still could not see him here in this dark, a fact now I know as a kind of blessing.

God, in his infinite and terrible mercy, decided the sorrow of a parent's face at the news of the death of his child was too painful a prophecy for the child I was to see.

He'd known even then that I would know this pain, and know it soon enough.

"My Mahlon," Momma said out of the darkness of her own shadow, the words filled with the work of love she'd given my older brother his whole life long, love given and given and given and now lost.

"Mahlon," I whispered, and thought of my older brother, thought of him in Italy somewhere, thought of the pencil-thin movie star mustache he'd shown off his last trip home just before he shipped out. I thought of his smile when I swore I'd never tell about him and Lula Beauchamp, and thought of the birthday feel I'd had when he'd finally left.

And for no reason I know I looked up then, to the night sky above us, the purple gone of a sudden, replaced just that quick with this night.

Here were the beginnings of stars, the faintest splinters of light that came up every night I'd ever been alive, a fact which only just this second seemed a loss for how little I ever looked at them.

Here were stars, fixed and shining, each in the same place I'd ever seen them, me nothing beneath them for the fact I never looked at them, took them and their placement up there as much for granted as the next breath I'd take in.

Taken as much for granted as a brother.

"Mahlon," I whispered again, and felt the fear welling in me grown too huge to hold on to, and then it burst, and I cried, and I cried, and I lay my head on my momma and daddy's legs, blinked at the tears out of me.

And saw shimmer for an instant off to the side of us all, there in the grass and shrouded in the weak light out of the kitchen window, Eli in his white shirt, standing, watching.

His arms were crossed, his feet squared to us. Then he let his head down, and I saw his shoulders move ever so small, his own shiver of grief for my brother. Eli, crying too.

He turned, disappeared from the light, and was gone, and I closed my eyes, felt Daddy's hand to my hair again, heard Momma's cries, and heard myself whisper, once more before those slivers tore my throat to the empty shreds they were sure to be, my older brother's name.

"Mahlon," I whispered.

Chapter 5

It was Eli to name our baby, him choosing to keep a secret from me the notion until the day he was born in May 1953, at Cooley Dickinson Hospital here to Northampton. We'd tried out names but hadn't found anything we wanted, and then, me finally coming up from the anesthesia I'd been put under to a swirling room of white and light and silence, I looked to see my husband beside me.

"Let's name him Mahlon," he said, and nodded once.

There was no smile on his face when he'd said it. But neither was he sad for what the name meant, who it had been.

The truest name ever given, for the fact we'd

known we loved one another on the night my daddy'd been handed the telegram. That was the day we charted our lives from, despite its being marked forever with death.

We'd been living in Northampton six years by then, since a year out of the Navy, when Eli and his best friend from the service, Lonny Thompson, decided to go in together, start up their own plumbing business back here to Lonny's hometown.

Six years in a place more foreign even than Portsmouth, New Hampshire, where, at least, with all the military everywhere, people were from more than the one place we all lived. In Portsmouth I had girlfriends from Georgia, and Tennessee, and Kansas and Idaho and one even from California. Eli still worked building submarines that first year we were married, and I'd worked myself at Grace's Five and Dime on Queen Street, the war over and folks happy.

But Northampton was different altogether for how close and quiet the people here were, as though the winters we went through were some kind of sign to them to keep the doors of their hearts closed for the cold wind a possible friendship might blow through. Which is why the girls I met and made friends with I held as close as I could, Hilda and Phyllis and Carolyn, and Mary Margaret. The plumbing business worked well enough, houses being built after the war slowly but surely. Little developments sprung up all around Springfield and Holyoke, enough old buildings needed repairs and renovations right here in town.

It was an adventure we were on, this living so far and away from our home, and making our money, and trying to set up a family, and just enjoying each other. Before Mahlon was here we went out nights to Springfield to the Highland Ballroom to hear the big bands that passed through, once Jimmy Dorsey, another time Kay Kaiser and his Kollege of Musical Knowledge, another time Spike Jones; we even a time or three took the train all the way in to Boston to the Ritz-Carlton, once even to the Totem Pole Ballroom, and always with Lonny Thompson in the lead, him with some new hometown girl he was working on that particular week.

We took the train home to South Carolina now and again, always stopped first to Georgetown for a couple days to visit Eli's people, then headed on down to Charleston for a couple three days more, days filled with just setting and visiting. We watched the lives of our parents move on, heard them blister us again and again for not yet having any grandkids, heard

less of it as they finally realized this wasn't
something going to happen, most likely, for the
news from the doctors we'd been given.

And though Momma and Daddy, and
Mr. Stackhouse and Momma Jasmine, Eli's
momma, begged and cajoled us to move back
there to home, the fact we'd set up our lives in
our own place, had our jobs and friends and
everything, all of it made by ourselves and for
ourselves, gave us to know we could only stay
in Northampton.

Which is all to say, finally, that though we
loved and held close our two families back
there to South Carolina, we didn't really look
back, once we'd gotten married and'd moved
north.

ELI AND LONNY'D MET working inside the
hull of a sub in the shipyard the first day they
got there, and there'd been no separating them
from there on. He'd even come with Eli down
from New Hampshire to be best man at our
wedding in June of 1946. I'd never met him
before he stepped off the train behind my Eli
two days before the wedding.

My eyes, of course, were on my love, my
Eli, this beautiful man, a man now with genuine shoulders and a jaw sharp as granite, no

longer the boy in blue jeans and rubber boots at the stern of a shrimp boat.

He'd joined the Navy not but a month before V-E Day, nothing to hold him back once he'd turned seventeen. He'd given the news of it at the dinner table on an evening not at all unlike the one we'd discovered each other at a little less than a year before, and I'd known in the way my momma, and especially my daddy, took the news that in fact there was a kind of relief for it. They knew by that time we two were going to be who we ended up being, a married couple setting off to find our own lives together. And Eli setting out for the armed services first meant their sixteen-year-old girl wasn't getting married anytime soon.

"I enlisted yesterday," Eli'd said from across the table. He was sitting straight and tall in his chair, and had hold of the table edge with both hands, afraid my daddy'd come down hard on him for leaving him high and dry for a crew. Eli quick looked at me, hoping for something to hold on to other than the edge of the table.

I'd nodded, small but certain, and gave him a smile.

We'd talked of it for near as long as I'd been talking to him. The two of us walked every night since that first one, and held hands now in plain view. He'd told me a hundred times of wanting to leave and find something to do with his hands of his own. He was becoming a man, had to find his own way, and the service was how to do it. The war was almost over then, winding down everywhere you looked, and the skills he could learn outweighed the possibility he might find his death, the way my brother had.

I held the smile on him, nodded again to try and hand him as best I could some hope and help.

Momma let out a heavy breath, leaned back in her chair. Her eyes went first to mine, then to his. She brought her napkin to her mouth, started to crying and smiling.

"Knew it!" Daddy near shouted, and slapped hard his hand on the tabletop. He took his napkin from his lap, threw it on the table, and crossed his arms. He looked at me, then to Eli. He was smiling.

Now here was Eli in his sailor uniform, the navy-blue blouse and bell-bottom pants, the white stripes sharp lines on the big square collar, clothes I'd never seen him wear save for the photographs he sent home.

But here were his same eyes, eyes that pierced me and held me even before he dropped his seabag beside him and took me in his arms and kissed me, no matter the whole world was watching: Momma, and Daddy, and Momma Jasmine and Mr. Stackhouse and his little stepbrother, Gordon Junior, all of us there at the station in Charleston.

Here he was, home to marry me.

He held me, and he kissed me, nothing in the world close enough to touch us. But when we were through, and he let me go and pulled away, smiling and smiling, the world started seeping back in. Everybody moved to Eli then, our mommas both crying, Gordon Junior touching at the sleeves of his uniform like it was the hem of the Robe, Mr. Stackhouse and Daddy slapping his shoulders like he'd been the one to beat Hitler himself single-handed.

That was when I saw behind Eli another man in uniform, his head down and him smiling, hair combed back, hands behind his back and holding his seabag.

Eli turned from me, one arm still around my waist, to Lonny. "Here he is," Eli said. "Lonny Thompson, the Yankee loser I've been telling you about," and Eli reached out his free hand, slapped him on the shoulder, and laughed.

Lonny smiled even broader, shook his head. "I'll bite my tongue right now about that Yankee stuff," he said, "seeing as how I'm down here in Dixie." He let go the seabag with one hand, put his hand out for me to shake. "I don't know what he's told you about me," he said, his eyes on me and then Eli, then me again, "but all I've heard about you is how beautiful you are." He took my hand, and I felt how strong it was, and how callused, just like Eli's. "Turns out," he said, "all I heard is the truth."

We shook hands, then let go, but only after Lonny'd let his eyes hang on mine a long moment.

"Watch out that smooth talk don't get all over you," Eli said. "Goes down sweet, but it'll ruin you. Like sugar in a gas tank." He laughed again, and Lonny's eyes were down from mine, and he slapped at Eli.

We were all of us together, already a family there at the platform of the Charleston station. Gordon Junior touched at Eli's sleeve again, while Daddy started up talking to Lonny about the submarines and what all was going on up there to New Hampshire. Eli held tight to his momma, who set to crying again, which made Eli hold on even tighter, nowhere in him any way to tell he'd ever been a boy too stunned at his own daddy's death to believe his momma could marry someone else.

It was love I saw in how tight he held her, love I saw in his momma's arms around him. Love in all this, all of it: this family.

★ ★ ★

SEVEN YEARS LATER Mahlon was born, and
named, and then he was grown up, in the same
old way everyone complains of the years passing without your noticing it: first he was walking, then bringing home worksheets to color
in, and here came Cub Scouts and Little
League and band and Boy Scouts and a paper
route.

Then here he was in the kitchen, home
from his classes at Holyoke Community College, on his lips word of a girl he'd met in his
freshman composition course. A girl with eyes
he couldn't believe for how beautiful they
were, and with a brain, and a laugh, and hair
he wanted to touch the minute she'd sat down
at the desk beside him.

Ruth.

Ruth. An only child just like my Mahlon.
She was a girl from up in Ashfield, a hill town
she lived in until her momma died when she
was twelve. She'd moved then with her daddy
on down to Holyoke, so he could be closer to
his work as supervisor at Chicopee Mills.

Ruth, an independent girl made so by the
death of her momma, and the death of her
daddy when she was a senior at Springfield
High. So that when my Mahlon met her that

day in college it was her will and backbone and spirit perhaps he saw and fell in love with so quick. A spirit I fell in love with as well the first time I took her hand in mine to shake when we had her over to supper not but three weeks after they'd met.

She'd stood in the doorway of the old house on 116, behind her the failing light of an October early evening, beside her my son, beside me my Eli.

And I saw her eyes, saw in them what Mahlon'd seen from that first day: a woman, with her own mind, and a heart that could hold Mahlon close enough to let him know the love I'd known with my Eli.

She'd had on a gray sweater, a plum muffler, and blue jeans. She'd had her hair pulled back, and I could see in how Mahlon couldn't take his eyes off her that this was a done deal, the two of them. Done and done.

Mahlon'd said, "Momma, Daddy, this is Ruth Denton," and smiled, like the words were some kind of preamble he'd had to memorize and'd finally gotten right.

"I'm so happy to meet you," she'd said. The usual words, but filled with her eyes, and given the truth for the smile she gave.

She put out her hand, and I took it, felt the firmness of it. I let go, and she offered it to Eli, who nodded, smiled, said, "We've heard a lot about you."

They'd come for supper before going in to town to see a movie at the Academy of Music. They never made it, the four of us up late into that autumn night, talking, getting to know one another.

Becoming kin.

They married, struggled to get on their feet, struggled too through the discovery of cysts on Ruth's ovaries. She'd had, finally, to have a hysterectomy at twenty-five, no hope from then on out for having children of their own.

It was a struggle they'd made it through, too, until they saw it was enough, however selfish the world might've felt it was, to just be the two of them together, and to live the rest of their lives with and for each other.

Then gone was my Eli.

It was Lonny to comfort Mahlon when Eli passed, the two of them just heading out to the Quabbin to walk and to talk a couple afternoons a week on the paths and trails that laced the reservoir out there. Mahlon'd known Lonny since before he could remember, shot his first deer with him, Eli that day at the head of the next draw over on the land Lonny owned out past Belchertown, the luck such that Mahlon had decided just to set up with

Lonny instead of his daddy, and here had come a buck, and Lonny'd let Mahlon have him.

Mahlon'd even thought for a while on becoming a plumber because of Lonny, though the partnership that'd gotten us here to Lonny's part of the world split up in 1952, only a few months before Mahlon was ever born. That was when Eli'd opened up his own garage down on Lower King, Lonny staying with pipes and plungers and whatnot.

Then, in April, Lonny'd been diagnosed with his cancer, and Mahlon was up to his place two or three nights a week after work, just to talk. No more walks out to the Quabbin.

But it was Mahlon to die first.

AND WHERE IS the husband's arm around the shoulder of his wife as she whispers her son's name?

Where is my Eli, and where is my comfort?

And now I knew the foolishness of a girl's being born again. I knew, in the cold light of this November morning in Massachusetts, that the next new world I'd seen upon coming up from the warm water off Sullivan's Island wasn't one that would not change. It was a new world, shot through with change, filled

with it and the certain curse of the fact we all
of us lived hoping, dumb as the sheep God said
we all were, that life would go on in grace, and
that joy was something we could hold tight as
the hands of the ones we loved most.

What was my story, but one of grief, my
song one of sorrow?

Chapter 6

RUTH AND MAHLON'S HOUSE was four blocks off Main, back behind the old elementary school and the graveyard beside it. Like all of them in this part of town, the house sat ten feet away from the houses on either side, only enough room on the one side for a little strip of grass, on the other a driveway that hugged the house and led to the garage behind it. Most all the houses, too, had been broken up into two or three apartments each, theirs no exception.

They'd rented out the downstairs for a few years to a young couple, then those kids had a baby, the husband got promoted, and they bought a house a little farther out. Then, as though all things worked together like some sad trail of stepstones across a creek, Eli died of his heart attack, and here Mahlon and Ruth were with an empty downstairs. They asked me to come live with them.

A couple hundred yards away, at the end of Walnut on a raised platform of dirt, were train tracks separating this neighborhood from King Street and the Dunkin' Donuts and video stores and Cumberland Farms and whatnot of downtown all over there. The first few nights I was here, I'd come awake to the low rumble of a train heading into town and passing on through, then listen to it just as hopelessly fade away.

Once that rumble was gone, I'd listen for the sound of Eli breathing next to me. But instead of the warm and sweet in-and-out of air from him I'd hear the creak of the bed through the ceiling above me, Ruth or Mahlon turning in their sleep. A small sound, but a comforting one, a quiet twist of metal that gave me the good knowledge I wasn't alone.

Some nights, too, I'd wake to hear the two of them making love, the small untroubled sound of the bed moving up there slow and gentle, sometimes in there too their voices, pitched quiet and distant and twined together all at once. Voices I couldn't recognize for the fact these were the ones they saved for when they were alone and together like that, and though it may seem strange for me to say that there was pleasure in listening to my son and his wife hold each other and love each other, there was a kind of pleasure nonetheless.

It was the pleasure of my own history with Eli, our own making love. Not the colorless love we made all those years it took us to find Mahlon, love at times desperate for the fact we'd been told by most every doctor from Springfield to Hartford we'd never have children. Love senseless and remote for the goal to it, one just past our reach but one we longed all the more for: conceiving a child.

Nor did the sounds from upstairs bring me the pleasure of remembering the early days and the eager way we had at each other, we two drenched in each other's arms, smiling and breathing in and in and in and smiling still for it. A smile that started the first night we were together, our wedding night—June 24, 1946—when we were finally alone in a room in the Fort Sumter Hotel there at the tip of Charleston and White Point Gardens. Outside our window on the fourth floor lay the whole of Charleston Harbor and the huge live oaks that filled the park and those grand mansions like brick-and-stucco peacocks along the Battery.

A view I didn't see until the next morning, when I woke up to find first light creeping in through the curtains. I'd stood from the bed with no clothes on at all, a move I'd never made in my life before, standing naked at a window with not a thought in me of why this wasn't something a woman ought to do.

Because it was love I'd just then known, the all-night-long burst of it, the startling surprise of pleasure we'd waited all this time to know from each other worth all that wait, worth the promise revealed in the two of us together, him inside me, me with my arms around him: we were meant only for each other. Last night I had been a virgin, and this morning I was my Eli's lover, and I felt in the light on my skin and the sky out there as broad and full of early light as any sky could ever be, that the rest of my life was certain to be this full of bliss, this full of love.

Then here was Eli behind me, close to me, him naked as me, and I felt a hand at my waist, and here was his other hand, out in front of me. In it was a round box a little smaller than a shoe-polish tin, wrapped in silver paper and tied off with white ribbon.

He put his chin on my shoulder, formed his body to mine. I held the box, said, "For me?"

"No one else on earth," he said, both hands around me from behind. "Open it."

"As if I wouldn't," I said, and reached to his cheek, touched him. Gently as I could I untied the ribbon, carefully lifted free the tape at either end.

"Your wedding present," he said. "Not much to look at, but it's what a sailor could afford."

It was a round blue velvet box, and I lifted the lid.

There, centered in white satin, lay a locket, the kind you pinned to your dress. Gold, simple. No filigree to it.

I lifted it free of the box, held it up to this morning's light in through the open window.

"It's beautiful," I whispered.

"Now you got to open it up." He reached to my other hand, took the box, and tossed it on the bed behind us.

I unhitched the tiny clasp, opened it up to see my Eli, his face no bigger than a quarter, clipped from one of his Navy portraits. "My handsome Eli," I said, and held the locket up with both hands.

Across from his picture the locket was empty. No engraved words, and I said, "What will we put on this side?"

"Whoever we find," he said. "Whoever it is God gives us to take a picture of."

"And what if there's more than one?" I said. I put my free hand to his hands at my waist, dangled the open locket before us both, before us a day breaking clean and pure and only for us.

"Then we'll have to get you another one," he said. "But keep this one close," he said. His voice had gone to a whisper, his hand up to my own hand, the two of us holding now the locket. With his thumb he pushed it closed, until it snapped shut in my palm.

"Keep this close," he whispered, and turned me to him.

"I promise," I'd whispered, and without another word we were back to the bed, and to each other, me holding tight to that locket, and this beginning.

BUT THE SOUNDS I heard from the bedroom above me, and the pleasure I found in them, weren't about any sort of love Eli and I'd known on our honeymoon, or like we'd known trying to make the child God might give us.

The pleasure I found in the sounds from above me was the memory of those times of my own with Eli, when we were adults, Mahlon growing up and our lives running what felt at times all on its own. Those sounds of Ruth and Mahlon brought me those moments in the dark of our bedroom in the old house on 116, the two of us at the end of a routine day discovering each other new, the person in bed next to me somebody I'd known and forgotten and'd found again.

And each time we did this, met each other in the dark and drew into the other's arms for the comfort and warmth needed those particular nights, we'd whisper to each other, "Nice to meet you."

A habit born out of need, one for the other, spoken in a kind of code deciphered in the dark to reveal the secret we both knew all along: *you have my heart.*

WHEN FINALLY Ruth made it downstairs, I was in the kitchen, setting out something for us to eat so's we'd at least try at some breakfast: toast, juice, half an orange each. Who knew when there'd ever be biscuits again.

She had on a heavy cable-knit sweater, cream-colored and with a high neck. Her chestnut hair fell down about her shoulders in a way made it look even more beautiful, and she had on jeans, her slippers. She wore no makeup, and stood for a moment looking at me, her hands in her jeans pockets.

I was at the table, in one hand the plate of toast about to set down. But I just held that plate there above the tablecloth, white with here and there bright red and blue and yellow tulips. Because I couldn't move. Here was my son's wife. And my son was gone.

Here was started the first day of the end of my life here.

"You look warm," I said, and smiled. "That sweater."

She tried at a smile, rubbed her nose with a Kleenex balled up in her hand. Of course her eyes were red and sharp and swollen. Of course.

"Toasty," she said, and nodded at me, at what I held in my hand: the plate of toast. She tried at that smile again.

I put the plate down, shook my head the smallest way. "That's a good one," I said, and took my seat, directly across from Ruth's plate.

Ruth didn't move, only stood looking at the head of the table, where there was no plate, no napkin, no knife to spread fig jelly from the jar at the center of the table.

"You've got to eat something," I said. I leaned forward a bit into her line of sight. I nodded, still looked at her. I put my hands to my lap, looked to her chair. She moved to the table, sat down.

I put a hand on the table, held it out to her for the morning blessing we said each day.

This was Mahlon's job each morning. Asking God to take care of us, see us through in His mercy to the end of this day, and to keep us safe.

I held my hand out, palm up, and looked at Ruth. Her eyes were to the window, the light coming in stone-bright and hard. Outside lay the end of the driveway where it wrapped around the back corner of the house, and the little garage, the white clapboard of it, the shadows beneath the eaves.

Outside lay nothing.

I bowed my head, still with my hand out on the tabletop in hopes she might take my hand, and I prayed.

"Dear Lord," I said, and stopped. Just those two words out of me. Nothing else, because nothing else came.

Then here was Ruth's hand in mine, sudden and warm and solid. Enough touch for me to go on. Whether I believed this God could bless us and keep us or not.

"Dear Lord," I said again, and held tight to Ruth's hand, felt her fingers go tight around mine, and even the pain of that hold felt, in its own jagged way, good. "Bless this day. Protect us." I paused, heard clear as him being here with us the same petition Mahlon made every morning—*Hold us in your hand, and forgive us our sins, for we are sinners and fall short of Your glory*—but chose not to say his words myself.

Because though it was true, and we were all sinners, at this moment, on this morning, I wondered who held God accountable when it so fell that He was the one who sinned against us.

My Mahlon was gone.

"Amen," I whispered.

I opened my eyes, looked up at Ruth, her hand still in mine.

She was turned to the window, her eyes on the same nothing out there. She hadn't closed them, hadn't bowed her head, and I admired her for that. For keeping steady the gaze when everything around you is swirling up and around and away from you.

"I was thinking," she said, "up in the shower." She paused, took in a shallow breath. "I was thinking about Mahlon, and me. About how we had this little ritual." She was staring heavy now out into that light, didn't blink or even, it seemed, breathe.

I watched her, waited without breathing myself. This was news about my child. This was news.

"We never told anyone about it. Didn't have to." She paused. "Because it was ours. Because we did it."

And though I wanted this news, it came to me the brittleness of whatever she was about to do. It came to me in the light in her eyes, that blue-green lit with this day and the glisten of tears about to come, that this was something maybe she ought not offer up. Maybe this was something she should save, and savor.

Maybe this was something might could break in the telling of it, the way I might begin to lose altogether if I ever put to spoken words those moments in the dark when Eli or me would reach to the other, whisper *Nice to meet you,* that code no one else in the world could ever know.

"Don't," I said, against my will, for this news was what I wanted. I wanted whatever portion of my son, whatever mote of his presence I could see. That was what I wanted.

But this was hers.

Her eyes went to mine quick. She blinked, blinked again, that glisten still hanging on.

"Don't say it," I said. "You hang on to it for

the treasure it is," I said, my voice gone, not even a whisper for the fact my own heart was breaking yet again.

"But it's only—" she started, but paused an instant. She took in the smallest of breaths, and I saw her shiver, in her the shock of seeing what it was I was keeping her from doing. She saw I was after helping her save her husband, to keep him alive.

"It's something you own. That memory," I said. "What it is you did. It's something you own," and I swallowed hard at the words.

She nodded, once. The move wasn't much more than the shiver went through her for recognizing what I meant in all this. But she nodded, and my heart kept right on breaking.

THE ORANGE WAS tasteless in my mouth, mealy, an early navel way too early. I'd bought it a week or so ago, back when the world was open to possibilities. When an early navel might be, despite all odds, true to its flavor and purpose.

I put the orange back on the plate, only one wedge gone from it, there with its peel in three pieces like bright shards from a broken bowl. I looked over to Ruth's plate. She hadn't touched anything, the toast long gone cold, the orange still its perfect unbroken bowl of color, the cranberry juice in exactly the same spot I'd placed it.

"Maybe I'm just a little too full from all the casseroles the girls've been bringing," I said. I stood, picked up the plate and glass. "There's enough food in the freezer and fridge to last us a month." I put the juice to my lips, took a small sip. It'd gone warm, the sweet-and-sour of the cranberry dulled for it.

I went to the sink, put the plate and food inside it, still held the glass. I would finish it. I would empty the glass, give my body whatever it was cranberry juice, whether warm or cold, could give it. Then the glass was empty, and I took it from my lips, looked at it for a moment.

It was an empty glass, and needed to be put away. Everything I had needed to be put away, from this glass to the all of what was in the front room to the bed I slept in every night. The same bed Eli and I met each other new in each time we spoke our secret words.

I rinsed the glass, pulled from the cupboard door beneath the sink the dish towel hanging there, and heard in the same second the odd split of bright sound Ruth's chair made as it scraped across the floor. She stood from the table, came to me at the sink, dropped her own toast in, but set the orange on the counter beside the sink, and the juice glass. Her glass was empty, too.

"They gave me two weeks off," she said. I turned, looked at her. Her eyes were to the orange there, as though it might speak to her, surrender some wisdom or secret as to how it could sit there, as bold and bright as it was even after it'd been cut in half. "But maybe I'll go in before that," she said, and paused, let her eyes come to mine. "Maybe I'll drive over tomorrow or so, see if I can't get back to work a little sooner."

Her eyes on me were a test, I could see. She was asking me something in her words. She was after something.

And it came to me: she was asking about being a widow. She was asking what it was you were supposed to do now.

How do you live now? she was asking.

You move home, I wanted to say to her. You try to breathe, I wanted to say. You finally reckon with how life is nothing more than whistling in the dark, I ached to tell her.

But I said the easy thing. Because I was leaving here, and leaving her.

She was still so young. She was intelligent, and beautiful. She could stay here, live out her days, and maybe one day the weary pain that shouted out from her blue-green eyes might disappear.

I said, "It's God gotten me through this long. His tender mercies that's gotten me through these eight years. He'll be here for you, too." I put a hand to her face, felt how soft her cheek was, how young and sweet and beautiful just that touch was. "Hollow words, I know," I whispered. "But two weeks won't begin to touch it. Two weeks will seem like a year and seem like a day. You got to trust in God to see you home."

She looked at me, tried once more at a smile. But there was nothing for it, and it disappeared in a moment, crumbled into itself. She leaned into me, and we were holding each other one more time.

How many more times would we hold each other? I wondered. How many, before I left her here, to her friends, and to that job, and to this house and this neighborhood and to the low cry of trains that trembled through town each night? How many, before I left her to this light?

I did not know, of course. But here was one of them, the two of us together now, this holding each other, though Ruth could not know, the first of my good-byes.

And the doorbell rang.

We pulled away at the same instant, looked at each other, and Ruth took in a quick breath.

"I'm wagering it'll be one more casserole," I said. "Probably Mary Margaret, or Hilda. They both said they'd be by today." My hands were to her shoulders, in one of them still the dish towel. I smiled, said, "How much you want to bet it's another plate of Mary Margaret's famous pierogis?"

Ruth sniffed, wiped at her nose again with that same Kleenex. "Peach Gazda's coming over today, too," she said. "She ate half those pierogis Mary Margaret brought over day before yesterday." She gave a small laugh. "She loves them."

I was already headed out the kitchen into the foyer. "Mary Margaret'll be happy to hear that," I said, and nodded. The notion of Peach, one of Ruth's friends and a fellow cashier from work at the Stop & Shop, coming by to help us eat yet again seemed a good one. Soon enough Ruth would be here without me.

This was where she was from, where she was born and raised. She would stay here, both in her home and surrounded by her friends.

She would find, somehow, how to breathe.

And Mary Margaret had begun to help me breathe again, too: she'd been the first one I'd called once I'd been able to think to phone someone, and then here she'd been to the house, outside this same front door that cold night, her bundled up in her heavy jacket over her nightgown, and tears already behind the thick glasses she always wore. Before she could even get off the muffler she'd had knotted beneath her chin we were holding on to each other, and crying. Then Hilda and Carolyn and Phyllis got here, and then the all of us tended best as we could to Ruth. But it'd been Mary Margaret I'd asked to spend the night here with us, and Mary Margaret to stay, the two of us in my bed down here, and lying awake and awake and awake.

I was at the door then, looked to the window to quick catch a glimpse through the sheers of who it was out there, whether Mary Margaret, or Hilda or Peach. We could warm up what was in the fridge, I was thinking, if it was her. But it was Mary Margaret I was hoping for.

But then I saw the shadow through the sheers of somebody else. Not one of the girls, but tall, this shadow. This was a man.

I pulled the door open, not sure who it might be, but in me all the same a solid black brick of pain for who I knew it was.

Here he was, between us now only the glass storm door. Dressed the same as he always had, a gray down vest over a red-and-black plaid wool shirt, gray work pants, old work boots scuffed and muddy. He still had the same old glasses he'd worn since a couple years after the war, the old-fashioned plastic-framed kind that started out thick at the top and thinned down to wire at the bottom edge. In his hands was his same old hat, the Red Sox ball cap he'd worn forever, even as far back as when he and Eli'd come into Grace's Five and Dime in Portsmouth, the two of them asking after free chocolate sodas, me obliging them.

Lonny Thompson.

Here he was, and it seemed he may well have already passed away himself for how thin he was, how drawn his face, those glasses huge on his face, as though the frames'd grown somehow. The neck of his shirt seemed too big, too loose, and his shoulders'd all but disappeared. Wisps of white hair hung about his nearly bald head, age spots littered across the wrinkled skin of his forehead and cheeks and ears.

He was dying of the cancer.

But here were his eyes, the warm brown of them behind those glasses, no matter how drawn he was, no matter how very near death this man was.

I hadn't spoken to him much other than

hello and good-bye in more than fifty years. Not since a spring afternoon in 1952. Never mind he was my husband's best friend all those years. Never mind it was my son to find comfort from this man once his daddy'd passed away.

Now here he was to my front step, between us the thin glass of the storm door, and all those years.

I heard from behind me a startled breath in, on it grief and surprise both. I didn't need to look behind me to know Ruth was right there, right there, come to see who was at the door this next day.

Then she let out a sigh, one from deep in her soul, a sigh hollow and full and quiet and quick and sad, all at once.

This was the man her husband'd been visiting before he died. Here was the reason he was dead now. This man.

Lonny's eyes broke from mine to Ruth behind me, and I turned, looked to her as well.

She was leaned against the doorway, both hands to her face, held there as if in a prayer, her fingers just touching, as though she might be afraid to utter the prayer that might be on her lips.

She looked from Lonny to me, and here was the shine in her eyes, the glistening evidence of the grief I'd heard in her quick breath in. She closed her eyes, then let her head drop, her chestnut hair falling off her shoulders to shroud her sorrow.

Slowly I turned back to Lonny. His eyes were still on Ruth, but then he looked at me.

That was when he swallowed. I saw the work of it, the way his Adam's apple labored with the effort, and saw too the thin indentations high on his cheekbones, lines that ran from just in front of his ears and down to the edges of his nose, where oxygen tubes had left their marks all these months.

Mahlon had told me how bad he'd gotten. He'd told me about the oxygen, about how he and Lonny took small walks now and again, and how it'd gotten to where it was only out onto the porch of his house that they two could make it before Lonny'd give out.

He'd driven all the way here, behind him the old blue Dodge pickup as battered and beaten as it'd ever been, LONNY'S PLUMBING AND HEAT-ING painted on the door.

For a moment I wondered what it had taken to drive all the way down here in the shape he was in. But, just as I'd known it was him for the shadow he'd cast through the sheers, I knew it was a kind of love that'd gotten him down here.

It was love for Mahlon that'd gotten him here, love that had inside it a love for my husband, his best friend his whole life.

It was a love for me, too. Love that meant no matter the sin in the world there was still a love larger than the mistakes any of us made.

And it was love for Ruth, because she was Mahlon's wife, and he knew how much Mahlon loved her.

I saw all of this, and saw too our one trip all the way to the Totem Pole Ballroom in Auburndale, come to me now fifty years later, and the sofas they had in there in rings, tiered down to the dance floor. I saw we three—Lonny, and Eli, and me—and saw too the date Lonny'd brought, her already dancing with somebody else not but a minute after we'd sat down on our sofa and ordered up drinks from the cocktail girl. Lonny had on a blue pinstripe suit, I saw, and already was glum over the bust this evening would be, even with Benny Goodman playing in the packed-out place.

And I saw me standing then and putting my hand out to Lonny even before the drinks'd come in, but not before looking a moment at Eli, nodding to him, our eyes meeting a moment. I saw the smile on Eli's face as he nodded back, figuring out what I wanted to do: give poor Lonny a dance.

And then I saw me turn to Lonny, whose eyes were still to the dance floor, looking for that nameless girl gone from my memory all these years later.

"Let's dance," I'd said then, and held out my hand to him, and now here he was standing in his blue pinstripe suit, and smiling, the evening not a bust after all.

And we'd danced, making sure to flounce our way right on past the girl, who'd taken up with a stubby Merchant Marine of all people, one it was plain to see couldn't dance to save his life.

But we'd danced, and we'd laughed, and later on Eli had cut in, and then, the night over, and Lonny having danced with at least a dozen girls, we'd headed home. We'd left that girl we'd come into the ballroom with there at Norumbega Park, and'd laughed about it all the way home.

I'd danced with him, this man who now labored so just to swallow. This man who stood before me now, dying.

His eyes came back to mine, and he swallowed again, all that labor once more. The hand with the Red Sox cap in it came slowly up to the glass, and he touched his index finger to the glass, then his next one, and now he dropped the cap, let it fall to the ground like a banner surrendered, his whole hand to the glass of the storm door.

I looked in his eyes for a long while, felt inside me the same cry Ruth'd let out, the hollow of it, and the fullness.

And I looked at that hand, the same one I'd held a moment too long there at the train station all those years before.

Only a hand. A man's hand, the hand of someone as much a part of this family as any blood relative might ever be.

Though it was cold out there, and though it was warm in here, there was no halo of condensation around his hand, no wisps of gray warmth out of him to leave as evidence he was even alive.

"Forgive me?" he said, the effort of the words even more than he'd needed to swallow. His voice was thin, empty, as though the glass between us and the cancer inside him had robbed the words of any meaning, despite how hard he'd worked to deliver them.

I put a hand to my face, a move too quick and sharp for the all of what he was asking: forgiveness, for being the reason my son was dead.

"Lonny," I began, but heard out of me nothing more. Only his name, spoken and left alone.

That was when I heard Ruth crying from behind me, a quiet sheet of grief just here with me.

"Lonny," I tried again, "maybe not now. Maybe later on we can all . . ." I said, and then the words gave out altogether, and I was only left looking at him through this glass between us.

Here was Lonny, asking for forgiveness.

God in His heaven, and nothing right with the world.

Still he held his hand to the glass, and I looked at it one last moment before I turned away, slowly pushed closed the door until it latched hard and certain.

I went into the kitchen. Two plates lay on the counter, beside them the sorrow and bright promise of half an orange.

Light fell through the window.

Chapter 7

WELL, UH, HILDA?" Mary Margaret said, and I saw a broken smile play across her face, her eyes blinking too many times for the work it was just to lead off a hand. "What do you bid?"

Bird in Hand was the game we played every Tuesday night, a game involves bidding how many hands high and low you could win, and then the all of us yammering on through every minute not given over to making that bid.

It was a game for old women, and that's who we were. Old women sitting around a dining room table over to Carolyn's house on Florence Center Road, the little split-level ranch

she'd lived alone in since her husband Virgil
died in his sleep fifteen years ago.

Mary Margaret held her cards out in front of
her like she always did, the cards too low and
away from her face despite the fact she wore
those trifocals now. We'd told her enough
times she shouldn't hold her cards that way because it was too easy for us to see, and so too
easy for us to be tempted to cheat. It was we
women, too, who'd finally talked her into
those trifocals for the fact she couldn't see a
barn beside her. But the old habits die hard,
and so we all knew just to look low, duck our
eyes when she held them out that way.

"Because if you don't, uh, get a move on,"
Mary Margaret said, and tried again at a smile,
a signal to me she was about to attempt to be
funny, "then we'll have to ask you to, uh, get
the Hilda out of here."

"Ha!" Hilda let out from across the table.
"Mary Margaret is trying to make a joke out of
my name!" Her German accent cut the words
into hard pieces of separate sound, though
she'd been here in the States for nearly as long
as I'd lived in Massachusetts. "What a joker
you are," she said, and shook her head at Mary
Margaret, screwed her mouth up as though the
last thing she'd do would be to give a smile.

"A joke out of Mary Margaret," Phyllis said,

her sitting here to my right. She let out a short laugh herself, then *tsk*ed. "Even a blind squirrel finds an acorn now and again," she said, and then Hilda let out a real laugh, and she and Phyllis shook their heads at this whole notion of Mary Margaret, and a joke.

I looked at Mary Margaret, here to my left, saw she was blinking even faster now, the butt of her own try at making light of the fact Hilda wouldn't yet commit to bidding.

These were our Tuesday nights playing Bird in Hand.

And this was my dear, fragile Mary Margaret. My best friend. The same woman who'd lived next door to Eli and me when first we got to town. Like me, she was a new bride, married only a year before to Tommy Blizniak, just home from the war, where he'd been in the South Pacific with the Seabees. She was a girl who'd never left the Connecticut River valley, her life spent on a Hadley onion farm until she was nine, when her parents were killed in that train wreck on the New Haven line. It was the first time she'd ever spent a night without her parents in the same house with her, them headed to New York City for their very first time away, and it was that loss, a matter of fact hard enough and heavy enough to make her second-guess every move she'd make from then on out, that opened the door and invited that breakableness right on in. A loss so real its presence was still right here with us, seventy-some years later, with the hesitant call for bids to start.

Now Tommy lived over to Willow Springs, the nursing home off River Road, where on good days he can recognize Mary Margaret. Sometimes he'd even smile at her and maybe nod, the stroke two years ago so strong it was a miracle, the doctors'd all said, he was even alive. She lived next door at Willow Woods, the assisted-living apartments with its own cafeteria and TV room and library. She wasn't in bad shape at all, nowheres near the bulk of the people living in there. But it was next door to Tommy. The accommodations were good, the food hot, the laundry folded for you, and help anytime you needed it.

"Two and one," Hilda finally said. "My bid is two and one." And just as her accent hadn't dulled any in all these years, her hair was still the same blond, her eyes the same piercing blue they'd been when we met in 1951 at a rummage sale out to Belchertown. At the exact same moment, we'd both picked up an opposite corner of the same Swallows Flying quilt for sale at a table. We'd looked up at each other, got to talking about that pattern, and'd been friends ever since.

"Two and one," she said one more time, and glared across the table at me, her partner for this round, and of course I could see in the cut of those blue eyes what she was saying: *you bid higher.*

But I only smiled at her, sat back in my chair, looked at this room on the night I had news to give them of how my life was going to change.

The walls were cluttered with drawings and watercolors and collages and all else from first Carolyn's grandchildren and now her great-grandchildren. She had nine so far, though at sixty-eight she was the youngest of us all. When you walked into each room here you sometimes felt you were walking into a grade-school classroom the day after the art teacher'd come through. Even in this room, the dining room with its wood-paneled walls and china hutch, she'd tacked a string of construction-paper turkeys to the walls at the ceiling, each one made from the handprint of a child and pasted with paper feathers of every wild color.

I'd be lying if I said that all this evidence of the life that had come from her and Virgil— those nine great-grandchildren, the fourteen grands from the five children she'd bore—had never gnawed at my heart for how Eli and I'd had only Mahlon, and that he and Ruth'd never even been able to find their own. But on this night there was in all these decorations the certain innocence there had always been. Here were children's hands. Here was evidence of joy.

In every one of those turkeys, and in every Christmas reindeer head, those children's hands the antlers, and in every autumn leaf ironed between sheets of waxed paper she'd taped to the windowpanes on the front door, there was only love. Pure and simple and true, so that on this night I could not bear any ill will at all, nor envy, nor pity for myself. Here was love, as it had ever been and always would.

Precisely what I felt for these women, my friends.

Tonight was the second Tuesday after the funeral, Thanksgiving a week and a half away. It'd been a given we wouldn't play cards that first Tuesday, no one even suggesting it, though Mary Margaret and the girls'd visited every day since the Hadley police officer'd pulled up to the house.

Nor had we taken up with the quilting yet. Nobody'd said word one on this matter, either, but we all knew that tomorrow we'd be either to my house or to Phyllis's, our two quilting corners. Then we'd settle back to work, as though this evening's jawing and messing were a kind of starting line for the rest of all our lives.

Or the finish line for the last eleven days.

"So then it was all I could do not to give that knucklehead grandson of mine a handful of slap," Phyllis started back up, just like she always did: she'd begun to tell us a story fifteen minutes ago, this one all about her grandson and his monkeyshines, then let it trail off like she did for the rest of whatever anyone was after talking about, only to start in as though she'd never stopped. Even though it was her turn to bid, she was just getting around to her story, like always. "Sammy's here at my door at one thirty in the A.M.," she said, "and asking can he camp out in my front room because he knows his father's going to cuff him good if he shows up at his own house like this." She shook her head, her perfect white hair cut close. She looked at me, smiling, as if I were somehow in on this conspiracy we'd already heard her tell of three times so far tonight. "Imagine this kid!"

She had on a pink pastel sweater, pastels all she ever wore. What with that close-cut hair and those colors, no one of us could ever manage to tell her she wasn't a teenager anymore, despite how much White Shoulders perfume she wore. She was a heavy girl, always had been, and held her cards so close to her chest it seemed near impossible for her to truly know what she had in her hand for the barest glimpse she took of the top edges of the cards.

She had her own story, her own woes, this grandson she was talking about, Sammy, not the first or last of them. He was thirty-two, still lived with Phyllis's oldest, Jack, and his wife Miriam. Thirty-two, and still so afraid of his daddy he wouldn't go home drunk.

I nodded at her, smiled myself. But I couldn't muster any picture of Sammy, because tonight my head was filled with the notion that I was going to tell them.

Tonight, I would tell them I was going home.

"It is your bid," Hilda said, for Phyllis, of course, but still glaring at me, waiting for me to respond.

I looked at her, held her eyes a moment, thought to wink my left eye the way I do when I can bid higher. We all have our own signals, and we all know every one of them, too, so that if I were to wink that left eye, or the right to show her I couldn't carry the hand, it wouldn't be anything but headline news here at the table. We'd been playing near as long as

we'd been quilting, and we all knew that
Hilda's glare like that meant what it did, and a
smile meant otherwise; Phyllis touched the
bridge of her nose for low, tugged her left ear
for high; Carolyn signaled she couldn't go
higher by just letting out, "But I just can't go
higher," as though in her honesty we'd forgive
the slip, her always surprised when we carried
on about how she just couldn't say such a
thing. Mary Margaret, her cards flat and facedown on the table once she'd made up her
mind how to go, puckered her lips when she
knew she could carry the hand, made a quick
tsk when she couldn't.

It was a language we all spoke, our own kind
of card-game code that showed we were all of
us keeping secrets in our own way, but keeping no secrets at all. We knew how to read one
another the way dear and old friends can read
each other, for better and for worse, in win-
ning the hand and in losing it all the same.

But this night was not every other night, and
though I hoped there was a code I knew of for
saying good-bye, there came at me the truth
that there was none. Only the cold words I'd
have to line up and give out to them all, my
dearest friends on earth.

Any second now Carolyn'd come on out of
the kitchen with a fresh batch—the third

tonight—of cocktail wienies baked in little crescent-roll scraps. Carolyn was a little slower than the rest of us but, bless her heart, she was the sweetest of us all. Wienie wrappers—her name for them—was the only appetizer she ever made, each one skewered with a toothpick, the lot of them served up on her best china platter. We had wienie wrappers and nothing but every fifth Tuesday, because it was the hostess's job to provide the goodies.

Still, these eleven days after the funeral, the girls brought food to us, sat with us, watched us eat and carried on with us and around us. Eleven days of food, more of it than our house'd seen since when Eli passed.

But it'd started to work, that company and the good fact of food shared by friends who loved one another and looked after one another enough at least to lead me here. I wanted to be here for cards this night eleven days after my son's death.

And it'd started to work on Ruth as well: she was out to the movies with Peach Gazda from work right this moment, the two of them over to the cineplex at the Hampshire Mall.

Ruth'd had her visitors, too, mostly friends from work who showed up bearing their own gifts of food and flowers and company. The house'd seemed more a swirl of life than I could ever remember, people in and out and in and out again, everybody smiling or not smiling or talking or not talking. But all of these girls there, with us.

And still I hadn't told Ruth of what I'd planned, and in fact had already started in motion.

I'D WRITTEN my Eli's stepbrother Gordon Stackhouse, Junior, the stepbrother Eli'd left up in Georgetown to come work for my daddy. The only relative I knew of we had left down to South Carolina, a man a few years younger than Eli. It was a Christmas-card relation anymore, the only touch we had on each other's lives the trading of cards and a few little lines about what all had happened in the last year. He was a good man, a deacon in his church, two sons and one daughter, all grown. Gordon and his wife Melba'd sent flowers when Eli'd passed away, and the two of them always made certain somehow to have their Christmas card to our house the week after Thanksgiving.

And so I'd written him and Melba, let them know of the passing of my only child, and to ask too for any ideas they might have on where I might could find a place to live in Mount

Pleasant. As though these two items—my child died, I wanted to move home—were a kind of explanation one of the other, and so bore no need of comment by me.

I'd written the letter the third morning after the funeral, the sun nowhere near up yet, me alone at the empty kitchen table, the only company that smell of coffee, Ruth still asleep as she should have been. When I'd finished writing it, I'd held out in front of me the yellow sheet of stationery with the curlicues of daisies all around the edges, my hands shaking with what I was after doing.

But even with the way my hands shook with that letter, I was certain already there was a new place being prepared ahead of me. I knew it, knew it in the same way I'd known the memory of light, whole and perfect and real, that first morning after. I saw in the words I'd committed to ink and paper that purple light at sunset, saw myself a little girl inside it, and saw myself, too, as me, this woman with knotty hands and what felt like too much knowledge of the sorrows God could visit upon you. I was there, the both of me, home to South Carolina, and that light.

That was last week. Three days after the funeral, me out to the mailbox and pushing up the red flag, sunrise still only a whisper of gray in the sky to the east.

STILL HILDA GLARED at me across the table as though I hadn't gotten her message—*You bid higher*—me not yet winking right eye or left to let her know what I could do.

Phyllis took a quick peek at the top of her cards, held them tight to her chest again. She was looking at me, waiting for my wink, one eye or the other.

I looked again at my hand, saw the same set of cards as when first they'd been dealt by Mary Margaret—three twos, two aces, and a king. Plenty to outbid Hilda. Plenty to take the whole hand.

But I didn't wink. I gave her no signal, and now I could feel Mary Margaret's eyes on me, too. They were waiting, watching me. They knew me. These were my friends.

"Naomi?" Mary Margaret said near a whisper. She leaned in a little closer, tried at that broken smile again. "Are you, are you okay?" she whispered.

These were my friends.

That was when Carolyn came in from the kitchen, in her hands the platter of wienie wrappers. Right on time. "Look what I found out in the kitchen!" she said, eyes to the platter, smiling at all those toothpicks standing at attention.

But then she looked up for the silence that'd taken over the room, and quick stopped not but three paces in. She was behind Hilda, saw all eyes were on me. "Oh," she said, her eyebrows up. "Excuse me," she said to me, and nodded once hard, as though she were some loud visitor in her own home.

Phyllis let her hands holding the cards slowly fall from her chest, the cards open for all of us to see, clear as Mary Margaret's. But it was only me to see them, the others still looking at me.

"Your cards, Phyllis," I said, but she didn't move, her mouth open a little, her eyebrows together the smallest way.

"Naomi," she said, her voice pitched at the same whisper as Mary Margaret's, then Hilda whispered, "Sweetheart," the word two words inside her accent. But both words soft and untroubled.

I looked to her. She'd fanned closed her hand, the cards looking from here like only one, held tight in both her hands. She tilted her head, that glare she'd given gone.

"We love you," Carolyn said, her voice full

and true. "You know that," she said. "That we love you." She nodded hard again, as though this sealed things among us all, and then she smiled, moved the platter from one hand to the other. All those toothpicks, hovering just above and behind Hilda.

And then I felt a touch at my wrist, soft and purposeful at once.

Mary Margaret.

I turned to her, her hand out to me and touching me, and I let go my cards altogether, just let them drop to the tabletop. I tried at my own smile, grabbed hold of Mary Margaret's hand with my own fingers, the pain in them nothing for how hard I held on, and how hard she held on to me. The pain was nothing at all.

Here was Mary Margaret, her mouth closed tight but smiling, the wrinkles beside her eyes magnified for the glasses. But her eyes, the gray-green of them, somehow all the more alive.

We were all alive. Here. Now.

She whispered, "We do." She nodded once, just as Carolyn had, in the move nothing tentative or weak. This was truth. "We love you."

"I'm moving back home," I said, the words out of me too quick, too quick, but out of me easy and powerful and clean, the way a knife just sharpened will betray you and slice a

finger, the blood blossoming from your finger-
tip in a moment of red so beautiful you have
no choice but to marvel at it, the color and
brightness of it, before you even feel the pain.

There was nothing then, no smiling, no
nods. No codes or secrets or even breathing, it
seemed. Only those handprint turkeys above
us all, evidence of the innocence in a child's
hand, the magical way the outline of who you
are can become something else altogether.

Just like me here before my friends. A moment ago I was a friend, and in this silence I
knew I was already a traitor.

Mary Margaret let go my hand, pulled it
only a hair away despite how I'd held on to it.
The movement was so small, quick, and clean
itself I wasn't sure she'd really let go, and I
looked down at our hands just to make certain.

They were apart, there on the tabletop.

I looked up to her face, her eyes on me
through her glasses, eyes already filled with
tears because of me, and because of this
betrayal.

I was leaving her, and she was already leaving me.

"You have to go home?" Carolyn said, and
half turned back to the kitchen, her eyes still
on me. "Because I can put some of these up in
a Tupperware for you." Her eyes narrowed a

bit, her eyebrows furrowed with thought, piecing out what every other friend here had already.

"To South Carolina," I said to them all, and it occurred to me inside the swirl of all this betrayal that this was the first time I'd spoken this truth. The first time I'd let myself say out loud what I knew I was going to do: *I'm moving back home to South Carolina.*

I looked again at Mary Margaret. She was sitting up straight as she could in her chair, her hand even farther away, her eyes blinking again, holding off the tears welled up there.

Then one fell, slipped out from beneath her glasses, and trailed down her cheek.

I reached up, reached to her face, leaned toward her and toward her, because I had it in me to wipe that tear away. I wanted to let her know this was a good thing, that my going home was something not worth letting tears spill over.

I reached, saw my hand rise from the table, from the cards and the coffee cups and napkins with toothpicks laid neatly on each; I saw my hand rise for this history of all we women together all these years, these sisters of mine, and saw my fingers unfurl, the knuckles thick with age, until here was just my index finger, reaching to Mary Margaret's face, to that tear and its

trail down her cheek. Then here was my fin-
gertip, nearly there, nearly there, to try and
wipe away the pain I'd inflicted on her, my
oldest friend, my dearest friend.

But then, in the instant before I touched her
face, she turned her cheek from me a fraction.
Her eyes were still on me, that tear's trace gone
untouched by me, my old finger left alone and
useless, robbed of its purpose.

And I saw just then that my touching her
wasn't a move I'd intended as comfort to Mary
Margaret, but as a comfort to me.

It was me betraying her, with my heading
home.

Mary Margaret's jaw set hard, her teeth
clenched, her mouth pursed up. None of it
anything I'd seen on her face before. Never.

But here it was, that word again: *betrayal.*

She said, "What about Lonny Thompson?"

Now it was me to pull away, to haul in a
breath as sharp as broken glass, to watch my
hand crumple in on itself and draw away from
her altogether. The word *betrayal* was now a
double-edged sword: I could betray her, and
she could do the same to me.

"Mary Margaret?" Hilda said, and Phyllis
said, "They were such dear friends, Eli and
Lonny," and Carolyn said, "If you have plumbing problems, my son-in-law Gary's the one to

give a call," and I turned to them all once more, and the world came back to me.

Here were these other friends, all with concern and puzzlement on their faces, their eyes going from me to Mary Margaret and back again for whatever strange connection this was: I'd told them I was leaving, and Mary Margaret named Lonny first thing.

I sat up straight as Mary Margaret, stunned and surprised into this moment of time for the fact it was Mary Margaret, finally, to speak in code of how we would say good-bye. She knew me, knew my sorrow and regret. And she'd laid it bare open, a wound gaping and still just as raw as the day I'd told her of it, no matter the years and other sorrows that'd rained down on us both.

She'd spoken the code: *you have betrayed me.*

And now Hilda, and Carolyn, and Phyllis all seemed suddenly too far away, as far from me as I was from that sun outside Mahlon and Ruth's bedroom that first morning after.

As far away as I'd been from Lonny when I'd closed the door on him, his words to me the same ones I wanted to give to Mary Margaret first, and next to these other women: *forgive me,* I wanted to say.

I put my hands to the edge of the table. I looked at them all, watching me, and felt my legs begin to move of their own. I felt myself push on that table edge, felt myself begin the thoughts that involved making my hand go to beneath this chair to pick up my purse. All this thought, in just this instant. I was leaving. Now. Good a time as any.

And the doorbell rang, split this moment in two, same as it had when Lonny'd shown up at our door. A doorbell ringing, cutting us all in two.

Carolyn said, "I'll get it," as though nothing had passed here at all. She came around Phyllis's end of the table and then behind me, still with the plate of wienie wrappers in her hand, and into the foyer.

"Why do you want to go back there?" Phyllis said, her words hushed. She reached to me, held hard my right hand, hers warm and soft and gentle. Hilda said full-voiced, each word clipped as it'd ever been, "You have not been there in many years!" Slowly she shook her head.

Mary Margaret looked away, brought her hands to her lap. Her chin was turned from me, almost touched her shoulder for how low she brought it.

I heard the front door open, felt the quick push in of cold air from outside even before I had time to answer either of them, though there were no words to speak.

"What a surprise!" Carolyn said, and we all turned to see who was here.

Peach. Ruth's friend from work. Who she'd gone out to the movies with this evening.

She stood just inside the foyer, held her purse by the strap with both hands so that it hung down in front of her. She had the same blue parka she'd had on when she'd come to pick up Ruth, and the same black slacks, her hair the same lacquered flip, and I wondered why I was tallying all of this up, and I realized it was because of what was missing: Ruth.

Peach was trying hard to smile, her eyes already to mine and nervous, and now I was standing, my purse forgotten, these girls forgotten.

I said, "Ruth?"

And Ruth edged in beside Peach, poked her head in the doorway.

It was all I could see of her, just her head, that hair of hers long and falling down in a straight line from the collar of her red parka, her skin pale, her mouth working up a smile.

But there was nothing of a smile to it at all.

Because her eyes were telling the story right then, and I knew again why my son loved her, knew it for her eyes, and knew too the sorrow there, genuine and still unsolved.

She was looking at me.

What was it going out to a movie could do for you? I wondered, me headed for the foyer, across those few feet between us toward her pale and lonely face.

And what was it playing cards with friends could do to solve the sorrow all your own?

"We had dinner over to the Friendly's at the mall," Peach said, her voice pitched low and quiet, as nervous as her eyes and smile, "and then we went into the theater, and halfway through the movie she just stood up and started out. I thought she was going to the bathroom and I sat there for fifteen minutes before I—"

"Naomi," Ruth said, and Peach hushed for the word out of her. Ruth was still working that smile, biting down hard on her cheeks, the corners of her mouth up in a grimace she hoped would pass for a smile.

She held out a hand to me then, and now her hand was in mine, cold and thin. I could feel the small bones there, as though I were holding in my hand a shivering sparrow dropped from a tree for the cold, but still alive, and not yet given up.

Carolyn stood with the plate in one hand, the other holding the doorknob, on her face a sweet smile, her forever happy to have someone to her home, no matter what the occasion. "We've got hot coffee and wienie wrappers and a good game of Bird in Hand going on," she said. "We'd be pleased for your company!"

Peach looked to her, let out a quick breath, as though this'd been the news she'd been waiting for. She stepped one foot farther into the foyer, and though I'd been betrayed by my best friend only a moment before, still I made to pull Ruth inside this house with its food and warmth and friends.

I wanted to bring her in here, the only place I knew could even come close to being safe.

And it seemed for that moment she would come inside, that we could step into this home cluttered with handprint turkeys and waxed paper autumn leaves, and feel that we were a part of this all. We were in fact safe from the accidents waiting just outside the spill of light from this open door, accidents that lay hidden in the darkness out there, lined up to gut our lives with whatever next surprise God was wanting to hand us.

Ruth's eyes were hard on mine, in them the barest beginning of relief: there was trouble in being alone even if it was with a friend. Maybe trouble wouldn't find her here, with all these women inside a house that wasn't her own.

That was what I saw in her eyes, the very beginning, perhaps, of hope.

I felt her fingers quicken in mine, felt her hold a little tighter, felt her begin to move toward me, and inside.

But then Mary Margaret—my Mary Margaret, my girlfriend, my trust—called from behind me, "What does Ruth think about you moving back to South Carolina?"

She knew me, Mary Margaret did. She knew me for the coward I truly was, knew me to have lived a lie my whole life—I was a faithful wife, a good woman—and for that fact of who I really was she knew, too, that I wouldn't have the heart or courage to let Ruth know what I was going to do.

Because I hadn't yet told Ruth.

Mary Margaret knew me.

That relief, that barest of glimmers, bled out of Ruth's eyes in just that instant, soon as the words out of Mary Margaret registered.

I looked at Ruth's eyes, saw her lips move, and the whispered words that came with that movement, *What did she say? What did she say?*

Now it was my hand quickening in Ruth's, and without letting my eyes fall from hers I said to Carolyn, still with the doorknob in one hand and the plate of wienie wrappers in the other, "You take care, Carolyn. We'll be heading on back to the house now." I reached my free hand to the coat tree beside me, pulled from it my old black wool coat. Here was a rush of movement behind me, the girls all getting up, words bubbling as they made their way around the table to try and persuade me to stay for whatever reasons they had, and now they were touching me, everything commotion, Peach talking too.

But here were Ruth's hopeless and puzzled eyes on me, her hand growing even smaller in mine.

"You'll be needing this," I heard beside me, and quick turned to Mary Margaret.

She stood an arm's length away, her jaw set even tighter, her chin still turned. In her hand was my purse, held out to me like it was an old loaf of bread gone moldy, ready to be tossed in the trash.

I took it from her, grabbed hard at it, the move too fast and tough for my fingers to feel anything but pain. I turned, pushed through them, my coat not even on, and stepped out through the door and onto the front porch.

Ruth turned with me, her hand still in mine, and the news finally came to me that yes, I would have to tell Ruth, would have to let her know I was heading home to light and water and the smell of pinestraw in the hot summer sun.

She was still a young woman. She had her friends here, her home. She had to stay here.

"Call me," Peach said from behind us, and Phyllis said, "We'll talk to you tomorrow." Hilda put in, "Please make certain to be careful!" and Carolyn, her words smiling and surprised, I could hear, at this sudden turn of events in her own house, said, "Quilting tomorrow at your house or Phyllis's?"

I let go the question, no words to answer. Quilting. What did that mean?

"What was she talking about?" Ruth said then. "About South Carolina?" and though I knew she was looking at me, waiting, waiting, all I did was to hurry a little faster down the walk, and away from the light spilling out that front door.

"Just let's go on home," I said. "We need to be home," I said, and felt the cold of this night slice into me with the truth of who I was.

A liar. An adulterer. A coward running for a home anyone with a lick of sense knew wouldn't be there once I arrived.

Chapter 8

BLESS YOUR HEART," I said once we were in the car. "Bless your heart. Maybe going out and all was just too soon. Just too soon to be going to the movies." I turned on the headlights, eased my old Electra away from the curb.

Wind tossed leaves across the street in front of us, the small bit of it lit with the headlights. They were single leaves, the last ones that'd hung on to the trees and made it through the fall, when all the hardworking people who lived in these houses we passed had spent Saturday mornings raking up the ones that'd given up on time, then bagged them and set them at the curb for the trashmen to pick up, or simply burned them in great heaps out back.

They were single leaves, gray, dead as dead could be as they skittered out in front of this car, no triumph at all in hanging on to the last. Nothing good about not dropping on time, with the rest of them, weeks ago.

I turned right off Florence Road and onto Route 9, headed back toward downtown through Florence Center, past the park. Then here were the brick dormitories and cross-walks and what have you of Smith College all clustering up.

I looked at it all, the windows lit in the dorms, and the big white houses that in the dark out here seemed as white as day, like they were stronger than the fact of night. This was the hub of town, the reason we were here, if you read the newspapers the way they wanted you to read them. Smith College was the cen-ter of the universe, though it was nothing more than a finishing school for the confused and rich, for girls who, when their cars broke down, handed over to my Eli a credit card and a shrug when he told them how much it would take to fix.

Then we passed through the blinking yellow light out front of John M. Green Hall, the au-ditorium a hulk of shadows, those pillars out front like the ribs of some huge dead animal all shadowed over.

Over fifty years I'd lived here, and I'd never been inside.

But why would I have? This was Smith College, and the closest I would have ever come to this place had to do with my age when I'd moved here. That was the most I'd ever have in common with the place: the fact I was a young woman once who was old enough to have gone to college here.

I was married. And I was after having a child with my husband, the one I loved with all my heart, and did until he died. College hadn't mattered, and never did.

I was in love with him, and we'd had our lives put together since that evening at the table back home to Mount Pleasant, him smiling at me, my momma dropping her fork, my daddy with his eyes wide open to us both.

We passed the museum at Smith, Main Street easing down the hill and to the left. We got the red light there just before the street drops into town, and the boutiques and cafés and gourmet cooking stores and art galleries. The whole street—four lanes wide, crosswalks ready and willing to hold out a helping hand to the pedestrians always out—was lit with streetlamps, washed everything in a kind of orange glow, the street and all its fashion laid out like presents under a Christmas tree for someone else. For the wealthy folks who'd settled in up here over the last twenty years, looking for what it meant to live in a hometown.

Because that was what they all wanted, and what we all wanted: a town to call home.

Here was why I wanted to leave. Here it was: I wanted my hometown.

"It was the dark of it," Ruth said, and I turned to her. She was sitting up straight in her seat now, eyes to the stoplight out front of us, just looking at that red as though it were listening to her. Red light glistened in her eyes, wet for her crying.

"It was the dark inside the theater," she said. "The way the lights went out, and we were all left sitting there watching something going on on the wall. Watching these people live their lives." She paused a moment, swallowed, and I could see her jaw set, the muscles working a bit in the light from the lampposts outside.

She turned to me. She bit her lips together, swallowed again. "It was too much what I've been inside every day so far. Too much like it."

The light changed, and the green washed her face in a shade that seemed to hide her beauty and love and life even more deeply inside herself. But still I could see the glisten in her eyes, the tears there.

I nodded. I said, "I understand."

She turned away, looked ahead again. She nodded one time, the smallest nod imaginable.

So far it'd been me to try and teach and comfort her about what it might mean to be a widow, to love and lose and know it would never be back again. But she'd taught me this time.

She knew death herself, knew already what it was to lose your momma and then daddy, though she never spoke of it to me. We never talked about either of them, and through all these years I'd never once brought it to her, the fact she didn't speak on it. All I'd known was what Mahlon had given me, and most of it early on, when he himself was finding out about her when they were dating.

Her mother had had ovarian cancer, and'd died at home the way she wanted, there to Ashfield, the hill town up off Route 9. Ruth had been with her when she passed, and then Ruth'd moved with her daddy on down to Holyoke, where he worked Chicopee Mills as a supervisor. He died when she was a high school senior in the mill fire in 1974, to be taken care of for a year or two by an aunt and uncle in Hadley, until she moved out and started on her own.

And met Mahlon in an English class in college.

She knew already the truth of loss. This was, just like she'd said, all like sitting in the dark and watching a life played out just beyond your reach, that life your own.

I waited for one more nod from her for the peace it'd give me, for the comfort of it, however glancing. But she did nothing, only looked out at that green light.

And I drove, down off the hill and into the narrow valley the buildings and shops and apartments Main Street all made. People moved on the sidewalks, inside stores and buying things and eating things and laughing and talking, even this late of an evening. Even with a wind that tore at the last single leaves on trees, and carried them out and away.

There was life out there on this street, with it and inside it and through it all this wind, this dark, those leaves now and again. Inside and through all of it the truth that life went right on, even when you lost your heart.

THERE WAS no reason to it, Lonny and me. And no excuse.

But I only know this fact now that I can see as an old woman, a woman old enough to know that when we are young and make the mistakes we do, we are still fool enough to fool ourselves. We are so much more willing to believe ourselves, believe the lie we give ourselves to crawl out from under the fact we are sinners and sinners first, no matter the way these days that word doesn't ring with anything but the dusty sound of old people.

Sin.

When we are young, it means, *I have made a mistake.* When we are old, it means, *I have separated myself from love.*

So that what I told Mary Margaret one afternoon in April of 1952, the two of us having coffee over to her kitchen, the daffodils outside her window up and bright yellow and more alive than I'd felt myself for years, was the story of a mistake, and not the separation from love.

It was the story of Naomi, that same girl, and how she and her husband had been told by her doctor there wasn't any hope. It was the story of how they'd left this doctor, the fifth one they'd seen in four years, every one of them with the same story to tell them both, and how they'd walked down the three floors of the gray stairwell of the doctor's office there at the hospital in Springfield. Her husband, her

Eli, had walked behind her slower and slower, until when she'd reached the bottom floor he was a whole flight above her.

She stood at the door out of the stairwell, a door painted the same dull gray as the rest of her life now that she'd been given this news again and always. She was waiting for him to open the door for her, her Eli the gentleman he was and always had been and always would be.

But he was so many steps above, so many steps away, that this Naomi took in her mind to open the door herself, and reached out to the old tarnished doorknob, and pulled it open, felt in her face the quick shove of hard cold air from outside, felt it through her altogether.

A different kind of air this morning. Early April air, on it somehow the kind of hopeful wet and softer edge, the air no longer the same solid and hopeless cold it'd been since early December.

There was hope on this air. There was life to it, somehow.

She pushed the door open, stepped out into the parking lot and the gray sky. She didn't bother to gather her coat close about her neck, but let the cold course through her deeper and deeper. She heard behind her the door close of its own, her husband so many steps behind her.

He'd said nothing to her as they drove home, up the gray and brown valley, the thin road before them simply another shade of gray they had to cope with along with the rest of the gray that was the all of this news: there was no hope.

They said nothing, as though there had been an agreement between them forged in the secret the doctor had revealed to them, the secret that their bodies had betrayed them despite the love they had for each other. The doctor's words were so loud in their hearts now and for the final time—money had run out for the number of doctors they had seen, for the costs of such specialists—that the notion of words they could pass between them seemed as hopeless as the gray woods outside the window as they drove, as hopeless as the gray sky above this all.

But there had been this air, the feel of it, the possibility.

That was when, in the telling of this all to Mary Margaret only days after the fact of the mistake she'd made, Mary Margaret, her friend, her love, her listener, had reached a hand out to her across the table in her kitchen, and had taken Naomi's in hers. She'd smiled at her, and said nothing. She was there to listen, and to listen.

Once home, they had sat in the cab of the pickup, still no words between them. And then this girl, this Naomi, had opened her door, felt in that instant the same cold and full air, the same hope that seemed just past where she could touch. She felt that cold and that wet, felt it around her legs, and here at her throat, and on her face, and she'd turned to him, her beloved, and had put her hand to his there on the gearshift. He hadn't yet turned off the engine, and she felt through his hand the tremble of the engine, and thought too she could feel the tremble of his heart.

She looked at him, looked at him, waiting. But his eyes did not meet hers, only looked out the windshield at the house before them. He let out a quick and stiff breath, blinked one time, twice, and then a third, the last blink long and purposeful, she knew, his eyelids closed and quivering.

He wasn't going with her inside the house. She knew he wouldn't accompany her on the trek through this hopeful air that mocked them both, and into their hopeless house and along the hopeless hallway and into the hopeless bedroom, and to that hopeless bed they shared.

Because this was what she wanted, she'd known only then: she wanted him, now. She wanted the two of them together and in each other's arms, and him inside her and her with him as close as they could ever be. She wanted him because, with this news of the end of their lives, it seemed the only way she might live to take the next breath would be to feel him sharing with her in this hopelessness. She wanted him inside her, his mouth beside her ear, hers beside his, his arms holding her, and him inside her while she held him.

She wanted to hear the quick breaths in and out they would make, what on that night in Charleston, outside their window the whole of Charleston Harbor and the huge live oaks and grand mansions like brick-and-stucco peacocks along the Battery, had been a kind of music, the two of them breathing in and out hard and quiet and with a kind of joy that made no accommodation to the truth of the world, the sorrow in it and just outside their window.

She wanted to share with him this new world, the hopeless one.

But then, her hand still on his, his eyes closed, lids quivering for just this moment, she knew he was gone, and even before he opened his eyes she lifted her hand from his, from the trembling of the engine and his heart both.

He didn't look at her, and she closed the door, eased it shut without slamming it hard so that there would be no reading into this any anger on her part at the way she would enter the house betrayed as she'd just been. But it was betrayal she'd felt, full and true and hopeless.

Mary Margaret held her hand. The daffodils seemed to shout for how bright a yellow they were. Their coffee grew cold. The radiators hissed. Mary Margaret held her hand.

Eli backed out of the driveway, pulled away, headed off down Jackson Street toward where only he knew.

And Naomi'd stood at the steps up to the house, watched him turn off Jackson onto Elm, the only evidence he'd ever existed the thin pale blue of exhaust that hung like the smallest ghost down at the corner, where he'd gunned the engine as he turned.

She looked to the house, to the pale yellow clapboards, the windows on either side of the door, the curtains inside, the rooms past them darkened, unknowable.

No one's house she knew.

She turned, headed on up Jackson toward Market, walking.

She walked. And walked. And found herself at a house she knew. A house on Third Street,

a house she'd been to only a few times for the
fact the man who lived inside was a bachelor,
her husband's partner in the plumbing business,
a wartime pal who'd never gotten married.

She went up the steps to his door, his house
a small one with only one window to the left
of the door, dull green asphalt shingles for siding, no curtains in the window.

It was lunchtime. His own pickup sat at the
curb out front. He was home.

He'd held her hand a moment too long back
home in Charleston, there at the train station.
His eyes had held hers a moment too long.

She hadn't slammed the door to her husband's pickup, the one that had turned onto
Elm and left behind a blue cloud of smoke.

She saw her hand go to the door, the scarred
and weathered door of a house in which a
bachelor lived, saw her hand, saw it.

And saw before she'd touched the wood the
door swing open and wide, to Lonny Thompson, smiling at her, a napkin in his hands and
wiping.

He smiled, looked past her either way up
and down the street, and she saw on his face a
kind of puzzlement, wonder at why she was
here and how her husband was not with her.

"Naomi?" he'd said when his eyes finally
came back to hers. "You all right?"

And that was when she had cried, fully sobbed, and fallen into his arms, this man, her husband's best friend, his partner, his best man.

THERE HAD BEEN no joy to it. There had been no love to it, nor any ecstasy. There had been only two people inside a house on Third, two streets over from the railroad track. A house with dull green asphalt shingles for siding, inside it a woman, this Naomi, whose folly would haunt her the way a scar will haunt you, its lasting mark nothing you can do about save for trying to hide it. There had been only a woman, angry at her husband and the fact there was no hope for any children, no hope for that kind of love she had hoped for, an increase, she'd believed, of the love she had for her husband, and he had for her, by bringing into this world one from them both.

They had tried for years. They had tried, and failed, and her husband's hand not taking hers there in the cab of the truck, and the air this day that seemed full and possible, and the gray sky seemed all of it betrayal enough to make her seek out this man, her husband's best friend.

A good man. A man who believed in the words she gave to him as she'd cried once she was inside his house, the door closed solidly behind them, and as she pulled him to his own bedroom, and as she tugged at his belt and shirt, the man too stunned and too much of a human to understand that this betrayal could be stopped, and perhaps himself a moment too lonely inside the all of his life, a man who could believe as he reeled and swallowed and then, finally, began to hear the words she gave him, words she knew were a lie and yet which fed this moment, allowed it to grow and breathe and live of its own until the two of them were there on his bed, their clothes still on, her finding him and taking him in and crying all at once, him still stunned and lonely and a human being.

The lie of her words: *I've wanted you. I've wanted you always, since the day at the train station.*

The sound the two had made, their breathing, was no music, but the sound of chaos, of the breaking of lives, a sound even more hopeless, she heard in the midst of it all, his mouth beside her ear when finally he'd given in to her in his loneliness, than the gray sky outside this house on Third, more hopeless than the inside of the truck cab on the way home, more hopeless than any doctor's words.

More hopeless even than the closing of

her Eli's eyes to her, than his trembling hand
under hers.

It was hopelessness that had driven her to
Lonny Thompson, hidden behind her own
eyes the hope like a ghost, like cold wet air at
the throat, that perhaps she would conceive in
this act of separation.

She wanted a child.

And then it was over, and she opened her
eyes to a man she did not know, his eyes already open and wide in astonishment at this
moment, at the sudden shift in the earth's axis
here at lunch of an April day.

Lonny Thompson. Her husband's best
friend, a man he'd met in the hull of a submarine. A man at a train station who'd held her
hand a moment too long.

The reason she had moved here, her husband this man's partner.

Lonny Thompson.

No one she knew.

She left him there on the bed, still with his
puzzlement and wonder, and had walked on
home to that house on Jackson, and climbed
the five brick steps to the front door, entered
her house, and went to the bathroom, where
she had run the water for a bath too hot to
bear, and she had climbed in, bearing it, bear-

ing it, and washed herself and washed herself and washed herself, as though in the washing she might kill what might have already been created inside her, and in the hopes, too, she might find beneath the skin she washed off, nearly boiled off for how hot the water was, someone new, instead of this woman she knew even less than Lonny Thompson.

Naomi. Who was she?

A mistake, she had told Mary Margaret. A mistake, and she had cried.

And of course it was a lie, calling sin a mistake, when it is always and only a separation from love. A separation made by this woman, this hopeless and crying woman who would, in the telling of this to Mary Margaret, find herself saying it was all a mistake, that it was a mistake and something she would wish to take back, because she loved her husband, her Eli.

She loved him whom she had betrayed.

And Mary Margaret had never told, never once spoke of it.

Daffodils still shouted outside the kitchen window. The radiator still hissed.

This girl, this Naomi, cried, and Mary Margaret listened.

★ ★ ★

ELI CAME HOME that evening to the house dark, no lights on. He'd walked in the back door, like every evening.

Naomi, he'd called. *Naomi?*

He moved through the house, checked room and room and room to finally find her here, in the bathtub, water gone stone cold. She was shivering, and he knelt to her as soon as he'd seen the shadow of her in the dark, found her with one hand holding tight to the edge of the tub, the other clutched in a fist at her chest. He leaned quickly to her, touched her cheek and forehead, felt how cold she was. He stood, her hand in his, and pulled her from where she had tried to wash herself free of her mistake.

And then he had lifted her fully, taken her, wet and shivering, into both arms and lifted her free of the cold water, stood her on the bath mat, toweled her dry all there in the dark. Then he'd lifted her again, her still shivering, still shivering, and carried her to their bedroom, where he lay her in their bed, pulled over her first the sheet and blanket, then the Wedding Ring quilt her mother had made for them.

A Wedding Ring quilt. A gift, made in love for love.

Her love, her Eli, turned from her then, and left the room.

The girl had watched him leave, afraid for what would be the first of every time he ever left her again that it might be the last time, that the mistake she had made might have been found out and the back of the man she loved moving away from her might be the last she saw of him.

He left the room, her there in the dark growing darker each moment her mistake pressed down upon her, almost taking her breath from her—the shivering would not stop, would never stop—until it seemed in fact her breath were leaving her, that she would never breathe again for the mistake she had made, and the fact he was leaving her, as he had every right to do. Every right in the world to leave her alone, with her mistake.

But then here was movement in the dark before her. Here was her husband, her Eli shrouded so deeply in the dark and her mistake that it seemed the boy she'd squinted into sunlight all those years ago might have been a dream. But here he was inside this moment of darkness and mistake, his arms full with other quilts brought from the hall closet, and then this dark figure—*This is my husband,* she marveled, *This is my love*—leaned over her and lay first one quilt, and another, and another, heaped them all on her to warm her. All of this in the dark for the failing light of the world outside their window, the hopeless and sorrow-filled world out there going dark upon them all.

But here was her husband, showing her his love despite that hopelessness. Despite the slight ghost he'd left behind when he'd gunned the engine, and despite the way he'd closed his eyes and held them closed.

Here he was, bestowing love on her, inside a hopeless house that would never be a home, both for what they could not make between them, and for the mistake she had made just this day, this most hopeless of all hopeless days.

When his arms were empty, he reached to the corner of all these quilts, and pulled them back, a move that seemed remarkable for its strength—to be able to pull away so much warmth, she thought, to be able to lift with such ease so much love—and he climbed into bed next to her, still in his clothes from this day, still in his uniform shirt, the name *Eli* stitched in red thread above the left pocket of the gray shirt, still in his gray work pants. He'd kicked off his shoes somewhere before this moment, she felt with her toes as he moved in next to her, and he smelled of coffee and cigarettes and of soap from when he'd washed his hands just before heading home from the shop. All these same smells he carried with him every time he came home from work, and she marveled at these smells, too, and how easy they came with him, how simple and true they were, how much him they were, how much Eli.

His clothes were rough at first, and cold, though she knew how much colder she herself must have been to his touch, and he pulled the quilts back over them both, and turned to her beneath them all, and took her in his arms, and held her.

She moved in close to him, and closer, felt her skin prickling over not in cold but in response to the depth of her mistake, herself huddled inside herself and her mistake to have betrayed such a man as this. Her skin prickled over, grew taut for it, fairly bristled at this gentleness, this act of love she bore witness to, and she felt the pain of her skin against him, a jagged and sharp pain that had, she knew, nothing to do with the roughness of his clothes against her skin, but had everything to do with her own heart, with the wound that her whole self had become. The all of her, fresh and stinging and raw, her whole self a wound, she knew at the end of this day that would haunt her the rest of all her days.

And then, in a kind of miracle she knew even in that moment to be precisely that, a kind of miracle, her skin against his seemed to begin to heal, to soften, to gain warmth from the quilts, from his arms, from him.

Eli. Her husband. Her love.

That was when she allowed open her hand, clutched tight in her fist what she'd pledged to keep close.

For before she had gotten into a tub of water too hot to bear, she had burrowed in her bottom clothes drawer, found back in the farthest corner she could possibly find to have hidden it.

A locket. Gold, and simple. No filigree, no engraved words.

But the empty side of the locket too empty to keep close to her these last few years of trying, and trying, and trying yet again to fill it with a photo of whoever God might give them, so that the empty side had become to her a kind of curse hidden away in anger and sorrow and failure.

She had found it where she had buried it, and then had climbed into that tub, and bore that heat, but not before she lay the locket, still closed, on the edge of the tub, balanced there while she washed herself and washed herself, and while inside the washing she prayed to God to be forgiven, and to be allowed no child inside her for what she had done. And still she washed, and prayed, and washed in the hopes she might kill whatever child might now be materializing in the empty side, and she prayed she might be forgiven of this death as well, washing herself in water too hot to bear in the hopes when she opened the locket she would not find in there that child.

She'd watched the locket, and watched it, and when she finished washing, the water already on its way to tepid, she reached to the locket, and opened it, and found a dark kind of miracle, the miracle that was no miracle and the same miracle she had lived through all this while: there was only her husband inside, opposite him nothing.

There was only herself, fresh and stinging and raw, a wound waiting for the miracle of healing.

She held the locket out before her, looked at both the man and the emptiness beside him.

She held it, and looked at it, while the water had gone from tepid to cool to stone cold, and while dim light in the single window above the toilet failed to the utter black in which her husband, the man across from the empty side, had called to her.

Naomi? her husband had called.

She snapped closed the locket, clutched it in a fist she held to her chest, her other hand tight to the edge of the tub. And she'd waited, hoping for him to save her.

They didn't make love, there in the dark that night. He didn't take off his clothes, and she did not reach to him in a way that would signal him she wanted anything other than this moment, this beginning to heal. And he did not touch her with any signals himself, any moves that would mean he wanted more than this moment himself.

But for a moment she let open her hand, and saw in the darkness there was only enough light to see the locket, there in the pale of her hand, a locket plain as her hand was her own.

She closed her fingers around it again, but now it was different. Warm somehow, despite the cold in her.

They lay there, until morning, and began their lives again.

ALL THIS—all this—I had told Mary Margaret. All this Mary Margaret knew.

All of it taken in with the holding of my hand not but a few days after it had all happened, the yellow daffodils full and whole and bright outside her window.

Eli's and my lives began again.

I watched and hoped and prayed and cried for my period for the next three weeks, and then it came, welcome as a sailor home from war.

Eli and I didn't touch one another other than to hold each other to sleep for two months after that night, as though the two of us knew there was a passing of something between us. Some dying, maybe, of our old selves away from the hope we'd had and into this new world of no children.

Then, three months after we'd started making love again, three months after a night in which I trembled and he trembled and we both cried out of the fear we had for whatever might happen next to us, whatever world we were about to enter—three months after that first night back together, months during which we made love as though we had never done so before, reborn in us as well the discovery that we had each other, that the one either of us held in their arms was the bedrock and foundation of the way we would know the world for the rest of our lives—three months of that kind of lovemaking in which we were making love to and with each other, my period did not arrive.

Two months later Eli and Lonny Thompson ended their partnership.

Then here was Mahlon.

I never asked Eli about the breakup of the partnership, never asked after whose decision it was to have Lonny stay with the plumbing business and Eli strike out new with the garage on Lower King.

I never asked him, for fear there would be some question from him that might somehow undo me, expose the mistake I had made, reveal to him the scar of my sin against him.

And Mary Margaret never said word one to me about any or all of this. Never.

Until this night, when she'd asked her small and simple and treacherous question: *What about Lonny Thompson?*

And here had been brought back to me my sin, the act become now, with my age and sorrows, not just the mistake it had always been, but the separation from love it had always been as well. Me, from Eli.

Mary Margaret had betrayed me. In asking she'd intended not an answer from me but to remind me of my own leaving her, my own betrayal moving home to South Carolina would be.

Don't leave me, she'd said with that question.

But I was leaving her. No matter the mistake this was, no matter the separation from love it would be. No matter Mary Margaret's sin against me. Or mine against her.

And still there lingered in me the fact of her words, the cold of them, the stark and solitary notion:

What about Lonny Thompson?

Chapter 9

I HEARD THE SOUND in what I thought was
sleep: *tap tap tap,* then *tap tap tap* again. I
wanted to give the sound to a dream, to find it
perhaps Mahlon at a door, or even Eli, knock-
ing so gently and quietly and wanting in to
see me.

But then I found my eyes were open, that I
was not inside sleep. Neither Mahlon nor Eli
were here to find me.

It was my bedroom door, and here came
once more *tap tap tap.* I turned, saw pale light
frame the door, the door ease open.

Ruth.

She leaned in, her hair falling from her
shoulders, her face gone to me. My glasses

were on the nightstand beside me, and the
light from the kitchen fell in from behind her.

She was inside my room, reached a hand to
me, moved toward me.

"Naomi," she said. "Come with me."

I said nothing, as though perhaps this were
the dream I'd believed it wasn't. There was no
choice to this, I saw. Here was my son's wife,
his love, offering her hand to me in the mid-
night dark of my bedroom, and I took it, felt
how warm it was in mine.

Ruth. My Ruth.

WE'D DRIVEN the rest of the way home in silence, down through Main Street, then under
the railroad overpass, left onto Market and on
down to Walnut and into the driveway that
hugged the house on the left side, then into the
turnout behind the house, the square of pavement where for years we'd wedged all three
of our vehicles: my Electra, Ruth's Corolla,
Mahlon's Chevy pickup.

Now Mahlon's pickup was gone, towed
away from that spot on River Road, where the
black ice had been. Neither Ruth nor I'd laid
eyes on the truck. It was gone, and for a moment I'd thought of Eli, and the shop, and the
wrecked vehicles he'd have out back, pushed

up against the chain-link fence that separated his lot from the railroad tracks. Even then I'd stayed away from those things when I'd come get him for lunch or to just stop in and tell him I loved him, each wrecked vehicle I could see out my windshield a life changed, and never for the better.

Mahlon's truck was gone, so much more room here behind our house, as though this were itself some kind of blessing, not having to nose our vehicles bumper-to-bumper just to fit.

I turned off the engine, and we'd sat there a few moments in the dark, the engine slowly ticking down, the cold of the evening leaching in through the windows. The house, outside Ruth's window, hung high above us, white clapboard glowing in the night like a ghost itself, hulking and hard and all angles.

Her hands were together in her lap, clutched in them the strap of her purse. I reached to her, found one of them, felt the cold of it. She looked at me, let go the strap, and held my hand. "Maybe it's just too soon," I said once more, trying the empty words out on her again like some sort of sales pitch for a product she'd had no choice but to buy.

Then we went in, up the steps into the back of the house, where my kitchen sat. We took off our coats, and I hung them on the pegs just inside the door, and we'd leaned into each other, and we held each other.

She'd let go of me first, pulled away, but held my shoulders a moment longer. For an instant I'd seen in her eyes on mine some recognition of something else between us. Not the movie, and the way the world happened out of our reach now that our husbands were gone. And not the notion this was all too soon to be going out.

It was something else I'd seen in her eyes, something I could not name.

And then I had walked with her to the bottom of the stairs, let go, and watched her walk upstairs to her and Mahlon's floor. She took each step slowly, looked back down at me once when she was a few steps up, but not again. Once she made it to the top, I'd called, "Goodnight," and she'd said "Goodnight" without turning to me, and she moved into her room.

NOW HERE WAS her hand warm in mine, nowhere near the cold it'd been when I'd found it in the car.

With my other hand I found my glasses on the nightstand. She turned from me, and we moved through my room, out into the kitchen, where my own radiators hissed not at all any different than Mary Margaret's had a morning so many years before.

"Ruth?" I said.

She was in a flannel gown and her old mint-green bathrobe, her fleece-lined slippers. I'd not even a moment to put on my robe or slippers, but that did not matter for the warmth in the kitchen, a kind of warmth I recognized immediately. One that went past radiators hissing, and I glanced to my right to the stove. The little red light above the knob was on, the oven heating up.

This was the feel of the kitchen every winter morning when the three of us were in here for breakfast: the radiators, the oven, the dark outside.

I looked to the clock on the stovetop: 2:41.

"Ruth?" I said again. "Honey?"

She looked at me still, and here in the kitchen light I saw that same look in her eyes as when she'd pulled away. Still I could not find a home for that look. There was nothing on her face I could read, only her eyes on mine, and now I was troubled.

She led me to the table, pulled out my chair without a word, and I sat.

Here was the table, the vinyl tablecloth, white with those tulips scattered across it. Here was Mahlon's place to my right. And here, opposite me, was Ruth's place, her chair. Where we'd sat the morning after the funeral, and we'd tried to eat a piece of toast, an orange.

And then Lonny'd knocked at the door.

I looked up from the table, from those tulips. I wanted to find Ruth's eyes, to try and understand in them what we were after doing here.

But she was already to the counter, and I watched as she opened the cupboard beneath the counter, reached in, pulled out a bowl.

My flour bowl. The one I kept filled with flour and draped over with the tea towel, white with thin blue stripes.

My flour bowl.

My biscuits.

"Ruth, honey," I said and started to stand, "you want me to make some biscuits I'd be glad to," and now the sense of this all started to come to me: she was in her grief, and wanted back to before.

She wanted Mahlon and her and me to be here at my table of a morning, with fresh biscuits and coffee and warm maple syrup to drizzle over those biscuits.

But Ruth quick looked to me, said, "Naomi, sit," the words sharp though not mean. Just quick, and I saw she meant it.

I eased back into my chair. I was to bear witness, I saw. Just bear witness to whatever she needed to do.

"I want you to listen," she said. "I want you to know some things." She didn't look at me, and set the bowl out on the counter, and now there came to me the smell of coffee, or the recognition of it, the smell so much a piece of all this it didn't even register.

I looked at the Mr. Coffee on the counter to her left, tucked under the cupboard. She'd already brewed a pot.

She pulled the tea towel off the bowl, folded it in quarters, and set it aside on the counter, her moves careful and slow, then opened the cupboard above the Mr. Coffee, brought out the tin of baking powder. She pulled off the plastic lid and reached in with two fingers, pinched up powder between them, dropped it into the flour there in the bowl. She snapped back on the lid, put it back in the cupboard, brought out this time the little round can of Crisco.

"I've watched you do this for as long as you've lived here," she said. She reached in a hand to the bowl, fluffed around in the center of it. "Maybe you never thought I was watching, but I was."

She set the Crisco on the counter, went to the fridge, pulled out a single egg from the rack in there, then the green and white carton of buttermilk, untouched since Mahlon'd died. Eleven mornings, until this one.

I felt how empty my hands were in this, how helpless in what she was doing, and I looked at them there on the table. My old woman's hands.

Ruth cracked the egg at the sink edge, just like I did, so's not to get any raw egg on the edge of the bowl, and she opened the shell, let slip into the flour the egg.

She said, "I even watched you do this a few times over at the house on 116. Quite a few times." She paused, looked in at the bowl, the shell halves in either hand. "So it's not as though this is any secret."

She dropped the shells in the sink, picked up the buttermilk carton, tipped in what looked to me the precise amount I tipped in every time.

"Ruth, I'd be glad to help you—" I started, but she quick turned to me once more, cut her eyes at me again to signal I was to sit, and listen. Still there was no anger in how she looked at me, nothing in how quick she turned to give me any fear.

There was only need.

I swallowed, nodded. She had things to say.

She went to the oven then, took the potholder from the magnet hook on the front of the oven door, and opened the door, reached in, pulled out my old iron skillet, already heated up, in the bottom of it, I knew, a little dribble of oil all set to receive.

She placed the skillet on a hotpad I only now saw set on the counter beside the bowl, then peeled the plastic lid off the Crisco. She dipped her fingers in, pulled them out, on them a dollop of lard. Just enough.

She set the can on the counter, with the Criscoed hand reached into that bowl one more time, and now she was working her fingers in there, a kind of work I knew by heart. She leaned a hip against the counter, her hair up on her shoulders now. Here was the fine line of her nose, the fine line of her lips, her eyes on the bowl and her hand in there.

This was my daughter-in-law, in her mint-green bathrobe and flannel gown and fleece slippers.

Ruth.

She said, "Every Thursday morning Mahlon

made his delivery to the Stop & Shop, and I watched for his truck. I'd see from my checkout stand his truck out the front windows, and he'd pull around back to the dock." She paused, took in a small breath. Her voice had gone higher, tighter for the labor these words were to give. Still her fingers moved. "Didn't matter whether we'd had a fight that morning or if his delivery schedule was so jammed he didn't have a spare second, we made certain—"

She stopped, and her lips trembled the smallest way.

And now I knew, in the pitch of her voice, in that tremble, in the way she'd had to swallow hard, take in a breath to get this all going, what she was after here.

"Ruth," I said, "Ruth, don't tell me. It's your treasure," I said, and heard the struggle it was to say these words myself, the pitch of them just as high and lonesome and full of need as her own words.

Because she was going to do it. Here she was, going to tell me the ritual she and my Mahlon had between them. Here she was, going to give me her portion of my son, and I made to stand yet again, heard beneath me the scrape of the chair. "Ruth, child," I said.

She put up her free hand, held it out like a crossing guard for just a moment. She wanted to speak. She needed to speak. And I sat back down, put my hands to the tabletop again.

She put the hand back to the bowl, held it, took in another breath.

I looked back to my hands, still useless. Older than my momma's had ever been allowed to grow, but in them the knowledge Ruth herself was finding now, in kneading these ingredients all together. This knowledge—this unwritten piece of family history—had found its way into my son's wife's hand and heart.

And she was about to give away a piece of her own history, her own heart.

Nice to meet you, I heard whispered so quiet and so deep and so warm in my ear that I knew Eli was still with me.

She moved her fingers in the bowl, moved them, then lifted out what seemed a kind of strange and natural blessing: here came a biscuit, white and wet, a disc not a half inch thick and a thumb's length wide.

She held the biscuit there in the air, her eyes focused on it and her lips still trembling, like the piece of dough might reveal to her a path through this moment less painful than it had to be.

I bit my lips together, laced my fingers together.

Nice to meet you, I heard my own heart whisper.

She said, "Every Thursday, once the back-room manager was unloading the truck, and once I'd gotten someone to cover for me at the checkstand, I'd make my way to the backroom, and I'd accidentally bump into him in one or the other of the dark rows back there. Those pallets of toilet paper and dog food and bleach all stacked to the ceiling. And he'd kiss me, and I'd kiss him back, and then we'd get back to work."

She looked a moment longer at the biscuit, almost in wonder, it seemed, then set it in the skillet. "That's all," she said, and she looked at the biscuit there. Though from where I sat I could not see the biscuit in the skillet, I knew that, yes, it had to be with wonder one would look at such a thing: nothing more than flour and egg and lard and buttermilk and baking soda.

But given love, the blessing of hands willing to work, and a warm kitchen filled with the good smell of coffee, it was a history.

"Just every Thursday, his lips on mine," she said. She turned to me, her blue-green eyes as clear and crystalline as they ever were.

My Mahlon'd loved her from the minute he

met her. In her eyes was her good heart, constant and certain.

"Just the smallest kiss," she said, her voice down to a whisper now, "but I knew he was there. I knew it was for me."

Here was Mahlon, given back to me. A gift from the woman he loved.

Here was Mahlon, a coffee cup in his hand at this same table, winking and smiling at Ruth every time he said anything about Thursday deliveries, and here was Ruth smiling for that wink every time.

It was a kiss they shared.

I nodded, my lips still together, and I wondered what she could see in my own eyes, wondered if she could see the way I missed my Eli, and my Mahlon.

I wondered if she could hear as clear and true as I could mine and Eli's own secret history: *Nice to meet you, Nice to meet you.*

Ruth turned to the bowl, reached in, lifted out a few moments later another biscuit, and another, until there were six nestled in the old skillet.

Then she had the skillet in her hand, opened the oven, slid it in, closed it back up.

She went to the sink, rinsed her hands, dried them on the towel hanging from the cupboard knob beneath the sink. Then she took up the tea towel from off the counter, let it fall open. She draped it over the flour bowl, put it back away under the counter.

All of it smooth as if she'd done it every morning. Smooth as if it'd been me to do it.

She came to the table, her eyes hard on me yet again, and she sat.

I had a piece of her heart right in my own with what she'd told me of her and Mahlon. A treasure, shared now.

She reached across the small space between us, took hold both my hands with hers. She leaned in, closer. She said, "I will go with you when you leave here."

I took in a small, quick breath, blinked once, twice, three times, all in a moment.

What does Ruth think about you moving back to South Carolina? Mary Margaret had called.

What is she talking about? Ruth had whispered.

And I really was a coward, and Ruth was stronger than I might ever hope to be.

She'd given to me the secret history of her and Mahlon. She'd given to me too my own history in the making of biscuits, history she'd made her own when I'd thought it would die with me. She knew I was leaving, and in her grief at the death of her beloved, she was brave enough to give these back to me.

I said, "Ruth, child," and I let go her hands with one of mine, reached to her face, touched my old fingers to her cheek. "Ruth," I said, "you can't go with me. You can't. You are a beautiful girl. You have your life here. I'm old, and I can't say where I'll—"

"Naomi," she whispered, and the word shut down my own words, lined up and hollow and cowardly as they were.

She brought a hand to mine at her cheek, held it there. She let her eyes close a long moment, opened them again.

She whispered, "Where you go, I will go. Where you live, that's where I'll live too." She paused a moment, took in a slow breath, let it out just as slow. Still my hand was at her cheek, her hand holding on to mine. "This is a pact between us. Here. Now."

I took in a breath. I smelled the coffee here, smelled the faintest glimmer of the biscuits beginning to rise. Now I knew what I could not name in her eyes before this: I saw me in her. I saw my own history, saw Mahlon, saw light down through boughs and scattering on the pinestraw. I saw light.

It was me she was giving back to me, I saw, right there in the blue-green of the eyes my own child loved.

She said, "There's nothing here for me," her voice still small and whispered. "I have no family. But it's not because I have nothing else that I'm coming with you. It's because I have you." She brought my hand from her cheek, and we laced our fingers together there on the tabletop.

Who was Naomi? I wondered. Who was she to be so blessed as to have a daughter such as this?

"So your family will be my family," Ruth whispered, "and when you pray to God for his mercy, then I am praying with you, too. Because there's nothing can come between us anymore. There's nothing can do that," she said, her whisper beyond a whisper, even quieter. But here with me, still as quiet and certain as Eli's voice in my heart, *Nice to meet you.*

"There's nothing but dying can come between us," she whispered, "and we've both faced that already." She paused. "We're here. We're together."

I let my eyes fall from hers, to our hands on the tablecloth. Tulips, red and yellow and blue, spread across the field of white. And our hands, together.

Here was hope.

The biscuits would be done soon enough.

And then we would eat, no matter what time it was. No matter the hard fact of death we both knew.

I looked from our hands, up to her eyes, that blue-green that was my own blood. I took in a breath, felt no treachery in the words I was already lining up. There would be no loss of my own treasure, I saw, in giving them up, no loss in the story they would tell once they were gone from me.

There was only love.

"Sometimes," I began, and let go for her the story of Eli, and me, and finding each other in the dark of our room at the end of a day, and the introductions we made one to the other.

Nice to meet you.

Nice to meet you.

And I told her, too, of the code this was, the secret we knew these words meant all along: *you have my heart.*

And Ruth, my Ruth, my daughter, understood.

PART II

Kin

Chapter 10

ISTEPPED OUT of the car, the air cold on my legs even through my slacks and long coat. Fifteen degrees on the marquee out front of the bank at Main and King on my way here. Yet another sunny day.

I did not know if or when, once we were gone from here, I'd be back.

We were leaving tomorrow.

This was the cemetery out past Florence, the spread of headstones like a kind of granite carpet. First week of February already, and still no snow since back to November, which seemed no more than a God trick to me: he'd allow snow to kill my son, then keep hold of it every day after in order to keep this world I walked through as bare and open and keen a wound as my heart.

But we were moving tomorrow. We were leaving here, headed for that light, that water, the harbor and creek and shrimp boats and pinestraw, all of it, and that fact made the trees up the hill at the edge of the cemetery still as leafless as ever feel like a trick I hadn't fallen for.

This morning at breakfast, before Ruth headed to work for her last day at the Stop & Shop, the two of us with the little we had left of our lives in boxes around us, the movers due any minute to pack it all away and start on down to South Carolina, I'd told her I wanted to go here alone today. I told her I wanted to see them by myself once the movers had done their work, once this house'd been emptied of us.

Though she'd nodded and smiled at me as if she knew exactly why I wanted this solitude, truth was I had no idea why I wanted to be here without her. I only knew I needed to do this, to be here with them. Just me.

We were leaving tomorrow.

I pushed closed the car door, looked across the hood for a moment back toward the entrance a couple hundred yards down the one-lane asphalt road through the cemetery. Down the hill stood the wrought-iron entrance gates, running away from it on either side the stone fence that separated this place from Route 9, the two-lane that led away from here and all the way into Pittsfield, fifty miles away.

Mahlon used to make deliveries to grocery stores all the way out there. From Easthampton to Pittsfield and back. All on that highway down there.

But on Thursdays, he was over to the Stop & Shop on upper King. On Thursdays, he was in the backroom, and he was kissing Ruth, and I smiled thinking of this.

From where I stood I could see on the other side of Route 9 the state park, and I could see from here, too, the plunge and the barnlike building next to it, where you changed and kept things in the lockers inside. The pool itself was empty, the palest blue, lounge chairs stacked in high piles and pushed up against the barn. Every time I stood here I couldn't help but think of summer afternoons when we'd lay out, Eli and me, on the lounge chairs, and watch Mahlon and all the rest of the kids jumping and swimming and fighting. Then we'd head home to barbecue steaks or burgers or whatnot.

I lost the smile, remembering what was gone.

I turned, stepped onto the grass from the crumbled edge of the asphalt, and started up the easy slope toward where they lay. My knees were aching with what we'd accomplished, the work of putting our lives into boxes and selling off what we didn't need, my fingers sore as well.

Yet it wasn't a pain would keep me from doing what I was here for: visiting Eli and Mahlon this last day. I hadn't been here in five days, a kind of sin couldn't be averted, what with all we had to do and had done. But it felt a sin nonetheless.

Ruth and I'd visited here every day for the first month after Mahlon was gone, then every other day once Ruth'd gone back to work the second week of December. Then here had been Christmas, next New Year's. We'd gone up here both those days, and Thanksgiving too, laid out flowers from Forget-Me-Not on Main, never any plastic nonsense even though the cold always had its way with whatever we put out.

But the cold and what it did to the flowers didn't matter. What mattered was that we'd been out here. We'd even started bringing patio chairs, the green and white lattice ones we kept in the basement all winter long, the day after we'd sat up eating biscuits and drinking coffee. Ruth'd been the one to rummage around in the dark and cold down there to find the chairs, right where Mahlon'd left them, behind the card table and the ladder he'd used every fall to put up the storm windows.

WE'D SOLD OFF the ladder and that card table and most everything else we could at the tag sale we had out front of the house two weekends ago. Everything from the dining room table and chairs to the three boxes of old paperbacks, Zane Grey and Louis L'Amour and Larry McMurtry and everybody else who'd ever written a western, it seemed, all of them Eli's and Mahlon's favorites both. We'd even sold half our sheets and towels, and some of our hotpads and tea towels and old extra Tupperware we'd neither of us used anymore.

All of this evidence of our lives, sold off to people who'd been parked out on the street before daylight that morning. Early birds ready to pick through our lives for a good deal on a copper teakettle, a power saw, a card table and ladder.

It was the selling of the furniture, though, that felt the most strange that day. Ruth and I took turns bringing in interested people, strangers and friends alike—Peach had ended up buying the two end tables from my sewing room—to walk through our home, touch the furniture, sit on a chair, rub a finger on the waxed tabletop. Even climb onto my bed and lay out on it shoes and all, what one girl not twenty years old did in my own bedroom.

Here was a girl in an orange parka, blue jeans, and clogs, lying in my bed, thinking on whether to buy it or not, her hands beside her and pushing down hard and pushing again.

A moment stranger even than selling the house itself, which happened almost in a blur. Phyllis's daughter-in-law Miriam, a realtor, bought it herself three days after we'd posted it with her. She'd use it for a rental, she let us know, once she partitioned off the downstairs from the up. Just like it'd been when Ruth and Mahlon'd bought it all those years ago, and I couldn't help wonder if she wouldn't set up in our house that knucklehead son of hers, Sammy, the one who at age thirty-two still lived with her and Jack, and who'd show up drunk at his grandma Phyllis's doorstep too afraid of his daddy to go home.

While Ruth or I brought people into the house to look at our furniture, out in the yard the girls manned the tables, Phyllis and Hilda and Carolyn keeping an eye out for us to make certain we got the best money we could.

Mary Margaret hadn't come, even though I'd called her and asked if she'd be able to help.

"My Tommy's took a turn," she'd nearly whispered into the phone the day before the sale.

I hadn't seen or talked to her since that night playing Bird in Hand. Since the night she'd betrayed me with my own history. She'd neither come to another quilting session nor to a cards night, Tommy and his condition, one of the girls would always update us, taking a turn, and taking a turn, and taking a turn. The girls, too, visited her to her little apartment at Willow Woods, and Tommy in his room as well.

But I hadn't.

By the end of the day we had only the sofa and chairs in Ruth and Mahlon's front room, and both our beds—the girl in the orange parka hadn't wanted it, for no reason she gave. We kept the fridge and microwave, the kitchen table and chairs. We kept our clothes, of course, and our quilts, dishes and pots and pans and my sewing machine and the chair for it. We kept three lamps, and one lone end table, my dresser and Ruth's both.

And those two green and white lattice patio chairs.

Last night I'd said good-bye to the girls. We met over to the Friendly's on King for Happy

Ending sundaes, each girl handing me a card and hug and us holding hands together for what all had passed between us all these years.

Carolyn's son'd loaned her his digital camera, and the waitress took too many pictures of us for the fact none of us could help but blink for the flash. Then Carolyn passed around the thing so's we all could look at one another right there on the spot. No need even for paper with this camera, for a permanent sort of record of us having been together this night.

All these lives, boiled down to dessert and four women around a table laughing and crying both while we looked at an electric picture of ourselves trying to smile through this end of things.

Then we'd made our way to the door, the girls picking up the tab between them, though I'd made something of a fuss about that. We put on our scarves, tied them off beneath our chins all at once just before we went on out the door. We had done this a thousand times before, sat here and yammered and ate ice cream and all left at once. The same old wind down from Canada whipped along the valley and King Street and right through us once we were on the sidewalk and heading for our cars. Still we chattered and hugged again, and chattered and hugged yet again.

But this time we'd ended up standing beside Hilda's old Honda station wagon, and now she was opening the hatch, and reaching in, and the girls' chatter all stopped.

She held out to me something in a white plastic bag, big and square, and I cried right then, my hands deep in my coat pockets and unwilling to move, unwilling to take this gift.

A quilt. Wrapped the same as we wrapped every other one we ever made once it was finished.

"You look at it," Hilda said in that German accent, each word strong and solid, the pitch and spirit a kind of song I was already missing. She pushed it to me, the bag touching my chest now. I saw in the light from the lamp-posts out here Hilda smiling at me, her eyes piercing me same as always, the blue of them a gray out here, but piercing all the same. "You open it," she said.

"It's a brand-new pattern," Phyllis said, and put an arm around me, we two side by side. "Not another one like it. We had a devil of a time, what with the stitches around all those curves."

Here was a quilt. And here were my hands moving all of their own up to the white plastic, peeling back the edge of it to reveal to me their gift.

Now the girls worked to pull it out of the bag along with me, and I could see it was a kind of Star pattern, but with only a single big star at the center. We unfolded it, each girl holding a corner and stepping away from each other to hold it out full.

"Not much to make of it in the light out here," Carolyn said. She stood directly across from me, Phyllis the corner to my right, Hilda the one to my left, the empty plastic bag tight under her arm. The wind puffed at the quilt, made it shiver a bit.

It was a Star, all right. Big and sharp right at the center. But around it was a ring of something I couldn't recognize for the dark, and the shivering quilt itself, and for the tears in my eyes: some foreign pattern radiated out from the star at the center.

Carolyn said, "Sometimes I might come off a little slow on the uptake," and she paused. I looked up at her. She was smiling and smiling, the knot of her scarf a little cockeyed beneath her chin. The girls were grinning at me too, proud for this moment, and now I was smiling with them.

"But I've seen at least six dozen times," Carolyn said, "how you look at those Thanksgiving turkey handprints I got running along the molding in my dining room. And those reindeer heads the grands turn up with too, the ones have their cutout handprints for antlers. And I came up with an idea."

"Yes, this pattern was all of her idea!" Hilda said. She nodded hard at me and at Carolyn and me again.

And now I recognized what this pattern was encircling the Star at the center of the quilt. Handprints, a single circle of them, cut out of all kinds of fabric. Eight of them, left and right alternating, the fingers pointing away from the center.

A halo of hands around the Star.

"These two here," Phyllis said, and nodded in front of her, "are mine."

I swallowed hard, took in a breath.

Hilda put in, "The work of those stitches around the fingers, oh!" She nodded to the fabric in front of her. "These are mine right here."

"And mine are right here," Carolyn said. She nodded like the other girls to the spot in front of her where two hands reached out. "We had a heyday cutting and piecing and trying to get the circle of them all set just so."

I took in another breath, like I'd had the wind knocked out of me.

"You shouldn't have done—"

"Now stop this," Hilda said, and nodded hard at me. "We love you."

"We all do," Phyllis said quick after Hilda, and then Carolyn said a little slower, a little quieter, "We all four love you."

I blinked, swallowed, felt my hands go tight on my corner of the quilt.

Eight hands.

We all four love you.

I looked down at the hands in front of me, two hands reaching out toward me from that star. Right and left.

"I might seem a little slow," Carolyn said again, "but I can pay attention." She nodded at the two hands out in front of me. "Those are Mary Margaret's," she said, "and it doesn't take an astronaut to see it's no coincidence you were the one to end up holding that corner."

"We did not have this planned!" Hilda said. "It is the luck of the draw that you are holding that corner!" she said.

Phyllis looked at me, her eyebrows together. "We all know there's something passed between you both," she said, and now she was moving toward me, the quilt collapsing, and all three took that as their sign, too, to commence folding up this quilt, all of them moving slowly toward me, carefully folding.

But my eyes were to those hands held out to me. Mary Margaret's hands. They were falling, it looked, with folding the quilt.

"It is something she will not talk about," Hilda said, a softer edge to her words, a sadness that seemed to sand away the strict sound of her voice. "We are very sorry that you have not been together as you have always been for these weeks before you are leaving."

"But she wanted her hands here on the quilt," Carolyn said, and now the girls were here before me, nearly huddled around me. The quilt had been folded neatly already, but with no thought to putting it back in the bag. They were holding it, the three of them, an offering to me. "And she made it with us," Carolyn said. "All of us made it for you. And we're hoping you'll go over to her—"

"When did you find the time to do this?" I said, my words too loud out of me, and turned from the matter of Mary Margaret.

"There's always time to make a gift from your heart," Carolyn said. "It doesn't take an astronaut to know that, either," she said.

"That's rocket scientist," I said, and tried to laugh. "You mean a rocket scientist," I said.

But the girls were silent. The wind picked at the ends of their scarves there at their throats, their mouths thin lines, their eyes on me.

I reached up, wiped at my own eyes, at the cold of the tears welled up there. I said, "This is a gift I will treasure." It was all I knew to say.

Then we hugged, this one last time. It was me to start it, and I reached out first to Phyllis, who held me to her too tight yet again, the scent of her White Shoulders welcome and beautiful.

"I love you," she whispered. "You be careful now and make sure to call us."

"I will," I whispered back.

Hilda'd gotten the quilt into the plastic bag while I'd held Phyllis, and when I turned to her she handed off the quilt to Carolyn. Hilda put her hands on my shoulders, and looked at me. She was searching my eyes, I could tell, for more than the way I'd ignored their words on my best friend.

She would find nothing, I willed myself. She would see only my love for her, this woman I'd met at a rummage sale in Belchertown fifty years ago.

Hilda smiled, a slow and genuine one. She pulled me to her, and I held her. She said, "My prayers are with you," her voice warm in my ear, and I said, "Thank you."

Then here was Carolyn. She held me close, too, and held me, then finally let go. She smiled, said, "If you get the urge, just call me and I'll send you my recipe for wienie wrappers." She touched at my cheek with her thumb, shook her head the smallest way. "You don't want to hear this," she said, "but until you talk to Mary Margaret, there will be no comfort for either of you. You can't walk away from—"

"Carolyn," I said, then, "Please."

She looked at me, blinked twice. She nodded, and held me, held me, and whispered no more on the matter of my life.

Then we let go, and as we waved to one another and moved for our cars, it was as if their hands fixed on that quilt, that halo, were drifting out on water, out and away, never to touch again.

Chapter 11

THE QUILT WAS still on the front seat of my car, there in its white plastic bag. No chance I'd let movers take that with them.

Those green and white lattice lawn chairs were still in the trunk too, beneath our suitcases all packed and ready to go. Even leaving my Electra had been arranged, Ruth and me deciding her Corolla would be the better choice for us to keep. Phyllis's Miriam had once again come to the rescue: on our way out of town tomorrow morning I'd drop it off in the lot out back of her realty office over on Pleasant, slip the keys in the mail slot. She'd do what she could to sell it for us.

The movers had come right on schedule,

packed us away, our lives tucked inside a truck in less than three hours. We had a room all set for tonight at the Clarion Inn, there at the end of Lower King, just before you got onto 91 South.

I walked up the hill, passed the gravestones all inlaid in the gentle slope, brown grass edged up to them, that grass crisp underfoot. So many names, so many lives, so many families.

Now here I was, at my feet their black granite gravestones, both edged in the same brown and hopeless grass. Set at the top of both stones were the little vases, one for each, inside them one red rose apiece, the cold having done its work to make the flowers hopeless as the grass.

Here they were. My husband, my son.

I looked at the stones, read yet again their names, their dates, and the inscriptions Mahlon, Ruth, and me could come up with when it was Eli, only Ruth and me when it came Mahlon's turn.

Eli's read:

Beloved husband
Beloved father

Mahlon's was a kind of echo that spoke the same truth of who he was:

Beloved husband
Beloved son

The words seemed small and feeble. Only words, no matter they were carved into stone. What made the words anything more was me standing here, inside me the history of who the men beneath me were.

Paperbacks, a power saw. A ladder, a card table. A dining room table and chairs we'd sat at through an exact number of Christmases and New Years and Thanksgivings. A number I might could come up with if I stood out here and sifted through history long enough.

All of it sold off, so that we would leave here as free and clear as Ruth and me could make ourselves.

WE'D DECIDED on the tag sale that night in the kitchen once the biscuits came out, and once I'd warmed maple syrup on the stove in the little pan I always used. Then we started in on our three biscuits apiece, and our coffee, even though it was three in the morning, and we talked.

I told her of the light that'd come to me the morning after the funeral, light scattered like diamonds at my feet on the pinestraw, and I told her of the warmth I'd felt even in the cold of her room.

I told her of the letter I'd already sent to Gordon and Melba Stackhouse down to Georgetown, and how I'd let them know of Mahlon's passing and asked after any ideas they might have on finding a place to live in Mount Pleasant. I told her too of how I'd stood at the mailbox and put the letter in before she'd ever even gotten up, and how my hand'd shook as I'd written it, me so full of fear and hope.

And I told her how it'd been in her tears, and the black dress she'd worn to sleep the night before, and in the thin frost on the roofs I could see out her and Mahlon's window, that all of this had been brought to me, the notion I could move, and I apologized again for thinking to leave her here.

She'd only smiled at me, nodded, said, "Don't say you're sorry again."

Then an afternoon two days later, Ruth upstairs and taking a nap, me in the front room and just starting to straighten up the piles of folded material and baskets full of scraps and heaps of batting—I'd told the girls at quilting that morning they might could take off my hands the supplies I kept here, though none of them volunteered, only smiled and nodded and looked at one another as though saying nothing might be a way to keep me here—the phone rang.

It was Gordon.

"Hey, Naomi!" Gordon said in that big way he had, and here he was with me, the boy a little shorter than Eli, stocky and wearing glasses and with a quick smile. Here he was in just these words, his voice just the same, though the last time I'd spoken to him must have been when Eli died. Eight years ago, but here warm and pleasant in my ear was his drawl, the same as mine. On just those two words a world of familiarity and comfort.

"Gordon," I let out, and I cried, right there into his ear without any more word than just his name. Suddenly I was more full of fear and hope than the morning I'd mailed the letter, the all of it bursting forth just now with the fact of this call.

"Now, gal," he said, and I heard him sniff, pause a moment while still I cried. "Melba and me want you to know how very sorry we are at Mahlon's passing on," he said. "We want you to know what a special boy we always knew he was."

"Thank you," I said between quick breaths in, "thank you, Gordon, thank you."

"You just take a breath now," he said, "and a sit-down before you get yourself all worked up," and I smiled, took in a breath slow as I could.

I sat on the sofa, despite the piles of folded material that took up most of the cushions, and I touched at my eyes, made to take in another deep breath. Then I was off, told him about the accident, about the funeral, and about how big a hole there was in every day now. I told him about Ruth, and the two of us together inside this house.

Gordon listened and listened, put in now and again a memory about Mahlon, and about Eli, and then he put on Melba, who managed only "Bless your heart" before she started in to crying, which started me up again, and then I told her all I'd told Gordon.

We were silent a few seconds, the two of us about empty of everything but what my letter'd said: how could they help us find a place to live in Mount Pleasant?

"Naomi," Melba said then. "About moving back down here."

Here came a heavy click, and Gordon's voice on the extension: "Now what's all this business about you wanting to leave your Yankee home, Sister?"

That was when I'd laughed, felt the hope in me fill, felt the fear begin in the smallest way to fade.

It was a name he'd given me a long time ago for no good reason I could say, save for the fact I was his stepbrother's wife. A sister of sorts.

But it was the sound of it that mattered, that human voice, and the fact someone I could call family was saying it. Even though Gordon was Eli's stepbrother, the son of Gordon Stackhouse, Senior, who married Eli's momma and'd taken her away from Mount Pleasant on up to Georgetown, here was the closest thing to blood I'd know.

Besides my Ruth.

The two of them started to jabbering at once all about why couldn't we move in to Georgetown, and how they'd already rounded up an *Apartment Finder* magazine for Mount Pleasant, but they had one for Georgetown County too, and would I think on that, please? They'd gotten the Mount Pleasant one from their daughter Jocelyn, who lived down to West Ashley on the other side of Charleston from Mount Pleasant, and who was a dental hygienist with three kids of her own and her ex-husband gone these five years now. "But it was good riddance to rotten fish," Melba said, and Gordon put in, "You got that right," and I laughed yet again, the feel of it in my chest almost too foreign to recognize, some language I'd known but forgotten.

"Our Jocelyn's got her older brother in Mount Pleasant to take care of her," Melba said, "our boy Beau who's a captain at the fire station there off Six Mile Road to Mount Pleasant. He's the one who tossed out that worthless husband of hers when push finally come to shove," she said, and the two were on another tear about Beau, then went back to why couldn't we live in Georgetown near them like family was supposed to do, and they'd have called sooner than this but the letter got snagged somewhere along the mail route and then they'd not been certain what to say if they were to call, what with how sorry they were about Mahlon's passing on and how happy they'd be for us to move down there and back to home.

Words to me, and for me, and with me. All from two people I was sorry now I hadn't stayed in touch with more than those Christmas cards. This was a blessing, the sound of these voices, voices rich with love and news and those drawls, all these words from them piling up and up, me still with that strange feel a laugh gave me, distant and familiar at once.

I laughed again, listened to them go on about their third child, their son Robert, a manager at the Piggly Wiggly in Georgetown and who knew people in Mount Pleasant might could set up a job for Ruth, because she was a cashier, wasn't she? Robert'd be happy to land her a job right there in Georgetown if we'd think on settling there near family.

And it was then, me settled on my old sofa with these voices singing in my ear, this news about Robert and a Piggly Wiggly, that I finally heard the leap they'd already made. The one I hadn't allowed in me until just two mornings before, when Ruth had told me she would go with me.

They'd already begun to make plans for Ruth, had known even before I did that she would be with me.

Then I'd looked up from the daze I'd been in listening to all this commotion, all this life, to see Ruth herself, up from her nap and sleepy-eyed, but with a look of surprise to her.

She stood just inside the cluttered room, and while Gordon and Melba still went on, apologized again for not calling sooner for their being joyful and sorrowed at once, I looked at her, saw her beauty yet again and that puzzlement too. Suddenly this room was so crammed with all my quilting business I wanted then and there to toss it out to the street, so close was the idea of moving, so clear the path home.

"Ruth's right here," I said, without even waiting for one or the other of them to take a breath. "You want to say hey to her?"

Ruth's eyes grew even larger, and she quick reached a hand to her forehead, rubbed it, ran it back through her hair, as if she needed to clean up for a family she'd never even met.

"Why certainly, yes!" Gordon'd said, and Melba said at the same time, "Bless that girl's heart, put her on!" and I stood from the sofa, handed the receiver out to her, smiling.

"Who is it?" she mouthed.

"Gordon and Melba," I said full-voiced. "They want to say hey to you."

For a moment she didn't move, only looked at me. Then slowly she started around the baskets, and the sewing machine, stepped over the pile of batting, all with her hand already out, on her face still the puzzled look, her eyes on me.

She whispered, "I heard you laughing."

I said, "Good," and handed her the phone.

She took it, held it for a moment more, that puzzled look nowhere near gone yet, the sound of my laughter as foreign to her as it was to me.

Her eyes were still on mine when she put the receiver to her ear, said, "Hello?" It wasn't three seconds before she'd smiled.

I PUSHED my hands even deeper into my coat pockets against this sunny cold. I'd made ready to move us from here, to leave Eli and Mahlon both alone here in a strange land. It was done, Ruth my partner in it.

And now it seemed Ruth's smile as she'd listened there on the phone, and the voices of those I knew and the promise we'd find people who loved us, was why we were leaving here.

We were leaving here to try to be happy. But we were leaving Eli and Mahlon.

I looked at their gravestones against the grass that bordered each. Brittle grass. Dead, until sometime later this year, when it would send creepers out onto the granite, looking for a way to cover up those names. To wipe away those words.

I bit my bottom lip, held it tight in my teeth, and felt the pain. But I held on to it, let myself feel it as deep as I could. We were leaving them.

I looked up from the gravestones then, to

the line of trees up the hill, the stone fence of the cemetery in front of them all. The stones were piled one on another, like any of a hundred thousand stone fences I'd seen in the years I'd lived here. A stone fence, a wall I'd looked at from here who could say how many times in the last eight years.

But this day there seemed in them something else, a familiar and lost feel to them, the careful and confused pattern those stones made with one another in order to stand straight and firm and to stay that way.

And then I knew why I'd come here, and come here alone.

This was the wall I'd built between me and my sin. Between that betrayal of my husband and my love for him. A solid wall, a working wall. A wall that had stood our whole lives long, but that I'd always been able to see beyond, a wall past which were the leafless trees of my own betrayal I could see every day of my life.

We were leaving here to try to be happy.

Then the fence, the trees past them, the brown grass and all the gravestones everywhere around me washed over in wet, my eyes veiled suddenly in my own tears. I swallowed, took in a quick breath. I looked down at my husband's gravestone, in the next moment fell to my knees, the pain nothing, nothing, and I brought my hands from my coat pockets and leaned forward until they settled on the stone, the cold and black of it. I touched the first two words of his inscription, those feeble words meant to capture a glimpse of who my husband had been when he was alive for as long as it took words to be wiped from stone.

Beloved husband

"Forgive me," I said.

Because I had never asked him for this when he was alive, though I'd asked him for it every day in my heart.

This was why I was here alone.

I was still a girl shivering in stone-cold bathwater, still me huddled inside me. Despite Mary Margaret had never said word one to me on it and still stayed my friend. Despite I'd never spoken to Lonny again save for the usual hellos through all these years.

I was still a girl shivering, still only me huddled and hollow, despite even the gift of our son, and the blessing of his wife.

"Forgive me," I said once more, my fingers still to those stone words about my husband,

and reached across the grass to Mahlon's stone too, felt the pain of my stretching to touch his own history, his being the beloved husband and son he'd been. Then I was touching those words, just as cold and solid as the record of my husband's life.

"Forgive me, both of you," I said, the world still washed in my tears, in my trying to breathe.

But they were dead.

Every dream I'd had of finding a life blessed first with a husband, next with children to call my own, then perhaps the blessing beyond blessing of a grandchild whose handprint turkeys or reindeer antlers I might could dress up my dining room with so's I might see that blessing every day and know God was here with me, the bestower of all these blessings—all this had been taken from me by that same God. The same God to give it all.

And this was why I was leaving, I fully saw. Why that light from home so filled me, gave me such desire to head back there, why the world down there seemed so filled with joy and life. Why the voices I'd heard on the other end of the telephone line all these weeks of planning and planning and planning seemed so able to save me: there was only me left here, shivering and small and unforgiven.

Better to call me empty, for all God had taken from me.

Still these twin gravestones were washed in my tears, the stones still so cold, still so black, and now I felt the pain in my knees begin to creep in, and the cold of the ground, and the burn of that cold in my fingertips.

"Naomi," I heard whispered from behind me.

Before I could turn to the word, here was a hand out in front of me from behind. A hand thin and trembling and white with the same age my own hands'd taken on, and I turned slowly to see whose hand it was, though I knew already and refused in the same second to believe it.

Here was the sleeve the hand seemed swallowed by: red and black plaid wool, and next I saw the old scuffed work boots and gray work pants, the gray vest and that wool shirt. Here was his Red Sox cap, those old-fashioned glasses.

He was bent to me, one hand to his knee, the other still held out to me to help me up.

Lonny Thompson.

Even closer to dead than when I'd closed the door on him that first morning after the funeral. The ball cap was too big on his head, his hands too small, the glasses even bigger now for how much he was being eaten away by the cancer.

"Naomi," he whispered again. "Take my hand," he said.

And I'd no choice but to think again of us there at the station in Charleston the first time I met him, and the way we'd held hands a moment too long.

The sun still shone down hard on us. The cold still shot through us. That stone fence still stood.

I leaned back from the gravestones, my hands to my sides. I put one to the grass to steady myself, pushed hard on that hand and struggled up inside this pain, struggled and struggled, until first one foot was beneath me, and I stood. All without his help.

He was still leaned over. He looked up at me beside him, both hands to his knees now. He was breathing hard, and I saw again the indentations on his cheekbones, the thin lines where the oxygen tubes ran.

He'd walked up here, and I turned to look down the hill to where sat a burgundy Monte Carlo, right there behind my Electra.

Mary Margaret's car.

Even from here, with my tears and the pain

in my knees and the cold light cutting through me, I could see Mary Margaret inside and leaned over the wheel, watching.

"It's me needs forgiveness," Lonny managed out, his voice thin as his hands.

I turned, started down the hill.

Chapter 12

I MADE IT to the car without looking at either of them, kept my eyes to the brown grass before me, weaved my way through these headstones, through all these dead, and through the pain in my knees.

But when I came around the hood of the Electra, I let myself look up the hill at Lonny.

It felt like sin, looking at him. But I looked.

He'd only gotten a few yards down, and'd stopped, leaned over again, hands on his knees, his chest heaving with all this. Then, once I made it to the driver's side and opened my door, I let my eyes go to Mary Margaret's. This too felt like sin, simply letting my eyes go to hers.

She was staring at me, her forehead and eye-brows above her trifocals quivering and skittering again and again in just the second or so I looked at her.

Here were her hands, holding tight to the steering wheel. Those same hands as on my quilt. This proof of her love.

I looked away, because now I knew it was in fact a sin. My letting our eyes touch, and not saying good-bye, was as clear a separation from love as I could make.

I had the car door open. I had our bags in the trunk. I was leaving.

I looked inside the car, saw there on the seat the quilt in its white plastic bag. And despite myself, and despite my will, despite the stone wall I'd built stone on stone, my heart broke.

I saw in that instant what a hand held out to you meant, and my heart broke again, and again and again, and one time more. All for the way her forehead and eyebrows moved, for the fear and loneliness and confusion and betrayal I saw there. And for those hands holding on to the wheel as though it was a friend she would lose and didn't want to let go.

Because none of who I was right this moment was lost on me. None of it.

It was me needed to ask forgiveness. Me, too, who needed to let Lonny ask after mine for his being the reason my Mahlon was out late on a night in November. I knew all this.

I closed my car door, took one small step away from the car, and let my eyes go back to Mary Margaret's.

She let go the steering wheel, climbed out, and here we were in each other's arms, the sweet softness of my dearest friend and the sad silver whisper of her crying in my ear. We held each other.

"Forgive me," I whispered to her, the words nothing but joy out of me. Not the bitter herbs I'd thought they might be, nor the broken glass or boiling pitch I'd figured these words might all be.

Then my heart broke again into too many shards to count when I knew how sweet these words would have been to give to my Eli. To ask forgiveness of that sin against him, when he'd lived beside me and with me and inside me all the days of his life.

"Your Ruth told me you would be here," Mary Margaret whispered. "I will miss you so."

"I'm so sorry," I said, and we pulled back from each other, still with our arms around each other. "I'm so sorry," I said again.

Her mouth quivered a moment, and I saw by the wrinkles beside her eyes she was trying at a smile. "You know I love you," she said, and I nodded quick and hard and smiled too. I said, "I love you, Mary Margaret." I paused, took in a breath to begin the work of explaining myself to her, the work of giving out words that spelled nothing but *I am leaving you*.

But before I could say a thing, she reached up a hand to my mouth, put her first finger to my lips.

"You hush now," she said, and nodded herself. "If I could go home, I would too." She still smiled, but here was the tremble too, her mouth quivering. "I love my Tommy," she started, "and always will. But if I could, once my Tommy passes away, I would go back to my old house in Hadley," she said, the words trembling themselves, "and I'd be a little girl on the afternoon before my mother and father took that train." She paused, swallowed. "I'd be sitting at the table in the kitchen, watching my mother bake her gingersnaps for me so I would have some while she was gone."

She broke then, and I brought her to me, held her close again.

"It's all right," I said, though I didn't know what was right here at all. She was still an orphan even now, seventy years after the fact. I said, "Thank you for the quilt," and she managed to let out a small laugh, even inside her crying. She pulled away again, looked at me, shook her head.

"You should have seen us all working on that thing to get it done for you on time." She sniffed, rubbed at her nose with a Kleenex she'd brought from her coat pocket. "Carolyn had this grand vision, and it turned out fine." She shook her head again.

And before I could say a thing more about the quilt and folding it open there in the dark parking lot, before I could say anything on those hands, the beauty of that circle of them, here was Lonny beside me, his hand touching to my shoulder, his face closer than it'd been in half a century.

Here he was, the man who'd been my husband's best friend, and who'd been like a father to my Mahlon once Eli was gone.

All these years of all our lives passing and passing before us all, when all we were was flesh and blood and memory and loss.

He was a man. A man I'd sinned with against the one man I loved. But he was a man, and only that.

"Naomi," Lonny said, and took in a breath after just the one word. "We need to talk," he said, and now slowly, slowly, Mary Margaret let go my arm, slowly moved away from me. I glanced to her, saw her smile at me, give the smallest nod.

They'd talked of this private need, I could see in her eyes. Now she was at the hood of her car, moving away from me. Still she smiled at me as she started across the pavement to the grass, and on up the hill to where my Eli and Mahlon were.

She was my friend.

"I know it was wrong of me," Lonny said, and I looked to him, saw him breathe in and out.

I said, "You just relax a minute. You just breathe." I paused, reached to his arm, let my hand touch him, the rough wool of his red and black plaid jacket.

His arm felt like nothing, like inside the sleeve might only be a bird wing, or the thinnest branch.

He troubled up a smile, seemed somehow to stand taller. He took in another breath deeper, though I could hear the shallow purchase it made inside him. He squinted his eyes a moment, opened his mouth even wider, breathed in again.

"Your Mahlon passing," he said, and leaned back against the car, closed his eyes. "It's a great misery to me," he said, "that he's gone. He was the nearest thing to a child I ever had."

He breathed in, and again. "Even so, I'm sorry he was up at my house that night. If he hadn't of been, he'd be alive right now." His eyes were still closed, but seemed to shut even tighter with the words, the work of them. Or with the work of bringing to bear the memory of my son, alive.

Lonny loved him. And Mahlon loved Lonny, too.

I said, "Lonny," the word strange and brand-new and ancient in me at once. "Lonny," I said, "that's enough. He loved you. He was where he wanted to be that night."

There they were: my words, the release of them a kind of miracle for the way they released, too, my own sore heart and miser's desire to keep hold tight as I could my Mahlon's death.

I'd wanted him with me. But he hadn't been. Instead, he'd been at this dying man's house, and ministering to him in the only way really mattered: keeping company.

Lonny's eyes fluttered open. It took a moment for him to find me here beside him, my arm on his. Still the pain of this all was on his face, as though his words and mine both were of no help. His mouth was open, eyes squinted nearly shut, the rattle of his breath a ghost inside him.

He reached to me, took my hand on his arm in his own hand. The touch was nothing, the same ghost as struggled on every breath.

I said, "Lonny," as though to stop him, to let him know nothing else was needed from him, and then I said the other words, the ones I'd held tight to all these long months.

I took in a breath of my own, and said, "I forgive you."

He looked at me, still breathing in and in, as though there weren't enough air in the world to fill him up. Then tears came at the corners of his eyes, there in the creases of pale skin, skin thin as frost on a November morning rooftop.

"Thank you," he said. He looked down, reached his free hand to the corner of one eye, then the other, let that hand fall again to his side. "Thank you," he said again, even quieter. He breathed in, and swallowed.

His eyes met mine, still in them the wet of tears welled there. He said, "I want you to know how much he loved you, and Ruth." He paused, breathed. "He was happy."

Slowly I shook my head for him to stop. Not for this good news of my son, but for the work of the words he put out. For how hard they came to him.

He was near to dead as a man might be. And

here he was beside me, lining up his own words to give me what had to be his own treasure, his own secret story of my son. His own memory and heart.

Nice to meet you, I heard yet again from my Eli.

"We talked about the Red Sox folding in the playoffs," he said, and a small smile came on him, more creases in that thin skin. He shook his head. "Same as ever." He paused, swallowed. "And we talked about the snow, about how early it was on us. Not even Thanksgiving yet."

He looked at me again, blinked. The tears were gone now, his eyes suddenly a kind of clear I only remembered from the old days. Sharp, and solid, and true. My husband's best friend.

"I didn't make it to the funeral," he said, "because I knew it was all my fault. His being there at my place and heading on home down that road."

"Lonny," I whispered, "Lonny, you have to stop this talk. Mahlon was up there because he wanted to be with—"

"It's two things in my life," he cut in, his eyes tight on mine. "Two things that I kept from you," and again he was winded. I pressed my hand harder on his sleeve, wanted him to stop this path he was walking with his words. Still there was nothing to him inside the sleeve. Only frail bone.

"I forgive you," I said again.

"Stop," he said, then, "hold on," and he sharpened his eyes on me, his mouth a thin line. "You just hold on to those words," he nearly whispered. "You just wait until I tell you what I need to tell you."

He was breathing in harder even than before, and I could see how the words he'd lined up were ones he'd measured and weighed and held on to for longer than I could know.

Maybe forgiveness wasn't enough, I saw with the labor in him, in those creases, in the sharp edge of his eyes. Maybe it was speaking words he needed, and I thought of Mary Margaret, and the joy I'd felt in simply saying *I'm sorry* in her arms.

"Two things," he said. "First is having Mahlon there to my house that night, and not calling up earlier in the day to tell him to stay home for the weather. For that snow and all." Slowly he shook his head, looked to the ground before him, that cracked and crumbling asphalt. "I could of done that," he said.

I whispered, "Mahlon loved you."

He nodded, still with his eyes to the ground,

and sniffed hard. Then suddenly he let out a sob, hushed and hollow, his mouth crumbled into itself, jagged and soft at once, his eyes shut tight inside all the wrinkles, and his shoulders gave way, shivered.

He tried at a breath, at another, and still that hollow sob came out. I held even tighter to him than I dared, both hands to his arm and holding on, holding on. My own throat welled up, the knot there ready to let itself out in my own sob, and I let go one hand, reached to hold him as best I could in my arms, this big man who'd sunken into himself with how near death was to him, and with the sorrow of this grief on him.

But even with my arms trying to hold him, and even in his shivering, he didn't move, as though he had an iron spine, his feet anchored to the ground. Still he sobbed, still his shoulders shook.

I let go, pulled away, but still held my hands to his arms, him square in front of me now. His eyes left the ground between us, met mine. He gained a breath, finally, and whispered, "I break a promise with these words to you." He let the words out evenly, gently, his jaw set. "But it's a promise I should of broken a long time ago."

His face was wet for the tears, his cheeks flushed the palest pink for all this was to get out. For all this work.

But what was this work?

What was this promise?

He swallowed, blinked. "Second thing," he said, "is Eli knew about you and me."

And my hands on his arms were away, and my face, the skin there, pinched and burned, and I heard out of me a single small *oh* of sound, all of it in the single instant past his last word. All of it in the single shallow gap between one heartbeat and the next.

I saw myself from very far away, saw Lonny from even farther distant. I saw we two from miles away, we two discovered.

Oh, I let out again, though it seemed not of me, seemed from years distant, lifetimes distant.

He wavered in my eyes, quickened in my eyes, tears here and here and here, and my face pinched and burned, my hands empty and away from him but still held up, as though there was something to catch, something big and wide and everything.

He tried to gather himself, his mouth trying to set itself straight, the thin muscles in his jaw working. He said, "He knew because I told him." And here was his sob again, that hollow rush of sound out of him.

But there was nothing in me.

"I told him because he was my friend, and because it was wrong, and because we both knew it was from the second I answered the door that afternoon." He took in a ragged breath. His eyes went to mine a moment, an instant, terror in them, and loss.

What was this news he was telling me, and where could I place it?

Where was there left to hide from me, and my separation from love?

"I told him the afternoon it happened," he said, his voice as ragged as that breath in, as clotted and mottled and full of death and loss as it could hold and not be dead itself. "I went to the shop a couple hours after you left," he whispered, "and he was there and busy with his hands on something. Busy working. Cut-ting pipe at the bench for some project we were working on. But I could tell he'd been through something." He paused, closed his eyes again. He took in a breath. "I could tell he was lost, and I cannot say now or ever why I told him, save for the fact he was my friend, and I'd betrayed him and the love you and he had for each other." He paused again, and here was the sob again, hollow and dead and dead and dead.

I was miles away. I was years away from this all. Still my face pinched and burned, and still I searched for somewhere I might hide.

He coughed, thick and wet, breathed in again. "I waited for the cutter to shut off, the saw to run down to where he could hear me between cuts. And that was when I told him, when it was quiet. And I told him because it was wrong, and because he was my friend. And I apologized to him, and I told him it wasn't you. That it wasn't your fault."

He opened his eyes a moment, looked at me. But I could see he was somewhere else as well. He was gone from here. He wasn't looking for anything from me now. He was only speaking truth.

He was only speaking his life, and the misery of it.

"He didn't do anything when I told him. He just stood there looking at the cutter, the pipe, the vices on down the bench. And then he turned around and looked at me. Then he walked over to me, and he hit me." His eyes were still on me, but through me. He was inside himself, inside his story, and what separation from love he'd been living all this time too.

"Knocked me clean to the floor. He didn't say anything, just stood over me a minute, looking down at me, and I didn't do anything but look at him. And I told him I deserved even worse. I told him I deserved more from him for what I'd done. And then he walked away, right on out the shop door, and he got in that old truck of his, and he drove off."

He was looking through me, I knew, because I wasn't even here.

I was in the bathtub, water gone stone cold. I was shivering, and here was Eli kneeling to me in the dark, finding my hand holding tight to the edge of the tub, the other clenched at my chest. I was with my Eli, who leaned quickly to me and touched my cheek and forehead to feel how cold I was, and he stood, my hand in his, and pulled me from where I'd tried to wash myself free of my mistake.

Then he was lifting me fully, taking me, wet and shivering, into both arms and lifting me free of the cold water, and now I was standing on the bath mat, Eli toweling me dry all there in the dark, then lifting me again, me still shivering, still shivering, and he was carrying me to our bedroom, where he lay me in our bed, and pulled over me first the sheet and blanket, and then the Wedding Ring quilt my mother had made for us.

While tight in my hand was a plain gold locket, only one photo in it, the other side empty as I'd prayed it would be.

"I didn't even leave the shop that day," he went on, though I was nowhere near. "I stayed there on the floor until it got dark, found an old blanket in the utility closet, wrapped myself up in it."

He paused, focused a moment on me, as if I were there in front of him. He said, "I don't want any pity from you. I'm not telling this to you for anything I want from you. I just want you to know who you were married to. The man you were married to."

Eli was leaving the room, and I was there in the dark growing darker each moment my mistake pressed down upon me—the shivering would not stop, would never stop, ever—until it seemed my breath was leaving me, that I would never breathe again for the mistake I had made, and the fact he was leaving me, as he had every right to do. Every right in the world to leave me alone, with my mistake.

"But this is the part I have to tell you," he said, and breathed the same clotted breath in. "I have to tell you, because he was a better man than either of us could ever know. And even better. And Mahlon just like him. That was why Mahlon was out to my house. Because he was good. He was good. Just like his father was good."

He paused, put a hand to the thin and creased skin of his eyes, rubbed there.

He said, "Next morning he came in to work and found me there sleeping on the floor. He nudged me with his foot, and I woke up to him standing over me again just like the afternoon before. And he looks at me, and he says, 'We got work to do.' " He paused, shook his head again, tried to breathe. "And he goes straight over to the cutter bench and picks up like nothing happened."

He stopped. He looked at me, tried at finding me.

"But this is what I have to tell you. This is the promise to him I have to break, and should of when Eli passed away." He swallowed, his Adam's apple a hard knob at his throat working to move. His eyes were full again, his breathing heavy and clotted still.

I was a shivering woman in a bed, my husband leaving the room, and with him every right to leave me forever, clutched in my hand a locket, half full, and half empty.

His eyes went to me one more time, and he sniffed, blinked. "That morning," he whispered, "I stood up from the floor, and I said his name one time out loud before he could start up the cutter. But before I could say another word he stopped, and then he looked at the wall, and he said it."

He stopped full then, his lips tight between his teeth. He'd stopped breathing, was holding silent for this. For whatever he needed to say, even if I was nowhere near.

Lonny opened his mouth, grabbed at air, grabbed at it, each snatch a tight fist in his throat.

Then he gave it away, handed the words to me, the ones that made this shroud of sorrow wrapped around me nearly choke off whatever joy I may have had for moving away from here.

Even though the news was what I'd longed to hear for the last fifty years. Even though it was what I longed to hear even unto a few minutes ago, when I'd been on my knees at my husband's grave.

He said, "Eli was just looking at that wall, and he says, 'I forgive you, and I forgive her. And you will never say another word about this for the rest of your life. Because I love her too much to let her know I know.' "

Now pain came upon me, sudden and full and certain, pain more than any I'd known before, pain greater even than the terrible but passing kind I'd gone through in the birth of my child; pain deeper than the pain I'd known when I'd found my Eli in our bed, breakfast on the table and me coming in to our room to find him gone, dead beneath the sheet and blanket, me thinking in the kitchen he was just a little tired maybe, sleeping in a little bit before getting up to face that day; pain keener even than when I'd received the news from the policeman who'd come to my door that night in November.

Here was pain, all of it in this instant summed up and weighed and measured against all the sorrow of my life—here was our back porch in 1944, a yellow telegram in my momma's hand; here was the phone call from my momma in 1956 that Daddy'd passed away; here was Gordon Stackhouse calling not but a year and a half later with the same news on my momma.

Here was the all of it.

Yet this news should have been joy. It should have been joy, this forgiveness.

I shot my eyes right then to the graves, to Mary Margaret standing there up the hill, her head bowed, hands deep in her coat pockets. There was my Eli. Right there, right beside my Mahlon, just below that ground.

"I should of told you that same day," he whispered.

This should have been joy.

"No," I heard myself give out, a surprised word surprised not by joy but by terror and sorrow and distance from me and my whole life.

He'd known, and'd forgiven me. And I had never known.

"He was a better man than we'll ever know," Lonny whispered. "He even kept us in the business together another eight months or so, trying to keep things working between us. It was me to ask him could we split the business, him to give it over to me and start up with the garage instead of starting up his own plumbing business."

"No," I said again, louder now, though it was still a nothing sound out of me, no more than a splinter of a word, a dead spark falling to the ground. Not enough even to register with Lonny, lost in his reverence for my husband and in his own condemnation.

This was what I wanted. This was the news I'd prayed for my whole life long. Given to me by God a lifetime too late.

Here was movement in the darkened doorway of our bedroom. Here was my husband, my Eli, his arms full with quilts brought from the hall closet, and then this dark figure—*This is my husband,* I marveled, *This is my love*—

leaned over me and lay first one quilt, and another, and another, heaped them all on me to warm me, while the hopeless and sorrow-filled world outside grew dark upon us.

Here was my husband, already forgiving me. He knew even then, and chose to cover me with quilts.

And when his arms were empty, he'd reached to the corner of all these quilts, pulled them back, and lay down beside me, his clothes rough at first, and cold, and he pulled the quilts back over us both, and turned to me beneath them all, and took me in his arms, and held me.

"No," I said yet again. Lonny blinked hard then, looked at me. He leaned in closer, and I could smell death on him hard and certain.

"It's a promise I've kept that day to this. A promise to a friend who stayed a friend, though it was never the same after that. A promise no one else knows was made. Not Mary Margaret. Not Mahlon certainly. Nobody. Even if it was a promise I should of never kept at all. A promise to hide from you how much he loved you."

He reached to my hands still up and empty between us, and took them in his. His hands were cold, and thin, his grip no more than the dying man's hold they were.

"Now," he whispered, "can you forgive me?"

The words fell on me like cold bricks, like an abandoned house falling down. My life, falling down on me.

I swallowed hard, took in a quick breath, though I was still nowhere near. And because I wasn't here, I was able to say with my next breath out, "Yes, I forgive you," and to believe I meant it in this moment. They were words I'd spoken, I knew, but I was nowhere near.

I brought my arms down, his hold on them giving way, and now tears fell free from his eyes, and he smiled.

He was still alive.

"Good-bye," I said, and felt myself back away from him, felt the muscles in my face try at working into a smile of my own, though I was having none of it. "Good-bye," I said again, and nodded, said, "Thank you," and now his smile was gone, replaced with puzzlement at my words, for me backing away.

But it was me who was more puzzled than he would ever be.

My husband had forgiven me.

I took another step back, and turned from him, heard him say "Naomi" once before my back was to him, and now I looked up the hill, took the handle of my car door and opened it.

Mary Margaret stood up there at the grave

of my forgiving husband, and my good son. Her head was turned to us down here, and now my free hand was up, and I waved at her, called out "I love you, Mary Margaret!" then "Good-bye!" all as though I might see her at quilting tomorrow, or cards next week.

She quick put up a hand and waved at me, smiled: no more than reflex at my own mechanical moves. But I would never see her again, nor Lonny.

I climbed in my car, my knees in pain that was no pain for the real thing in my heart and head, and I worked harder than I ever had before to fit the key into the ignition while Lonny stood outside my window. He spoke my name again and again, a word worn out for the life it'd expended here in Massachusetts, a nothing word as meaningless as *Thank you* and *Good-bye* and *I love you*.

This should have been joy.

But I did not know what to do with this forgiveness, did not know where to place it, or where to hide from it, or how to hold it.

Finally the key turned in my hand, the Electra started up. Lonny took a step away from my window, and Mary Margaret started down the hill, on her face a look of surprise and betrayal yet again, behind her my good son, and my good husband.

Here was my Eli, beside me in bed, all his clothes on, and here again was the pain of my skin against him, a jagged and sharp pain that was the wound my whole self had become. The all of me, fresh and stinging and raw.

Already forgiven.

Where would I place this fact? And how could I hold it?

And this word yet again: *Naomi*.

I put the car in gear, eased forward and away and down the narrow asphalt lane toward the gates that opened onto Route 9, and a way out.

Chapter 13

I HEARD RUTH in the hall, heard the key in the lock, heard her pause for a moment before finishing the work of turning it.

I was in our hotel room, in a chair by the one window, the drapes pulled open so that I could see the last Massachusetts day I'd spend here fall into dark. I hadn't yet taken off my coat, hadn't turned on a light. If in fact I'd planned to turn one on at all.

The door opened, and here she was. My Ruth.

She stood in the doorway, framed in the light from the hallway outside. Just like the night she'd come to my bedroom, pulled me into the kitchen to make me those biscuits.

The night we'd decided to leave together.

She was in her uniform from work, the green vest, white blouse, those black slacks. Her coat was over one arm, in that hand her overnight bag. In her other hand she held the key, clutched there too the ribbons for three Mylar balloons, bright metallic red and blue and gold. They floated just above her head, printed on them all bon voyage.

"Naomi?" Ruth said, as though it might be somebody else here in this chair. Some other old woman.

"It's me," I said.

I'd driven here from the cemetery, and parked, checked in. I got the quilt in its white plastic sack from the front seat, then my overnight bag from the trunk, set them both beside each other on the bed in here, and I'd sat down, and I'd waited. Three or four hours.

From here I could see I-91 through the leafless trees, the long and narrow off- and on-ramps made for this exit. Back to my left were the hills just south of town, to my right the empty stubble of cornfields past the parking lot. I'd sat here, and watched those hills go black. I'd watched car headlights cut on one at a time until there were none left with their headlights off.

I watched until the empty fields were still empty fields.

Ruth pulled closed the door behind her, the balloons bumping against one another to make a strange sound in the room. She flipped the switch there at the door, and on came the light directly above her.

She moved into the room, set the bag on the bed beside the quilt and my own bag, dropped her coat there too. The key still in her hand, she went to the closet door, wrapped the ribbons around the knob, let them go, one last jostling of air.

She went to the dresser, bent to the lamp, but before she twisted it on she paused. She was looking at me.

I nodded. She could go ahead. I could sit in lamplight now. Because she was here.

But she didn't turn on the light. She stood bent to the lamp a second, then two, then slowly she stood, edged back to the bed, sat down. She let out a heavy breath, put her hands to the edge of the bed like she was holding on. Like she might herself float up and bounce along the ceiling like a Mylar balloon.

And it occurred to me maybe she hadn't been looking at me at all. That me nodding at her to go ahead and turn on the light wasn't what she'd seen at all.

Maybe she was inside herself, same as me on this night before the next life. Maybe she was after the comfort of this darkness, and the way it kept outside of you who you were.

Maybe she was hiding, too.

I took in a breath, said, "Good to see you after a long day."

"A long one," she said. She shook her head carefully, in a kind of disbelief. She let go the edge of the bed, brought her hands to her lap. "They'll be sending my last check down to the apartment in Mount Pleasant. They've got the address and all."

I said, "I think the girls have already sent cards to us down there. Care packages, I figure."

"You know," she said, and it was as if she hadn't heard a word from me. She was on her own, I saw. She was somewhere else.

She'd lost her Mahlon, I saw.

"Everyone thinks we're crazy," she said. "I could feel it at the party today. And I've felt it all along. Even Peach, who hasn't said anything but how happy she is for us." She looked at her hands, laced them together in her lap.

My Mahlon had held those hands. He'd kissed them. He'd placed the ring on the left one, that ring still there, shiny in the light from there at the door.

"They think we're making a mistake in all this. In leaving so soon." She paused, breathed in. "Maybe in leaving here at all."

I said, "Do you?" I blinked, swallowed. "Do you think this is wrong?"

She was quiet a moment, and looked up at me. Then she looked away, to the balloons.

But it was somewhere else she was looking, I knew.

Her eyes lingered in that other place a moment, and I felt time fall away from the two of us, and all the plans we'd made, all the arrangements, all the work of leaving here. All of it just fell away.

I was in a bed heaped with quilts, my skin raw and jagged.

She looked at me, let out a breath. I could see in the light she was smiling. This woman, this beautiful woman, the wife of my dead son, smiling.

"I want to see that sunlight you're talking about," she whispered.

Now here was that light again, the scattered diamonds at my feet, the warmth of it, and the scent of pinestraw, the prickly carpet of it. Here was light, inside this dark and dead hotel room in a dark and dead town. Brought to me by my Ruth's smile, her words.

"I want to know what that's about, that

light." She shrugged again. "Crazy would be to stay here." She looked from me to the window, and I looked out then, too.

Here were black hills, an interstate. Empty fields.

And I knew right then, knew it clear as the fact I'd known I wasn't ever going to get up and turn that lamp on, that Mary Margaret was sitting beside her Tommy over to Willow Springs, her arms crossed and holding herself, and waiting.

I saw her, waiting.

I saw Lonny Thompson home to Sunderland, him in his hospital bed set in the front room, the television playing a Bruins game, oxygen tubes on him so's he could take in what last breaths he had in him.

And I saw my Eli at the other end of town, saw too my Mahlon, their gravestones set in the dry dead grass in a cemetery surrounded by stone walls as black as the waiting world this night.

Here were black hills, an interstate. Empty fields, all of it bathed in the failed light of a snowless February day.

Where could I go to hide from me? And where could I place the fact of my forgiveness?

I turned from the window. Here was Ruth, looking at me. She was waiting, too.

Where you go, I will go, she'd said. *Where you live, that's where I'll live too. This is a pact between us.*

For a moment I saw the two of us in our cars right now, headlights on and me in the lead, snaking through the streets of this town toward Phyllis's daughter Miriam's realty office over on Pleasant. I saw us pulling in to the lot out back, leaving my car parked there just like we'd planned to do tomorrow morning. I saw me bent to the front door of her office, slipping in the keys through the mail slot, then Ruth weaving her Corolla along those same streets and out to the interstate.

I saw us looking at all these old buildings, these landmarks out of our lives, one last time.

But I didn't want even that. Not even in the dark. It was the light. Still and always.

I swallowed, said, "We'll leave the keys to the Electra at the front desk. We can call Miriam's office tomorrow morning, tell her she can pick it up here."

And Ruth, my Ruth, already with me as quick as if the idea had been her own, nodded once and stood, all of it one move, all of it a single thought and action at once, and I knew it'd be wasted words even to ask if she wanted to change out of that uniform.

We'd find a place down the interstate. We'd

pull off someplace away from here, someplace neither of us'd ever spent a night before, and find a room, and we'd sleep.

Already she'd picked up her coat and shrugged it on, then took up her overnight bag and mine both, a bag in each hand, and I stood for the first time since I'd entered this room.

I reached to the bed for the quilt in its white plastic sack, picked it up. It seemed heavy to me, seemed made of more than cloth.

I turned from the bed, saw Ruth paused at the closet door, and those balloons. I said, "Let me get those for you."

"No," she said. "They'll just be in the way."

But she stood there a moment more, her eyes lingering on the balloons, and then her hand was to the door, and she opened it.

I OPENED my trunk, and we pulled out our suitcases to move into Ruth's, no words between us while cars passed and passed out on the interstate. Then here were two green and white lattice patio chairs in the floor of the trunk, revealed by the work of our own hands.

We said nothing, the two of us staring down at the chairs, the only light the pale yellow of the trunk bulb.

I reached to the trunk lid, and pulled it

closed, the sound hard and solid in the parking lot. Too hard. Too solid.

Ruth looked at me, nodded. We picked up our bags, headed for her Corolla three slots down.

We made it all the way to Maryland before either of us said a word about a place to sleep.

Chapter 14

WE WERE UP before daylight, and I could see even in the pale glow from the night-light in the motel bathroom the smile on Ruth's face, the two of us looking at each other, giddy for the prospect of whatever might come next.

We drove, me one hour, Ruth the next two, and so on. We stopped in Richmond, gave a call to Gordon and Melba to let them know we were a day ahead of time, that they needn't do anything special, that we could stay somewhere on the road down if they needed the extra day. None of which they were having. Before I'd even finished explaining why we were early, that we simply couldn't wait another second to get home, they were on both extensions again, just like that first time they'd called.

"Only thing is, Robert's got to work today," Gordon said, "so he won't be over till later," and Melba put in, "And Jocelyn won't be up from Charleston with her kids until tomorrow, and of course Beau's working his shift to the fire station so he won't be here at all," and the deal was done. One night early was even better than they could hope for, despite it was only the two of them to be the welcoming committee.

Then here we were to Florence, South Carolina, and Highway 701 around four in the afternoon, the only thing left to drive a two-lane road and fifty-three miles through the old world of who I was.

Here was light, the old charm of it, the afternoon warmth and softness and bright memory of it all. Here were fields gone fallow for winter but still velveted over in green, smack in the middle of February. Here were live oaks spun with Spanish moss, and longleaf pine all heavy with themselves, their boughs above us as we drove like some kind of guardians over this road, protectors from the light that fell through them and onto us.

We had the radio on, and just then the

weatherman said it was "a cool sixty-three degrees, tonight's low down to a brisk fifty-two,"
and both Ruth and I laughed out loud for that.
"Fifteen   degrees   yesterday,"   I   said,   then
hollered out, "Sixty-three in February and
sunny, and green everywhere!" We both rolled
our windows down, put out our hands to catch
the wind. My hand sliced through it like I used
to do when I was with my daddy and momma,
my brother Mahlon and me in the backseat of
our old Ford. I felt as much like we were flying right then, my hand cupped and moving of
its own in the wind, as when I was five or six,
and we were driving over the old bridges into
Charleston proper from Mount Pleasant for
whatever reason.

I looked over at Ruth, her right hand on the
wheel, her left out her window and doing the
same. Just flying.

We drove, the road leading one way and another in long, gentle curves, while we passed
barns fallen in on themselves, and dead farmhouses, and empty shacks, all of them with
vines grown up and through and out the windows and holes in the roofs and around crumbling chimneys. Kudzu, dead for winter,
seemed to strangle all these dead places, brown
tendrils for all the world like long fingers holding tight.

But there were new barns, too, and full alive farmhouses with screened porches and gravel drives lined with oaks themselves. There were trailers dropped here and there, and ranch houses, the occasional gas station and general store, each with a couple three cars or trucks parked out front. There were perfect little gardens out front filled with daffodils—daffodils, already up in February!—and old tires split open and painted white and filled with those daffodils as well. Old refrigerators and washers sat up on broken-down porches, and yards with grass cut so fine you'd swear it was carpet you were about to set foot on.

All of it—the dead and alive places both— just like I remembered.

But there were other things, too, I hadn't thought of, things of course I knew would be here but wouldn't allow in for the weight of all I placed on my memory, and the weight of my desire for a world lit by a sun more forgiving and faithful than the one too weak to melt off black ice.

There were satellite dishes, of course, little ones fixed to a chimney or off the eaves, and big ones set out in the front yard like some sort of lawn ornament you might be proud of. Out front of a lot of houses were these little four-wheel vehicle things for riding off into the woods, what looked like overgrown go-carts. Beside or inside most every one of those gas stations was a video store, the windows plastered all over with movie posters.

But what had I expected? There were video stores every hundred feet in Northampton, not to mention tattoo parlors on every corner, and what seemed a new sushi bar opening every other weekend. All of it played out in a town I'd lived in for more than fifty years, a town that, when we got there from New Hampshire, was not much more than Smith College and onion fields.

A town not a whole lot different than the Mount Pleasant I'd left.

Time moved, whether you liked it or not.

And so as we came closer and closer to Georgetown and Gordon and Melba's, there were more and more clues the world down here hadn't stayed still: trees started giving way to billboards for Hardee's, and McDonald's and Taco Bell and another fast-food place called Bojangles' that sold chicken and biscuits, and I tried to imagine that—fast-food biscuits—and fairly shuddered at the thought of it.

There were billboards for lawyers who'd help if you'd been in a car wreck, and billboards for chiropractors who'd fix you after that wreck. Strip malls started up, with more of

those video stores, and dry cleaners, and bar-
gain shoe stores and even more video stores.
Gone were those general store gas stations, replaced with minimarts at corners, all of them
built on big concrete patches, the station logos
and colors all too big and bright to believe, all
of them sparkling and shiny and strange here
on a country corner.

Then we were in Georgetown proper, 701
dead-ending into 17, Old Georgetown Highway. We got a red light, beside us suddenly that
McDonald's, across from us the Bojangles', and
an army-surplus store and a Burger King. Here
was a Ford dealership too, and traffic and traffic and traffic, all of it sprung on us in the kind
of ugly and startling surprise time passing can
only be. And farther off to our right, hulking
like some ugly green and corrugated monster,
stood Georgetown Steel, the huge plant right
here in town a fact I'd forgotten, and then I
remembered the paper mill too a little ways up
the river, and the horrible smell off that place,
a smell seemed to soak into the walls when the
wind was just right.

Georgetown. We were here.

"You ready?" Ruth said, and I turned to her.
She had her sunglasses on, like I did, and
smiled.

She'd never met any of these people. She'd

heard talk, certainly, but always and only that. She'd spoken a time or two to them on the phone since all of this plan had begun. But there was now the true specter before her of family, of people who were a part of her and of me and of Mahlon and Eli she was about to put faces to, and for a moment I feared Gordon and Melba'd hug her to pieces, squeeze the wind out of my Ruth.

There had still been in her a fear, I'd known, that'd rendered her frail through this all. Through the sale of everything we could, through the brochures and whatnot of the apartment we were moving to, through even that last lingering look at the balloons before she told me they'd be in the way.

I reached over to her, took her hand, squeezed it hard. "Never more ready," I said, and hoped she'd believe the lie.

GORDON AND MELBA WERE out the door before we'd even parked beneath the bare crepe myrtle that leaned over their driveway, the two of them headed toward us like horses out the gate to start on the hugs and tears and crying I knew would come.

Gordon looked all the world like his daddy, Eli's stepdaddy Gordon Stackhouse. He had the same bushy white eyebrows crept down almost over his eyes, and that bald head save for a crazy wisp or two right there above both ears. He had on green coveralls, short-sleeved and with a built-in belt. An old man's outfit, but it was the same old Gordon, the grinning little boy we'd have to deal with when we came up the odd Sunday afternoon for dinner and a visit.

And here was Melba, her joy and big heart and arms open wide. "Bless your heart!" she hollered and then she was at Ruth's open car door, Ruth climbing out, keys still in her hand, sunglasses on. She had only one foot to the ground, but Melba's arms were already around her.

Melba closed her eyes as she rocked. I could see tears on her face, in the wrinkles beside her eyes and down her cheeks. Her hair was the same hennaed red as last I'd seen her, maybe forty years ago, and her arms had the wattle of an old woman's, just like mine. Ruth got her other foot out of the car and onto solid ground, and here were her own tears, and I watched from my seat Ruth's arms go slowly up and around Melba's, saw her drop her keys for surrendering to such a hug.

Now Gordon was here at my door, opened it for me, helped me up careful from the car seat, then I gave up to his open arms as well, all of us wordless and crying, the car doors standing wide open.

"Sister," he whispered as he held me, "we're so glad you're home."

I smiled up at him, not in me the nerve to correct him, me too thankful just to hold my Eli's kin in my arms.

Almost home, I wanted to tell him, but did not.

Slowly we made it up onto the porch and into their house, the same house Eli and I'd come to visit in those dating days. Gordon'd inherited it back in 1967, when Mr. Stackhouse passed. The house was a small thing, set back off 17 on the other side of the Georgetown River and out of the mess of that downtown, back on a narrow asphalt road heaped over with live oak boughs.

The front room was cluttered the way old people's homes will be cluttered with the furniture it took a lifetime to gather and none of which you'd ever let go.

Unless you were leaving your old life behind.

The sofa was covered with a brown and white checkered afghan blanket that might've been here the last time we'd visited, or might not, I couldn't recall. Beside it a black Naugahyde recliner with arms so worn out the doilies pinned on to cover them up were nearly worn through themselves. Woodpaneled walls were covered with family pictures, all framed eight-by-tens.

And there were model wooden ships everywhere, a passion of Gordon's I'd forgotten in all these years. Behind that recliner three shelves went up the wall, on them eight or nine glass cases each a different size, each built to fit only what they held: a ketch-rigged sloop, an old CrisCraft, a yawl, a catboat, a simple dory. All of them rigged, sails set or oars to the gunwales, decks varnished. All of them beautiful.

Then the surprise of knowing what these boats were called came to me: I knew a sloop, a yawl, a catboat. They were all boats my daddy'd taught me when I was growing up, when some days he'd taken me out on the *Mary Sweet,* and we'd see them in the harbor.

That knowledge now here. Just like that.

"I forgot about all this," I said to Gordon, "the model ships," and turned to him. He was smiling, looked up at the shelves himself, Ruth looking too. "These are beautiful," she said.

Melba stood at their TV cabinet across from the sofa, set on it a glass case two feet tall.

"This one's my pride and joy," she said, a hand to the top of the case like she was a game-show girl.

Inside was a fully rigged trawler, the hull a perfect kelly green, its seines all up in that same way I'd always thought of as hands in praise. Ruth and I stepped to the case for a closer look, saw the stern deck had in it rows of tiny wire crabpots too, and lines coiled, even the smallest rigged fishing poles set into rod holders on the gunwales.

"This was my daddy's baby," Melba said, "the *Rebecca*. Took my Gordon three years to get this one set, and he gave it to my daddy the day he was done with it. You should've seen my daddy bawling when he got this. Such a sight," she said, and shook her head.

"This is beautiful," Ruth said. "This is perfect."

I looked at Melba, her smiling big as ever, eyes to the ship. "It truly is," I said.

"Don't suppose you'll recall what this one's about," Gordon said from behind us, and we turned. He stood behind the recliner, his hands up to the far corner of the top shelf, and the smallest case up there, maybe a foot long and only six inches tall. From my height I couldn't see what was in the case, only watched as he lifted the whole thing off the shelf, gentle as could be. He turned to us, stepped out from behind the recliner, smiling down at what he had.

A submarine.

"Oh my no," I said, and now here it was between us, all of us looking at the model like it was a campfire could keep us warm.

It was small, rough-carved from a two-by-two, and painted sloppy, the top half of it gray, the bottom black, and with a tower looked nothing more than a knot out of pine plank. Up from the tower and off the bow were toothpicks, painted gray too: a radio antenna, a bowsprit.

"First one I ever did, and looks like it too," Gordon said. "After Eli went on up to New Hampshire." He paused, still smiling down on it. "Did this when I was twelve and so damned jealous of Eli off to building subs and me so proud of him at the same time. My stepbrother." He shook his head, glanced at the *Rebecca*, then over his shoulder at the shelves. "All this come out of this punky thing," he said, looked at the submarine again. "All of it out of Eli heading off to the war."

With his words I only now remembered hearing about that submarine, back when Momma'd sometimes trade letters from Eli's momma once Eli was in the Navy.

"Beau found it in a shoe box out to the garage when he was staying here with us after he and Valerie," Melba said, and stopped, took in a quick breath, like it'd come to her as a surprise, the words she'd spoken. She reached up, scratched at her nose. "Beau built the case for it himself and made a present of it back to his daddy on Father's Day that year," she said, and nodded.

"Looks mighty puny," Gordon said, and looked up at me, still smiling. "But I got Eli to thank for all this," he said. "Or him to blame, one."

"He'd be proud to see all this," I said, and knew it for truth. I smiled at him, nodded.

"He's got his ships," Melba said, "but I got my kids, and my grandkids to show off for you," and Gordon said, "They're mine, too!" and turned, gently placed the glass case back on that top shelf. Then Melba took hold my hand and brought me to the sofa and the pictures that carpeted the wall above it, Ruth right here with us.

Melba and Gordon both narrated at once, as though one were afraid the other might leave something out: here was Jocelyn's senior picture, twenty years ago already, she didn't go to the reunion seeing's how she'd got word her ex-husband had plans to show up, and here were her kids' school portraits this year, Zachary in eighth grade, Brian in seventh, the two of them just too close together and don't they look like twins? and little Tess in third, and doesn't she just look too thin to you for a little girl that age? And here's Robert—that job at the Piggly Wiggly here in town's waiting for you, has your name on it, Ruth—and his beautiful wife Ellen, she's a ball of fire and a giggler from the get-go, you can see it in her eyes plain as day, and here's their Emily girl, who's almost grown up in tenth grade this year and gone through two boyfriends already, and here's little Ashley their princess and won't let anybody forget it neither, she's in second grade, wears a little rhinestone tiara around the house, I told you she was a princess; and here's Beau in his uniform at graduation, we were so proud, and this little Polaroid here is Beau and Ollie, just about a month before, Ollie'd've been eighteen in October this year, and the only thing can keep that Polaroid from fading is to hide it away, which we're not about to do.

There on the wall, nearly a secret for how small it was against all these eight-by-tens, was a framed Polaroid, the image on it nearly gone full to the green and yellow tint these things get swallowed by. But you could see it was a man smiling, in his arms a baby, black-haired like his daddy, Beau.

Ollie. Beau, and Valerie.

And it was to my shame that I remembered only then the story from all those years ago: how their first grandchild, Ollie, had passed in his sleep at five months, not a year later Beau and his wife Valerie breaking up over it.

Ruth said, "We're so sorry," and I turned to her. She was looking at Melba, and I saw in her eyes she knew the story herself. She'd been married to Mahlon four or five years by the time this'd happened.

We were a family all the way back then.

Melba nodded, rubbed at her nose again. I could see her eyes were wet for this giant fact made new once more with our being here. She gave a quick smile to Ruth, nodded once more. Enough words on the matter, I could see.

But I went ahead, said, "We are sorry," and felt the shock of guilt again for having forgotten over all these years that loss.

Melba's eyes met mine, and she smiled.

Then we were ushered to the dining room at the back of the house, though not a room so much as where the table sat, the kitchen to the left and part of this end of the house.

Set upon the table was a dinner for Thanksgiving and Christmas and Easter all at once. To the right was a sideboard, centered on top another huge model ship, a five-masted schooner set to sail right through its glass, crowded around it even more food, and the two of them set to narrating the dishes like they were those family photos: here's Ellen's shrimp and grits with Tabasco same as her momma did, she brought it over an hour or so ago, they'll be here in a little while; and biscuits and cheese grits and green-bean casserole, ham sliced off the bone and a whole fried turkey breast I cooked up special out in the fryer in the garage, no trouble at all; and those sausage balls Jocelyn's ex-husband made for us every year, the recipe a keeper though he certainly was not, and Beau throwing him out on his head finally, thank you very much; here's green salad and a purple Jell-O mold with cottage cheese and apples and walnuts, Melba's momma found that recipe in of all places on the back of a Rice Krispies box, you're supposed to put Rice Krispies in but my momma knew what to put in and leave out; and sweet-potato pie, you remember your momma and sweet-potato pie, Naomi? of course she does, why would you ask such a thing? and mashed potatoes and gravy and another plate of biscuits, and pitchers each of sweet tea and unsweetened both—

"Just in case this Massachusetts girl here doesn't know what's good for her," Gordon said from across the table, Ruth beside him and Melba next to her, an arm around Ruth's waist as simple and true as if they were dear friends from many years past.

"I've been drinking it sweet since the first meal I ever ate at Naomi's house," Ruth said to him, and smiled at me. "And if anybody's a Massachusetts girl it's her. She's been living up there since before I was born."

"This girl's a sharp one," Melba said and laughed, pulled Ruth closer. "Just like we'd heard all these years, all of it true, and her even more beautiful than anyone told us."

I stood across the table from the three of them, me somehow settled into place here when we'd first turned to the heaps of food from all those pictures, all that family.

"She's a keeper," I said.

Here we were, their home, and all the words, all this food, all the family photos, the model ships, and those worn-out doilies and bare crepe myrtles outside and even Gordon's eyebrows and Melba's hennaed hair all music to me.

All a song I'd forgotten for the years gone from this place.

I looked at Ruth, still smiling. She'd

crooked an arm around Melba herself, natural as could be.

I said, "How did you ever put this all together a whole day before we were supposed to get here?"

Melba laughed, said, "When's putting together food for family ever been a difficult thing?"

I shook my head, smiled down at the table so full. "You shouldn't have," I said. "But we're glad for it."

I looked up to her, still smiling.

And saw behind the three of them drapes floor to ceiling, huge magnolia blossoms on a sea-green background, and it only occurred to me now that last time I was here, all those years ago, there used to be a door off this room, one that led out to the backyard and the dock, a rickety old thing that angled over the saltmarsh hay and yellowgrass to the creek back there.

Without a word I went round the end of the table. Gordon leaned forward and peeled back a little piece of that fried turkey, and Melba and Ruth watched me head for those drapes.

"It's still there," Melba near to whispered, and there seemed some magic passed between us. And not just with her, but with Gordon, too, who turned from the turkey. Then slowly he went the couple feet behind him to the drapes, reached inside the edge of them, pulled the cord to open them up.

They'd replaced the door with a sliding glass window, and when the drapes pulled back full the memory of being a girl to Mount Pleasant and those walks in the woods was all the closer. So close I could feel the carpet of pinestraw beneath my feet, could feel the warm light down through the trees.

The yard swept out from beneath their own pines and live oak to the marsh a hundred feet or so away. There was the dock, the planks on it mottled and warped, I could see even with the sun already down. The creek was narrow here, the dock maybe fifty feet long and narrow itself, more so than I could recall. Nowheres near enough room for a boat to put in.

But we'd thrown castnets off the end of it, Eli or Gordon or even me, and I remembered of a sudden the cinch rope clenched between your teeth, the gathered net with its lead weights as big as your finger sewn into the hem all the way around draped over your arm, in each hand an edge of the hem itself. Then you threw it all out in a circle on the water before you, what every time I ever saw made me think of a petticoat thrown full on the floor, those weights swirling out over the water to drop, if you did it right, into a perfect circle, then disappearing. Next came the pull of the cinch rope once you felt the net settle to the bottom, and the hauling in to find treasure, whether shrimp to eat or mullet for bait, sometimes even a spottail bass.

And here in me was the memory of the crabpots we'd drop in out there, and the cannonballs we'd do when the tide was in. We'd found our fill of blue crabs and shrimp, and our fill of fun jumping off back there while Eli and I were dating, little brother Gordon always wanting to pull his stepbrother under but Eli always stronger, and older, and just as mischievous as Gordon.

Now here was the same Gordon beside me, with his daddy's eyebrows, eyes the wet and rheumy of an old age we'd never even considered might could find us those days out off the dock.

I put my hand up to the glass, felt the cool of it, saw where my gnarled fingers touched at the glass that there was a shadow, a ghost outline up off the tips of them. Condensation on the glass.

I was still alive.

I felt Ruth's hand to my shoulder, all four of us looking out the window now. Across the creek the trees were a tall presence of green above the grays and yellows of a saltmarsh in February, and I watched while in the growing dark of our first day back there came at me the mystery of empty woods, of light leaving for the day. The green trees over there were turning color, changing to a kind of blue headed toward black, the curve and texture, the pitch and reach of the boughs out toward the creek above the marsh all swallowed in the failing light. Above it all night edged on, the lavender and gray of it, not even a star out yet.

"Almost home," Ruth whispered in my ear, her breath warm, a comfort.

And just then, from across the creek and deep inside those trees, that wall of them no longer trees for the dark but a mystery deeper still, a light came on.

Not just one, but a gang of them.

There, off to my right and across the creek and through those trees, sat a house not a hundred yards away, lit up with a string of floodlights shining up on it from the ground. I couldn't see the all of it, only could tell it was a house, a pale green one, built up high.

"Leastways you can't much see them in daylight," Gordon said, his voice gone to gravel. "But then those dusk to dawn lights go on, and there they are." He paused, swallowed. "None of them yet got a dock permit, though who knows how long before the wetlands commission people cave in."

Then another set of lights came on to my left, and another straight out off the end of the dock, all of them set up to show off a house hidden in the woods.

"My," I whispered, and now the weight of the thousand miles we'd driven in these two days hit me, and I felt my knees and the pain in them, and the ache in my fingers.

I felt on me what I hadn't thought of this entire day, or at least hadn't allowed to let myself think on.

It was the weight of forgiveness in me I felt, the surprise of it, delivered so late and so full, around me these people I loved who had no notion of who I truly was, of what I'd done. And with no notion of how I'd lived my life with all this, and how only yesterday at my husband's graveside I'd been delivered of it.

Forgiveness lighting up my sin, illuminating it like brand-new houses hidden in ancient trees.

Still I did not know what to do, or how to hold on. But still I left my hand at the glass.

"There's thirty of them back in there," Melba said quiet, on her voice a kind of marvel and sadness at once. "Every one of them sold before they even broke ground."

"My," I whispered again, though the word out of me was so quiet I believed it was only me to hear.

Then Ruth squeezed my shoulder the smallest way, and I felt her lean into me. I knew she'd heard me, and had heard on the word the weight of these miles, and the revealed mystery of empty woods.

But she hadn't heard the other weight. Of forgiveness.

People lived in those woods.

"Almost home," she whispered again.

Chapter 15

THE FRONT DOOR BANGED open, and we all turned to it.

Here running in was a little girl, white-haired and with a rhinestone tiara on her head and wearing a pink tutu.

"Mamaw! Papaw!" she shouted, her arms up for Gordon and Melba. But her eyes were on me, and Ruth, and me again, all before she fell into Melba, who hadn't even the time to bend to her. She wrapped her arms far as she could around Melba's middle, her cheek pressed hard against her tummy. She was grinning up at me, a spray of freckles across her nose, her teeth two perfect white rows save for one gap on the bottom.

"You must be Ashley," I said to her, and smiled, leaned a little over to her.

"Thank you," she said, and giggled. She quick turned her face away from me, pressed just as hard and holding on just as tight to Melba.

"Ashley, this here's your aunt Naomi," Gordon said, and bent to her, hands on his knees. "And this is your aunt Ruth, too."

She whipped her head back to me, glanced at Ruth. "Y'all aren't sisters!" she said, and giggled again, this time louder, and before I could say a thing here came Ellen, lugging a huge casserole dish with two hotpads. She had a grin plastered on her face and was looking at Melba. She shook her head, then gave a quick nod back over her shoulder, a signal something was up with whatever was coming after her.

Then she looked at Ruth and me, and the smile wasn't plastered anymore, but real.

"Welcome home!" she said, and wedged the casserole onto what little room was left on the table. "You never met me, but we've heard a lot about y'all," she said, and came to me, gave a hug, and did the same for Ruth.

Her hair was in tight curls I couldn't say were permed or natural, and she had blue eyes, freckles all over. Already she was giggling just like they said she would, over what I couldn't say.

Right behind her through the door was Gordon and Melba's boy Robert, a man I recognized mostly from the photos of him here on his momma's wall, but somewhere inside his smile and eyes the same baby in diapers I'd seen last time I'd been here. He was still in his white shirt and red tie from work, sleeves rolled up, his nametag there at his breast pocket. He wore glasses and had those eyebrows well on their way to the bushy of his daddy's, and he looked beat for a day's work. Now he was hugging me, and shook hands with Ruth, but not before he glanced to Ellen, then to Gordon and Melba. He made a smirk, quick shook his head.

"All's I got to say," he said, and crossed his arms, looked at Ruth and me both, "is just never have a teenage daughter. That's all." He laughed a little, and Ellen giggled, while the front door stood open, waiting for their other girl, Emily.

"She broke up with her boyfriend today," Ellen said. She looked at Melba, had her hands together in front of her, the fingers just touching.

Melba said, "Bless her heart."

"Her boyfriend's nickname is Fatback!"

Ashley shouted, still holding tight to Melba's middle. She let out a squeal of laughter, her eyes on us.

"Y'all just shut up!" came shouted from outside the front door, and we all turned to see nothing. There was just that voice, on it a girl's pain and exasperation both.

"She's sitting out on the porch," Robert said, took in a deep breath through his nose, let it out. "She can hear us." He rocked back on his heels, then forward.

Ellen said, "She'll do this sometimes."

Robert said, "You got that right."

"She'll be okay in a minute," Gordon said, his voice easy now and a little too loud. Papaw's voice, I realized, just in case she was listening for him.

"No need for worrying," I said. "I was a teenage girl once, too," I said, and thought of my brother—*I ain't listening to Little Orphan Annie! You got no choice but to give me your last piece of bacon!*—and my own cries of exasperated pain at being part of a family.

"I've been there too," Ruth said. "There's nothing worse than a broken heart." She smiled a little, looked at Ellen, who smiled back.

It was just something to say, I knew. Comment on a teenage girl, on it nothing meant but commiseration: teenage girls are a handful.

But then Ellen let drop her hands, slowly moved to Ruth, and gave another hug, this one longer, surer.

"We are truly glad you're here," she said, and pulled away, "and we're sorry for the grief you've had to bear." Ellen looked at me, still holding on to Ruth. "Both of you," she said, and turned back to Ruth.

Ruth looked at her, and to me, on her face surprise, her eyebrows slowly gone up, her eyes opening wide, and she bit her lip.

"We all are, sweetness," Melba said, and put a hand to Ruth's shoulder, rubbed it careful. Robert said, "Yes, we are," and Gordon said, "We're glad you two are home."

Ruth's chin trembled. She quick looked to them each, met them all with her eyes. She took in a sharp breath, pulled Ellen to her, and she cried, silent and full, her shoulders quivering for it. She held tight to Ellen, and cried.

Then Gordon was holding me, this Stackhouse man squeezing me hard to let me know it wasn't lost on anyone the grief I had to bear right along with Ruth.

"Y'all are momma and daughter, not sisters!" Ashley squealed, down below this all, and Gordon let go. She was still clutching tight her mamaw, still grinning.

"I guess you got that right, little missy," Gordon said.

I leaned to her again. She didn't turn away this time, and I touched her hair, felt how soft it was, how fine. I gave a little tickle behind her ear.

"Momma and daughter," I said.

And of course she giggled.

GORDON SAID GRACE, all of us holding hands. Ashley, to my left, squeezed tight, Melba's hand in my right warm and big and holding even tighter. But I didn't mind a bit the pain on my fingers. Not a bit.

And then we ate.

Then ate more.

Eventually, too, Emily came in from the porch. She was a beautiful girl, the same spray of freckles across her nose as her little sister, and with the same white hair, hers parted in the middle. No tiara, and thin as a stick.

She smiled at me and at Ruth as she walked through the family room toward the table, no one saying a word for her quiet entrance. They all knew how to handle this, it happening enough times before.

She had on a white top with spaghetti straps, and a short short red skirt, the number 71 on the right thigh. The same heavy patch of a number you might see on a letterman jacket, and I couldn't help but wonder what sport it was a girl wore something that short for.

She went straight to the kitchen behind us, on the counter piled the plates and silverware and napkins and dishes of food we'd had to move to make way for ourselves to sit.

Everyone at the table watched everyone else, though all of us were eating: Gordon with another tear of that turkey to his mouth, Ellen with a spoonful of cheese grits, Melba and Robert and Ruth and Ashley all eating.

Ashley, though, even with her mouth full, was ready for something, grinning while she chewed on a biscuit she held with both hands. She rocked in her seat, her feet swinging back and forth beneath her. I could see in her eyes, and that grin too, that she was ready, waiting.

All I'd wanted was just to say hello. I wanted just to let Emily know we were happy to be here, glad to be a part of all this food, and this family.

So it was me to open my mouth first.

I set down my forkful of broccoli-cheese casserole—what Ellen'd toted in when they arrived—and turned in my seat. Emily was leaned into the open refrigerator, nosing around for something. That white blouse had pulled up in back some with her leaning, and there across the seat of the skirt, in those same letterman jacket letters, was the word abercrombie.

"What sport do you play over to Abercrombie?" I said.

She stood from the refrigerator, turned to me, in her hand a bottled water. "Ma'am?" she said, her face all a question.

"Is that the name of your high school?" I asked, and gave a quick twitch of a smile. "Abercrombie?"

Ashley squealed, shouted, "Abercrombie and Fitch! She plays for Abercrombie and Fitch!"

"What?" I said, and turned to the table to see the all of them broken up into laughter.

There was a joke here, and me the butt of it. I quick looked to Ruth, who was laughing and wiping her fingers, her mouth closed tight for the food in there, and Gordon was at it too. Melba managed out "Bless your heart!" to me, and covered her mouth, propped an elbow to the table, and kept on laughing.

"It's clothes," Emily said to me. "A clothes company. Just a clothes company," and though

I could see the impatience in her, still a corner of her mouth was up in a smile she didn't want to let out.

"She used to play for Fatback, but he kicked her off the team!" Ashley squealed, and Emily shouted through clenched teeth, "Daddy!" and Robert put in, "Careful your mouth or you're in the car, Ashley."

But they were all still laughing, even Emily now, coming round the end of the table with her bottled water and a plate and silverware, and then she settled in beside her daddy, who speared a slice of ham and set it on her plate.

"Daddy!" she said, and tried to hold off another smile.

"Pork is our friend," Robert said, "and you need some meat on you, I'm here to tell you."

"A and F! Aunt Naomi thinks she plays for A and F!" Ashley shouted, still rocking, still with that biscuit clutched tight.

I was an old woman, no doubt to it. And this was a story they'd tell on me for years to come.

Emily put her elbow to the table, covered her eyes, shook her head.

Robert spooned up a good lot of cheese grits, served it onto Emily's plate without her seeing. Gordon, smiling, shook his head, and pointed at me with his fork. And Melba, and Ruth, and Ellen, and me too, all laughed, and all ate.

Aunt Naomi, Ashley'd said, and I tried to recall when I'd ever heard that name.

Chapter 16

LIGHT FROM those houses across the creek banged into the bedroom, even with the curtains pulled tight. Ruth and I shared the queen bed in here, the house with only three bedrooms. One of them—Jocelyn's old room—had been turned into a workroom, Melba's sewing machine and Gordon's workbench and tools in there now.

This was Beau and Robert's old room, though there was nothing to it of a boy's life anymore. The curtains at the two windows were more of those magnolias from the dining room, only on a pink background you couldn't say was pink in this dark. But you could see those magnolias, big and white and floating there, the light from across the creek leaking in all the way around. On the wall opposite the windows was the closet door, beside that the door into the bathroom. It was a teeninecy thing, only a shower stall big enough to turn around in. A toilet, a pedestal sink, a door into the other room so the kids could share it between them, though now it opened into that workroom.

At the foot of the bed was a white hope chest, on it our two overnight bags; against the wall across from it stood a white chest of drawers, above it a mirror, above that a white shelf. Set on it were a dozen or so of those crocheted toilet-paper cover dolls, the crocheted piece a hoop skirt over the roll, at the top a plastic doll head crocheted right into it, bonnet and all. There hadn't been boys in here for a long time.

After dinner we'd visited for an hour or so, Ashley lying on the floor in the middle of us all and whispering to herself the storybook she had in front of her. Emily sat out to the dining room with her back to us and reading a novel. We'd just talked—about fifteen degrees in Northampton yesterday, and the manager at the Piggly Wiggly to Mount Pleasant and her phone number, how Jocelyn's boys Zachary and Brian were trying to get into the magnet school and how Emily wanted to get two more piercings for her ears. Just talk, the last bit thrown in too loud by Gordon just to get a rise out of his granddaughter.

She didn't bite, not even a sigh for it.

I'd started to nod off a little, the words and voices all melting into one another in that way that made no sense but which you were listening to all the same. Ruth's voice was in there and fearless, talking about something, and Ellen with a word and Robert with a few and the all of them laughing of a sudden.

I opened my eyes, startled I'd fallen asleep.

There was Ruth at the dining room table with a washrag, wiping. Water ran in the kitchen, the sofa and recliner empty.

Ruth saw me, smiled. "Didn't want to wake you," she said. "Another of these long days we keep having." She nodded, headed into the kitchen.

Ellen and Robert and the girls were gone, Ruth and Melba at the refrigerator arranging things to fit all the food we had left. Gordon stood at the sink, wiping dry a pan.

He smiled, nodded. "I heard you sawing logs in there," he said, shook his head. "You'll be dreaming on cheese grits and shrimp in no time, once you hit the hay."

Now here I lay, my hairnet on, glasses on the nightstand beside me, flannel nightgown warm as toast. Wide awake, as if that little nap after dinner'd been enough for a whole night.

I could tell by her breathing beside me that Ruth was awake, too, the two of us side by side and on our backs. It was in the shallow depth of each breath she took in, let out, as if she were waiting for word from me to let her know we could talk.

But it was her to speak first.

"Do you remember that feeling?" she whispered, then paused. "Of being a girl," she went on, "and everything in the world was meant to embarrass you. Like Emily was tonight."

It was a question out of midair, but we were here, in the middle of the night in a house gone quiet, in what might as well be a foreign country. For that it seemed as logical a question as any.

"I remember," I whispered back, "but I thought you'd be thinking on sleep this time of night," and she quick gave back, "I'm sorry, Naomi. I thought you were awake."

"Haven't closed an eye yet," I said. I let out a little puff of a laugh. "Guess we're too wound up from the day."

"Yes," she said. "And being here." She paused, took in a breath. "Just being here," she whispered.

She was quiet a second, then whispered in a

voice seemed almost amazed, "Did you know she was the one who brought in the overnight bags from the car?"

"That child?" I asked, my whisper almost too loud. I hadn't given the bags being in here a thought when we'd come in for bed. They'd just been there.

"Yes," Ruth whispered, still with that kind of amazed wonder. "While you were asleep on the sofa. We were rinsing dishes and from nowhere comes her voice, 'Can I help?' And Melba and Ellen and I all turn, and she's standing there with that look on her face. Like she's bored, with her head tilted down, and her arms crossed." She stopped, slowly shook her head. "But she's looking at me, and Ellen and Melba knew she was and so they didn't say anything." She paused. "She was asking me if she could help me," she whispered. "And so I tell her if she really wants to, we haven't brought in our bags yet. My hands are wet with the dishes, so I nod to my purse hanging off the back of one of the chairs, and tell her the keys are in there, and if she really wants she can bring them in for us."

She went quiet, shook her head once more. "She got the keys, and did it."

I thought on Emily, on that exasperated pain I'd heard in her voice—"*Y'all just shut up!"*—and the embarrassment and antagonized way of life my brother'd held me under.

"Talk to me," Ruth whispered. She rolled over toward me, pulled the sheet and blanket tight to her chin. "I need you to tell me stories," she whispered. "Of when you were a girl."

"Honey?" I whispered. I looked at her, tried to push up on an elbow and made to turn over to her. "You all right?"

"I'm fine," she said. She reached a hand out from under the covers, put it to my shoulder to signal me to lie down. Here was her chestnut hair moving in the near dark, the silk sheaf of it off her shoulder as she reached to me. Here was her hand too, soft and warm but pushing to let me know she was, in fact, fine.

And so I lay back, and I looked to the ceiling, at the fan up there, and I looked at the curtains, those magnolias floating like a raft on that light from outside.

I was quiet a few seconds, wondering what she was after.

But she'd asked me to speak.

"Every day," I started, not certain where this might lead, but whispering nonetheless. "Being embarrassed," I went on. "I knew it chapter and verse. There was my brother, for starters, and him harassing me like brothers will." I stopped, listened for her to see if she were going to put in something of her own.

She was silent, still with that shallow breathing in and out, and I knew then what she needed: stories, just like she'd said. A way to start to live down here. A way to start to breathe, here in a foreign country.

And there washed over me my life as a girl, a place so far removed and kept so far away with how many miles we'd lived from here, the all of it brought me now with fried turkey and cheese grits, with the single word *y'all,* and the simple gift of sunlight dying over a saltmarsh, and a girl beside me needing stories. Never mind they were about the embarrassment a girl feels, because we all feel it, no matter what country we're from.

She needed stories, because we were almost home.

"But I was embarrassed about him in other ways," I whispered, and took in a deep breath. "He slept in a shack out back of the house. Because our house was so small, and it was my job to wake him up, me to walk out the back door and down the three concrete steps off the porch and then knock on his screen door." I was quiet, felt in me the old rush of blood, the sense of burning came with shame. "I was so ashamed of my brother sleeping in a shed, that

I woke him quiet as I could so's nobody in the houses around might could hear me. Knocked light as I could on that screen door, whispered in to get up. Me looking around to the neighbors' houses for someone watching me. I knew we were poor, and everybody near enough to see me out their window was, too. Plenty others had sheds or shacks or whatnot family lived in. But that didn't matter, because it was me out there having to wake my brother."

I went quiet, listened for Ruth, for some word, or the deep rhythm of breaths that would signal me I'd talked her to sleep.

Then I heard from the foot of the bed her rubbing her feet together under the covers.

She was listening.

"Eli used to jab a pencil into my shoulder from where he sat behind me in school, him and all his friends laughing him on to it," I said. "Which embarrassed me, them laughing and this annoying boy behind me positively misbehaving. You couldn't do anything for it but raise your hand and tattle, which I wasn't going to do. Which is why they did it to start with. Because they knew they'd get away with it." I paused, thought of Eli a moment, slowly shook my head, smiling to myself. "That was back when he was a nitwit. Before I got hold of him."

"Back before 'Nice to meet you,'" she whispered. On her words was a smile too, I could hear.

I was quiet, thought on her words, on that night when I'd told her of our hearts' password. For a moment I felt a quick trace of pain, a shadow of it through me. This was our secret, I thought. Mine and Eli's, and now she was using it back to me, like it was a phrase you could utter as you please.

But it was only a shadow, and passed as one.

I whispered back, "Yes, before."

I lay there again in silence, Ruth's feet still. "And I was worried over my bust," I whispered, and let out a quiet laugh. Ruth whispered a laugh as well, and wiggled there beside me, settling in. "Or the lack thereof, like every girl starts out. But I worked myself into a fit wondering when they'd come in, and all I'd wear were these loose-cut blouses had a Peter Pan collar, so no one would notice I was empty up top. Then when they started coming in I tried to talk my momma into making me a couple more in the same style but even bigger, even looser, so's nobody'd notice I actually had them finally." I paused, let out a quiet laugh again. "My daddy heard me the afternoon I tried to talk my momma into this plan, and he shouts from the other room, 'You'll wear the clothes you got till your bosoms pop the buttons, and then all we'll do is use fishing line to sew them buttons right back on!"

We both let out a laugh, then shushed each other and laughed and shushed again, like two girls at a pajama party. "And the tomfoolery of it was," I finally got out, "was that nobody noticed when I had nothing, and nobody noticed when they came in. But you couldn't tell me that, and I wouldn't've believed it if you'd told me. Because I was a girl, and I was embarrassed at it all." I took in a breath. "Especially my daddy making comment on my bosoms."

I let out a heavy sigh, shook my head again.

Ruth rolled onto her back. She took her hands out from beneath the covers, put them behind her head. "I haven't come close to even thinking about any of this in years," she whispered.

She was looking to the foot of the bed now, that chest of drawers, the mirror, the shelf of toilet-paper cover dolls above it all.

"The whole time growing up we had one of those things. Those toilet-paper hiders. I never knew if my mom made it or not." She paused. "I never saw her crochet, or knit. But she sewed things."

She looked to the ceiling. "I was embarrassed about that thing. That one of my friends would see that thing sitting on the back of the toilet and make fun of it. It was this bright magenta yarn, and the doll face always just smiling. It sat on the toilet tank for as long as I could remember. When we lived in Ashfield, and then after my mother died and we moved down to Holyoke, here it was on the tank in the bathroom there, and I was still just as embarrassed." She paused. "And it was still there when my dad died in the mill fire."

She stopped, thinking on what she'd just said, I could tell. On the path she was about to head down, and there was to her whispered voice the same kind of marvel as when Melba'd told us how many houses were buried in the woods across the creek.

We never talked about her momma, or her daddy.

Yet there wasn't any sadness to her voice, like there'd been in Melba's. There was just a kind of awe, and quiet.

"I remember walking to school when I was a freshman, and wearing brand-new clothes I didn't know worked or not," she whispered, and now it was me to roll over onto my side, and face her. I tucked my hand under my pillow, looked at her profile, watched her mouth move with her words. "When my mom died I was twelve, and I didn't let my dad or anybody buy me any clothes for a year."

She took in a breath, held it, held it, then whispered, "She used to make me clothes I didn't want to wear."

I readied for tears, but none came, on her voice still that sense of marvel, and no sadness.

"Then she died," she went on, "and we moved, and I didn't trust anything. I wore those silly clothes she made me even though I didn't want them. But they fit through the rest of that year, in eighth grade." She stopped, blinked. She breathed out. "She'd made me bell-bottom pants, but they were this horrible green. And there was a vest she'd made me out of blue calico with little red rickrack all the way around. Two gingham blouses different colors, and another one out of that unbleached linen. Another pair of pants, orange this time, with patches sewn onto them. 'Right on,' was one of them, and 'Sock it to me,' and a peace sign." She paused, swallowed again. "I hated them. But my mom had died, and she made these things." She stopped, then whispered, "I didn't want to betray her."

I thought I heard a twist in her voice then, a bumping up against something. I reached to her, put a hand to her elbow beside me, and she turned to me. I could see something of a smile on her. "I'm fine," she whispered. "I am." She turned to the ceiling, here again her profile.

"Then I outgrew them," she went on. "Right about May, and somebody must have told my dad, because one Saturday morning a week after school's out he wakes me up and tells me we're going shopping." She turned her head to the shelf again, those toilet-paper dolls. "That's when it hit me. Not having a mother. Because I didn't have one to measure up to anything, whether or not she would approve of it."

She took in a breath, let it out through her nose. I touched her elbow again, patted it the gentlest way I knew how.

"I don't know how to say this," she whispered, and paused, still facing that shelf, those dolls. "But it hit me, that I would buy clothes with my dad, and he would say yes or no. There wasn't my mom to say yes or no. And I wouldn't know what was right or wrong for it. Whether the clothes were something my mom would let me wear, or if it was something I'd fight with her over wearing because she wouldn't let me. There wasn't my mom to say yes or no, even if I wanted to get the no. So I didn't trust anything. I didn't know what to trust, or who. And it scared me."

She swallowed, harder this time, and turned back to the ceiling.

"So I just bought things. We were down at Holyoke Mall. Dad and I just going into Steigers and Penney's both, and I'd see something and go try it on in the dressing room, and I'd come out without wearing it for him. He'd just nod when I held out to him what I wanted. Because he had no idea himself." She paused. "Because he had no idea what was right or wrong himself. He didn't have my mom to ask, either." She paused again, let in a long breath, held it again, and let it out. "Sometimes I'd come out of the dressing room," she whispered, even quieter now, "and I'd catch him sitting there before he saw me, and he'd have his elbows on his knees, and his face in his hands."

She stopped, those last words out of her down to nothing. I patted her arm again. This was what she'd bumped up against, I knew. Her momma, her daddy.

Herself, alone.

I left my hand there on her arm, just resting there. As if I could do anything for her, but to listen.

"And then I wore those clothes that year," she whispered, but the words back to that whispered pitch we'd held so far, like that had been the bottoming out of this all: her daddy, with his face in his hands, and her seeing him.

"I wore those clothes my freshman year, and I never knew if what I wore worked or not, and I'd walk to school down Ivy to Springfield High, and wonder what people's mothers told them to wear and what not to. Nobody made a peep about anything I ever wore. That was what scared me most. And embarrassed me most. That none of it made any difference." She paused. "Just like you, and those blouses, and nobody noticing what you didn't want to show off."

She stopped, looked at me. "Does this make any sense?" she asked.

"How'd you choose that plum muffler and gray sweater you wore the first time I met you?" I whispered, and tapped her arm with my fingers. "When Mahlon brought you out to the house on 116 to meet us." I paused. "Do you remember?"

Because I did. Here she was, on the front steps up to the door at the old house. A beautiful young woman in a gray sweater, a plum muffler, and blue jeans. Her hair pulled back, and Mahlon with no way he would take his eyes off her.

They'd been a done deal, the two of them. Done and done, right there on our front steps.

She looked at me a long moment, then back to the ceiling, recollecting. "I," she started, but then held off, blinked. "I thought he would like those together," she whispered, much quieter for whatever of it she was seeing right now. "I knew I liked them together. That they looked good together." She blinked again, turned to me.

"You two were already good as married that night," I whispered. I reached to her hair now, with my fingertips stroked it there at her temple.

"I picked those out," she whispered, and smiled at me, "because they worked."

"So maybe it was your daddy to trust you first. Maybe he saw you could be trusted," I said.

"Yes," she said. "May be," she said, and looked up at the ceiling again, slowly blinked.

We were quiet, and now rising up from the next room came the sharp gray rhythm of Gordon's snoring, and I whispered, "Oh my."

"We're never going to get to sleep," Ruth whispered, and rubbed at her nose. "But I don't mind." She was smiling again, and looked away, at the shelf, those dolls. "And all of this because of Emily. Abercrombie and Fitch, just broken up with another boyfriend. A little sister bugging you to death." She paused, whispered, "That was funny, you asking her what team she played on," and she gave out a quick, quiet laugh.

"I always like to entertain," I said, still with my fingertips to her hair. "Last I heard, Abercrombie and Fitch was some kind of stodgy old men's store. How was I to know it was selling skirts so small you could use them for a potholder?"

"And still she said 'Ma'am' when you asked her that question. Even with being a teenage girl in an A and F skirt, and with an ex-boyfriend named Fatback." She paused, and I could feel in my fingertips her slowly shaking her head. "She still said 'Ma'am.' "

She rolled over to face me, her hands tucked beneath her cheek on the pillow, my own hand at her temple even more full in her hair. I didn't move it.

"When I first met Mahlon, I thought he was some wiseguy. We'd sit in freshman comp and every time the teacher called on him he'd say, 'Yes sir?' and it was always that, Yes sir, No sir.

And I just always thought he was jerking the chain of that old professor we had in there, or that he was brown-nosing him."

I could see every feature on her face, and her hands there against her cheek, the collar of her flannel nightgown, all for the light in from beside the curtains. She was beautiful. Of course my Mahlon would love her. Of course he would.

"Then one day after class I was a couple people behind him in the cafeteria, and first the woman grilling burgers asks if he wants any cheese on his, and he says, 'Yes ma'am.' Then he comes up to the cashier, and she looks at his tray and says, 'Is that everything?' and he says, 'Yes ma'am.' And it was only then I figured out he wasn't doing it to get anything from anybody. He was just being polite. That it was just how he talked to people, and it knocked me down."

"Back before he kissed you in the backroom on Thursdays," I couldn't help but whisper.

She was quiet a second, then whispered, "Yes, before," and she was smiling.

Then here was Gordon snoring again, that gray saw. I pictured him on his back, the way Eli would be when he started up his own snoring, and I saw Melba in bed next to him, wondered if she would do like I did every time he started up and reach a hand over to him in the dark, jostle him a little so's he'd roll onto his side.

And I thought of Melba, and that snapshot, a Polaroid giving up its recollection of that moment of Beau and his baby boy a little bit each day, until one day that picture would be just a notion of a picture for the sunlight in on it, and then only a memory in Melba's head.

I whispered, "I forgot about Ollie. And about Beau and Valerie." I paused, sniffed. "That's something embarrasses me. Something I'm ashamed of."

"It's all right," Ruth whispered. "Now you remember. That's what matters."

"Yes," I said. But I should have recalled that piece of Gordon and Melba's life, that shard that still gave pain enough to bewilder Melba even to today.

"Ollie would have been seventeen right now. Only a year older than Emily," Ruth whispered, and here was that same awe, that wonder. "I remember him because that was when Mahlon and I were trying so hard to have a baby of our own. We used to be a little bit jealous, because we'd hear from you about Eli's stepnephew, this Beau, and this Valerie being pregnant, then this little baby boy named Oliver being born." She paused and, still with her hands beneath her cheek, turned her head the smallest way, looked at the ceiling again, like she'd heard something somewhere in the house.

She whispered, "We went to work more than ever then, and then Ollie passed away from SIDS." She stopped again, moved onto her back. "Maybe two months after that we found out about the cysts."

And now slowly, slowly, she was sitting up, her hands to her lap, her legs moving out from under the covers until she was up Indian-style on the bed.

"Ruth?" I whispered. I struggled to sit up, too, tried to push myself up from my side. I wanted to sit with her, and wondered what'd made her sit up this way, wondered what it was she might be seeing.

But here to my shoulder was the pain of that work, and of my age, and it was nighttime, and we were in bed, and so I lay back down, watched her. Despite all the words we'd passed, and despite these stories.

She was looking at that shelf. She whispered, "I wonder where it is right now. That doll." She paused, and I heard her swallow. "The one I grew up with, me so embarrassed about it for no good reason at all."

I said nothing, only looked at the shelf, those

crocheted dolls. The room seemed bright as day for that light across the creek, and how long we'd been talking, eyes open wide.

I thought of those lights, shining up on the houses. And I thought of embarrassments, and being a girl. What had gotten us on this long path it seemed we'd now nearly talked out.

And I thought of the one embarrassment I most wanted to tell her, the black stone caught in my heart. The story of me that went past that word *embarrassment,* and past the word *ashamed* and on past *betrayal,* and that broke right on through *sin.*

Only to land on *forgiveness.*

Forgiveness, illuminating my sin, like brand-new houses hidden in ancient trees. Me with no words I could whisper to let any of it go.

Ruth turned around on the bed, still Indian-style but facing me now. "This is good," she whispered. "Being here." She paused, took in a deep breath. "Remembering about Ollie, and seeing Emily, hearing her say 'Ma'am,' reminding me of Mahlon." She was smiling full on now. "I can feel it already," she whispered. "This is good," she said, "our coming here."

I looked at her, a young woman this night allowed to touch on her momma's dying, and maybe her daddy's trust, and allowed to whisper a few words on her love for my Mahlon.

I was jealous.

Still, I nodded, agreed with her by letting my eyes close against that light of forgiveness. It was all I could think to do.

Now here were her fingertips, just touching my temple, the small bit of hair the net didn't protect.

Chapter 17

W HEN I WOKE UP, the bed beside me was already empty, and I could hear talking from out in the front room. Slowly I pushed myself up, sat for a few seconds on the edge of the bed, facing those windows, all those magnolias.

If I had my way, and despite how cold a sentiment it might have been to hold, we wouldn't spend this day here to Gordon and Melba's. No matter the food, no matter the hospitality. No matter they were kin.

We were only an hour or so from Mount Pleasant. Only an hour from the next story.

But the movers weren't due in until tomorrow morning, and here we were.

I reached to the nightstand, put on my glasses, then took the first few steps of what I knew would end up a longer day even than yesterday.

I went to the window, reached to the cord behind the one side, and pulled it open.

Rain. A middling kind, not loud enough to wake me. But enough to give the water out to the creek, what sliver of it I could see from here, a soft sheen to it, no single drops.

I looked to those trees across the marsh, and those houses. For the life of me, no matter how hard I tried to see, and squint, bob my head one way and another, even touch my nose to the glass with a notion I could see better if I was closer, I couldn't make out any one of them.

Just trees.

RUTH AND MELBA SAT at the dining room table, coffee mugs before them, both smiling up at me, Ruth especially. They were both still in their robes, too.

"Morning, Aunt Naomi," Ruth said. She took a sip, her eyes on me over the top of the mug, still smiling even through drinking coffee.

"I was just telling her about when Gordon

broke my arm in eighth grade," Melba said, "when he pushed me off the culvert over to Layton's Creek the first day of summer vacation."

"It was Shine Morrison pushed you," Gordon called out from the workroom in a flat pitch that said they'd been through this a thousand times too many, told this one time more for Ruth's ears to hear. "It was me to haul you in from the creek and save your life, but it was Shine Morrison pushed you in."

Melba narrowed her eyes, shook her head quick. She leaned to Ruth, put a hand up to her mouth to whisper a secret: "It was Gordon," she mouthed. "He had a crush on me."

"It was Shine Morrison had the crush on you," Gordon called. "It was me to marry you, but Shine Morrison had the crush on you first. And if you'd have married him instead of me, you'd be living with that plug-ugly cellular tower in your backyard right now. So count your blessings."

"It was Gordon," she mouthed.

Ruth stood, coffee mug in hand, and came around the table. "They should be ready about now," she said, and now she was in the kitchen. She bent to the oven, and pulled it open, set the mug on the counter. She grabbed a hotpad from the counter, and pulled something out.

There on the counter beside the mug was an old mixing bowl, a tea towel draped over it.

She closed the oven door, and turned to us.

A skillet of biscuits.

"She got a wild hair this morning, wouldn't let me make my own," Melba said. "She told me she wanted to make a batch of Naomi's biscuits her first morning here to South Carolina."

A perfect batch of biscuits, browned just so. Done exactly right.

Ruth looked up at me. "What do you think?" she said. She was still and all just a girl, I saw. Wanted a good word on what she'd done, and who she was.

"They look good to me," I said, and smiled. "But they're not my biscuits. They're my momma's."

"They do indeed look good," Gordon said from behind us, and I turned. He was already dressed for the day, the same sort of short-sleeved coveralls, but these blue. The hair above his ears was as wild as ever, in one hand a coffee mug, in the other a slip of sandpaper.

He was looking at Ruth, nodded at the pan. "But if that batch there tastes half as good as they look," he said, "won't be long before they'll be Miss Ruth's biscuits and nobody else."

Melba stood from the table, went to him. "What's wrong with my biscuits?" she said, and snatched the coffee mug from his hand.

"It was Shine Morrison pushed you in. Me to save you," he said, slowly shook his head at her, and then she was at the coffeemaker, filling his mug. He looked to Ruth, winked, glanced at me, winked again.

Ruth said, "They'll always be Naomi's." She was smiling at me.

But it was a different smile this morning, I saw. More to it, suddenly, than I'd seen even yesterday, when she'd stood with her arm crooked around Melba, natural as could be. More to it than even last night, in the dark that was no darkness at all.

I can feel it already, she'd said.

"I told you this girl's a sharp one," Melba said.

I said, "Don't I know it."

THE BISCUITS WERE good. They were excellent, light and moist. Done exactly right, and we ate three apiece, drank coffee until the second pot was gone, and called that breakfast. Melba put on a pot of decaf, and still we sat, and talked, while outside still it rained.

The day moved on, slow as I figured.

One by one we girls took our showers, and while I waited for mine I stood with Gordon in his workshop, watched him sand on the hull of a ship he told me was a Dutch fishing boat.

He was sanding with paper looked like only paper, no grit to it at all for how fine it was, and talked on about the history of the Dutch boat, the fact the hull itself was wide with not much draft for the shallows up there, the keel gunwale-mounted so's they could drop in and lift out to allow for those shallows.

He told me, too, of how this one was to be a gift for Robert's fortieth birthday next June, and how a while back he'd made a bark took him two and a half years to build. So happened he finished the last coat of varnish not but a week before Beau's birthday, his fortieth, and so he decided he'd make a gift of it to his oldest child. Since he'd done that for Beau, he'd realized just to be fair he'd have to build one for next Robert, then Jocelyn.

He told me this all in a voice so quiet, so calm, I had no choice but to understand the why behind spending so long on a model ship. There was peace to it, the comfort of holding in your hand something you were making, and now I was missing already the girls, and our quilting, so very much like what he was after with building ships: being at work with your hands to provide something, finally, good.

I watched that paper on the hull, the way because of the grit it seemed to me only a few grains of wood fell with each pass. Same as the way this day was passing, even if there was comfort to watching him work.

The shower cut off in the bathroom next to us. Ruth was finished.

"My turn," I said, but Gordon didn't seem to hear, only worked that wood, grain by grain.

THE RAIN LET UP near three, the clouds still hanging low and dark, right when Robert and Ellen and the girls all arrived back to the house. Ellen toted in a Tupperware tub, and another casserole dish, Robert with a pork loin he'd picked up at work this morning when he'd checked in.

Ashley had on her tiara still, but wore instead of the tutu a Snow White costume from Halloween. Emily had on a pair of blue jeans dipped so low on her hips you wondered what kept them from dropping to her knees, and not a minute after they arrived she disappeared somewhere in the house. Ashley camped out in the middle of the front room floor again, a different book this time.

A while later Jocelyn made it up from West Ashley with her own kids—Zachary and Brian, eleven and ten, and seven-year-old Tess, who was, as warned by Melba, too thin to believe. All three of them ran straight through the house when they got here, hopped over Ashley and headed right to that sliding glass door.

Robert sat beside me on the sofa, a napkin of sausage balls in his hand and a glass of sweet tea on the end table next to him. Gordon sat in his recliner, where he'd been parked since lunch: leftover turkey, cheese grits, green salad.

The kids running through didn't say word one, and then one or the other of the boys slammed back the door so hard in its track the whole window quivered.

"Whoa now!" Gordon hollered out, and the boys and Tess froze with his words, especially Tess, whose thin golden hair swirled around her head with how fast she turned to him.

"Where's your manners?" he said, stern and silly for it, I knew. He was pulling their legs, but the kids weren't certain he was.

"Take them to the woodshed," Robert said, and grinned, picked up his tea.

All three of them looked at me sitting on the sofa, not yet up to say hello to Jocelyn, whenever she'd be in. I tried to stand, pushed on the cushions beneath me with one hand and pulled on the arm at the same time.

Suddenly here were two crew-cut blond boys at either side of me, both taking hold of a hand each. Just as Gordon'd pointed out, the two were so much like twins I had no idea which was Zachary and which Brian. Both had the same hair, and wore striped T-shirts, baggy denim shorts came down past the knee, and flip-flops.

"We must use the force," the one to my right said. He was looking to the other one, who looked to him and grinned. "Force we must use, yes," he said, his voice a high-pitched old man's, and he nodded.

They both closed their eyes and grimaced, made that same high-pitched voice, but in only a grunt. Slowly they pulled, though I was already near to standing. Then they were laughing at each other, and here I was, standing up.

"Nice to meet you, Aunt Ruth," the one on the left said, and before I could tell him I was Naomi, the other one said, "Meet you nice it is, Aunt Ruth," in that same voice.

They both bowed, then turned to Robert, saluted at the same time. "Captain Scoobee," they said, "we salute you," and turned, set for the sliding glass door.

I looked at Robert, who slowly shook his

head. "They do that every single time I ever see them," he said.

Now here stood Ruth, in from the kitchen. She was bent to Tess, and smiling. "I'm Aunt Ruth," she said, and held out a hand for her to shake.

Tess wore a little shorts and blouse set, bright pink with light pink daisies all over it, her skin near the same golden color as her hair. She hesitated a moment looking up at Ruth, confused. She glanced at me, then at Ruth, and her hand. She shook it once, and looked down.

"We knew you were actually Aunt Ruth," one of the boys said, and moved toward Ruth. "But there has been a terrible collision at the pod-related quadrant of the ninth dimension."

"You are actually Aunt Naomi," the other one said. "We don't mess with the ninth dimension. Not since what happened last time." He reached out to Ruth and shook her hand, and the other one did the same. "Nice to meet you, Aunt Naomi," they both said at the same time, and looked at each other, laughed.

Tess backed away, her hands in front of her and up to her chest, her eyes on Ruth.

"Hello, Tess," I called out.

She turned to me quick as when Gordon'd hollered out, her face stricken a moment with what looked like fear. Her forehead and eyebrows quivered an instant, and she looked away, out the sliding glass door standing open. But it was a look took hold of me, in just that instant of it.

I knew that look. I'd seen it before.

Gordon was up from the recliner, moved to Tess, took her hand gentle as anything. "That's really your aunt Naomi," Gordon said, quiet, and pointed at me.

She glanced at me again, then at Ruth over her shoulder. She looked more fearful than ever, even more confused, her eyebrows together, mouth closed tight. Then the boys busted past Tess and Gordon both, out through the sliding glass door and headed for the dock.

"Where's your castnet, Pappy?" one of them called out behind him, and Gordon shot back, "It's Papaw or nothing," to which the other one shouted, "Pappy it is, boys!"

Gordon looked at me, Tess's hand in his, his eyes open wide. He shook his head. "Those boys is off their nut about a half mile," he said, and Robert put in, "You got that right, Pappy," and laughed.

Gordon turned, then he and Tess both were out through the open sliding glass door. "Let's go show those boys how to throw a castnet," he said to her, and she nodded up at him.

I looked across to Ruth, raised my eyebrows, gave the smallest shrug to say *Is she just shy?*

Ruth shook her head, shrugged back.

"She's never recovered from that divorce," Ashley said, her words matter-of-fact, and we both looked down at her on the floor between us. She had the book open, lay on her tummy and up on her elbows, her chin in her hands as she read. Her legs were bent at the knee, feet up in the air and locked together, just rocking easy as you please.

"She doesn't say much at all," she said, and reached down, turned a page. "And she eats like a bird."

"Careful your mouth, Ashley," Robert said.

"Careful your mouth, Ashley!" Ellen shouted from out in the kitchen, listening to every word that'd passed out here.

Then came "Thank you very much, little Doctor Laura," from the front door, and here was Jocelyn struggling in same as Ellen had last night with what all she'd brought.

"Hey, Aunt J," Ashley said, and turned another page.

Robert and I and Ruth and now Ellen out from the kitchen all went to Jocelyn, in a fuss took from her arms first what looked a Tupperware pie keeper, beneath that a casserole dish, beneath that a cardboard box. Slung on one arm was a backpack, on the other arm two more, and once we'd lifted it all from her—it was me to get one of the backpacks, Tess's, I knew, for the bright pink of it, the other two camouflage—Jocelyn made like she was about to fall down, wagged her arms out in front of her, rolled her eyes and took deep breaths.

She was a redhead same way her momma was, though hers was styled a little more, and had a wave to it. She was a little heavy, but wore those tight black stretch pants, a man's white dress shirt with the tails hanging down to cover her up some.

"Welcome to the madhouse," she said, and came to me, gave me a hug, and then did the same with Ruth. She hung on to her a little longer, just looking at her, slowly shaking her head.

"What you been through," she said, and pulled her close again.

"Boys, now careful!" Gordon shouted from outside. We turned, saw through the open glass door one of the boys with his arms around the other from behind, holding him out over the water. Both of them laughing.

Gordon stood shaking his head. He'd let go Tess, her hands up to her chest again, fingers laced together, her chin down. She watched the two of them, on her face the same fearful look as just a moment before.

"It's like this twenty-four-seven," Jocelyn said, in her voice a kind of tired surrender. She crossed her arms. "They were practicing that Aunt Ruth and Aunt Naomi mix-up the whole way up here," she said.

Gordon said, "Y'all want to castnet, you got to stop horsing around now," and the one holding the other backed up a foot or so on the dock, dropped the other in a heap to the boards.

Tess flinched when the boy fell, her hands gone from her chest to her mouth, her lips to her knuckles.

Then, bright as day, Jocelyn looked at us both again, said, "So we'll be seeing a lot of you both now! After school tomorrow I'll bring the boys over to your place to help start putting things away." She nodded once at me, then Ruth. "That's a promise," she said.

I looked at Ruth. She'd seen the all of what was going on out on the dock. She'd seen Tess's face, too.

But then she looked to Jocelyn, broke out a smile. "Sounds good!" Ruth said, and I said, "A promise is a promise," in what I hoped was just as bright.

Here came the rain again.

★   ★   ★

THE BOYS GAVE UP after one throw each of
the castnet out there in the rain, then came inside, wrestled on the front room floor. Ashley
cried when they rolled too close to her reading there.

Robert grilled the pork loin on the charcoal
grill out under the eaves.

Jocelyn opened up the cardboard box she'd
carried in, laid out on the table her Kitchen
Consultant Super Starter Kit from Pampered
Chef, a dozen or so kitchen tools and gadgets,
and the pale blue apron with the white logo on
front. She and Ellen and Ruth each looked
over all the gadgets and gewgaw, and Jocelyn
invited Ruth to her first party week after
next at a friend of hers right there to Mount
Pleasant.

Melba made hush puppies to go with dinner
tonight, and fried okra, and the boys ate their
whole meals using a spoon for a fork and a fork
for a spoon, and did it serious, without laughing, as though this were the most natural thing
on earth.

Emily made it to the table, sat beside Ruth,
who talked to her through dinner in quiet
words I couldn't hear for the general bedlam of
a dinner table of twelve. Emily gave up a smile

now and again for whatever Ruth said, and gave back her own words as well.

Tess ate two sugar-snap beans and a sausage ball.

The boys wrestled on the front room floor after dinner.

Ellen and Ruth cleared dishes while Melba and I rinsed and handed them into the dish-washer.

Robert left to make a run by the store, see if they'd handled the freezer thaw well enough.

Jocelyn sat at the table and talked about each item in the Super Starter Kit, from the Crinkle Cutter to the Lemon Zester/Scorer to the Large Round Stone to the Apple Corer/ Peeler/Slicer, the company's "signature item," and if her ex-husband would just make his payments she wouldn't even have to be doing any of this.

The boys wrestled on the front room floor.

Robert came back, and Ashley curtsied for me in her Snow White costume when it came time for them to leave for home.

Emily came out of hiding—she'd disap-peared after dinner—to give me the lightest hug you could give and still touch on her way out the door.

Ellen kissed me good-bye and hugged and hugged, said, "We'll get down there to see

you, but you got to promise you'll make it up
here to see us!" and Ruth and I both promised
we would.

The boys stood quiet when it was time to
go, called Gordon *Papaw* and hugged both him
and Melba tight, on the boys' faces the sad fact
they had to leave here, head for home.

Jocelyn packed up what she'd brought, no
help from either boy, then promised one more
time she'd have the both of them over to the
apartment once they were out of school tomorrow, to help put things away.

Gordon carried Tess out to Jocelyn's car, her
falling asleep on the sofa not ten minutes after
supper.

I excused myself for bed.

IF I'D HAD MY WAY, we wouldn't have spent
this last day here to Gordon and Melba's. A day
whose every minute'd fallen like a single grain
of wood off the hull of a ship.

I turned out the light, climbed up into the
bed, and lay there, listening to them talk out to
the dining room table, the murky rumble of
three voices that went up and down and fell
together and broke out in laughter.

Light still leaked out beside the curtains.

We'd be seeing more of Ellen and Robert,

their girls, especially Emily, given her place in Ruth's heart already. Certainly we'd be seeing Gordon and Melba.

And Jocelyn, who lived the closest in of all. There would be the oddball handful those boys were.

And Tess, and I thought of that look on her face, the look I knew: her forehead quivering an instant, the muscles there skittering for fear, and confusion.

For loss, I knew.

She's never recovered from that divorce.

Now I knew where I'd seen that look before. It was in Mary Margaret, whose loss of both parents made her second-guess every move her whole life long, a loss that opened the door and invited brittleness right on in.

Here was Tess, her own door already opening.

And I thought of Ollie, and Beau in his father's garage after Valerie had left him, him trying to solve his own life out there, only to find a piece of his daddy's life, that carved sub. I thought of him making it new for his daddy, building a glass case for what'd been Gordon's first effort to deal with his own kind of loss: his stepbrother, my Eli, gone off to war.

Loss was alive down here too. Of course I knew that. You'd have to be a fool to believe otherwise, to think that loss lived only where you left it.

But all I wanted, this moment, now, was to see that light, and the way it fell through the pine and live oak, palmetto and magnolia and water oak too, light sifted down through the woods to spread like scattered diamonds on the ground, bright broken pieces of light on pine-straw so many perfect gifts of warmth.

Tomorrow, I'd be home.

Ruth would be in here soon, and so I started to breathe deep, tried to get some kind of rhythm so that I might be asleep, or at least sound like it, once she got in here. I didn't want any whispering tonight.

I closed my eyes, took in a breath, and another.

Here was rain on the rooftop now, loud enough to hear. Middling gone to hard.

Chapter 18

T HE WIPERS BLURRED most all the ride down.

It was all different. And all very much the same.

Highway 17 was four lanes now, a wide grass median in the middle, ten yards of grass back to the woods on either shoulder. When I was a girl the whole fifty miles or so from Mount Pleasant'd been a two-lane shrouded over with live oak and pine, save when it cut low across the marsh on stubby pylons, the road hovering just above the saltmarsh hay.

Now it was just a straight line, or nearly so, and sixty miles per hour. But still nothing but woods, even if so far back from the road.

Still it was marsh too, the highway shooting out across it always a kind of surprise. Grays and browns and rusts suddenly beneath us, ahead of us the dark line of trees, a smear of black through the rain, waiting.

Same as when I was a girl, but different.

MELBA'D MADE US a breakfast of eggs and bacon and more biscuits—hers, which didn't rise quite as high as mine, but were still a delight. While we ate, Gordon'd gone over the directions we'd been given by the apartment people again and again. He'd spent twenty minutes talking about other ways to do it, pursed his lips, shook his head, shrugged, scratched at his ear.

All this to say, finally, "Yep. That's how you get there."

Melba'd teared up there at the table, and me too, and Ruth as well, three women still in their robes and crying and smiling and laughing. Gordon, in his short-sleeved coveralls— the green again—carried on about how we'd see one another more than we cared to, no need for tears now that we'd be only fifty miles between us. We'd be tired of each other by Christmas.

Ruth'd showered and dressed, came out of

the bedroom in her blue jeans and a green cotton sweater. The same outfit of old clothes she'd worn the day of the tag sale back in Northampton. She had her hair pulled back in a tight ponytail same as she'd done that day, too.

She stood in the open door a moment, in her hands her overnight bag. She glanced back into the bedroom at something, looked at Melba a second. There was something a little nervous to her, her smile a little anxious.

But it was her clothes I was worried over, what she'd chosen to wear this day.

Gordon and Melba and I were still nursing coffee at the table, and I said, "Ruth, don't you want to put on something nice?"

She glanced one last instant behind her into the room, looked at me, gave a little shake of her head to let go whatever it was in the bedroom had hold of her. Maybe, I thought, it'd already occurred to her she'd put on the wrong sort of outfit.

But before she could say anything, Gordon let out, "This girl's a step ahead. She knows this is moving day," and he cut his eyes at me, winked. "More than it is any sort of fancy trip."

Ruth nodded, set the bag down beside the

sofa. "This is going to be one long day," she said. "Just thought I'd dress ready for it."

"You're right," I said, too quick. I looked back to my mug, empty save for a dribble at the bottom. I shrugged, said, "You're right. It's true."

"Melba?" Ruth said then, and crossed her arms quick, smiling. She looked down, and I could see she was blushing for something, embarrassed.

"Sweetheart?" Melba said.

"Can I ask you something?" Ruth backed into the bedroom, arms still crossed. Then she put up her index finger, crooked it a couple times to motion Melba in with her. "In here?"

"Of course, sweetheart," Melba said. She stood from the table, glanced at the two of us, her eyebrows up, wondering what this was about. Then she was at the bedroom door, and inside, the two of them out of sight.

"You know it's likely going to be even more work for the fact you got Zachary and Brian to contend with, putting things away," Gordon said, and laughed a sad kind of way.

I looked at Gordon, said, "You got that right, Pappy," and he let out another laugh, said, "You sound like you never even left this place, Sister."

"Oh why darlin', yes!" Melba squealed from in the bedroom, and then came, "Bless your heart!"

Here was Melba strutting out of the bedroom, chin up in the air, and with a smirk that was a smile too. She narrowed her eyes at Gordon. "We have a connoisseur of the finer arts," Melba said. "A woman of taste, unlike you, Mister Gordon Stackhouse, Junior."

Right behind her came Ruth, smiling as well. She had her hands behind her back. "I asked her for one," she said to both me and Gordon. "Hope you don't mind," she said.

She brought a hand from behind her to show us a bright red crocheted toilet-paper cover doll, roll and all.

"Oh my no!" Gordon shot out. "Why on God's green earth would you want one of those horrible things?" he said, and shook his head.

"I have my reasons," Ruth said, "and we need to start thinking about how we're going to decorate."

"If that's the case, and this woman didn't twist your arm over it," Gordon said, "then take as many those awful things you want, please!"

"This breaks the set, you know," she said to Gordon, and poked a finger to his chest, her

smiling full on now. "Won't be any takers for
the rest of them at our estate sale, which is
what I know you were counting on for the
kids."

"Thank you, thank you," Gordon said to
Ruth over Melba's head. "She made every one
of those in a fever forty years ago, which is
right about how long I've been waiting for
somebody to come along—"

"You built that shelf for them, didn't you?"
Melba cut in.

"I was only—" he started.

But my eyes were on Ruth, who was looking at me through all this, Gordon and Melba
eye to eye now and having fun for it. Ruth
held it up a little higher for me to see, and I
went to her there at the bedroom door, took it
in my hand.

An old crocheted hoop skirt, a plastic doll
head on top, bonnet and all.

"Closest thing to magenta I could find," she
said to me, quiet, and I nodded, looked at her.

"Our first housewarming gift," I said, and
smiled, handed it back to her. I glanced back to
Gordon and Melba, still at each other.

And I left them there, went into the bedroom.

My eyes went right to that shelf above the
chest of drawers and mirror, to the hole in the

line of dolls. Certainly, this was good. My Ruth, finding which way she could a piece of the momma she didn't have.

And though this would be, like Gordon'd said, a workday more than anything else, maybe even more than we'd planned for the fact those two nutty boys would be there to help, still after I'd showered I put on the outfit I'd planned to wear all along, packed special for this morning. I might could change into something old once the movers were gone and we were in the apartment. Or I might could just wear what I wanted the whole day long. It was my own choice.

This was the day I would gain back a piece of my own home. Even with the rain.

So I went to the overnight bag, brought from deep inside, where I'd laid them both flat so's they'd stay neat, my good navy-blue wool slacks, and the white knit sweater, red roses round the neck. The sweater Ruth and Mahlon'd given to me the birthday before Eli passed.

I put them on, and looked in the mirror.

I was an old woman, her gray hair in need of a styling in the next day or so.

An old woman, wrinkles beside her eyes and down her cheeks, her nose bigger the way old people's noses went. An old woman with a wattle to her throat, her eyes the same rheumy wet behind her glasses as her husband's step-brother's were going.

But I had on this sweater, the red roses on white that ringed my shoulders like a spring garland. Eli's favorite sweater of mine, so much he'd give me a kiss at the back of my neck every time I wore it.

The last time a week or so before he passed away. I hadn't worn it since.

Then I reached into the overnight bag again, dug down even deeper, to the little zippered pocket hidden along the seam on the side. A pocket meant for hiding things you wanted kept hidden.

I found the tiny zipper, opened it, reached in.

Here it was, just as I'd secreted it in there the morning before we'd left, Ruth to her last day of work, me headed for my last visit to Eli and Mahlon. Precisely where I'd placed it, before I'd found out all I'd been forgiven.

I'd wrapped it in a pink Kleenex, the round velvet box, lined in satin, long lost somewhere along the path of this life, and I peeled back the tissue to reveal to me the locket.

Still only a gold locket, still no filigree to it, nor any words engraved.

I hadn't worn it since the day of the funeral, hadn't looked at them inside it since the morning after, when I'd sat on my bed, convinced already of the truth I'd get here to home one day soon. That I'd return to those colors it was enough just to look at to have them live in you, and to the water, and that light up off it, and that joy.

I hadn't opened it for all of what God'd given me, then taken away. I would open this locket, I'd decided that morning after, and look at these two faces again only once I'd gotten home, the looking at them a gift.

I pinned it to the sweater, right there at my heart, and turned, looked in the mirror one more time.

Here was the locket, keeping close.

I was still an old woman, I saw. But maybe now, with being here, this day, I might become Naomi again.

THEY MADE no fuss when I'd come out of the bedroom. Melba'd smiled, said, "Bless your heart, you look wonderful," and came to me, hugged me, teared up yet again.

"My my," was all Gordon said, a hand to the back of a chair, the other on his hip, him smiling.

"Oh, Naomi," Ruth said. She had her purse over one shoulder, had a beige plastic grocery sack in her hand, inside it, I could tell, the doll. She came to me, took over that hug from Melba, then pulled away, still holding me, her eyes to the roses. "That sweater," she said. "I thought it was long gone."

Then her eyes landed on the locket.

Her smile seemed to quiver. She blinked, looked to the locket, to my eyes again.

She knew how close I'd kept it all the years she'd known me. I'd worn it every day, though she'd never said a word on its disappearance. And had done me the honor of never asking after it.

She nodded, let her hands fall from my shoulders to my own hands, and took them, gave that smile one more time.

I looked past her, to Gordon, said, "Brother," and I let the word hang there a moment for what I meant with it. I'd never called him that in my life.

"Brother," I said again, quieter, "I need one last favor of you."

He'd let go the chair, both hands to his sides, almost like he was at attention.

"Sister?" he said, and tilted his head a little, listening.

"Tell us," I said, "how to find the house on Whilden." I paused, nodded at him, tried a smile. "The old house," I said.

He took in a breath, let it out in a low whistle, and now slowly he came to me. Ruth stepped aside, and here were his hands on mine, him looking down into my eyes. We were all together, a cluster of kin, Melba with a hand to Ruth's back, Ruth beside me, Gordon before me.

He said quiet, "I was wondering when it was coming to this." He paused, took a look at Melba for whatever she might give him in a glance.

Melba nodded to Gordon, then closed her eyes. She let her chin down a little, like she might be saying a prayer.

Gordon looked back to me, swallowed. "Sister, no one here's had the heart to ask you what needs asking. Because of what you and Ruth both've been through, and what you lost." He glanced to Ruth beside us, then came right back to me. He swallowed again, working up for these words.

"Sister," he whispered, "why do you want to go there?"

"Because it's home," I said, simple and straight, but soft as I could. There was no way to put to him my notion of light, and those colors.

And of finding Naomi.

"I can get you to the old house," he said. "I

can draw you a map easy as putting pencil to paper." He shook his head slowly. "But you're trying to find something don't exist. You won't recognize a thing." He worked up a smile. "This here is home," he said, "or near as you're going to find it."

"This is almost home," I said. "But it's not my home. It's not our home, however much we love you."

"We love you," Ruth said beside me, her voice an echo of mine and her own words both. She reached a hand to Gordon's arm, smiled to Melba. "We love you both," she said. "But we have to go." She paused. "We have to find out."

I looked at her, stunned into silence for what I'd known all along: that she was with me in this. Yet here was Ruth, with me. Here was my treasure, despite the treasure I could not share with her, the story of the forgiveness I'd been afforded.

Despite, too, my jealousy, for how quickly it seemed she was touching her own life, finding it here already.

I turned to Gordon, still no words in me.

"Naomi," he whispered. "I'll get you to that house." I could feel his hands tremble holding to mine, saw how full his eyes were. Not the wet of old age, I knew. But tears, readying.

"But," he whispered, "it's only the Lord can bring you home. Only Him in His grace can give you the peace you're looking for."

"He's the one," I said, and suddenly with his words I squeezed tight his hands. It was only pain in my own hands. Only that, and I squeezed harder.

"He's the one," I said again, "who left me empty enough to go looking. And I believe I'll find it. I will."

"Naomi," Melba'd said, and touched my shoulder, rubbed gently there. "Don't talk like that. He's not gone."

"Didn't say He was," I said, too quick yet again. I hadn't looked at her, my eyes still on Gordon's, and then I'd felt the cold surprise of a tear down my old woman's cheek, my own eye to brim first. "Mahlon's the one gone. And my Eli gone all over again for it. I said it was God who'd left me empty." I paused. "So maybe you ought to just call me empty instead of Naomi."

Ruth had looked at me then, on her face a kind of quick puzzlement, but with her hand still to Gordon's arm. She'd glanced then to Melba, to Gordon again.

"Help us, Gordon," she'd said. "Please."

★ ★ ★

GRAYS AND BROWNS and rusts. A smear of black through the rain.

Here were the colors I'd wanted to see.

We passed through McClellanville and the single flashing yellow at the only corner—a Texaco station and general store on the left, an Amoco minimart on the right—a half hour after we'd left, just like we'd been told by Gordon and the apartment people both. Then here was more marsh out either side of us, rusts and browns and grays again, above it the gray of this rain.

Up ahead on Ruth's side and a hundred yards out rose a tuft of trees like a rooster's tail up off the marsh, one of the million nameless little islands everywhere.

"When I was a little girl," I said, and paused, heard in the space the words out of me made that they were the first ones spoken since we'd climbed in, backed out of Gordon and Melba's driveway. "Grown-ups used to tell us stories about the Mothers and Fathers," I said, quieter. "Haints of the first slaves. Supposed to be buried out to one of these little islands three hundred years ago." I nodded at the island, right out her window now.

She glanced at it, then to me, back to the road. "Haints?" she said.

"Ghosts," I said, and smiled. "Hadn't

thought of that word in fifty years," I said, and shook my head. "When the first fireflies showed up we'd be out in the backyard, my brother and me, trying to gather up enough to make a lantern out of a Mason jar. And my daddy'd sit out on the back porch, and tell us the Mothers and Fathers would haunt you if you were out in the woods too late. Every year he told us that one."

I shook my head, looked out the windshield for the next smear of black that meant the woods were coming up. And that we were one stretch closer. "Supposed to have green eyes lit up in the dark like fireflies, but they'd chase you through the woods," I said.

"Sounds like one of those stories they tell you to keep you out of trouble," Ruth said. "We had Elder Hosmer, who back in the French and Indian Wars went crazy for whatever reason, and scalped his wife and two daughters." She shook her head. "That's one they told us up there in Ashfield to keep us from running off into the woods alone. Like your Mothers and Fathers."

"Maybe so," I said. "But it still scared the bejeepers out of us."

She looked at me. "Bejeepers," she said. "That's a new one. And haints." She paused a moment, leaned her head to one side. "And when will I get to start saying Y'all?"

"The first time you say it and don't know you did," I said, and smiled, looked at her.

She nodded, smiled, eyes to the road. "That's the trick, I guess," she said.

We were quiet, and now here was the line of woods, a thick wall of black that seeped to the darkest green as the highway slipped closer to them.

"Naomi," Ruth said, and I looked at her, her eyes to me and to the road and to me again.

She said, "You know it won't be the same." She paused, let her eyes linger on me a few moments before she looked back to the road. Out her window the gray above empty marsh gave way to the smear of trees. "It won't be the same as when you were a girl," she said.

I looked away, out my own window. "I'm not a fool," I said.

"I know," she said, and already I was sorry for how my words'd snapped out of me.

"This is good," she said, in what sounded like an answer to a question hadn't yet been asked. "All of it already. Just like I said the other night." She paused. "But we just have to know. We just have to understand that this is new," she said. "All of it. We have to understand it won't be like either one of us thinks it will be. That it will be new, and good because of that."

The rain started in even harder, and the wiper jumped to high for it.

I knew she was right, me wound too tight for what all I'd allowed myself to imagine: a hometown like the one I'd grown up in, and the old house kept up neat, living in it a family might let us wander in and look around.

Maybe even buy it.

All the while Eli and Mahlon keeping close, right there at my heart. And the blessing of Ruth beside me, a family member I could give back my history to.

Of course it was all nothing but a dream. Gordon knew I'd been dreaming it, Melba too. Everyone did, I was sure, right on down to Ashley, who knew the story of her cousin Tess without missing a beat.

Now Ruth knew too. Maybe she'd known all along that I dreamed my dream to fool myself away from what I knew would come: things changed.

But you can tell yourself one thing to stop from believing the other, and still believe.

"And I want to know what you were saying back there, about God," Ruth said.

I looked to her.

Now there was trouble to her, like I hadn't seen before. Her eyes, the blue-green of them, seemed sharper somehow, and she was shaking her head the smallest way, her eyes to the road. "Because I don't know what any of that means. What the two of you really meant back there," and now I thought of that puzzled look to her face when I'd finally let out that I was empty.

"To me," she said, "it was always just what you and Mahlon and Eli believed. It's what gave you hope." She paused, regripped the steering wheel, adjusted herself in her seat. "But when you say to Gordon that God's done with you, whatever God means to you. And when I know your whole life you believed in Him. Well." She shook her head again, slower, but something to her eyes still just as sharp, just as pained.

"That means," she said, and now her chin was trembling. "That means you're giving up hope. But what else is it that's gotten us this far?"

"Ruth," I said. "Ruth, don't—"

And now she eased on the brake, glanced in the rearview mirror, touched on the turn signal. We were slowing down, onto the shoulder, and we stopped.

She turned to me, her chin still quivering. "You told me the morning after the funeral," she said, her voice ragged and quiet now, her eyebrows together, "that God and his tender mercies—that was what you called it, his tender mercies—had gotten you through the eight years since Eli died. But the only mercies I've gotten," she said, "have been from you. And now what I've found down here, with Gordon and Melba and everyone else."

She stopped, took in a breath. For an instant I wanted to wedge in the rest of what I'd wanted tell her before she'd pulled over. For an instant I wanted to finish the sentence I'd begun:

Ruth, I wanted to say, *don't look to me.*

I am a sinner, forgiven a lifetime too late.

I am empty.

"So it's too late for you to tell me you have no hope," she said. "It's too late. What you place your hope in, I do too. And so if you take away your hope, then what do I have left?"

Emptiness, I wanted to say

Naomi, I wanted to say.

But instead, I was the same coward I'd always been.

I said, "Remember what Mahlon prayed every morning?" I nodded, reached a hand to Ruth's face, held her chin, still quivering. "He'd pray, 'Hold us in your hand, and forgive us our sins, for we are sinners and fall short of Your glory.' Do you remember that?"

She closed her eyes, sniffed. She nodded.

"That's what I believe," I said. "That He holds us, and He forgives us. And we're still sinners who fall short of Him. That's what Mahlon believed, too."

I was not lying. To her, or to God. Or to me. That was what I believed about who God was. But I also knew He took away what He pleased, and no one held Him accountable.

I let my hand fall from her chin to the seat between us, and her empty hand there, and I held it.

Enough of a gesture to have her smile at me, and believe me.

THERE WAS NOT much to our arriving. Only me, reading directions, and Ruth driving.

And rain.

I recognized nothing.

There were traffic lights, to begin with. Lights so far out of Mount Pleasant I'd thought perhaps they were for some new town that'd started since I was gone. Then here were more traffic lights, and an outdoor mall with chain stores and restaurants straight out of Springfield and Holyoke, then more traffic lights, another outdoor mall, and cars swarming up around us, and still all this rain so much it was hard to make sense of anything.

Now here was the entrance for the apartment complex out my side, where we'd be back sometime soon to meet the movers and the manager, and I peered off to my right as best I could through a thin line of trees, and through this rain, to see a parking lot, and buildings. Pink, I thought.

Now we were under a freeway, then rounding up the onramp to join it—a freeway, in Mount Pleasant—all of it just as Gordon'd said, and then here was the end of the freeway at another stoplight, an Exxon minimart on the right, a car wash on the left. We had two more lights before we'd even get to Coleman Boulevard, the one name Gordon'd finally hit in all this that I recognized.

Coleman, where Mount Pleasant Academy was, and where Eli Robinson had sat behind me, jabbed me with a pencil.

The light changed, and we passed any number of antique stores, an auto-parts store, another restaurant, and a smaller strip mall, and went through those two lights.

We made it to Coleman.

"I walked to school on Coleman Boule-

vard," I said. The street we were on made a T
with it, and I leaned forward, saw between
swipes of the wipers a store in front of us across
Coleman, something old-timey, red and with a
tall storefront, but nothing I recognized.

We made the left onto Coleman, and I
turned in my seat, looked behind me and to
my right, leaned forward to see out Ruth's
window.

"What?" Ruth said.

"I think that was Old Georgetown Highway," I said. "That road we came in off the
freeway on. That was Old Georgetown Highway. Or at least some little piece left of it."

She smiled, shook her head, squinted out the
windshield again. "You need to calm down if
this is what you're going to do every time you
see something you know."

"I'm not even sure that was it," I said, and
faced forward, settled myself. "School was back
that way, I think," and I pointed a thumb over
my shoulder. "This goes on out to the bridge
over to Sullivan's Island," I said. "It's a draw-
bridge, turns sideways instead of up and down.
It was the strangest thing we ever saw when the
WPA came out and put it in, and we'd ride our
bikes down here just to watch it turn."

Still there was nothing I saw that I knew.
Still there was all this rain.

"Here it is," Ruth said, and we turned, as Gordon'd warned, at a restaurant that looked like an old 7-Eleven.

McCants Street. Cloaked over with live oak. Where, a mile up the road, Eli and I'd walked our first walk together, all the way to the end of the road. Where we'd stood at the dead end, before us the lavender harbor.

And now, suddenly, the rain eased up, then stopped altogether, as if we'd put in a request for it, this last few blocks to where it'd all begun.

I could feel the blood in me rising for this all.

The street shone with the water, and though there was none falling, still we'd get splattered with it when we ducked under live oak, water dripping heavy off the leaves, and now there seemed somehow light coming through from above, the gray going white while we rode slowly along.

We passed a couple three apartment complexes on the left, some older homes on the right. Here was the water-treatment plant on the left, too, and the ball fields, just like Gordon'd said there would be. All of it new.

Then the road changed, went from the sturdy black asphalt it'd been into rough, and gray, and older. Trees seemed to swallow us up even more now, too, and then here was the cemetery, to my right, the old one that school was let out one day a year so we children could clean it up.

A low white fence outlined it, like ever, more live oak inside the yard, gravestones at cockeyed angles for the roots, and then here we were past the end of the fence, more houses now. Still none of them coming to mind.

Then, here on the corner on my right, stood a white post four foot tall, stenciled on it in black letters the words venning road.

"One more block," I whispered, and Ruth turned right onto Venning, a long block that would lead us, finally, to Whilden.

Venning. The street Eli and I'd walked onto out the back of our yard that first night, when the treefrogs above us had started up the story we both knew was ours already, the sudden whirl and purring drone of them all about we two.

There were houses here, clustered in close like the houses here had always been, but still I did not recognize them. They were beautiful homes, even in this gray going white. Homes with shiny brass kickplates on wide black doors, curved tabby driveways, bright white porch rails, and Charleston green shutters.

But I did not recognize them.

"Slow down," I said, though Ruth wasn't doing much of any speed at all. It was only me, too ready, too ready, and I reached up, put a hand to the dashboard.

"I can't believe this," Ruth said. "We're here."

"We'll come up on the back of the property," I said, "up here on the right."

And now the light was changing fully, the clouds breaking open above us and around us so that suddenly, just as I'd dreamed it might, there really came that light down upon us. Here were the trees, those live oaks, spun in them the same airy twists of Spanish moss as had spoken that language of whispers I'd heard the first walk with Eli—*Eli and Naomi, Naomi and Eli*—and here were pines, and a magnolia in the front yard of a house out Ruth's window I believed just then I might have recognized. Even the grass and weeds edged up to the road all took on different greens, and from out of nowhere daffodils and daylilies I hadn't noticed in the yards of the houses we passed—was that the Howlands' place? or was it the Lambs'?— were out and full and dripping with the rain so that it seemed more like morning dew than anything else.

Here it would be, I knew. The place.

Home.

"Slow down," I said to Ruth one more time, though now we were crawling along. It seemed we'd passed it already, or that distances were larger now, because I could not see up ahead and on my right what I remembered of the house, beside us only an empty lot. We were almost to the corner of Venning and Whilden, and now I saw the white post not ten yards away: WHILDEN STREET in those stenciled black letters.

But here beside me was an empty lot overgrown with weeds, and I looked out my window, through the last little runnels of water from all that rain, to see just that: an empty lot.

I looked back and away from the corner, toward the rear of the lot. Here was a live oak, low and spreading. But nothing else.

I opened my mouth to speak, thought to ask Ruth to circle this block once and have another go at finding it, thought maybe too that they'd changed the streets, that the town may have renamed one or another, Whilden one of them.

But then I saw it.

A set of concrete steps sitting alone, ten yards or so from the tree, at the back end of this lot on the corner of Whilden and Venning. Right where steps up to a back porch would naturally be.

Three concrete steps, mossed over and trimmed in weeds, and empty.

I eased back in the seat, put a hand to the window, touched the glass as I'd done the glass door at Gordon and Melba's. But this time there came no shadow up off them, no ghost outline at the tips of my old woman's fingers.

Once there had been a white plank house here, a house up on a redbrick foundation two feet high, the front porch with a roof over it, out back a smaller porch without one. At the far rear of the yard had stood a low old live oak. Just far enough out from under its canopy so that acorns dropping didn't sound like firecrackers had stood a shed where my brother slept before he went off to the war.

And where a young man named Eli had slept, too.

The house was gone. Even the brick foundation, the only thing left those three steps from off what had once been a back porch.

"This light is beautiful," Ruth whispered. "Just like you said it would be." On her voice was that awe and wonder of a couple nights before.

She was right. There was beauty to this. But it was a different kind of beauty, what I could only think was a terrible beauty, a beauty God-given, God-prescribed.

Of course the only evidence of the joy I was after in all this would be those concrete steps, the ones on which I'd found my momma and daddy with a telegram. The moment when the name of our only child had been given to Eli, him even then just a boy. But enough of a man to pay attention to the loss he was watching, my momma, my daddy, and me beginning to grieve at the loss of Mahlon.

And of course this moment, and those steps, and Ruth and me and every plan I'd made on my own and out of God's hands would be bathed in this beauty, and in this light.

Here I was, delivered home by me.

I reached to my sweater, felt the locket, my eyes still to the concrete steps, and wrapped my fingers round the cold metal.

I held it, and held it.

"Is this the right place?" Ruth said from beside me, my back turned to her for my looking out the window. "Is it here anymore?" she said, a piece of that awe already fading in her voice.

I unpinned the locket, my fingers dull and slow, and then I had it in my palm. I looked down at it, there in the creases of my old woman's hand.

I could open it, or I could leave it shut. I could give them back to me. Or I could leave them with God.

I looked back out the window, at the empty lot.

And I opened it, looked at what was inside.

Two photos, each the size of a quarter.

"This is it, isn't it," Ruth said, not a question, but a fact.

I was quiet, still looked at the photos, at these images on paper. Only paper, even in this light. Mahlon's eyes not even open so I might see into him. And nowhere in Eli's face, that boy in a Navy portrait, anything other than Eli.

I'd believed I'd see in him my betrayal, and see in him my forgiveness, two facts out of my life that made me ashamed and afraid to lay eyes on him again, for how much I loved him.

"This is still beautiful," Ruth said, quiet now. For an instant, in the time between heartbeats, I thought she was speaking of my boys, of Eli and Mahlon both, and I whispered just then *Yes* only loud enough for my own heart to hear.

"It's still beautiful here," Ruth said. Here was her hand to my shoulder, holding on. "The light is just like you said it would be." She paused, held a little tighter to my shoulder. "And we're here," she said. "We're home."

I closed the locket, held it tight in my hand, and looked out to those steps once more.

There, on the top step, perched a mockingbird, dappled in light. He stood still a moment, and though he was too far away to tell from here, me in the front seat of a car just arrived from fifty years and a thousand miles away, I knew he was watching me.

He dipped down, quick tipped back his head, bent and tipped back again.

He was drinking from a pool of rainwater on the top step.

I turned from the window. "Did you tell Melba why you wanted the doll?" I said, and paused, took in a breath. "Did you tell her about your momma?"

Her hand was still to my shoulder, and I reached up, put mine on it, tight in my other hand the locket. She looked at me, tilted her head a little again, her blue-green eyes dead on mine.

"It's all right," she said. "We knew it wouldn't be the same. We knew that. We both did."

She was quiet, waiting, I knew, for something from me. But there was nothing I had left to offer.

Then she smiled. "I told Melba," she said, "it reminded me of home." She paused. "That's all."

"That's good," I said, and nodded. I let go her hand, faced forward.

Light fell.

PART III

Redeemer

Chapter 19

I WAS ON the park bench they keep inside the
Harris Teeter where Ruth worked, me
waiting for her to come off shift. We had just
the one car, and I'd had my Christmas shopping to do today—there were only six days left
before Christmas, and there was so much new
family I needed to get things for, from Tess
right on up to Gordon and Melba, when it'd
all only been cards all the years before this.

And now here I was, waiting for Ruth.

The bench sat up front of the store, against
the wall of windows, and faced in toward the
row of checkstands. Behind me the sun was
near down, and I could feel the heat through
the window on the back of my neck. Nothing

too warm, but warmth all the same, here at the end of a day that'd seen me deal with traffic from morning till now. Out front of me lay the wide plain of varnished concrete where people pushed grocery buggies on their way in or out, on either side of me silver Christmas trees decorated with red Harris Teeter ornaments and red lights.

The bench was meant for people just like me: old, and waiting, whether for the shuttle buses from the Franke Home or Sandlapper Estates, the posh retirement communities here in town, or for a taxi to haul you home. Or even for your daughter-in-law, working checkstand 7.

There stood Ruth, at number 7, scanning and scanning item after item after item. She had on the black slacks and white dress shirt the supervisors wore here, her hair in a loose ponytail. No doubt filling in for a cashier late into work.

We'd lived here coming up on a year already. Ruth'd worked the first three months or so at the Piggly Wiggly in the job Robert'd set up for her, just like Gordon'd promised on that first phone call I'd gotten back in November of last year.

Even though the job at the Piggly Wiggly over to that shopping center at Wando Crossing—there was a Wal-Mart in the same center, and a Marshall's, and a Rack Room and T.J. Maxx and a dozen other places to boot—had been good enough, Ruth'd found a better one here at the Harris Teeter back on Long Point Road. This was near where a handful of all the new developments had come in and, the manager'd told her, where she might could become a shift supervisor.

That was five months ago, and now here she was. Shift supervisor, promoted six weeks ago. When she'd worked at the Stop & Shop for fifteen years and never got past cashier. There'd been opportunities back in Northampton, sure. But she'd passed them up all along, wanting only to have as a worry the hours she'd have to fill.

But now. Now she was a supervisor, which meant she'd sometimes have to cover for a late cashier, sometimes have to bag groceries, sometimes have to fire and sometimes have to hire. She dealt with everything, from the circus of scheduling hours to grabbing a woman off her bike out front of the store when she'd walked out with a ham tucked into her dress, right on down to swinging a mop to clean up a dropped jar of mustard.

She was happy.

She was working, had friends she could call

up and have over for supper, had reason to wake up of a morning for the fact of a job, one that called on her to make decisions for herself, and expected her to make the right ones.

WITH THE MONEY from the sale of the house in Northampton, she'd bought a small place back on Rifle Range Road in a tract of homes called Quail Hollow, a house eighteen thousand dollars more and two-thirds the size of where we'd lived. A fifteen-year-old house with two bedrooms and an eat-in kitchen, a family room and a dining room, all of it built on a concrete slab. No basements down here.

But there was a yard to it. Not like the apartment complex we'd moved into that first day here—three hundred units in three-story stuccoed buildings all painted Lowcountry pastels and trimmed out with white gingerbread. As though pretty pinks and greens would erase the fact the complex was located directly across the street from Wando High School, a fact the management'd forgot to inform us of in all the paperwork we'd completed from Massachusetts.

The house had a yard, thick grass in the front and back both, and in the back three big pines giving off enough shade to let you sit out under them of an evening, provided you had the citronella burning. We had neighbors in close, just like in Northampton, but these were young couples with small children, and when you sat out under those pines you could hear the all of their lives: mommas hollering out for the kids to come in for dinner, daddies coming home to mow the lawn and edge it in whatever cool of the day there might be, the rumble of kids on Big Wheels up and down the street. There was the smell of fresh-cut grass, and that citronella, and smoke off barbecues most every night of the week.

And nobody in the neighborhood from Mount Pleasant, everyone from somewhere else: there were Jeff and Amy Adkins two doors down on the right, from Chicago, and next door on our left were Russ and Tina Deal from Naples, Florida. Across the street lived the Fortners, Allen and Lynn, from Phoenix, next to them the single fellow, Joel something, from Brooklyn.

They were neighbors, all of them. Polite, friendly. Sometimes we borrowed, just like in the old days, a cup of sugar or an egg one from another. Sometimes we barbecued together. When we moved in, we'd gotten a loaf of banana nut bread from the Fortners, and a lasagna from Joel. Jeff Adkins had mowed our lawn without our even asking the first couple of times, before Ruth'd hired a boy named Jacob from five or six doors down who'd left Xeroxed pieces of paper in everybody's mailboxes, advertising he'd mow lawns cheap.

I asked Jacob one day where he was from. "Ohio," he'd said, and went right back to tipping in gasoline from the red gallon jug into his mower, as though the question from this old woman was something he'd been asked too many times already.

Some days, too, light fell through those pine boughs to scatter at my feet.

All of this was good. I had in me no wish for different neighbors, for a bigger house, for a parcel of land large enough to lose myself on. For any more of this light.

Now Ruth got up each day, showered and dressed, went to work, either driving herself because there was no plan for me, or me driving her in for whatever errands I might have. Like today.

December already. Our lives in this new place moving just that fast.

One year and seventeen days since Mahlon died.

After she came off shift, we'd head home, where Ruth'd change into regular clothes and me rest a minute, take a look at the mail before we met with Jocelyn and her kids and some other friends of hers from church to go Christmas caroling.

All of which sounded good to me as well. I couldn't remember when I'd last gone caroling, didn't know people still did such a thing. We'd gone when I was a child, went house to house with a gang of kids from church, but that was the last I'd seen of it.

I would do this.

Still Ruth scanned, and the bagger, a young black man, placed each item into thin white plastic sacks, on each sack printed a green wreath, the words HOLIDAY WISHES FROM HARRIS TEETER in red inside the wreath.

The customer, a white woman, stood watching it all, her hair pulled back in a perfect blond bun, her lips a sharp line of red. In the buggy seat was a toddler just as blond as his momma, his hair in a perfect pageboy cut. He wore a blue seersucker jumper, I could see from here, and with both hands banged on the credit card keypad like it was a toy he wanted to break. His momma seemed not to notice a thing about all that, instead watched the numbers on the register pop up, then the bagboy bagging, then the numbers again.

Then they were finished, and the woman pushed the buggy out from the checkstand.

She had on riding pants, I could see now, and shin-high leather boots as well, those cream-colored pants tighter than you could imagine, her white blouse tucked in just so.

Now the child was kicking at her, his hands gripped to the buggy bar in front of him, his head shaking back and forth to make that hair on his head fairly shiver. Still his momma paid him no mind, just looked out past him toward the door like he wasn't even there with her.

I watched her a moment, then saw Ruth half turn to me, her still there in the checkstand. She gave the smallest smile, the smallest shake of her head at this woman in riding pants.

Mount Pleasant. Nowhere I knew.

But I smiled back at her, gave a little shrug. I was to be happy here. This was where I wanted to be. This was supposed to be home.

And I had been forgiven.

The bagboy moved three checkstands down, Ruth in her stand with a paper towel in one hand, a bottle of Windex in the other. She sprayed the scanner, leaned over with the paper towel, and wiped at it.

Her hair had grown longer, and she was still a little tan for the now and again trips to the beach on her off afternoons, trips she made alone, just herself and a book and a beach chair.

She was happy.

She looked over her shoulder at me, mouthed *Five minutes,* and smiled, then wiped at the scanner again, one last quick scrub of it.

WHEN WE'D BEEN at the apartment complex, I'd go with her to sit out by the pool, though through the summer there were days when it'd been too hot even to do that much, even leave the house, and I wondered at how we'd lived through summers when I was a girl.

I remembered the heat, of course, and the humidity, the way at night when I climbed into bed sometimes the sheets were damp for how heavy the air was. But there was always the lucky chance that sometime in the night a front might blow through, with it thunder and lightning and the blessing of rain. Then the air inside the house would go cool for it all, and those sheets became something I didn't want out of for the cool of them the next morning.

But there were whole days passed this summer when I didn't leave the apartment for the comfort of central air, when even the notion of going out to the metal hive of mailboxes a hundred yards down the sidewalk was too much to consider. Then I simply waited indoors until Ruth made it home, and watched TV more than I ever had in Northampton, what with the girls and the quilting and Bird in Hand.

Of course I missed the girls, though all of them were careful to write me once, sometimes twice a week each. Even Mary Margaret wrote, her careful hand on her lavender-scented stationery keeping me up to date on how many of Carolyn's wienie wrappers Phyllis had put away, and how Hilda's arthritis was making it harder than ever with a pair of scissors. And how her Tommy had taken another turn, and another.

All news from the old world, my girlfriends waiting anxious to hear from me about my life in return, even jealous, they let me know, of how good I must have it down here, all that beach and water and no snow at all.

But there had been more to my staying indoors for days than the heat, and the work of answering the news from friends.

Here with me every day since we'd left Northampton, despite Ruth's presence, and despite the joy of good words from the girls, there lingered in me each day the darkness of what I knew.

Still shooting through me each day, like the pain in my knees and hips and hands but deeper and truer and more stubborn than any physical pain I would ever know, was my trying to reckon with what I knew my husband had known, and had forgiven.

Because there was no reckoning with it. I'd been forgiven.

I lingered in the darkened rooms of the house in Quail Hollow, and watched TV, wrote those letters to my friends. I sat beneath three pines in a grassy backyard, citronella burning, children and husbands and wives not from around here but all living everywhere around me.

I did all this—I *lived*—as a forgiven woman, yet in me none of the fruits of forgiveness— peace, hope, and love—because the man I'd sinned against was dead, and there was nothing I could give him, and no way to give it to him. There was only this waiting for the day my own life would end, when I might see God, and give up to Him a curse face-to-face for leaving me this empty, and with this gift of love there was no way to say thank you for.

Even inside all this light.

Ruth finished with the paper towel, dropped it in the trash can beneath the register, set the Windex down there too, just in time for her to work the next buggy moving up.

Leading the buggy on in was a man, pushing the buggy another man, the both of them in navy-blue T-shirts and pants, on the left breast of their shirts a white insignia of some sort, the buggy full to spilling with food.

I looked over my shoulder out the window wall behind me, saw at the far end of the lot, back by the Bank of America, an orange and white EMS truck I hadn't noticed when I'd pulled in.

Now the five minutes I'd have to wait was ten at least, and I took in a breath, let it out slow, and looked back to Ruth.

She'd been turned to me while I'd looked out the window, I could tell, and I caught the last instant of her eyes looking for mine before she turned back to the men, and the long last chore left to her.

She hadn't smiled, hadn't nodded or shrugged or mouthed to me the word *Sorry,* like she might do.

No. There'd been something else to the look she gave me. Maybe something on the lines of nervous, as though she might think me angry at her for this turn. But I wasn't, never had been. Those afternoons I was here to wait for her I'd simply sit and say nothing, maybe get a free cup of coffee from the pump pot they kept on the little table at the entrance, back on the other side of the customer-service desk. Or maybe I'd head over to the magazine aisle and take a look at the nonsense fashion magazines for a minute or so, and wonder what from these ads Emily might have on next time she came over. But I'd never said word one when for some reason or another Ruth was a few minutes late.

Maybe she was worried over our being late to wherever we had to go for caroling, I thought. Or maybe she was mad at some late cashier she was having to cover for.

I looked at my watch, saw it still wasn't yet five-thirty, when she was due to go.

I looked up at her, hoped she'd try and look to me again, so's I could give a small wave, smile at her, signal her somehow I was fine.

She was turned away from me now, and seemed to stand taller. Her hands on each item were clumsy somehow, as though grabbing each can of soup or bag of salad took some sort of thought from her.

The first man was bent over, worked at lifting out items from the buggy, while the second man, redheaded with a crew cut and younger than the first, stood talking to Ruth. I couldn't hear what he was saying, but he laughed a single shot of a laugh, and gave a small sharp push of the buggy into the other man.

The first one, still bent to the groceries, flinched a bit, then stood, three frozen pizzas in his hands. He was taller than the redhead, had short dark hair sprinkled with gray and a mustache to match, and he reached over, banged the redhead over the head with the pizzas.

It was a slap between friends, but I could see by the way the tall one looked first to Ruth then the redhead then to Ruth and finally to the floor that he was embarrassed over this all. Still he held the pizzas in his hands, and the redhead said something, laughed again. The tall one quick put the pizzas on the belt, glanced at Ruth, then turned to the redhead, slowly shook his head. He was smiling.

All this while Ruth still worked at scanning what they'd picked up, her hands still that same clumsy and unsure, her back perfectly straight.

How long was all this going to take? I wondered. How long before these men filling up for the week would quit flirting with my daughter-in-law and let us be about our evening, and our lives?

If in fact that's what they were doing, flirting. It could have been they were just joshing each other, or putting on a show for Ruth. It could have been nothing at all, these men in uniform here to buy groceries for the firehouse.

But then I recognized the look Ruth had

given me a moment before, and I knew what the nervous glance on her face had been about: she'd looked back to me for some assurance that I was here for her in the face of this show. That was why her hands worked as they did, too, why she stood so straight as well.

She was afraid of all this. Of men making a fuss in front of her, even with the fact she still wore her wedding ring, and any fool with eyes to see would know.

But know what? That her husband was dead?

That my son Mahlon was dead, and she his widow?

The tall one had emptied the buggy, stood now at the foot of the checkstand, pulled from the bin beneath a paper bag. He started in on the groceries, while the redhead still yakked, both hands still to the buggy.

And the tall one just kept bagging, now and again glancing up at Ruth and at the redhead, shaking his head.

Now here was the bagboy. The tall one turned to him, and I could see him full on now. He smiled at the bagger, and I heard him say, "The cavalry has arrived," though he kept at filling his bag until he'd finished, then picked it up, set it in an empty buggy he'd pulled over

with him. I'd figured he would step back, let
the bagboy have at the rest of it, but he pulled
from the bin another bag, and kept on.

Finally, the tall one pushed the emptied
buggy into the jabbering redhead who turned,
and pushed the buggy on through. The tall
one grabbed the redhead's shoulder as he
passed by, said to him, "Bill, give this good
man a hand here," and nodded at the groceries.
He smiled at the bagboy, and moved aside to
let the redhead give a hand.

The taller, older one moved to the credit-
card keypad, pulled from his wallet a card, and
swiped it through, all the while glancing up at
Ruth again and again.

But Ruth didn't let her eyes meet his, instead glanced over her shoulder to me one last
desperate time, just an instant of eyes on me.
Her smile was a kind of fearful tremble, I could
see, as she pulled from the register feed the receipt he had to sign. Then her eyes to mine
were gone, back to looking at the receipt, and
at the pen she held out to the man, her fingers
just touching the very end of it, like it was a
match about to burn down to her skin.

My heart bled for her, put to this humilia-
tion—these men making fools of her through
no fault of her own, when they could see the
ring on her left hand. Especially the tall one,

who took the pen from that left hand, him still glancing up and up and up at her, while still my Ruth kept her eyes away. They were flirting, and I was the witness to it all, and my daughter's only protector.

Then they were finished, slips signed, groceries bagged, and in the same moment here was Ruth's relief, a young black woman with a cash drawer at her hip.

The redhead pushed the buggy toward the sliding glass doors, behind him the older one, who looked at the two-foot-long receipt, slowly folded it up, and placed it inside his wallet.

I watched them as they moved past me, oblivious to what they'd put Ruth through, and though the redhead didn't so much as breathe my way, the tall one saw me watching.

"Good evening, ma'am," he said. He gave a smile that seemed part familiar, part distant, as though he might be the least bit surprised by an old woman on a bench in the Harris Teeter. He put his wallet in his back pocket, and nodded. "Merry Christmas," he said, and he was past me, the sliding doors open.

It seemed there was goodness in his eyes. Nothing shifty to them, no malice to them, far as I could see.

But I thought of Ruth's hands trembling,

and the way she'd held the pen out to him, her fearful and grieved.

They were through the open door now, and the tall one put a hand to the shoulder of the redhead in front of him, whispered, "Who is that?" just as the doors whisked closed behind them, and just as he quick glanced over his shoulder, back into the store. Straight at check-stand 7.

I looked then too, saw that Ruth was already gone, the black woman ringing up the next buggy.

BEFORE RUTH COULD leave she'd have to sign in her cash drawer, then tie up for the next shift supervisor the usual loose ends of a day: who had called in sick, what sale item they were writing rainchecks for, all that.

More waiting. And so I stood, slowly made my way outside to the sidewalk in front of the store.

There they were, pushing their cart toward the EMS truck, and I could hear even from here the loud laugh of the redhead. He started running with his buggy ahead of the tall one, then stood on the bar at the bottom of it and coasted, still laughing.

Men.

The shopping center was built in a square around the parking area, on each of the two dozen or so lampposts red lights strung up in the shape of Christmas trees, all of them on in this dusk. From where I stood just here, outside one of the two Harris Teeters the town had— there were also three Piggly Wigglys, four Bi-Los, and two Food Lions, with a Publix thrown in for good measure, each with a shopping center of its own—I could see straight across from me that Bank of America where the EMS truck was parked, beside that a soup and salad café, next a prissy odds-and-ends boutique. Next was a toy store that specialized in scientific products, next another café, the Hound and Duck, all meat and potatoes.

In the row of stores to my right was a Starbucks, a day spa, a hair stylist, and a Heavenly Ham shop; to my left was a cell-phone store, a package store, a real estate office, and a mortgage company.

And this was only half of the center. On the other side of the row that held the cell-phone place was another square just like this one, all the stores over there clustered around a Steinmart the way all these were around the Harris Teeter.

This was Mount Pleasant, and even then only a moment of it, a glance. There had to be three dozen of these kinds of places at least, and then there were the developments, those tracts where lived the people who shopped at all these places: Longpoint, and the Enclave, and Hamlin Square, The Meadows, Lake Shore, Mallard Lakes, Molasses Creek and Hobcaw Creek and Hidden Cove and Rice Hope and the granddaddy of them all, Snee Farm, where they had an Olympic pool and eight tennis courts, eighteen holes of golf and a clubhouse too.

And there was, of course, Quail Hollow.

All of these people, all settled in a town that, when I was a girl, I felt was my own private island, my own secret land. I could walk from my house to Shem Creek, walk barefoot, and watch my daddy pass by in his shrimp boat.

I could see my Eli at the stern, in his blue jeans and rubber boots, giving me the smallest of waves.

All that, gone. The only thing left a set of mossed-over concrete steps that led up to nothing. A mockingbird set upon it.

And here now was Ruth beside me, her purse strap over her shoulder, her face flushed for the hustle of getting away. I looked at my watch: five-forty. Not as late as I'd figured we'd be when those men had pulled up to the checkstand.

She said, "Sorry about that," and pulled out the blue knit scrunchy at the back of her neck, let loose her hair. Slowly she shook it out, with her fingers made to fluff it a bit. "Who knows what's coming through at the last second," she said, and let out a heavy breath, relieved, it seemed.

I was quiet a second, then nodded toward the EMS truck. Its headlights were on now, and slowly they pulled out of the bank parking lot. "Those men," I said. "No shame," I said, "flirting like that."

"Oh, them," she said, and the words came out quick, and thin.

I looked at her. Her eyes were to the truck a moment, then she was opening her purse, dropped in the scrunchy and reached in, pulled things this way and that, looking for something.

"They're harmless," she said. "They're in here once a week, stocking up," she said, and gave a quick smile, a little shake of her head. "At least that redhead is. The tall one's new."

Now here came beside us a woman in a white tennis dress, her hair the same perfect blond as the horsey gal's, but this in a flip, bobbing up and down as she walked.

Right behind her came the bagboy, pushing a buggy with a few sacks of groceries. "You take care, Henry," Ruth called out from beside me. She had her keys out of her purse, her eyes to the bagboy.

He turned his head as he pushed the buggy, climbed onto the rung at the back same as the redhead had. He was smiling, said, "Yes ma'am, Miss Ruth," and he nodded with his chin, one sharp jut of it.

She smiled, but then cut her eyes to something across the parking lot, beyond this Henry, and I saw a look come to her face, her eyebrows together in some kind of troubled consideration. Even in the dusk, I could see her cheeks still flushed.

I looked to where it seemed she was watching.

The bank parking lot, the two bright red sparks of the EMS truck headed away and out onto Longpoint Road.

"Let's go," Ruth said, and jingled her keys at me. "I'll drive."

"All right," I said, and swallowed. "All right," I said again, this time quieter, and I followed her out into the lot.

Chapter 20

I'M GOING to microwave some Spanish moss and send little bits of it back home to the girls in Northampton," Ruth called out from her bedroom. "Dorinda told me you could do that. Send it like little souvenirs in the mail."

I stood at the kitchen counter, my coat still on for how quick we'd be inside before heading to meet with Jocelyn and her brood. In my hand was the letter opener from the pencil can we kept beneath the phone, on the counter today's mail: the usual pound of catalogs, even with Christmas so close, and the bills we always had with us, today's dose Mount Pleasant Waterworks, South Carolina Electric and Gas, something in a business envelope but with the address handwritten.

And there were the cards we'd been getting most every day as well, two of them today. Like every year in Northampton, we hung them on a string above and beside the doorway into the kitchen, a kind of garland of cards that draped heavy the closer we got to the day.

Same thing here in this house, a string hung in the arch between the front room and this kitchen, the thumbtacks into the Sheetrock as easy as a hot knife to butter. Not like back home, where the walls were the old plaster kind and solid. Their first Christmas in, Mahlon'd had to drill the tiniest holes he could manage, then plug in a finishing nail at either side above the doorway.

Last year we hadn't even celebrated any of this, what with the plans for moving, and with the deep and cold feel in both our hearts that it wasn't a day worth celebrating for what we'd lost. We hadn't gotten any decorations out, hadn't bought a tree or put up even that card string over the doorway into the kitchen. Cards came, and we'd only piled them on the kitchen table, then went about the business of sorting what we wanted to keep, and what we wanted to sell.

Now we were here, in a house with a

smaller kitchen, a brand-new refrigerator in one corner, electric stove and oven instead of gas, pale blue Formica countertop, and stainless steel sink. A kitchen like any other of a million in the new tract homes that went up every day around here, like kudzu in an empty woods.

But there on the kitchen counter, in the corner next to the blender, sat Melba's bright red crocheted toilet-paper cover doll, roll and all. An attempt, I knew, to make this place feel more like the home Ruth wanted it to be. I'd told her a hundred times it was the sort of thing you were supposed to keep in your bathroom, but she'd wanted it out here.

"To remind me of Melba," she'd said more than a time or two, though I knew it was more about her own momma, and how she missed her, all of that carried in a strange memento sitting on our kitchen counter.

And now it was Christmas in full bloom. Just above the counter was a pass-through to the front room, a Formica counter three feet wide and open all the way to the ceiling. From here I could see the tree we bought over to the Lowe's last Saturday, hung on it every ornament we had, all done with Tess and Zachary and Brian while Jocelyn carried on about the Herbal Life franchise she was thinking on starting up—she'd been through Mary Kay and

Pampered Chef both since we'd moved here. I'd baked nutmeg cookies and made hot chocolate, which of course made the boys bounce even harder off the walls. And Tess didn't even finish a single cookie, no matter how hard I tried at getting her to eat.

Hung off the eaves out front of the house were three strings of icicle lights Ruth bought over to the Lowe's too, Allen Fortner from down the street helping out with his ladder, though I like to died when he was teetering up there, him a good two hundred fifty pounds and not much taller than me. But the lights'd gotten up, the tree set about with all we had. A sprinkle of presents lay under it already, one from Gordon and Melba, another from Robert and Ellen, a couple three from Ruth's friends at work. Me with one each from Hilda, Phyllis, and Carolyn. There was even a little round box under there for Ruth from Emily.

And here, in the doorway into the kitchen, hung the garland of cards. What seemed more than we'd ever gotten before for the fact we'd changed our lives in a way most all our friends couldn't imagine: *we're so amazed and glad for you that you moved back home,* Hilda'd written, and Peach Gazda'd said, *You are two of the bravest women I know.* Along with the card she'd sent a photo of Ruth's girlfriends from work, all of them in their uniforms—those Stop & Shop green vests and black pants—and jammed into a checkstand, Santa Claus hats on every one of them.

"What about the chiggers?" I called out to Ruth. "In the Spanish moss?" and I set aside the catalogs on the counter, and the bills, left myself the business-size envelope and the cards. "You want all your girlfriends back home to get an envelope full of chiggers for Christmas?"

"That's why you nuke it," she said back. I could hear on her words she was pulling on a sweater. "Once you nuke them." She was looking in the mirror, turning one way and another, sizing up. "Then you can handle the stuff because the bugs are dead."

"Sounds silly to me," I said.

Then she was moving through the bedroom, said, "Dorinda told me, too, that Spanish moss isn't even Spanish moss. It's just the name the Indians called it because the stuff looked like the beards on the conquistadors."

I looked at the first card, a big cream-colored envelope to Ruth. The address looked hand-written but not, one of these computer-generated things whoever sending it wanted you to think was personalized. But the hand-writing was too perfect, nowheres on it the odd flat loop or wavy line real people gave. I turned it over, saw it was from Harris Teeter headquarters up in Charlotte, and I set it down.

"You ought to get a job with the carriage tours downtown," I said. "You're a regular walking guidebook," I said, and now Ruth laughed from deeper inside the house, in her bathroom, pulling a brush through her hair, eyes to the mirror in there.

"Just stuff I want to know," she called out. "To find out about where we live is all." She paused, bent now to the mirror for a last touch at her makeup.

"Silliest thing I ever heard," I said, and held the business envelope out in front of me, the handwriting small and thin and hard to focus on for it. "I don't want anything to do with chiggers, dead or alive," I said, and slipped it into my coat pocket for later, when I could try and get a better look at it, or just hand it over to Ruth for her to read to me, like I sometimes had no choice but to do.

I heard Ruth laugh again at my old woman's words, and here in my hand was the last card of the day.

From Mary Margaret, I could tell, though the handwriting—the careful loops and shivering lines—seemed smaller than before, like they were shivering even fuller, and I thought of Tommy, in his bed there at Willow Springs, taking another turn.

I slipped the letter opener in and pulled it through, even this small splinter of work grown sharper and sharper in my hands every day. But this was a Christmas card, and from my Mary Margaret, and that kind of pain didn't matter.

I pulled out the card, on the front an old-fashioned painting of a shepherd on a hillside, a lamb beside him, the two of them looking to the star of Bethlehem, and I opened it.

And out slipped two sheets of Mary Margaret's lavender paper. They were folded in half, and as though it'd been settled years ago, lifetimes ago, they caught the air and unfolded themselves like birds just finding flight, and floated down.

It was an odd moment, the surprise of it a strange and mysterious one that seemed to last the entire day so far, me so tired at the shopping I'd done, and at the fiasco of those men after making time with my widowed daughter-in-law, and now with the prospect of Christmas caroling with Jocelyn and those boys of hers and sad little Tess and the rest of whoever else we were going to meet and have to charm and sing along with at a place who knew where—this was a sudden mystery, the way two sheets of paper inside a Christmas card from my friend could fall slow as snow in a Massachusetts woods, falling still and still, finally settling facedown right there on the counter before me.

All this, in only this moment.

I looked at those sheets, looked at them, the card in my hand and open, and still I looked at them, as though those sheets might right themselves and give their news out loud to me. But of course nothing happened, my old woman's surprise just an old woman's surprise, and I glanced a moment at the card, saw just below the verses from Luke about the angels and shepherds Mary Margaret's signature and nothing else—no note, not even the word *Love*.

I closed the card, set it on the counter, then reached to the sheets, picked them up, and turned them to me.

Mary Margaret's handwriting had gone to an even darker tremble, the address on the envelope—the shiver I'd seen there—only a hint at the trouble I saw in these words, and I read it.

December 14th

Dearest Naomi—

I am so very sorry to write you with this news. I did not phone you, because I thought I would not know what to say to you that would help, and there was nothing for you to do with this news except take it from me. But I want you to know I love you and that everything you ever told me I never told anyone else.

Lonny Thompson passed away last Wednesday in his sleep. He was in Cooley Dickinson for only two days because his doctor would not let him stay at home anymore. Then he passed away.

I know you both talked together that last day at the cemetery, but he never did tell me what he said to you, and I never asked him. I saw him three times after you left, when I went up to say hello to him in Sunderland. He said he was okay with how you left, but it never seemed to me that this was true.

I do not tell you this so you will feel bad, but so you will know that you and Eli and Mahlon were so very important to him. Still I do not have the right words. This letter has come out all wrong, so please forgive me.

The funeral was nice, but cold. A sunny day, and there were a good twenty people from town who came, including us girls. We sent flowers with all our names on it, including yours.

I love you, and my eyes are filled with tears as I write this to you. Will I see you again? I pray that I will.

Do you remember the day we met each other? I remember it, and hope the memory of it brings good thoughts to your heart. It does to mine.

Love,
Mary Margaret

Here, finally, was that word.

Love.

I hung on that word, hung on the sad scrawl of her hand giving it to me, hung on it for longer than the strange moment of these falling words from inside a Christmas card.

I hung on that word, because I did not want the others, though there was no surprise to them at all.

Lonny was dead.

"I'm just telling you what Dorinda said," Ruth said, and I looked up from the pages in my hand, saw her moving through the front room and toward me, when there had been nothing in the world an instant before save for that single and lonely and shivering word *Love.*

Love, I thought. What does that mean?

"But she moved down here from Wisconsin two years ago," Ruth was saying. She was at the pass-through, leaned toward me on it from the other side, her hands clasped together on the countertop there. "So maybe that's just some sort of joke on Yankees. Get them all to stand around nuking Spanish moss like it was a Lean Cuisine, then send chiggers on home to Wisconsin."

Here was Ruth smiling, her as beautiful as ever she'd been, her hair loose on her shoulders and gleaming even at the end of a day at work. Her cheekbones were touched with the smallest bit of color, her mascara the slightest shade of cinnamon, her lipstick a color so natural I couldn't say she was wearing any.

And she had on a Christmas sweater, a cream pullover cable-knit with a trim of poinsettias at the cuffs and along the bottom edge. Nothing loud or out of line, like sweaters I'd seen on some of these Mount Pleasant moms: circus red with giant snowmen appliqués, or Santa Claus climbing out a chimney big enough to fill the backside of a cardigan.

No. This sweater was just enough. Just enough. It was no wonder those men would pitch a fit over her.

And there was her ring, the single band of white gold anyone in the world knew meant love, no matter the people involved, and the way they could betray each other.

Mahlon had loved her. And she still loved him.

Lonny was dead, the last time I saw him alive the moment when he let me know of the depth of my husband's love for me. When he'd burdened me, and lifted that burden, with the good and terrifying news of my husband's forgiveness.

"You look beautiful," I said to Ruth, though the words came out more a whisper than anything else, and I felt my eyes begin to fill for it, felt the blood rush yet again to my cheeks, and I looked down from her.

My eyes had nowheres to go, but to the letter in my hand, and the news I did not want to hear.

Lonny was dead.

"Naomi?" Ruth said, and reached toward me, touched my shoulder through the weight of my coat.

And dead with Lonny was what he knew of my husband's good heart, dead with him Eli's forgiveness of him, and of me.

There was no surprise in this news at all, but in this moment, ushered in by Mary Margaret's words falling like snow to arrive here, now, I saw that there had been a kind of comfort in his being alive.

As long as Lonny was alive, so was my Eli's

forgiveness, because someone else knew of his heart. And as long as Lonny was alive, I could run from myself, from that piece of me that had sinned so fully and deeply against my Eli. That woman had still been alive, lived there in Massachusetts, a country I'd hoped would be as far from me as my childhood was from a morning in November, when a faithless sun had shone down on those frosted rooftops.

But I hadn't run from me. I'd only run from our home, and from the death of our son, and from God for having taken from me the last evidence of the love Eli and I shared.

And still God found me out. Still He was with me.

Still a mockingbird sat on concrete steps, and watched you, the two of you knowing full well the fool you truly were.

Ruth gently squeezed my shoulder through the coat, said, "Are you all right?" and I looked back up to her, smiled at her, at her beauty, and her life. I smiled at what she'd found here with no help from me but the push from a frightened old woman to move from the shadow of what I'd believed was my unforgiven sin, to the empty notion the sun could make me whole again.

When Eli, my Eli, had given me the gift of forgiveness even the day my guilt had begun.

Now here was Ruth, alive. She was, truly, beautiful.

And I saw only now the gift she was to me, brought here through gifts given me one after the other—Eli's forgiveness leading to the gift of Mahlon, Mahlon's love for Ruth leading to her gift to me, to words shared in a kitchen what seemed seven lifetimes ago: *where you go, I will,* she'd said. *But it's not because I have nothing else that I'm coming with you. It's because I have you.*

But it was me, finally, who had her. And there was only me to know of that gift that had brought us here, the gift, pure and perfect, of forgiveness.

A gift, I knew suddenly and fully, I could only do honor to by giving it away.

But how?

I couldn't tell her of how I'd been forgiven by my husband of my adultery, my breaking the bond of our marriage. How could that help, to tell her I'd sinned with Lonny Thompson, the one who'd been the reason Mahlon had been out on a night of black ice after an early November snow? How could *that* be the passing on of the gift my husband had given, to tell her of me, and of Lonny?

"I'm fine," I managed, finally, and folded the two pages in half quickly, just as quick put them in my coat pocket, me hiding yet again, this time from Ruth herself the news of the death of Lonny. And the news too of my being the single bearer of the gift of Eli's forgiveness.

A gift too good to keep hidden, I knew.

But what could I do? And how could I share it?

"I'm fine," I said again. I nodded hard once, my hand inside my coat pocket, clutched in it those pieces of lavender paper, as thin and frail as Lonny's arm through his coat that last morning, and as thin and frail as Mary Margaret's own heart.

As thin and frail, I felt, as my soul, burdened still with the weight of keeping a gift hidden, no matter how sweet, no matter how cleansing and pure.

Me, the only one left on earth to know, and no way to pass it on, as gifts are best received.

"If you say so," Ruth said, and smiled. She let go my arm, let her eyes hang on mine a moment longer before she looked down to the countertop between us. Then she reached from her side of the pass-through to touch at the catalogs, the bills, and took up the big cream-colored Christmas card. She looked at it only a moment, flipped it over to read the Harris Teeter address on the back.

"Same old same old," she said. "Just like

back at the Stop and Shop, a computer card to let me know how much I mean to the company." She shrugged, let it drop to the counter. "Who was that letter from?" she asked, and looked up at me, and in her eyes I could see there was nothing getting past her. We'd lived together this long. We knew each other.

And still I lied. "Mary Margaret's Tommy's taken another bad turn," I said. "Maybe the last one," I said.

"I'm sorry," she said, her eyes square on me. She touched at my arm again, leaned her head the smallest way to the right, in her eyes and her touch the truth of her concern, and now I felt even worse for having brought her to believe me.

Me, ever and always a liar, hiding.

Chapter 21

RUTH NUDGED THE CAR into a space that faced a low brick building ten yards or so away, a row of windows there, inside them all the curtains drawn. Between us and the building was a sidewalk and a strip of worn-down grass, everything a bright gray in the headlights.

"Where are we?" I asked, even though there was in me no desire to know. They were only words to speak, to try and hear if I could still manage not to lie.

Because I did not know where we were, only knew we were going Christmas caroling. I'd gotten into this car, sat beside Ruth as she backed down the driveway, then maneuvered us along one traffic-choked street after another to arrive here.

And my hand was in my coat pocket, holding tight those pieces of lavender paper.

"The Mount Pleasant Home," she said, and cut off the headlights, left us in a dark even more gray for a lamppost behind us in the small parking lot. Shadows were suddenly everywhere, we two in the deepest of them, together.

She looked at me. She had her coat on, her hands still on the wheel. The engine was still running, my feet warm for the heater blowing on them, though it was only fifty-five or so outside. Sweater weather back home to Northampton.

"Does she think this is really the last time? That he won't make it after this?" Ruth said. I could only see the vaguest features of her face, her hair, her a silhouette against her window.

"Who?" I said, still trying to piece out this all: where was the Mount Pleasant Home? And who was she talking about?

What did she know?

She was quiet a second. She gripped her fingers on the steering wheel harder, then eased, gripped again. "Tommy," she said. "Mary Margaret's Tommy."

"Oh," I said and took in a quick breath,

glanced forward out the windshield, then out my window, back to her, gathering myself for this lie, readying to move deeper into it.

"She doesn't think he'll make into January," I said. "Seems this time it may be for real. Not that he was ever faking, or that she was making it out to be more than it was."

"I never thought that," she said. She let go the wheel, turned off the engine, and in the silence I waited for the tick of the engine cooling down. Same as a night near a year ago, when we'd sat in the drive behind the house, all that room made for my old Electra by Mahlon's truck no longer there.

The same night Mary Margaret had called out to me, *What about Lonny Thompson?* while I ushered Ruth out Carolyn's door, Ruth home early from the movies with Peach.

We were all left sitting there watching something going on on the wall, she'd said about why she'd left the theater. *Watching these people live their lives.*

I looked at the brick building before us, that strip of grass, the sidewalk, still all gray. But now, with the headlights off, I could see light inside those windows, through the drawn curtains.

She said, "I think you should go up there." She paused. "When Tommy passes away." She looked down at her hands in her lap. "For the funeral. And to visit. And go see Eli and Mahlon."

I looked at her. That night it had been me to drive her home, me to sit at the wheel and listen for the ticking of the engine while she struggled in that darkness, watching everyone else's lives happening, her away from it and only watching.

She looked at me, her chin down, but her eyes on me. "Maybe I can get some time off work, maybe go with you. Or maybe you'd want to go alone."

Her words were a kind of test. It was in the way she held her chin down, her eyes on me, waiting for me to carry on with this bluff, or to give her the truth of what was wrong. She hadn't believed me after all.

I could tell her about Lonny. This as a means to tell her the real story: my Eli's forgiveness. I could tell her.

But the bluff held on. I was only watching my life happen on a wall, me in darkness.

I said, "She asked in the letter if I would do that. Come out." I smiled. "I'm glad you agree with her."

I could see in the shadows her mouth make a thin line, saw her bite her lips together. She nodded once more, and in one small move had the key out and her door open, the car filled with the pale yellow of the dome light.

"Tonight we meet the mythical Beau," she said, and turned in her seat, started out.

"I'll believe that when I see it," I said, and the words came out too loud, too much like an old woman welcome for the change in topic. I turned to my door, opened it, and started out, Ruth already around the hood and with a hand to my elbow before I was even standing, then closing the car door behind me.

I looked around then, still uncertain where we were. But then I knew: we were just off the biggest intersection in town, Bowman Road and Highway 17. I could see off to my right an Arby's, then the intersection itself, where Bowman crossed 17, with its four lanes and grass median and stoplights for every which way you were planning to turn. Past it all stood a McDonald's, beyond that the Kmart, its parking lot lamps tall as radio towers, it seemed to me.

Bowman Road, when I was a girl, had been the last oyster-shell road, an outpost branch off Old Georgetown Highway, nothing out here but the swamped headwaters of Shem Creek and shanties spread out like broken hopes of home. Now there was nothing left of the marsh save for what you might glimpse between the doctors' offices and quickie oil-change garages and all else around here.

Directly across the street from us stood East Cooper Community Hospital, three stories tall and brick, all set upon land all those years ago nobody would have thought to give a second glance to. It sat on a huge parking lot washed in a kind of dark orange for whatever sort of lampposts they had over there, a few cars clustered up close to the front of the hospital proper, the smoked-glass doors there. I could see from here too the emergency entrance on the left side of the building, wide glass doors under a canopy there at the far end of a long concrete drive almost straight across from us, all of it only a couple hundred yards away. An orange and white EMS truck—maybe even the same one—was pulled up and parked just out from under the canopy, its lights off.

And I could see, too, windows in the hospital over there lit up from inside.

It seemed convenient, a hospital this close to the nursing home, and I thought again of Willow Woods, where Mary Margaret lived, while next door to it stood Willow Springs, where Tommy and everyone else taking one last turn stayed.

I turned back to Ruth, looked at her. "Ten months we've been here," I said, "and we haven't seen Beau yet." I shook my head. "You'd think a relative would have a little more respect than that."

"It's been a rough year for him," Ruth started. "You know that. But tonight he's supposed to be here. He got a promotion to the station over by the rec center. He's got better shifts now, and Jocelyn said he'll be here."

"I've heard that before, too," I said, and we started up the sidewalk.

Because I *had* heard about Beau meeting us here or there or somewhere else over all these months. We'd spoken to him on the phone two or three times since we'd come here, the first time the day after we moved in when he'd said hello and apologized for not being able to help, then once this summer when he couldn't make it for a barbecue at Jocelyn's.

He'd called, too, when we were up to Gordon and Melba's for Thanksgiving, her table and sideboard and kitchen counters piled even higher with food than that day we drove in from Massachusetts. Even in the middle of all the confusion and cramped quarters of a house filled with so much family—everyone was there yet again, Ellen and Robert and Emily and Ashley, Jocelyn and her boys and Tess— Melba'd managed to have a place set for Beau and waiting at the table, his plate and napkin and knife and fork and spoon all set and ready, a little pool of calm water hidden inside a hurricane.

Gordon'd ended up waiting to start carving the fried turkey an extra twenty minutes, but then Melba, bless her heart, said, "Let's just go on and eat," though there wasn't any joy to her at all.

We all sat down, Gordon at the head and working away, to his left Melba, me to his right, everyone else spread around the table, Emily careful as ever to sit next to Ruth like she always did now.

There was only Beau's seat left, and then here was Tess, just climbing on up into his chair.

And the phone rang, right on cue. Zachary or Brian—I still couldn't tell which from the other—jumped up and answered it, plucked the receiver right off the wall phone there in the kitchen, Melba already to her feet.

"Why aren't you here on Planet Turkey with us, Uncle Beau?" the boy said, grinning at his brother still at the table, him with a turkey leg in his hands. "We're doing an autopsy on the first victim right now," he said, and Ashley, sitting there in an Indian Maiden costume she'd worn for Halloween and still wearing that tiara, shouted out, "That is so gross! People are trying to eat!"

Melba hushed them both, Robert whispering loud to Ashley, *Careful your mouth!* before Melba took the phone and grimaced a smile at the boy, then started in to talking.

We'd kept on eating, Melba moving out of the kitchen, her back to us. She seemed to want to find a corner for the quiet she needed, but the cord wouldn't reach. She'd only been able to face away from the table, and toward that high shelf above the recliner, where perched that submarine of Gordon's in its glass case. Beau's gift back to his daddy, all those years ago.

Then she'd turned to me, held the receiver out to me at the table. She was working hard at a smile, said, "He wants to say hey to you," and nodded.

I'd stood, come around the end of the table, and took it from her, but not before I'd touched at her shoulder, smiled at her.

"Aunt Naomi," he said, his voice strong and clear but quiet, the quiet that came from inside and had nothing to do with how you wanted to be heard. It was who he was. Same as I'd heard two times before. "Aunt Naomi, I want to apologize for not being able to be there," he'd said, and gone on for a minute or so about the why of work.

Then he'd said, "And I want you to know I love you, Aunt Naomi, and Ruth too. I just want you both to know that."

I said, "We love you too," and saw Melba and Gordon both smiling up at me, and we said good-bye.

I believed him, certainly. We were family. Still, I'd thought he ought to have at least called sooner. I sat back at the table, and only then did I catch the thin shine of tears in Melba's eyes, saw her pinch up yet another smile, touch at either eye. "It's been a tough row for him this year," she said, still with that smile.

Tess was sitting next to her, the commotion everywhere suddenly stopped for what everyone knew was something happening. Even the boys'd stopped tussling, their hands suddenly in their laps.

"Ollie's birthday was in October," Gordon gave out from the head of the table, his voice soft and low. He was looking at Melba now, smiling of his own, but not with tears. He reached to her, rubbed her arm slow and easy, tenderness to his smile and touch both. "He would have been eighteen," he went on, still with his eyes to Melba. "That's when Beau got on with the Georgetown department all those years ago. Back when all you needed was to graduate high school and pass the physical."

Gordon looked to me. He still rubbed slow and gentle at Melba's arm. "That's what he's been working on all this while. This year. The fact his own life took off on its own once he hit eighteen. And that's how old Ollie would've been." He paused, swallowed, looked back to Melba. "But he's coming through it. He is," he said to her.

Melba said, "I know it," and sniffed, looked up at Gordon. She reached a hand to his on her arm. "He sounds good." She squeezed his hand, and Robert said, "He sounded good when I talked to him on Saturday last week." He nodded to his momma, and Jocelyn'd put in, "It's just been this year," looked first to me then Ruth, as though her words were some kind of apology for her big brother.

Ruth and I both nodded. There was no apology needed. We both knew what grief was.

Yet there was still a piece in me that wanted to say maybe it was better if you went to those you loved, stayed near them. Maybe it was family, finally, that would help you through all it was God could hand you.

★　★　★

WE WERE AT the glass double doors of the building, the edges of the glass frosted all the way around with spray-on snow, stenciled snowmen and a Christmas tree sprayed on too.

The Mount Pleasant Nursing Home. Here was where we'd go caroling, and I looked through the glass, saw a long hallway with doorways spaced down it, a wheelchair here and there, at the end of the hallway a nurses' station, lit bright like it was the helm of a ship.

Just like Willow Springs. Where Tommy, in whatever condition he might be in, lay right now. Most likely with Mary Margaret beside him.

Ruth pushed the door open, and here was warmth, too much of it, and the smell of any nursing home I'd ever been in. Ammonia, pitched to one degree or another, and the smell of flowers, and of food somewhere. All of it wrapped in a warmth too warm, too forced.

It was, I'd known for the last thirty years or so, when friends of ours had started peeling away and into these places, the smell of death, no matter how careful the staff was, or how careless.

This was where any of us, all of us, might very well see the end.

We took a few steps into the foyer, and I

heard a commotion as familiar to me now as the sound of a lawnmower next door, or the smell of a barbecue: Jocelyn's boys, going at it like every time I ever saw them, and then here we were at a little waiting room off to the left, a room you couldn't see into from the front door.

There they were, on the carpeted floor of the place, laughing and rolling around with some big man I couldn't rightly see for them all over him, all three messing around on the floor of a nursing home and threatening to knock into a coffee table set up with a little Christmas tree and a dozen or so ornaments. There was a sofa in here, pushed up against one wall, two overstuffed chairs against another wall, but nobody was sitting. The boys both had on jeans and sweatshirts, and both wore Santa Claus hats, the furry red things with white trim and the little white ball at the tip. The man—Beau, I knew already—had on a green heavy sweater and gray turtleneck shirt, khaki slacks, and what looked like hiking boots. Past that I couldn't see a thing. Only the boys on top of him, him squawking out about how mean they were to him, and the boys still just pouring it on.

All three of them, laughing.

Here was Jocelyn, and Tess too, smiling

down at them, and darned if Jocelyn didn't have on one of those fire-engine-red Christmas sweaters, woven into it puppies chasing one another all up and down the arms and across the front, on every one of them bright ribbon bows for collars and tiny brass bells— real ribbons and bells, tied right into the weave. And Tess, in a green slacks and shirt set, on the left breast a little Christmas puppy, a bright red ribbon and little brass bell sewn on it.

She was smiling.

Nobody'd yet seen us for the fuss of the boys wrestling, and now they rolled in one clump too close to the coffee table, bumped it hard and sent the tree to tip over.

Jocelyn shouted in a tough whisper "Now, Beau!" and bolted to the table as though to catch what was already knocked down, while the boys quick sat up for what had happened.

This was exactly when Tess looked up from this all to discover Ruth and me standing here, and in that instant our eyes met.

"Aunt Naomi!" she let out, louder than any time I'd ever heard her, and for some reason I could not say she shot across the room to me, took both my hands, her smiling up at me big as I'd ever seen her smile.

"Why, how are you, Tess?" I asked, a little

stunned for this, and I heard from beside me Ruth take in a quick breath, as though she might be even more startled at sweet Tess letting out words this loud.

I glanced up to her and smiled, looked for the surprise I figured I'd see in her eyes.

But her eyes, too wide open, were to the room, her mouth a little open too, and I looked to the room, all the fuss suddenly quiet, and still.

Jocelyn was bent to the table, the tree—a plastic one—already righted, her looking up at us. And there on the floor, untangled now and silent, sat the three boys, Beau in the middle.

He had on a Santa Claus hat too.

The boys started in again, nearly leapt on him from either side, and Jocelyn stood up, talking already and headed toward us, Tess still holding tight my hands.

But I was looking at Beau, who hadn't moved, even with the boys pulling on him.

He was looking at Ruth, on his face the same look as she had, eyes open a little too wide, mouth open too.

I knew him.

"Uncle Beau is here, Aunt Naomi!" Tess said. She pulled at my hands a little, and though there was pain to this, I didn't say or do anything.

Because I knew this man.

But from where? I'd seen his picture enough times in the front room of Gordon and Melba's, that portrait of him in his uniform when he'd graduated from the fire academy. But the man in that photo was a boy, in his early twenties, not yet visited upon him the sorrows he'd come to know for the death of his son.

And there was that Polaroid, its fading colors giving away day by day the image of a man and his child, and I thought of the joy I could still barely see in him even with that fading, joy still clear and full at this baby boy with a full head of black hair there in his daddy's arms.

But that wasn't where I knew this man from either.

"He really does exist," Jocelyn was saying, "just like we've warned you all this time." She was at Ruth's side now, had hold of her elbow, and turned back to Beau, still on the floor, still not having moved at all.

Still with his eyes on her, his mouth open the smallest way.

He had a mustache, sprinkled through with gray, and it seemed there was goodness in his eyes, even though he was staring at Ruth.

Now it was me to take in a quick breath.

The fireman, at the Harris Teeter. The awkward one, the taller one, who'd looked at her and away and to her again, hoping, I'd seen, to make her eyes meet his, no matter the ring she wore.

While Ruth, my Ruth, trembling and fearful, had kept her eyes away from him, afraid of these men putting moves on her, and flirting, and meaning her harm and no harm at once.

The one who'd whispered *Who is that?* as the doors whisked closed behind him.

This was Beau, the fireman Ruth had known was new.

He moved, finally, got to one knee and pulled off his Santa hat even while the boys hung on his arms, and then he was standing, him taller, it seemed, for this small room, and still the boys jumped at him, held on to him, pulled at him.

He only stood looking at Ruth, the hat in both hands in front of him, wadding it, almost wringing it. His mouth moved, opened and closed once, twice, but nothing came out.

His face seemed to go red, a blush coming across him, and I knew it was for his having been caught out: Ruth knew him for the flirt he was around women.

Around Ruth herself. His stepcousin's widow.

I glanced again to Ruth. She seemed to

waver where she stood, as though she thought to take a step back for his standing up. In her eyes still on him was the same desperate and fearful look as earlier this evening, when she'd glanced at me to make sure I was still there at the bench, her afraid of these men making a fuss in front of her.

Here came a blush over her as well, her cheeks and ears and neck flushed with color, her eyebrows together in the same troubled consideration she'd given the EMS truck as she'd watched it leave in the dusk of this same evening.

She needed me, I knew. She needed me right then. Right now.

I moved to her side, Tess's hands still holding tight to mine, a sudden and heavy pain as I pulled her along with me, a pain too heavy and burdensome, but me without chance to let go for how much Ruth needed me.

"Did you get it?" Tess said to me, her voice still strong and a wonder for it, but I only quick smiled down at her, still in front of me and holding on tight to my hands, and her still smiling up at me.

Now Beau's eyes went to mine, and he blinked, his forehead pinched a moment for the fact he recognized me, too: the old woman on the bench at the Harris Teeter, the one he'd wished a Merry Christmas to as he'd folded up his receipt.

"Aunt Naomi?" he said, a question, certainly, and a surprise at once. He blinked again.

"What in the world is going on here?" Jocelyn asked, too loud as ever. "Do y'all know each other?"

"I'd say we do," I let out, level and calm. For Ruth, so that she might know I was with her, that I was even closer than standing beside her.

I'd said it cold as I did for him, too. Just so's he'd know I knew him.

"We go way back," he said, and now he was smiling at me, big and broad.

And true.

He stopped wringing the Santa hat, took two big strides across the room straight at me, and took me tight into a hug, me with only enough time to let go Tess's hands and turn my face from his chest so that I didn't smother in it, Tess squirming quick out of the way herself just in time.

Again he said, "Aunt Naomi," this time in a kind of quiet wonder, and still he hugged me, me so very small in his grasp. I breathed in his smell, took in the faintest trace of burnt wood.

He was a fireman. Of course.

He let me go, stood back from me and smiled still just as big and broad. Already

Jocelyn was laughing, and the boys were at him again, there beneath us all Tess, laughing and giggling at all this, all this.

"We go way back," he said again, now to Jocelyn, though his eyes were still on mine, his hands still holding on to my shoulders. "About an hour or so," he said.

"What's this?" Jocelyn let out. "What are you talking about?"

I said, "It was at the Harris Teeter while I was waiting on Ruth to get off work." My voice was just as level and hard, though nowhere in his eyes on mine was the kind of guilt that blush of his had betrayed. He was smiling at me, and smiling, and still holding on to me. "Beau here was with one of his men and buying groceries, the two of them giving Ruth here a hard time and flirting and all else."

His eyes seemed to flicker a moment, and the smile gave way a bit to puzzlement, and I could feel his hands go the smallest way loose on my shoulders.

And he let his eyes go to Ruth.

"It was Bill Dupree you were there with, wasn't it," Jocelyn said, and though I could see out the corner of my eye her cross her arms, put out her hip, still I was watching Beau, glad for the guilt he was onto now. Glad, too, it was me to bring it to bear on him.

I was here for Ruth. I was right here.

Then his eyes were to me again, the puzzlement gone, in its place what I could see clean and clear was regret. Plain and simple and true.

"I'm sorry," he said right out, the words no surprise at all for what I'd seen in his eyes. "Aunt Naomi, if Bill or I said or did anything out of line, I apologize. No excuses whatsoever." He looked a moment at Ruth, nodded.

"So it *was* Bill Dupree?" Jocelyn said, and I knew in that instant she was interested in him, knew too they were talking about the redhead with the crew cut.

"Will you introduce me?" Beau said to me, ignoring like any brother will his little sister.

He'd apologized. He'd meant it.

And now I had to think if he'd even done anything out of line at all. He'd tried to meet Ruth's eyes, and'd slapped this Dupree boy on the head with those frozen pizzas.

He'd wished an old woman he did not know waiting on the bench inside the Harris Teeter a Merry Christmas, and had called her *Ma'am*.

But he'd also whispered on his way out the door, *Who was that?*

I said, "This is my son Mahlon's wife, Ruth," and let my eyes linger on his a moment to let him know I was warning him, and to let him know who he'd wounded with his wandering eye.

But he was already turned to her, already smiling, that Santa hat back in both hands, him holding tight to it.

I turned to Ruth. Still she looked frightened, and still her cheeks and neck were flushed in color. Still her eyebrows were together, her worried and fearful.

But she was smiling, too. She was smiling now, and let out a breath, took in another, gave finally what wanted to pass as a laugh, but which seemed to me a means of relief.

Beau put out his hand to her. She paused a moment before she put out her own, let his take hold of hers. Their hands touched, and they shook, once. He quick let go her hand, then he turned to me, said, "I'm sorry, Miss Ruth, if there was anything I did or said or if anything—"

"Now please, y'all," Jocelyn cut in, too loud again, and she put her hands to her hips, quick shook her head. "If it was Bill Dupree involved, you know it had to be ugly," she said, "and it sounds like cotillion class around here with the introductions and apologies. This is just family!"

Beau, still with the hat in his hands, looked over at me, slowly shook his head. "You know, of course, that my lovely sister here was the only girl ever to flunk Miss Pansy's cotillion class."

Jocelyn pushed him hard with both hands—he didn't move, stood rock still—and the boys burst out all over again.

Yet even in the midst of all this going on, Beau looked again at Ruth, said in the softest way, and serious, "It's a pleasure to meet you, and I am sorry for your loss."

They were quiet words, said without a smile even inside the tussle and mayhem and noise of these people. This family. But I'd heard them, and Ruth had too. And I'd seen, too, that just as with his apology to me, he'd meant these words. He was glad to meet her, and he was sorry.

He was only himself.

Then the boys started in earnest, pulled at Beau to nearly topple him, and he staggered a bit, stepped back. Finally his eyes left Ruth, and he was smiling again, though the blush was still working strong on him. He turned from us, a boy hanging on each arm, their feet dragging the ground, and he let out a giant's laugh, deep and dark, entirely too loud for the front room of a nursing home.

That was when Ruth's arm looped into mine, and I felt her hold on hard to me, felt her lean in on me, my wounded daughter-in-law so close beside me.

I leaned into her, too, and looked at her. She was still watching him, her bottom lip between her teeth, her biting down hard. Then she turned to me, looked in my eyes, tried at a smile, all while Jocelyn went at Beau about this Bill Dupree, and how much of a dog he was for flirting like that, and asking in the next breath was he seeing anyone now. Beau just shook his head and glanced at her now and again with a look on his face to tell her what a fool she could be, the boys all the while getting louder by the second.

"Did you get it?" I heard Tess say, and felt her grab hold of my free hand, pulling on it. "Aunt Naomi, did you get it yet? Did you?"

I looked down at her, still there right beside me in her green slacks and shirt set, and I said too quick, said too hard, "Don't pull so hard on your Aunt Naomi's hand, sweetheart, it hurts when you do that."

I knew even before I'd said it I shouldn't have. She let go my hand in an instant, drew hers together at her chest and took a small step back even before I had the words all out, all the ugly of what was going on in meeting this Beau—Ruth's trembling, my cold words to Beau, that guilt I was pleased to see in the way

the blush worked its way on him—all of it was
still in me with those words to Tess, just hanging on and asking me whatever it was she
wanted to know. A girl so brittle of course all
it would take would be a word to break her yet
again.

"Tess, darling, I'm sorry," I started, "I didn't
mean to—"

"Here they are!" Jocelyn let out, and Tess's
eyes shot to behind me, and the ruckus started
anew with the sudden parade into the room of
more people. This was another whole family,
the Brookeses, Jocelyn let me know as she introduced me to the mother, bone thin and
with blunt-cut blond hair and a white sweater,
green corduroy slacks. We shook hands and I
took in the fact she was the wife of the doctor
whose caroling party this was, him somewhere
else in the building giving the heads-up to the
nurses, and now here was her son introduced
as well, him nearly tall as her and with the same
color hair and in jeans and a College of
Charleston sweatshirt; then another son maybe
the same age as Jocelyn's wrestlers, but this one
Japanese maybe, thick black hair and a green
dress shirt; and finally a girl maybe a little older
than Tess and in a bright red dress, little
Christmas tree appliqués along the hem, long
blond hair in curls down to her shoulder.

Through all this Ruth stayed beside me, though she'd had to let go my arm for shaking hands. And through it all too I'd tried to get a look at Tess, tried to find her to give her a smile. But then in paraded more people, and what seemed even more, until the room was a bright swirl of friends, some I was introduced to and some I wasn't, every name I got a name I knew I wouldn't remember two minutes from now. Tess'd faded into the room with these new people, even though the little girl in the red dress seemed herself alone once she'd shaken my hand. She'd stood beside her momma a minute or so, only to be caught up in the madness of the wrestling boys, and then they were all wrestling, the two new boys and the little girl, Tess nowheres I could see.

And slowly, slowly, Ruth drifted from beside me, while still I smiled and shook hands and let Jocelyn go on with anybody who had ears about us moving here near a year ago now.

Ruth was gone from me, and Tess was as well, and even though I was in the middle of a room full of people I felt my heart pull in me for the fact I seemed somehow still as alone as I ever had been. Maybe even more, for the meeting of this Beau, and for the letter in my coat pocket, and for the trembling of Ruth beside me, and for the lie I had given her about what that letter had said.

And for the way I'd cut short Tess, spoken to her as though she were a bother to my life, and not a child whose heart had been broken already.

That was when I caught sight of Beau behind and above the left shoulder of the next nameless woman Jocelyn was introducing me to, a woman with short gray hair and eyebrows too penciled in and who was going to get Jocelyn started up with something called Creative Memories.

There was Beau in the midst of the swirl, him meeting all these people, him tall enough so that I could see his eyes move now and again from whoever it was at hand and off to my right.

Here on his face was that blush, him nodding to someone I couldn't see and smiling, and then his eyes to my right again and then again.

"On Monday night? Then you'll be there at our next crop?" the woman said to me. I quick looked to her smiling too hard at me now, Jocelyn beside her and smiling just the same.

"Crop?" I said, and slowly shook my head. "A crop?"

Neither of their smiles faltered a whit, the two of them still just as bright and happy as could be despite the fact the old woman they were talking to had missed a step somewheres.

"The whole party," Jocelyn said, "where you crop pictures to fit in your Creative Memories album." She paused a moment, blinked twice. "Like we just said?"

"I'm sorry," I said, and smiled myself. "All these people, and the talking," I said.

But my eyes were already to Beau again, him looking to my right, and smiling at whoever, here still that blush.

And then, as if God had one more thing to show me about the way the world could be a dangerous place, a place filled with darkness and sorrow, God Himself ever and always a mockingbird on a stairstep left from a house long gone, I looked off to my right, and at this precise moment the people in my line of sight seemed somehow to part this way and that just the smallest way—a turn of the shoulders here, a turn of the head there—to reveal to me who Beau was watching.

Ruth.

She was nearly to the wall over there, the furniture and that little tree and coffee table and everything else in this small room swallowed up by all these people. From where I stood I could see she was listening to an older woman I couldn't say as I'd met yet, and she was nodding, smiling.

But then her eyes left the woman's a moment, just a glance up, and away, and right to Beau.

She was still blushing too.

"It's a precious thing," the gray-haired woman in front of me said, and I looked at her, saw her and Jocelyn both still smiling hard at me. "Cutting photos to fit those is a kind of cropping all by itself."

"What?" I said, and felt my legs beneath me begin to tremble. "What is?" I said, and let my eyes go back to Ruth. But the crowd had moved back in, and she was gone.

"Your locket," Jocelyn said, and now I could see her smile fall a little, puzzlement taking over. Both her and this woman's eyes went to my chest, and they both nodded. "Like we were just talking about?" Jocelyn said, and looked at me again.

"My what?" I said.

And then I looked down, saw what they were looking at: my hand was at the lapel of my coat, clutched between my first finger and thumb my locket, me holding on tight.

I hadn't even known I was touching it, hadn't registered the pain of holding on this hard.

I let my eyes go from my fingers, and to Beau, still there above and inside the swirl of this room. I let my eyes go to his shy smile, his blush, his nodding, and to his meeting all these people.

Someone near him, I knew, might take in the scent of burnt wood. But someone closer still would know he'd lost a child many years ago, and had spent most of this last one reckoning himself to that gift from God that would never go away: the death of a child.

Now my own pain came to me, and I knew in fact that my fingers were pressing too hard to the locket on my lapel, and to the photos of those I'd lost myself.

My husband, and my son.

I looked again to Jocelyn and the woman, nodded, agreed that a locket was a precious thing, agreed, yes, to attend the next crop, all while still my fingers burned on the locket, and burned, and while Beau smiled and nodded and talked, his eyes stealing again and again away from them all, and to my Ruth.

I glanced once more toward where I'd seen her. But I'd lost her, between us now too many people, and still my legs trembled, and still my fingers burned.

Chapter 22

THE DOCTOR WHOSE effort this all was leaned into the room, hollered over us all, and brought the loud to a stop. He wasn't but maybe five foot tall—his wife, the blunt-cut, bone thin blonde, had to be a half foot taller—and round as a melon, glasses low on his nose. His front shirt pocket was heavy with index cards, one for each of his patients, I imagined, and his Christmas tie—snowmen throwing neon ornaments at one another—too snug at his throat.

But like everyone here, there was something to him smiling. He started right away to parceling us out like we were Cub Scouts at a pack meeting, and I couldn't help but think of when Mahlon was a boy and Pack 32 would meet once a month over to the elementary school beside the cemetery.

His smile wasn't the pained and pasted on one you might expect for having to divvy us up, move us on through a nursing home too warm and full of the smells that made it a place none of us wanted ever to be. This was smiling true, and he went person to person around the room, each of us calling out to him the expected number we were to give—we were counting off from one to four—so that we'd be in even groups.

I listened for Ruth's voice, but as he went along the murmuring of us all started up. Everyone here knew the man, put in a word to him as he went along, and then he was at Jocelyn in front of me.

"Three?" she said, like it was a test, and the doctor nodded once, sure and certain and still smiling. Then he turned to me, smiling right into my eyes, and I let out "Four" almost too soft to hear.

"Miss Naomi?" he said. He put out his hand to me, and I let go the locket, put my hand to his without any thought at all, nowhere in the touch any pain.

"Yes," I said, puzzled and fearful I'd missed

yet again an introduction, a face I'd said hello to once already.

"Jocelyn's told us a lot about you and Ruth," he said, still holding my hand, "and we want you to know we're glad you're here with us."

I looked at him, looked at him. I made no move to speak, made no move to be polite and utter for this stranger words could get ahold of anything at all. There was before me only the something I couldn't name in the smile he still gave, and in the sound of these friends all piled in a room too small, before us all a mission of kindness that had to feel even to the littlest ones here a kind of chore more than an occasion for the joy it seemed was here with us.

He let go my hand, still in him the smile, despite this speechless old woman who hadn't the courtesy even to smile back at him. He nodded at me, said, "A lot of these folks are my patients, and they really appreciate our coming every year. They do." He nodded once more, then turned to the woman with the gray hair who cropped pictures for a living. "Five!" she said, and the doctor said, "Now, Connie," and she shrugged, said, "Six?"

"You're number one," the doctor said, and the woman laughed and Jocelyn laughed, and the three or four people spread out in front of me all laughed, and started back to talking, and smiling.

And smiling.

My fingers were already to the locket, holding on.

And I wondered: was this who I had become? Was this who I was now, at the end of my life? A woman who found a smile a remarkable thing? One who found the possibility of joy a suspect notion?

Was this, finally, Naomi?

"Thank you, everybody, for coming out tonight," the doctor shouted. He was in the center of the room, though I could only see him along and between the people before me. I hadn't heard Ruth's voice at all.

But there was Beau, across the room and to my left, in the back corner where the sofa and one of the chairs met. He was looking down to beside him, had his finger to his lips, shushing the boys, I was certain, his thick green sweater and gray turtleneck what I had no choice but to see was handsome on him.

He was handsome, and he too, even inside his shushing the boys beside him, was smiling.

"I need y'all to get into your groups," the doctor said. "Sharon's got the Xeroxes of the carols," and now his wife's hand shot up beside him, in it a sheaf of papers. "Let's get all the number ones on out the door and over to the south pod," he said. Somebody said, "We're number ones! We're number ones!" followed by a fall of laughter, and people shuffled through and between us and toward the entrance to the room.

Among them Beau, and I caught glimpses between people of the two boys still with him, holding on to his arms as they went.

He looked over to me once he was near the doorway out. He raised his eyebrows and smiled, nodded, then did the same for Jocelyn beside me, and they were gone.

Next came the twos, and the threes, and here was Ruth moving off with that group, wedged in the knot of people. She paused to look over at me. She was smiling, and put a hand up, gave a small wave, mouthed *See you later,* and I had to smile back at her, give a nod. She looked better somehow, as though she'd managed a few deep breaths in and out, though it still seemed her cheeks were too red.

But she was smiling, and once she'd waved to me her eyes cut to a woman pushed up beside her. Ruth opened her eyes a little wider to her, smiled a little broader, nodded quick: they were talking, the two of them.

Yet Jocelyn still stood in front of me, made no move to head out with her group, the threes, her eyes to the people moving off.

"That's you, isn't it, sweetheart?" I said. "Number three?"

She turned to me, quick put out a hand to my arm, gave a little shrug. She was smiling, but in her eyes was concern, her eyebrows together, that smile just a bit smaller than only a moment ago, when we'd been surrounded by folks.

"I don't want you to be left alone without any family, Aunt Naomi," she said. "I know how it can be when you're with a brand-new set of people. When it feels like you don't know a person in the world, and everybody else is carrying on like it's their birthday." She paused, let her whole hand hold on to my arm, as though she meant to lead me somewhere I didn't want to go. "Believe me," she said, her words pitched small now, somewhere I'd never heard from her. "I know what it's like to feel like that. And I just don't want you to."

"Too late for that," I said, my voice even smaller than hers, even softer than what little bustling was going on with the last of us left in here, the sofa suddenly with us again for the people who'd left, and here now were the chairs pushed against the wall, the plastic

Christmas tree on the coffee table still and all only a plastic Christmas tree.

All of it the same as the moment before we'd walked into a room with a man named Beau inside, waiting to break into my daughter's heart for nothing other than sport.

"Excuse me?" Jocelyn said, and gave a short shake of her head, squinted up her eyes at me. "What did you say?"

"I said you go on ahead. I'll be fine," and I reached to her with my free hand, touched at her own arm. I gently gave her the smallest shove away, just enough, I hoped, that she wouldn't see I meant it the way I did: I wanted to be left alone. And all of it saddled with a smile of my own.

"You sure?" she said. She tilted her head to one side, eyes still squinted at me.

"I'm certain," I said, and patted her arm.

She took a step from me, hesitated, shook her head one more time. "You'll be fine with this crowd," she said. "And you feel free to find us if you need to."

She smiled once more, and I thought I might've seen in her eyes some kind of relief: she was done baby-sitting me. She turned, called, "Marjorie!" and was out of the room.

★ ★ ★

WE MOVED ON out into the hallway, and to whatever pod it was left to us, led by the doctor himself. There were maybe eight of us, husbands and wives and children all dressed in greens and reds to one degree or another. They were all of them walking and chatting and making an occasional word to me, as though I were a part of them. I kept toward the back of the group, my eyes more often than not to the linoleum squares of the floor, careful not to look up for fear someone would see me and feel he had to bring me into the circle of friends they all seemed to have been their whole lives long.

But I wanted none of it. I wanted to be left alone, and kept my hands in my coat pockets, my coat still on despite the warmth in here, in my right hand the sheets of Mary Margaret's letter, the lavender of them something I could feel at my fingertips, and the thin loops of her frightened handwriting, even that word *Love* at the end of it. I could feel it all, there in the pain of my fingers pushed deep down into my pocket.

The doctor stopped at the first door on this hallway, a hallway the same empty as each one we'd walked so far, and gave us the routine we were to follow in each room: we'd sing three songs, the last one always "We Wish You a

Merry Christmas," the other two something from the quick list of lyrics printed on the sheets everyone but me had a copy of: "Silent Night," of course, and "Jingle Bells" and "O Little Town of Bethlehem" and five or six others. But it was always "We Wish You a Merry Christmas" we were to end with, and then we'd be out the door and moving on to the next room.

I knew already what to expect this night, knew from the years of visiting friends in homes just like this up in western Massachusetts, no matter if it was Christmas or the Fourth of July: we were here to see people my age and older, some younger, all marking time for what was coming at them next: death. Plain and simple.

We moved into the room, the doctor first, me last, to find a woman laid out as though she were already gone. She lay flat on the hospital bed, blankets heaped neatly so that all you could see of her was her head on the pillow. Her hair, what was left of it, was nearly transparent, a thin gray halo about her head, her cheeks sunken in and eyes closed, her skin yellow and gray both.

There was no one in the room with her, only a single potted plant on the nightstand to her right, above us a television turned to

Jeopardy! with the sound turned off, and then the doctor started right in with "We Three Kings."

He sang alone the first few notes, smiling and nodding at us all and at the woman, and then the room gathered in with him, and they were singing, first the adults and then the three children we had with us, a boy and two girls, none of them more than five or six and looking frightened for every good reason at the mystery of what lay before them.

Age. And being alone.

I feared the woman might startle at the sound of these voices in the room of a sudden and frighten these children even further, but in the same moment I thought maybe, truly, she was beyond hearing anything from us, her so very near her end.

We finished that song, started in on "Silent Night," and then the woman's eyelids fluttered.

They did not open, only quick moved as though struggling up from a dream she might be inside. Then her mouth began to move, her lips touching just barely at what looked like words, her still and never moving, no sounds from her.

For a moment there came a softer spot in the singing, everyone here seeing this happen, the movement of eyes and lips to a song we all knew by heart. The children looked at one another, still singing, and I watched from where I stood just inside the door a father place his hand on one of the girls' shoulder. He stood behind her, and let his hand settle there, while she looked at her friends. Then he patted her once, twice, and she looked forward, at the woman whose lips still moved, eyelids still fluttered, her singing in this way the carol.

And then we were done, moved out of the room singing "We Wish You a Merry Christmas" and into the hallway, no words between us on what we'd just seen, and now we were in a room where lay a woman with Parkinson's, her head moving in a slow quiver, but a smile on her still. She had her hair set fresh, as though somebody just today had come in and done it, the silver-blue curls perfect, and she wore a pink peignoir set, the robe tied off in a neat satin bow at her throat, both her hands clasped at her chest. She was sitting up full in the bed, and tried to sing along with us, joy right there in her eyes, though her words were only stumbling in now and again.

But there was something in the practiced way she held her hands at her chest, and how perfect her hair had been done, and even this peignoir set and that perfect bow that gave me to think she might very well be one of the women my mother washed clothes for from over on Bennett Street all those years ago. Back when our yard had been filled with lines of clean clothes like midday ghosts in the breezes off the harbor.

Then it came to me: all those Old Village women who'd paid my momma were dead, just like my momma was. If anything this woman might be a daughter of one of those families, maybe even someone I knew. A classmate two rows over from me there at Mount Pleasant Academy, a girl I'd always been sure to ignore for the fact my momma'd washed the very clothes she wore.

While my Eli sat behind me, jabbed my shoulder with a pencil now and again just to hear the laugh his pals gave when I jumped.

Here was my Eli, and here was me. Still just that girl sitting at the desk in front of him three years running.

Still ignoring the girl two rows over. Still acting like she wasn't alive, for the embarrassment that came upon me with how clean her clothes were, how white and crisp a blouse. Even if, right here and now, the distance between her and myself was so small.

I was after staying hidden, I knew, inside my desire to run from *me*, and from the gift I'd had all my life and hadn't had at all. The gift of my husband's forgiveness so deep it made no mention of my sin.

My song was one of nothing more than burden, my story nothing more than fear.

But they were mine.

We started in on the last song, yet again "We Wish You a Merry Christmas," the children already edging away from the foot of the bed, the parents looking toward the door and smiling one to the other for the good work they were proud to be doing this night.

And then the woman looked at me, our eyes meeting and holding a moment.

Our eyes were on each other, and though it seemed a curse in this instant, seemed yet again as empty and full a moment as a mockingbird on a concrete step, I saw in her eyes that she might just in this instant be the one to recognize *me*.

She was a woman I'd already assigned a house on Bennett Street, a classmate of mine wearing clean clothes at the expense of my momma's red hands. But she was looking at me, and smiling that joy out to me, joy borne of a visit by strangers, one of them perhaps she thought she knew.

And then she nodded, hope still in her, I saw, that indeed I might be someone she knew come to visit here in a place warmer now than it had ever been, more filled than ever with the smell of the end it surely was. She nodded.

And I let my eyes fall from hers, because I was after hiding.

I looked down from her eyes the smallest distance, until I came to her hands, still clasped at her chest in the same practiced measure of joy as when we'd first started singing. Here were her hands, pale white and thin.

As thin as mine. As bone thin and spotted as they'd been when I opened my eyes to see my pale hand sharp against the shoulder of Ruth's black dress that first morning after, the skin on my hands and this woman's both as thin as the frost on the rooftops outside Ruth and Mahlon's window.

But in this moment I saw too in my heart and head my momma's hands, saw just then her hands red from washing this girl's clothes and hanging them in the midday breeze earlier this August afternoon.

I saw my momma's red hands holding high a cast-iron skillet above a coffee can on the stove, my momma straining to pour off hot grease, the thin stream of it into the can still and forever like brown molten glass on this August evening. Here were my momma's hands again, the red of them, her wrists beginning to quiver for the weight of the cast-iron skillet.

No sir, I heard from the front room, then *Yessir.*

My Eli, and my daddy.

And here were my own hands—the hands of a young girl, me—taking up the skillet from my momma, and me settling it there on the stovetop, and then me—*me*—taking up my momma in my own arms, my hands gentle on her shoulders and holding tight this first evening I was no longer a child.

Here too were my momma's hands on my own shoulders, holding on even tighter than I was to her, but letting me go all the same.

She was letting me go in holding me this tight this August night, when I would begin my life with Eli.

And now, now, the woman laid out under blankets two rooms back, the woman whose lips moved just the smallest way, her eyelids fluttering like whispered words themselves, was my own momma.

And now here were ghosts cluttered around me, invisible but evidenced by the way they brought to me my life, and my loss, same as you couldn't see the wind that moved those sheets in our yard, but knew there was wind all

the same. Here they all were, in just this moment of a woman's eyes meeting mine, in a
nod of acquaintance, and in my eyes falling
from hers in cowardice, and in shame.

Ghosts: my momma, and my daddy. My
brother Mahlon, his movie-star mustache and
threat of a palmetto bug to my bed, and now
here were the ghosts of the girls, though they
were not dead, but lost all the same for the fact
of my making us move here and away from
them, in my will to do this a kind of death all
the same: here was Carolyn, and Phyllis, and
Hilda.

And here was Mary Margaret.

And here, I could see and not see, touch and
not touch, was my Mahlon, and my Eli.

Here too, though nothing more than a
breath in this wind of lost lives, nothing more
than a moment of air, was a boy in a fireman's
arms eighteen years ago.

Here was Beau's Ollie.

And I wanted to ask all of them, any of
them, wanted to shout to them and whisper or
simply speak with my heart so broken I could
barely breathe, How is it that the human heart
can live through all it has visited upon it?

How is it any of us end up here, at the tail
end of this life, without being crushed one way
and another by the sheer weight of the histo-

ries we all of us have lived out, and how is it
the human heart can endure in the face of the
truth history does not end until the last breath
we give out? How is it that joy and sorrow, like
twin stars, never touch each other, and never
disappear from the same night sky of our souls?

How is it, I wanted to ask and could not ask,
that the human heart endures?

But who could I ask? And who could
answer?

Then we were finished in this room, suddenly with me husbands and wives and children all alive, all alive, while sweeping beside
and around and through me were still these
ghosts, and now we were leaving the woman
whose eyes I could not meet, my classmate and
my stranger, the all of us suddenly back out
into an empty hall that carried in that emptiness as much of an answer to what I wanted to
know as any of these strangers I traveled with,
the all of us too burdened with our own histories ever to find an answer. We were moving,
moving, room to room to room, so that we
might visit people my age whose hearts had
not yet surrendered to the crushing weight of
sorrow.

"Just a few more now," the doctor said,
"then we'll be finished. Come on now," he
said, smiling and nodding outside yet another

door, gesturing us all in with his free hand, while still those glasses rode low on his nose, and while still his shirt pocket bulged with index cards, on each of those cards a history, an impending loss, a probable death. All carried in a shirt pocket, while still he smiled.

"This is Mr. Gervais," he said, herding in the kids first, the rest of us after, me of course and always last. "Mr. Gervais, and his boy Andrew," he said.

Ghosts surrounded me. They circled me, bounded me, clustered about me as slowly we moved into this next room, and now we were here.

And then suddenly, wholly, all of my ghosts were gone.

Here in the room lay a man in bed, the bed cranked up so that his head lay back against the pillow. Beside him sat another man, his son.

They were holding hands.

The father's mouth was open, his eyes taking us all in. He was no older than any of the others. No older than me. He had white hair and skin the yellow and gray of the first woman we'd seen. He wore a blue cardigan sweater, his blanket up to his chest. His son sat in a chair beside him, had on jeans and a plaid flannel shirt, had brown hair and eyes. No older than my own Mahlon.

Father, and son.

The son made to stand at our moving in, still with his father's hand in his, but the doctor said from behind me, "No, Andrew, no, you stay put."

The son was looking at the doctor, behind me here in the doorway for having herded us all in, and then his eyes met mine, same as the woman in the room we'd just left.

I was a part of this other group, these other people who seemed somehow happy.

He counted me among these people, I saw, and then the father looked at me and smiled, though his head did not move for what I knew now had to be a stroke. Just that smile, and the work of it, the effort and misery. But the joy, too.

The joy.

He smiled at me, gave to me in just that smile what he could.

A smile, given to me.

And already, even before the next carol had begun, my chest seemed to rock in me, and my eyes clouded over, and the pinch in my heart of my life without my husband and son became a vise cinching down on me for what I knew must be the very last time, the very last time. I knew this, knew it as fully as I'd known the light down here would never be what it

had been when I was a girl, and now I felt the
fact of my feet moving me backward, my
hands in my coat pockets pushed deep as they
could ever reach, Mary Margaret's letter like
broken glass in my hand—*Lonny Thompson
passed away,* I could feel cut into my fingers,
Lonny Thompson passed away—all of it, all of it,
swirling and circling into me with these two
men I did not know but knew all the same
looking at me, and smiling, one nearly dead
and the other only a moment of black ice away
from his own.

Father, and son.

Husband, and husband.

I felt all this, and knew suddenly and deeply
and fully what it meant to be alive, because I
seemed in this small moment so very far from
it: to be alive was to be the one in bed and to
have lived your life so that there would be
someone beside you, someone there to hold
your hand no matter the quiver, no matter the
cold of it or the dead white skin and frail bones
hiding underneath that skin. No matter the
cluster of ghosts you carried with you every
breath you took in.

And to be alive was to be the one in the seat
beside the bed, too, the one holding that hand.

To be alive was to live in a way such that
you were both of these people: the comforted

and the comforting, the loved and the loving, so that finally all you were, all that you had lived your life to become, the sum total of each sunrise and sunset you'd ever managed to witness, was to love.

To live was to receive love, and to give it away.

Forgive me, God, I believe I whispered, while all this swirled down and into me, and while still it seemed my history would crush me under the weight of my own unwillingness to give love away.

Eli had forgiven me.

Lonny was dead.

And I would be soon.

Forgive me, I whispered.

To have received the love I had from my Eli, and to have given it away. This was who Naomi was to have been, I saw.

Eli, I whispered, then *Mahlon.*

And then I felt the ground give way beneath me, this vise breaking me in half, and now the edges of the room began to whirl and pop, here at the center father and son, father and son, until finally it seemed my heart could no longer endure, and I fell away.

Chapter 23

N*aomi?*

Do you remember the day we met each other?

Where is my Eli, and where is my comfort?
And where is the husband's arm around the shoulder of his wife as she whispers her son's name?

His clothes are rough at first, and cold. He pulls the quilts back over them both, and turns to her beneath them all, and takes her in his arms, and holds her.

★   ★   ★

And her skin against his begins to heal, to soften, to gain warmth from the quilts, from his arms, from him. She begins to heal.

Eli. My husband.
My love.
I allow open my hand, clutched tight in my fist what I have pledged to keep close.
A locket. Gold, and simple. No filigree, no engraved words.

What will we put on this side?
Whoever we find. Whoever it is God gives us to take a picture of.
And what if there's more than one?
What if there's more than one?
Then we'll have to get you another one. But keep this one close.
Keep this close.
I promise.

Naomi?
Do you remember the day we met?
Naomi?

★   ★   ★

I remember a young woman married a little over a year, and moving in just this day to a home in a town she and her husband have been led to by her husband's best friend.

They will begin the rest of their lives here in this western Massachusetts town, in this quiet valley, in this part of the world she would never have believed she might live in.

Only a moment before, a heartbeat before, she had been a teenage girl in a light cotton dress, a girl who walked pinestraw littered through woods, a warm and prickly carpet beneath her, a girl born and raised in South Carolina light, in a small town on a deepwater creek that led to a harbor that led to the great green sea.

But here she is now, with her love, and a new life, in New England.

I remember, too, her husband had stopped for a while the unloading of boxes from the trailer they had hauled here, and had left her alone in the house to go see the garage he and his best friend had leased to begin their business together. She is alone, and emptying boxes, arranging their life just so, just so: they had pieced together the bed first, and here she is putting on the sheets, and in the moment when she lifts the top sheet, snaps it open over the bed to let it fall free and full to the mattress already covered

with the bottom sheet, there comes to her a moment
of her momma's life: the washing of sheets back
home, and hanging them on the lines out to the big
backyard, those sheets like midday ghosts in the
breeze off the harbor.

Only a moment, only a moment, and then the
sheet falls to the bed, and she smiles at her own life
set up now, and the adventure this all seems it will
be: life. Hers, her husband's. Their life.

Theirs.

She moves to the foot of the bed, edges between
boxes of clothes and towels and shoes to reach down,
tuck in the corners, making ready for when she and
her husband will climb into this bed together in their
new world, and start their life. She tucks in both
corners, then makes her way to the box set atop the
dresser, and she reaches in, brings from within it the
quilt her momma made for them both. A Wedding
Ring, bright piecemeal shards of color sewn into
rings against a white background, and I remember
how she turns with the quilt in her arms, and lays
it out on the bed, and with all the care she can give,
with all the attention and grace she can give, as
though this were a prayer in itself, she unfolds the
quilt, and sets it out on the bed, neat and squared
and centered just so, just so.

I remember she turns from the bedroom then, and
moves to go to the kitchen, but she stops there in the
doorway out, looks one way and the other, confused

just this moment at this new house, and which way to the kitchen, this house a new world all its own, terrain she will have to learn to navigate, after a year in a cramped apartment three hours from here.

But the kitchen is only just there to her right and through the doorway, and she goes into the room, maneuvers around boxes to the sink for no other reason than to look out the window above it, and to see this new world she lives in.

She will make lunch in a minute, she thinks, and she looks out the window above the sink, at the small strip of yard between her house and the one next door, the grass still green this far into fall, leaves off the trees already so that she can see the pale blue clapboard of the house next door. She can see too the last remnants of daffodils clustered beneath the bay window across from her, the plants only brown mops flat to the ground.

She can imagine them in spring, as she stands at the sink. She can imagine them full and green, their blooms shouting for how bright a yellow they will be.

And then she sees her, a woman, there at the bay window of the house next door, looking out at her.

Looking at Naomi.

She has black hair, and wears glasses in a thin metal frame. She has on a blue-checked collared dress, and holds back with one hand a curtain edge.

Then she seems to smile, though there is some-

thing brittle to that smile, and in the way she lifts a hand just barely, and seems to wave at Naomi.

Naomi waves back, too quick, she knows even as she lifts her hand, and the woman's smile through the window across from her seems to gain somehow, but then she lets fall the curtain edge from which she'd peered, and the woman is gone.

Just like that. As though it were a dream, but not.

And I remember Naomi knows something just then. She knows something of this woman's heart, knows there is something broken inside her, and she knows that this woman, her new neighbor, will not come to visit. It is as if a pact has already been sealed between them, with the fact of the woman's smile, and the fact of her hand raised in only the smallest way: she will not come to Naomi's house, as people in a neighborhood do.

She has seen the woman's face, her eyes, and the brittle there. She knows.

And sets about doing what she will to make a friend of this woman next door. A woman, she'd seen, no older than herself. Most likely a young bride just like Naomi is a bride, and already she has the oven on, and finds in the box set atop the kitchen table the canister of flour, and the tin of baking powder, the can of lard. She finds in another box, this one on the counter beneath the cupboards, her mixing bowl, in the box beside it her tea towels.

When they arrived this morning, they had found the icebox already stocked by her husband's best friend, inside it the buttermilk he knew they used for just what she was setting about to do, and eggs as well, bacon and cheddar cheese and butter and even four bottles of Coca-Cola, two bottles of Rolling Rock. There'd been no note on the door of the icebox, but they had both known who had put it all there. They had known.

He is a good man, her husband's best friend.

And now he has provided for her what she needs to make for the woman next door, her neighbor. Maybe, her friend.

She knocks on the kitchen door, at the back of the house, because this is the sort of friend she wants to be: a kitchen door friend, and she waits, waits.

And then the door opens, slowly, and here she is, the woman with black hair and glasses, that blue-checked dress.

Here is that smile, the brittle of it.

And I remember Naomi holding out to her a plate of biscuits, still hot, the plate covered with a blue and white striped tea towel, Naomi's hands beneath it warm for the warmth of the plate in this late fall day, and she thinks she might be able to see her own breath before her in this sun shining down on them both this first day in the new world.

My hands warm for the warmth of the plate this late fall day.

My hands.

"Come in," the woman says, and nods, seems almost to bow away from her, and she is inside, the kitchen warm and snug. A home.

"My name's Naomi," she says, and turns to the woman pushing closed the door behind her, and here are the woman's hands, reaching up almost hesitantly to take the plate, and she smiles again, says, "I'm Mary Margaret."

Mary Margaret sets the plate on the table there in the bay window, motions carefully for Naomi to sit, and then turns from her, opens a cupboard, pulls down two small plates. She gets forks from a drawer, pours coffee for them both from the percolator on the stove, all without word, and all without her eyes meeting Naomi's.

"You don't even know what I brought!" Naomi says and gives a little laugh.

Mary Margaret stops pouring coffee into the second cup, the pot poised over it. This is when their eyes meet.

Mary Margaret blinks once, twice, and I remember there is a moment that passes between us just then. There is a moment of time that will cement us together, through these early years of our marriage, when it seems the mystery of how a man and woman can live together and still stay in love might some-

times never be solved; and through the years when our children will swoop in and carry us away with them and these friends we have known all these years may receive from us no more than a passing nod as we drive past each other in cars on our way to other moments; and a moment between us that will sustain us somehow, somehow, through the accumulation of our histories, our sorrows and losses and betrayals and hands holding tight to each another, no matter the pain of how tight we hold on to one another.

There is a moment that passes between us that becomes friendship.

Mary Margaret looks at me, my words—You don't even know what I brought!—still hanging in the air like the breath I believed I might could see while I stood outside her kitchen door, waiting for her to ask me in.

She says, "You brought you." She pauses, draws in a small breath, on it a kind of relief at being able just to speak this way, to show in her words her heart, I can see. I see this, all in a single breath drawn in.

"You brought you," Mary Margaret says. "That's all that matters."

She smiles then, a smile that somehow gives way to what looks a kind of faith in me for simply sitting here, for bringing me here, to her table.

And there is nothing for me to say, the only words

to utter my hands to the plate of biscuits, and pulling
away the blue and white striped tea towel.

Then we sit, and we talk, and Mary Margaret
takes a biscuit, breaks off a piece of it, tastes it, all
the while on her face a kind of contemplation, and
she closes her eyes, smiles even further, even broader,
the two of us young brides who have been married
only a year or so—our anniversaries are three weeks
apart, we've already discovered—and suddenly she
stands, goes to a cupboard beside the sink, opens it,
and pulls down a bottle of maple syrup, then turns
to the cabinet below the counter, opens it, and brings
out a small saucepan.

In a moment she's settled the pan on her stove,
opened the bottle of syrup and tipped in a little, the
stove eye clicked on.

She looks back at me, says, "There's nothing
wrong with your biscuits. They're perfect. But this
is just the thing. This is just the ticket," and already
the syrup is warmed, and she brings the saucepan
right to the table, drizzles warm syrup on the biscuit
centered there on my plate.

And I take my fork, slice through and pick up a
piece, and taste it.

It's beautiful.

She stands before me, the saucepan still in hand,
her other hand to her throat and just touching, waiting for me.

Waiting for Naomi, a friend already.

"Just the ticket," I say, and I smile, and Mary Margaret smiles.

A smile is a remarkable thing.

And Mahlon drizzles warm syrup over his biscuits every morning because of Mary Margaret, our windows black in winter, gray and lavender in summer, with us the smell of coffee and biscuits, and plans for the day, talk of deliveries and rec-league softball games and the crafts fair over to the commons in Amherst.

Mary Margaret there with us every moment, for the gift of maple syrup, and here too my momma with the gift of biscuits, here as well my brother Mahlon with the gift of his name, and with us as well Eli with the gift of the notion to name our son after my brother.

Everyone, everywhere, all of them a gift, our lives from one end to the other, inside a world that never changed and a world shot through with it—ever and always a gift.

Naomi?

Do you remember the day we met each other? I remember it, and hope the memory of it brings good thoughts to your heart. It does to mine.

I remember this, remember it clear as sunlight down through pine, sunlight scattered like diamonds at my feet.

I remember.

★ ★ ★

How does the heart endure?

How?

It endures, because it is not alone. Because God is with us, the heart is never alone.

Naomi?

HERE WERE faces above me, faces I knew.

I knew them all.

"Naomi?" I heard again, and here was a face closer to me, closer, and I knew this face too, just as I knew all these faces clustered and hovering over me.

But I knew this face better. I knew this one, and I reached a hand from wherever my hand lay and touched his face, and I was smiling at him. Now he was smiling at me, his mustache moving with that smile, and his brown eyes moving, and he blinked, let out a breath. He reached to my face, too, and I felt his fingers, the rough of them, just touch my cheek, just push back a strand of my hair behind my ear.

And I took in the scent of burnt wood on him, as anyone could.

And I took in the sorrow that was all his

own, saw on his eyes the depth of what he knew about loss.

"Naomi," he said, still smiling, and he looked up and away from me to the faces above us, and said, quick and hushed, "Someone go tell Richard she's awake. Run."

I heard footsteps away. Beau looked back to me, said, "You just hold on, Naomi. We love you. Doctor Brookes'll be back in a second. He went to get a little bit of help. We're going to take good care of you, I promise." He nodded, still smiling, and quick looked back up and away, then to me again, nodded again.

And now I knew I was in Beau's arms, and that he was kneeling, me cradled in his hold, and I knew in the same instant his words weren't hollow comfort.

They were true. He loved me. He would take good care of me.

He was my kin, my family.

I was on the floor in the hall, I saw, above me the acoustic-tile ceiling and fluorescent lights, those faces above me the faces of those I'd sung carols with. Children's faces, and the face of a father who'd tapped his daughter's shoulder, and here were the faces of mothers and other fathers, and now here came the rush of footsteps down the hallway, and the face of the doctor, whose glasses now were pushed up

onto his nose, his eyes behind the lenses clear
and full of goodwill and care, and he was smiling too.

Then here were more footsteps, and now
here, here was the terrified face of my Ruth,
my daughter, the three of them—the doctor,
Beau, and Ruth—all above me and feeling too
close, too close.

But not too close at all.

"Naomi," Ruth cried, "oh, Naomi," her already kneeling and touching my face, and
searching me, searching me. Her forehead was
knotted up, her chin trembling with just my
name.

"It's all right," I said to her, though it seemed
I might not be saying anything at all, my voice
something inside someone else's dream.

"Oh, Naomi," she cried again, and now here
was Jocelyn above me too, all these faces in
close, and I could see behind her and above
now as well the faces of her two boys, Zachary
and Brian.

Zachary and Brian. Two boys.

And I knew them, knew the difference between them, now, now.

Brian's hair was a little thinner than his older
brother's, the blond of it a little shinier somehow.

Zachary had a freckle just below his left eye,

the smallest freckle I knew I'd ever seen, but a
freckle nonetheless. He was just the smallest bit
taller, too, and smiled a little more quickly than
his little brother, who sometimes seemed to
think a moment, hesitate a breath before letting loose with his own smile.

They were different, and it seemed in this
moment that I'd always known this, always
known, but'd never wanted to know. I'd not
wanted to bother to see what the difference
between these two crazy boys might be.

Two faces, wholly different, and new, and
familiar, all at once.

"Boys," I managed to whisper, and put my
hand up to them, or tried at least.

They smiled at me, leaned in closer among
all these faces. They were fearful smiles, full of
the strange and frightening fact of what they
were seeing: an old woman they knew, perhaps
dying, perhaps not. And they were here for it.

But they were smiling, and I knew them
both for the family they were.

"Oh, Naomi," Ruth cried again, still with
her hand to my face, and now here was a gurney from out of the blue, me being lifted onto
it, while my heart, enduring this as though it
were nothing at all, as if it were only a walk in
the woods down to a creek on a midsummer

afternoon, simply stayed with me, and endured, and endured, and endured.

"I'm fine," I whispered to Ruth, her eyes on mine and holding on hard. "You don't worry about me," I whispered.

She didn't smile, her mouth crumpled in on itself and tears falling free from the eyes my son'd seen his future in the first moment he'd said hello. Eyes I'd seen the truth and beauty of when she'd stood on our front porch the evening my Mahlon had brought her home to meet us.

Eyes right now, right now, with the same truth and beauty they ever held, and beside her Beau's eyes, the two of them above me and taking me in, taking me in, and I knew already.

I knew already.

Then I was on the gurney, the gurney then raised and clicked into place, while the faces parted, and now those tiles above me, blank as my heart had been all the months since I'd first decided to head home to the light down here, ran away above me, a long line of empty tiles and fluorescent lights and empty tiles giving way and giving way, one blank heartbeat to the next to the next to the next, while faces carried themselves alongside me: the doctor, who smiled at me and looked away and ahead of us, that smile gone until he looked back down at me and smiled again, the tie with those snowmen in a neon snowball fight bouncing with each step he took; and Ruth, her hand to my arm and holding on while she ran beside me, still no smile from her at all for the fear in her, I knew, suddenly and cleanly, that the one she'd come here with, the one she'd given herself to—*Where you go, I will go. Where you live, that's where I'll live too,* she'd said. *This is a pact between us*—was leaving her, and she would be left alone here, where the light I'd believed would save me had never shone down on me.

But I knew she wasn't alone.

The heart is never alone.

"Aunt Naomi!" I heard cried out beside me to my left, and I let my eyes leave the tiles above me, those dead heartbeats of the old life I was leaving behind me with each stride down this hallway, and I saw there, just a little beyond Beau, Jocelyn running too, and in her arms Tess.

"Aunt Naomi!" Tess cried out again, and she reached out a hand toward me. She was on Jocelyn's hip, her other arm around her mother's neck, holding tight. She was too big of a girl to be carried this way, and Jocelyn's face, I could see, was red with the effort.

But they were beside me. They were with me.

"Tess," I whispered, and I smiled at her, tried to lift my hand toward her, though she was too far away to touch, too far away.

"I'm praying for you right this minute," she said, and it was only then I saw she was smiling.

It was a smile free of fear. She was praying for me, and praying in faith, I saw in that smile.

Here was Tess, my brittle Tess, giving her prayers to the God I'd run from in coming here.

Here was joy, in giving me comfort, and her finding comfort in the giving: Tess, smiling.

"Me too," Jocelyn said, her face still that red, her hair moving as she ran alongside us. "I'm praying right now," she said.

"And me," I heard a boy call from some-where.

Zachary. I knew his voice.

"Me three," Brian called next, and I heard inside and around all this a murmuring of voices, and knew in the same moment there were people all around us as we moved, these carolers come to watch me hurried off to a hospital.

But they were all in agreement with Tess, I

could hear on their voices, their small words offered up to me. They were with Jocelyn, and Brian and Zachary, and with Tess: "We're praying for you," I heard, and heard again, and again, women and men and children alike as we turned left and into another hall, all of us hurrying.

They were all praying for me, and didn't even know me.

"You picked the right crowd to have something like this happen in," Beau said then, smiling broader now. He glanced down at me, and back up. "A doctor, a truckload of people praying for you, and all of it across the street from the hospital." He glanced down at me again, and let out a small laugh.

"Don't forget," the doctor put in, "and a fire captain thrown in there." He was a little winded for all this running, but he gave out a laugh too.

And somehow, somehow, I managed one too, a small and quiet laugh, but a laugh just the same, the feel of it in me almost too foreign to recognize, some language I'd known but forgotten.

"It seemed convenient," I said.

Both Beau and the doctor let out one more laugh, looked down at me at the same time, both smiling.

Ruth was still here above me, still running with us all, and I could see she was trying at a smile, trying at the smallest laugh. But there was nothing coming of it. Still she cried.

"I'm fine," I said to her, my eyes locked on hers. I whispered, "You don't worry about me. This is God getting us through. This is His tender mercies getting us through," I said, and smiled. "He's holding us in His hand," I whispered.

Her eyes hung on mine a moment longer, and though it seemed the joy I was trying to give her, the shard of hope that was suddenly in me with the good knowledge of what was to come of all this something I wanted to hand her like a Christmas gift she could unwrap and hold close—though none of that seemed to find its way into her eyes on mine, still I hoped, and felt joy.

Here was joy, because I'd been forgiven.

"Naomi," she said, her voice a whisper of fear and loss and sorrow about to be. "Naomi," she whispered, "what can I do?"

And I whispered to her a gift I'd been given myself so many years ago, words a treasure I'd been given so many years ago:

"You brought you," I whispered, and smiled. "That's all that matters."

She looked at me, puzzlement to her face for

a moment at this old woman's words, at the strange ramble I figured she was hearing out of me on a gurney in a nursing home.

But then there came into her eyes a kind of recognition, as though she knew what I meant, and as though perhaps her own words had come back to her—*Where you go, I will go. This is a pact between us*—and I believed I could see inside her eyes a smile all her own, and meant for me.

Then her eyes broke from mine. She was looking ahead of us, and now she peeled away from me for the fact we were bumping through a doorway, the ceiling above me giving way to a porch roof, the air out here suddenly cold and drenched in orange lights flashing all around.

But even inside all this, all this, I could see stars above me once we were out from beneath that porch, stars washed out and thin for all the light, and washed out too for the noise now of people hollering one thing and another about me and my pulse and blood pressure and more and more and more.

Here were stars, the faintest splinters of light that came up every night I'd ever been alive, a fact that only just this second seemed a loss for how little I ever looked at them.

Same as the night I'd looked up at them,

when the news of my brother Mahlon's passing came to us in a yellow piece of paper on that roofless porch, those concrete steps. Here were stars, fixed and shining, each in the same place I'd ever seen them, me nothing beneath them for the fact I never looked at them, took them and their placement up there as much for granted as the next breath I'd take in.

Taken as much for granted as the love of a daughter-in-law who still had so much life before her.

They were stars, never moving, fixed up there joy and sorrow both, and both beautiful and certain, fixed as ever they would be.

Stars, beautiful and certain.

Chapter 24

Fibrillation, Doctor Brookes called it once he'd gotten me settled into my room. Not a heart attack exactly, but an irregular heartbeat. Enough out of sync with itself to make me black out a minute, but even from that first word from him on what'd happened to me, it all seemed too much fuss.

He was leaning against the bed easy as you please, though his smile was gone, him serious and measured. It'd been a good hour or two since we'd busted in to the emergency room, where they hooked me up to an IV and a heart monitor, then set about to fussing and fussing over me. Then we'd gone into another room to take an EKG, and to another room where we'd simply stayed put, waiting for my room. I'd been tired through it all, but more than that: my breathing was short, and my chest seemed heavier, my heartbeat strange and foolish and stubborn in the odd way it beat inside. Through it all, too, here had been Ruth holding my hand, Beau alongside as well.

Then we'd made our way here, to a room with a window perhaps I'd looked at from the nursing home parking lot across the street earlier this evening, before the all of everything changed.

Because it had all changed. Everything.

The doctor had on a lab coat, his glasses back low on his nose. He'd finally loosened that tie, and shook his head slowly as he told me about the blood thinners I'd have to be on from now on, the beta blockers and the Coumadin I'd have to take. He told me of the ambulance ride we'd need to make over the bridges and on into the heart center at Roper Hospital downtown in a day or two. I'd be here at least five days, he'd already decided. I'd just have to stay put, to relax and get used to the relaxing.

Five days. I'd be home on Christmas Eve.

Beau and Ruth stood at the foot of the bed while the doctor kept on about how fortunate we were to have the episode happen where it had, though I'd only joked about the convenience of it when they'd wheeled me through the nursing home and out into the night beneath those stars.

But he was serious about everything he told me. I heard it in the way he'd said that word *episode,* on him when he'd spoken it no sense of the stuffiness of that word, the stiff sound of it out the mouth of a man I'd watched only a while ago holler about who was what number and where to get the Xeroxes.

What'd happened was serious, I could tell. And still it all seemed too much of a fuss.

"I'm just sorry to have to be one more index card for your shirt pocket," I said to him, and shook my head. I reached up even through the tired of all I'd been through that night, and touched at his shirt pocket. "Hope my card's not the straw that broke the camel's shirt pocket," I said.

He reached to my hand, shook his head at me, smiled. He said, "We're going to take care of you, Miss Naomi."

"But I'm fine," I said. Because I was, and I would be.

That was when Gordon and Melba and Ellen and Robert and even Emily all broke into the room in a careful rush, crowding in and touching at me and looking fearful and thankful and puzzled all at once. Doctor Brookes quick moved from the bed, took a step away, sizing up this new commotion.

Their faces were all to me, mouths open, tears welled up. Gordon leaned in close, had on yet one more pair of those green coveralls, this one long-sleeved for the fact of winter, the few wisps of hair on his head still wild as ever.

But here was fear on his face as he leaned in, touched at my temple. "You'll be fine," he said, and I whispered back, "Don't I know it." Gordon smiled full then, shook his head.

Melba'd already given in to crying, and took her turn, touched at my face, whispered, "You're in good hands." I nodded, wondered for a moment if she knew this doctor even though they lived all the way up to George-town.

Then I saw in her eyes what she'd meant, saw in the way she made her eyes hang on mine even full of her tears: it was God's hands she was talking about. She'd been praying for me, too, I knew. They all had.

"Don't I know it," I whispered to her as well, and put my hand up to her face. I cupped her cheek in my hand, held it there a moment.

Doctor Brookes said in a loud whisper, "Now she's got to rest, y'all. You can set up with her just a few more minutes, but then we have to move you on out. She's going to need her sleep."

"Fine," Ellen said almost in a whisper, and I saw her smiling at me down at the foot of the bed, her hands together in front of her, her curly perm curly as ever. Robert stood just behind her, his hands on her shoulders and him trying to smile. He had on his white dress shirt and tie, straight from work at the Piggly Wiggly.

Next to Ellen stood Emily in a gray sweatshirt and jeans, her hair just pulled back for how quick they must have left the house. Her eyes were red, too, and it gave me pause to think on that, a teenage girl crying over her daddy's step aunt, and I wondered what I might have done in the last year or so to deserve such attention, and came up with nothing. She was simply and always a confidante of Ruth's, the two of them every time they saw each other quiet and talking, and letting out a laugh now and again.

And I knew, too, that that boy Fatback was long gone, something Ellen'd whispered to me at Thanksgiving was due to no one other than Ruth, and words she'd given to Emily that Ellen'd never been able to pull from her.

Of course Emily stood next to Ruth, Ruth

already with an arm around her, the two of them facing me. Next to Ruth stood Beau, next to him Gordon, who'd come all the way around the bed to talk to the doctor. Gordon's arms were crossed, and he was looking over the doctor, grilling him in his way about what all was being done for me, and if they could bring me on up to Georgetown to the hospital there so's I could be closer to home.

And now here in the doorway was Jocelyn, Tess's hand holding tight to Jocelyn's left hand, Ashley holding tight to her right, and Brian and Zachary just behind her.

"Can we come in?" Jocelyn said, smiling hard for the duty she'd drawn in everyone being here with me: she was the baby-sitter.

Then Tess stepped into the room, her eyes right on mine. She was smiling just as free and clear as she had when she'd called out her prayer to me in the hallway of the nursing home.

Jocelyn had no choice but to follow, still holding Tess's hand. Jocelyn's circus-red sweater and all those bells knitted into the puppies' collars started in to jingling in the smallest, thinnest way as Tess led her in, and then here was Ashley, her without a tiara for the first time I'd ever seen. She had on a green and red striped sweatshirt and sweatpants, what looked like house slippers, her hair mussed from sleep on the way here.

Then came in my two boys, Brian and Zachary, their mouths thin lines, all seriousness and, for what seemed the first time ever, quiet.

They had on their Santa hats.

And room was made, room was made: everyone gave way for someone to stand in close beside them, until clustered here was the all of my family, sudden and perfect, and here with me.

Stars in a night sky, I thought. Fixed and certain, a bank of them spread around me, from Gordon right down to the youngest, Tess, here to my left in her green blouse, the little Christmas puppy's bright red ribbon and little brass bell on the left breast just peeking over the edge of the bed. She was in closest of them all, had snuck up under her grandma Melba's arm, her hand on the pillow beside my head, just touching my shoulder, just touching.

And Beau here, for the first time together with us all.

And Ruth.

Stars around me, I knew, and I knew suddenly, perfectly, that the light down here, the warmth of it down through pines and scattered at my feet, hadn't been the light I'd needed, no matter the way I'd believed it was.

No. Here was the light I'd needed: that of family, stars settled around me on a night when I'd been ushered by prayers to safety.

Family.

"*Did—you—get—it?*" Tess whispered, with each word a soft tap to my shoulder. She was smiling full, her eyes right on mine, touching at a secret between us, though I had no idea about what.

"Tess, now," Jocelyn said, "we don't need to be bothering Aunt Naomi over that. We don't need—"

"Get what, sweetheart?" I said, and remembered soon as I said it Tess pulling at my hand there in the front room of the nursing home, me shutting her down with my words, me too worried over how this Beau had wounded my Ruth.

"What I mailed you?" Tess said, still in a whisper. She leaned in even closer now, tapped at my shoulder yet again, and left her hand there.

I reached to her with my free hand, let it settle on hers, and I smiled. "I'm sorry," I whispered to her. "I'm sorry for being snippy with you tonight," I said, and now it was my own eyes tearing up in all this. "But honey," I whispered, "I don't know what—"

"Oh," Ruth let out from down at the foot of

the bed, then again, "Oh," and we all of us looked at her, saw her eyebrows up, her mouth open in surprise. Even Emily blinked at her, leaned a little away from her for the surprise of the word out of her.

She turned, this firmament broken of a sudden, and went to the corner of the room, lifted from there what looked like a white garbage sack. She set it on the chair down there, reached in, everyone turned and watching her, waiting for whatever this was about.

Ruth looked at us over her shoulder, a nervous sort of smile on her face for all this attention, then turned back to the bag, pulled from it my coat, the one I'd worn all night so far. The same one I'd had on at that bench at the Harris Teeter right on through to waking up on the floor of the nursing home, to find my world changed for the memory of Mary Margaret's words the first time we met.

You brought you.

Ruth lay the jacket over one arm, reached down into the pocket, and pulled from it the letter.

The lavender sheets were crumpled for how tight I'd clutched them, and the news of my being the only one left in this world to know the depth of my husband's love for me. She held them out, folded on one another, battered and creased at my own hands for the indictment of my heart they genuinely were.

Everyone's eyes were on her, and what she held in her hand, and though for a moment I thought perhaps there would come at me shame, that the discovery of the letter would let everyone here know of my sin, nothing came.

Here was peace.

Lonny had passed away. A memory had been bestowed upon me. I'd accepted the gift of forgiveness.

Ruth still had on that nervous smile, said, "You were holding on to these when you blacked out. They were in your hand." She lifted my coat from her arm, set it on the chair beside her.

At first I thought she meant the separate sheets when she'd said *they*, but then she carefully separated the sheets, picked them open ever so gently, and there inside those lavender pages, like a secret inside a secret, was an envelope, folded over on itself, crushed inside the pages from my holding too tight to the gift of forgiveness.

Ruth separated out Mary Margaret's letter, turned to my coat, and slipped the pages back inside the pocket, in her other hand now only the envelope. She looked to me while she'd done it, on her face a different kind of puzzle, and I knew already that somehow, somewhere along the long trip this night had become, us moving room to room to room, that she'd read the letter.

She'd read the letter, I could see on her eyes, and I knew right then, right then that I would have to tell her.

She made her way toward the bed, Doctor Brookes stepping aside for her. Gordon and Beau made room for her at the edge of the bed to my right, and now I remembered, as though it were itself a memory from another life, a moment out of someone else's life, me standing at the counter back at the house earlier this evening, and going through the day's mail, sifting through for whatever might arrive.

I remembered a business-size envelope, the handwritten address on it small and thin and hard to focus on, an envelope I'd slipped into my coat pocket for later when I could try and get a better look at it, or just let Ruth read to me.

Then here had been Mary Margaret's card, and that letter inside it, those two pages falling open and to the kitchen counter slow as snow in a Massachusetts woods. Gone from me any thought on an envelope put away for later.

Ruth put out her hand, held it out flat, and with her other hand unfolded the envelope.

"That's it!" Tess said from beside me. "That's it! That's it!" and she was tapping my shoulder again, her close in to Melba, who was holding on to her the gentlest way, a hand to Tess's hair and tracing through it her fingertips.

Tess was smiling, looking at the envelope, and Jocelyn put in, "You got to calm down now," her voice stern and quiet, then Zachary said, "Settle down," Brian dishing out for good measure, "Leave her alone, Tess."

"It's fine," I said to them all. "I'm fine," I said, and reached out my free hand to Ruth, took the envelope from her. But not before I let my eyes meet hers. I smiled up at her, nodded.

I had to tell her my story. I knew it in the fear I still saw there, and the puzzlement.

"Open it up!" Tess said, and now it seemed she might be jumping high as a kite if it weren't for Melba's holding her down.

Still I couldn't make out the address, the words just as small and thin. I looked at Tess, said, "Is this for me?"

"Of *course* it's for you," she said right back. "That's my penmanship," she said, and Melba gave out a little laugh, Gordon too.

"I'm afraid I need your help, sweetheart, to open it on up. My arm just isn't helping me much right now," I said, and nodded to where my left arm lay with the IV into it, the tape all over down there.

Tess quick leaned back, lifted her hands from where she'd leaned on the edge of the bed, as though she'd suddenly been burned. She looked at my arm, then me, then to my arm again.

The smile was gone, here again the kind of fragile I knew too well, too well. I whispered, "It's okay, honey. It's okay."

Beau said, "You go on ahead and open it for Aunt Naomi, Turtle."

Instantly Tess turned her head to Beau, a smile on her face again just that quick too, and she looked around at the all of us at my bed. We were all watching her, and she leaned her head a little to one side for the shyness sudden on her. Melba tickled a little under her chin, and then Tess put out her hand, took from mine the envelope.

I looked up at Beau, saw Ruth was looking at him, a small smile on her face.

"Turtle?" Ruth said. Beau shrugged, gave a little shake of the head, him still smiling. "That one goes way back," he said.

Tess already had the envelope open, the flap

torn off, and here she was pulling out something made of brown construction paper.

She unfolded it, unfolded it again, let blos-
som in her hand something I'd nearly ruined in
my hands for clinching it so tight. Then Tess
leaned onto the bed, and held out to me with
both hands her gift.

A brown construction-paper reindeer head,
its antlers cutout handprints.

Tess's hands.

Here was a red nose out of construction
paper, too, its eyes black circles drawn with a
Magic Marker on the wrinkled and creased
paper.

And here, written across the bottom in the
shape of a smile, was the word *Tess.*

I looked at it there in her hands, looked at it.
I felt my chin quiver, felt the smile I wanted to
give her tremble too, and I moved my eyes to
her, reached my free hand to her cheek,
touched the soft skin there.

How could I tell her of all the times I'd seen
these hung at Carolyn's house, given her by
her grandchildren every winter? And how
could I tell her of the Thanksgiving turkeys
they made for her as well, and of the autumn
leaves pressed between waxed paper and hung
like stained glass in her windows?

How could I tell her of the envy I'd known

all those years, when I'd known and known and known there would never be a grandchild for me?

And how could I tell her of how deeply I was thankful for her, and thankful for two boys I knew were two boys, and for a girl who knew she was a princess, and for a girl who counted my Ruth among her closest friends?

How could I tell them all how much I loved them?

I touched her cheek, felt the smooth of her skin, let my smile tremble and tremble.

"Do you like it?" she said, her eyebrows up, as though somehow she could believe I might not.

I swallowed, whispered, "More than you will ever know."

"Then I'll make you fifty of them," Brian said right out, and Zachary said, "I'll make you a hundred," and I saw out the corner of my eye, there down near the foot of the bed, two boys in Santa hats, one giving the other a small shove with his shoulder.

"Now, boys," Beau said, just like a good father will say, and Jocelyn said, "Boys."

"I'll make you a whole reindeer," Ashley said, her first words this entire time from down there between Jocelyn and her brothers. She was smiling, then yawned, and I nodded at her, said, "That would be fine, too."

"I'll make you one," Emily said, and I looked at her, me and everyone else, all our eyes suddenly on her.

"Not a whole reindeer," she said, and blinked at the sudden attention here. "Just the head," she said, her arms crossed, hip out in the teenage way she always did.

But I could see on her face she was serious in this. That there would be a gift coming from her out of all this as well.

All these gifts, and me here to receive them.

There was joy in giving comfort, something they all already knew.

I already knew how I could share the gift I'd gotten, that gift too good to keep. A gift of love so good and kind I could only do honor to by giving it away.

Here was home.

LATER, MUCH LATER, I woke up to voices, though in my sleep they hadn't been voices at all, but songs coming to me, as though across water, a great green sea; songs come to me from far away, no words to them at all. Only voices giving song.

They were songs I knew by heart, though they weren't songs of sorrow. They were songs of joy, of company, of friendship.

That was what I heard as I came up out of my sleep.

I opened my eyes to the hospital room. Morning light fell into the room through the window on my left. Though the blinds there were pulled, still sunlight made its sweet way between the slats, so that lines of shadow and light there across the blankets held me together, bound me up in their warmth.

Beneath the window lay a cot, sheets and blanket undone, Ruth's purse sitting on the pillow.

I let my eyes go to the song that'd brought me from sleep. There, past the foot of my bed, sat the two of them in chairs pushed up against the wall, Beau in the left one, Ruth in the right.

I lay there, careful not to move nor draw attention to myself waking up, because they were talking. And because I wanted to listen.

Beau was half-turned to Ruth, his face a profile against the dull yellow of the walls in here. He still had on his gray turtleneck and green sweater, his eyes thick and heavy, his face in need of a shave. He'd spent the night here, out in a waiting room, I knew, and now I could not recall when the rest of the family had left, couldn't recall any rounding up that'd been done by Doctor Brookes so's I could get some rest.

I'd only fallen asleep, and now I was awake, and listening.

He was talking to Ruth, his hands laced together in his lap, one leg crossed over the other, but with his eyes straight on Ruth. His voice stayed low and quiet, his words trailing together to give to me that song I'd heard in my sleep, and still no words came to me. Still it was only a kind of song, words carried one to the next in a peaceful string for how quiet he was speaking. A song I was happy to hear.

Ruth sat facing me, her arms crossed, her chin down. She was looking at the floor, maybe even had her eyes closed, and I could see, too, she was biting down hard on her lower lip, and now her chin touched her chest for how low she let it fall. She had on that same sweater from last night, the cream pullover cable-knit with a trim of poinsettias at the cuffs. But of course her hair was flattened out on one side, her makeup, the little of it she wore, gone.

She shook her head, and I thought I could see her smiling.

"It's true," Beau said, the first words I could make out. Still I didn't move, only watched the two of them.

Because I already knew.

Beau made to reach over to Ruth then, his hand slow out in the air between them. He held it there, held it, still with Ruth's eyes closed so that she could not know how he held it out there, ready to touch her arm, her shoulder. Ready to touch her.

But he brought it back, let it settle to his chair arm. He turned, and now he looked down, as if he'd been afraid to touch her.

And now I saw it wasn't a smile on her face, but her about to cry. She took in one quick, silver breath, on it the edge of tears, and then she stood, arms still crossed, and started carefully, quickly for the door.

But not before she paused there at the foot of the bed, and looked at me, checking on me.

I let my eyes close just soon enough, heard her take in another breath, this one even closer to the edge of sorrow she knew so well, so well, and then I heard her footsteps out into the hall, and away.

Then here came a sigh from Beau, deep and full and on its own edge of something. I opened my eyes again, saw he'd turned in his seat, had both feet on the ground now. He was leaned forward, elbows to his knees, his hands still laced together in front of him.

Then he bowed his head, took in a deep breath, let one more out.

Chapter 25

I SAW ON the clock the numbers 3:17, bright red and full of some kind of promise, even in the dark of my bedroom, even in the dark of all that'd happened since my son Mahlon had died, and since my Eli had died, and since I had sinned against him and God with what I had done with a good man named Lonny.

I saw in those numbers beside me on the nightstand something full of promise, as though in being forgiven and living in that forgiveness anything I looked at, any moment I let myself see, there was inside it the possibility for joy, for that promise, no matter how laced through and wrapped round with sorrow that moment might be.

They were only numbers on a clock on my nightstand, bright and red there in the dark. But there was promise.

And so I got up, though Doctor Brookes'd told me to stay put. But still I got up, because there seemed promise in this moment, no matter it was the middle of the night, no matter my doctor's orders, and I put on my glasses, then stood beside my bed, lifted from the foot my blue robe and slowly slipped it on, fit my feet into my slippers.

I'D GOTTEN HOME from the hospital near noon, everyone there to help, even Robert, who'd managed the miracle of a couple hours off from the Piggly Wiggly on a Christmas Eve. Here had been the fuss of it all once again, a parade of people on down the hallway of the hospital when all I'd needed was a car ride the couple of miles here to home.

But they'd all insisted, here with me Ashley leading the way, her tiara back on again and wearing a red felt cape, and Zachary and Brian with those Santa hats, the two of them pushing a wobbly-wheeled metal cart each, both carts choked with flowers of all sorts. There were cheerful arrangements of daisies and carnations, roses here and there, all laced through with little pine branches, the smallest Christmas ornaments, ribbons of green and red and silver and gold. They'd come from some of the families we'd caroled with, and friends from Ruth's work, even from neighbors up and down the street over to Quail Hollow, the Adkins, and the Deals, and the Fortners. Even a potted white hydrangea from Doctor Brookes himself.

And a dozen white roses sent from Phyllis, and Carolyn, and Hilda, and Mary Margaret.

I'd talked to Mary Margaret on the phone three times already, promised her soon as I was able that I'd visit her there in Northampton, and visit the girls, and visit Tommy too, who, she'd informed me when I talked to her just this afternoon once I'd gotten settled in, had taken a turn for the better.

"He wished me a Merry Christmas when I walked in his room this morning," she'd said, and I'd heard the smile on her.

And I would visit Mahlon and Eli, and Lonny as well. There were flowers I needed to give him, I knew, and time I needed to spend at my husband's and son's side, there in a cemetery with stone walls past which had been the leafless trees of my own betrayal.

But which now, I knew, I'd see as only the trees they were, green all summer long, that stone fence I'd built between me and my sin only a veil torn with my forgiveness.

There was time I needed to spend with them, and I would. And time, too, to spend with Mary Margaret.

We'd all moved down the hospital halls, Gordon behind me and pushing the wheelchair, Ellen holding the three Mylar balloons—red, green, and white—I'd gotten from the Creative Memories woman, Emily and Ruth already out to the parking lot and bringing up the car. Melba walked beside me on the left, Tess on the right, both of them holding a hand each, and I breathed in, took up the smell of the flowers on those carts just ahead of us, a perfume that seemed even more fragrant for the family all around me, if even in the midst of too much fuss, everyone here.

Everyone, except for Beau, who was on shift, and would be until the day after Christmas.

Beau, who'd spent more time in my room than anyone else, save for Ruth herself.

Beau, who I'd caught talking quietly with Ruth any of a dozen times since that first morning.

Beau, my kinsman.

They'd all stayed here at the house only a few minutes before heading back to their

Christmas Eve errands and whatnot, though they all wanted to stay. But the good doctor'd ordered quiet for me for the rest of the day, and Ruth'd finally herded them all out. They would be here tomorrow, Christmas dinner at our house for the fact Doctor Brookes didn't want me traveling at all. We'd see them soon enough, and then they were all gone, left to the rest of their Christmas Eve.

And perhaps that was what, finally, I'd seen in those red numbers beside me: we were here, to Christmas Day, a day of promise beyond promise. Three hours already in.

I moved for the door then. I had on my robe, and my slippers, my hair still in a net. I hadn't had it done since we'd moved down here, only had it cut now and again. I washed and set it myself now, and not even that since I'd been in the hospital. But this afternoon, once everyone was gone, Ruth had washed it for me in the kitchen sink, her hands gentle and careful and full of the love she had in her to give, and I'd wondered while she'd taken care of me when I might be able to tell her what I needed to tell her.

And when I might be able to give her what I needed to give.

But there had been to her hands in my hair

a kind of distance, a solitude she'd surrendered to, proof of it no more than the feel of her fingers in my hair, and the quiet she held within her while she shampooed, and while she slowly and carefully moved the towel about my head.

She'd said nothing, too, as we put the curlers in, no words either in the drying and combing, and then she'd finished, all of it enough to wear me out a little more than I'd thought it would. She'd brought me on back to bed, left me to rest with my hairnet on, and it came to me yet again that worrying over my hair enough to put it in a net might somehow be a sin, this vanity.

But I'd left the net on, like I did every time I went to bed, because it was what I'd always done. It was my life. Who I was.

A widow, who lived with her daughter-in-law.

A woman forgiven, and living in that forgiveness.

And then, as she'd left me there in my bed, her hand to the knob, I'd said, "Ruth."

She turned to me, tried yet again and as always she did now to bring up a smile. She raised her eyebrows, said, "Yes?"

"I love you," I said. "I want you to know that."

"I know it," she said, and'd come back to the bed, leaned to me, and held me close. "I love you, too, Naomi," she whispered.

Then she stood, and was gone, left to her the rest of her own Christmas Eve.

I TOUCHED the doorknob here in my bedroom, but turned once more to that clock, those bright red numbers filled with promise.

3:18, it read. I smiled, turned the knob in my hand, and felt the same sharp shards of pain I'd felt when a morning what seemed a century ago I'd stood at my Ruth and Mahlon's door, two coffee cups in hand, and the rest of my empty life to live.

But here was promise, and I turned the knob despite the pain, even smiled a moment for it.

I stepped out into the hall, saw already the pale and thin wash of colored light that made its way from the front room. I looked behind me, saw Ruth's bedroom door standing open at the end of the hall, darkness inside same as my room, and I knew now why there was promise in my waking up to here, and to now.

I moved along the hall, turned left and into the front room.

The Christmas tree lights were on, color bright and hidden and familiar and joyful all at once, colors that tugged at my heart. My old woman's heart that didn't know enough to let itself beat of its own accord, that didn't know enough of God's mercies to let itself seek the rhythm it had to observe. A rhythm that same God I'd believed had abandoned me had given it with my own first breath in, my history begun so many years ago.

It was a tug at my heart for all those who weren't here with me, but who I still loved and always would.

Here were only lights on a Christmas tree, nothing special at all or out of the ordinary, no more important in and of themselves than bright red numbers on an alarm clock early of a Christmas morning. Only lights, but they were here, where I knew now was my home.

Here too were those flowers, everywhere around: on the TV to my left, on the coffee table in front of the sofa to my right, spread out on the pass-through into the kitchen. Flowers, and flowers.

And there above this all, tacked to the walls up at the ceiling, along each of the four walls in here, circling the room entirely, were reindeer heads, their antlers handprints, what seemed when I'd walked in the door this afternoon home from the hospital a thousand of them, a surprise I hadn't been ready for at all,

Brian and Zachary in their Santa hats snicker-
ing behind me even before Gordon'd opened
the front door.

Reindeer heads, all tacked up and hanging
from the walls, each one different, some made
to look like pirates with eye-patches over an
eye, some with gap-teeth where they'd drawn
on a smile, some with cross-eyes or zebra
stripes or horn-rim glasses, one even with *x*'s
for eyes and with a tongue sticking out—
"That one was a roadkill we found," Zachary
said when he'd pointed it out there above the
hallway back to the bedrooms, and Jocelyn'd
reached out a playful hand and slapped at him,
said, "I told you to throw that one away"—but
all of them gracing this home like the good gift
of grace from God you couldn't buy.

"Those boys is off their nut about a half
mile," Gordon'd let out like he always did
when the boys were with him. And of course
Robert'd put in, "You got that right, Pappy,"
and laughed like he always did.

"There's mine," Ashley'd said, and pointed
to the closet door just to the left of the front
door, and there had been her own version of
what the boys'd done: taped to the door was a
full-size silhouette cutout of herself, her feet
turned out like she was standing on ground,

her arms out to either side. It was all on white paper, but the head yet another of the brown construction-paper heads with those handprint cutouts. "See?" Ashley'd said, and hurried to the closet door, Ruth pulling closed the front door behind us. "It's me," she said, and reached up on her tiptoes and pointed at the silver glitter tiara she'd put on it. "It's glue and glitter," she said, and smiled at me.

"It's beautiful," I'd said, and meant it, smiling at her.

"Mine's an ornament," Emily said, and stepped toward the Christmas tree then, pointed out like a girl not any older than her sister to one of the boughs. Settled there on the branch was what looked like a shiny sugar-cookie cutout of a reindeer head, but with all the details painted in: black antlers, black eyes, a red nose. She turned to me, smiling hard and embarrassed for it. She shrugged, said, "I made them in pottery class at school."

"She glazed and fired both of them," Ellen'd said from behind me, and I looked from Emily to the ornament, saw a second one hanging on the next branch over. Two reindeer heads: one for me, and one for Ruth.

"They're both beautiful as can be," I said, and looked at Emily, still with that little-girl smile. I reached out my hands to her, and she came to me, let me hold her a long while, this young woman with a heart big and sure.

"And there's Tess's," Melba'd said, and we'd let go. Melba stood beside me, her arm up and pointing to the first of any of these that'd been made for me, hanging there in the center of the garland of cards above the doorway into the kitchen.

Tess's gift, hanging there, simple and true, the word *Tess* for a smile.

All of them evidence of the innocence in a child's hand, the magical way the outline of who you are can become something else altogether.

It hung there still, here in light from only the Christmas tree at a little past three on Christmas morning, and would hang there as long as I lived, if I knew there wouldn't come another one. But there would, I knew already. There would be paper Easter eggs she and the rest of them might bring me to hang up, and Thanksgiving turkeys and perhaps even autumn leaves pressed between waxed paper, if they could turn up any autumn leaves.

But most important, these children would be here. Here.

I moved out into the room now, felt the joy of a Christmas morning I couldn't have imag-

ined when this story of joy wrapped round in sorrow had begun on a November morning a thousand miles north of here. Joy that'd seemed only a notion, something beyond any reach I could ever muster.

And now, here in the middle of this front room of what I knew was ever and always my home, that sun I'd headed for nowhere to be found beneath the stars fixed in the night sky outside, I could see Ruth.

She was in the kitchen, there at the sink, her back to me, her hands to the edge of the counter, her face to the window above the sink. She hadn't yet gone to bed, I knew: she still had on her jeans, and the blue jersey she'd worn all day long. She had on her slippers, her hair down about her shoulders, all of her given to me only in the light from the tree behind me.

She'd blushed when she saw him that first night, her cheeks and ears and neck flushed with color, her eyebrows together and troubled, her eyes too wide open, her mouth a little open too.

But she'd smiled when he'd put out his hand.

This is my son Mahlon's wife, Ruth, I heard from deep inside me.

And I heard whispered, this time even quieter, but even more certain, *This is my daughter.*

I'd seen Beau as well, seen the blush come over him, seen what I'd thought might be goodness in his eyes, and knew now had certainly been just that: goodness.

I'd seen his hand lifted to touch my crying Ruth the morning after I'd come to the hospital. I'd seen his hand held out to her, willing to comfort, willing to comfort, but holding back for his own fear, his own grief.

Here was the promise of this morning. Here was the way I could do my Eli's gift justice, and love my Mahlon as well. Here was how to give.

I moved to the doorway into the kitchen, above me now the garland of cards, Tess's reindeer head a kind of blessing beneath which I might stand and give comfort.

I stopped, put my hands together in front of me, laced my fingers together to let me hold on, hold on.

"What did he tell you," I said, "that first morning."

She didn't move, and I knew she'd known I was here, and I smiled for this, too, smiled at the all of the miracle of how I could find love in giving love away.

But she said nothing, only breathed in deep, let it out slowly.

" 'It's true,' was all I heard," I said.

That was when she turned to me, and though the light was low, I could see she'd been crying, standing there for as long as she had.

"I thought you were asleep," she said, and crossed her arms. She leaned her head to one side, looking at me, and I smiled, though I knew she could not see my face for the light behind me.

"No," I said.

She let her head fall then, looked at the floor between us, slowly shook her head. "He said," she started, and moved her hands up and down her arms as though she were cold. She took in a breath again. "He said that I was blessed. He said that I was a blessing to you. And that everyone could see how much a blessing I was to you." She paused, breathed out quiet and slow. She looked up at me, her hands still now, but holding on. "He said I was good."

"You are," I said, and though I wanted to move to her, to hold her and give her whatever warmth I might could give, something held me still, here beneath Tess's gift, her comfort in giving comfort.

"But I'm afraid," she whispered, the words slips of air edged with trembling. "I'm afraid of what I feel," she whispered. "And of forgetting Mahlon."

She stopped then, as though the name of my

son and her husband were some kind of miracle itself, a word with enough wonder in it to
keep us both from speaking more.

Mahlon, I thought, then, *Eli.*

Son and father. Husband and husband.

Blessings to us both.

I wanted to speak then. I wanted to tell her
my story, to tell her of Lonny, and the letter I
knew she'd read, and of the difference between
a mistake and sin, of the distance between myself and God I'd put into place with making us
move here.

I wanted to tell her my story. But my story,
I saw in only this moment and in the fact of no
words in me to speak all this, was forgiveness,
my song one of joy, what I'd thought was a
black stone caught in my heart only a hand
held out to me through all these years.

I was here to be a blessing, having been
blessed. Eli's gift to me, I finally saw, had been
my own life back to me, forgiven, and whole.

I said, "Don't be afraid. Because this is God's
mercies, too. What you feel is His gift to you.
It's His gift."

I stopped, still wanting only to hold her, my
daughter. But there were still words I had in
me, lined up suddenly and fully and a surprise.

"I want you just to remember," I whispered,
surprised and surprised at the joy in the words

from me. "Just remember now and again Thursday mornings," I whispered, "and his kiss given to you, the two of you stealing away. Remember that. And remember our mornings together, and the light through the window outside while we talked." I paused, took in a breath, felt it catch in my throat the smallest way. "And I want you to remember how," I started, and heard for a moment the next words lined up in me, and how they could seem silly in my speaking them. But I swallowed down that notion of silly, because it was love I was trying to tell her of. Love true and simple between two friends, love that was passed down to her husband, my son.

I whispered, "I want you to remember how Mahlon loved maple syrup on his biscuits of a morning." I paused, slowly shook my head at the wonder of this all. "Mary Margaret taught me that," I said, "the first day I moved in up to Northampton." I stopped, took in a breath of my own. "Back when we were brides," I said.

Ruth stood there, and I could hear her crying now, that broken silver sound, and I let that sound fill the air between us, let her tears go, for the right they had to be with us.

They were tears of joy, I could hear, for the remembrance of the joy of those moments between us. I let her cry.

And then, in a moment I could not measure, or anticipate, or figure could ever have come to me for how much I loved my son, I said, "Remembering Mahlon won't be a betrayal of him, or of Beau."

Now here between us was this new name. The name of the next blessing God had for Ruth, and I heard Ruth take in a breath, quick and full.

"You brought you here with me," I whispered, and though I'd feared now would be the moment my own tears might come, that tears might overwhelm me for what I'd known I would have to do from the moment there in Beau's arms in the nursing home, when I'd opened my eyes to see my kinsman, my family, still there were no tears in me.

Here was only joy, warm and solid. Here was comfort, in the comforting of my Ruth.

"I'm giving you back you," I said. "Because I love you. Because of the blessing you have been to me."

She came to me then, finally, stepped across a kitchen smaller than the one we spent break-fasts in together all those years, but the distance between us wide and uncharted, so that the moment it took for her to reach me seemed suddenly fearful and full of peril.

Suddenly, in the years it took her to reach

me across this kitchen, I knew my daughter, my Ruth, and the sorrow she herself had known so deeply her own life long: she'd lost her momma, and then her daddy, and then her husband.

I knew her.

And I knew the blessing she would be to Beau, and he to her.

Then she took me up in her arms. "Know how much I love you," she whispered in my ear. "Know how much," she said, and held me, and I held her too, held her, until slowly, slowly she pulled away, and brought her arms from around me.

She paused a moment before she let me go altogether, and I felt her give the gentlest squeeze to my arms, and then she let go, put her hands together in front of her, all the while her eyes on mine here in the dark of Christmas morning.

She held her left hand up between us. She'd lost the smile, but on her face no grief I could see. This was Ruth. This was my daughter. This was a woman I knew.

This was a blessing of God.

And then she did as I'd known she would, all of her own and with no word from me, between us the good knowledge that there was no sin in this, no betrayal nor distance nor loss.

There was only love.

She placed her right hand over the fingers of her left, gently eased off the wedding band on her ring finger, placed there so many years before by a man we both loved and ever would.

She placed the ring in my hand, then with her other hand curled my fingers slowly, painlessly over the ring, and now I could see the tears in her eyes, the shimmer of them for the light from the tree behind me. I saw her smiling, and saw tears.

I saw joy.

Joy I knew needed to be given away.

"You have to go to him," I whispered then, the words from me even more a surprise, and I swallowed, saw what had to be done, saw it clear as I'd heard the song of those tree frogs singing tree to tree to tree, telling a story Eli and I both already knew was all about us.

Ruth blinked, still holding my hand in both hers. She said, "What do you mean?"

"I mean you have to go to him. Be the blessing you already are, and let him be the blessing he's already been to you," and I thought yet again of his hand lifted to touch her, waiting, waiting.

"But—" she began, and stopped, her mouth open the slightest bit, and seeing, seeing.

"Yes," I said. I said, "This is good. Our being here."

It was what she'd said to me our first night to South Carolina, these the same words she'd spoken to me in the darkness of Robert and Beau's old room. When she'd told me of the death of her momma, and the clothes she'd made for Ruth, and Ruth's own fear she might betray her momma if she didn't wear those clothes. Then one day she'd outgrown them, and'd had to step out into trusting herself to buy the right clothes, without a momma to tell her what worked, and didn't work.

Here she was, on the front steps up to the door at the old house. A beautiful young woman in a gray sweater, a plum muffler, and blue jeans. Her hair pulled back, and Mahlon with no way he would take his eyes off her.

Here in my hand was their love, her wedding ring. Not an end to that love, but a moving through it, I could see, to the next story that would be all her own, the next song she would sing herself.

She'd loved my son.

"I—" she said, and her eyebrows gathered a moment, just a moment, her eyes on mine in this darkness that was not darkness at all, but its own light, its own song and story.

Then she smiled. And now here were her fingertips, just touching my temple, the small bit of hair the hairnet didn't protect.

I leaned my face into her hand, the warmth of it. My daughter's hand.

I said, "Now. Go to him. Talk to him." I paused, brought my hand to hers, held it there against my cheek. "He's at the station. It will be fine," I said, and I knew it would. I knew.

There was a different kind of sense to this all, I felt and took hold of, all in this vision of what could be: her, to his station, to begin the two of them now, now. To begin it, their own song. It was possible, here on Christmas morning, with the exchanging of gifts bigger than I could have ever hoped. I'd given her back herself in love, and she'd given me her wedding ring in love as well, all of it, all of it part of something bigger than we two and every soul that'd ever been, every being that'd ever loved: all of it part of the God I'd thought had abandoned me, the God whose mercy seemed hollow, and'd left me bitter, and empty.

And I could see in her eyes now and feel in her hand on my cheek that she saw the possibility as well. She smiled, whispered, "Yes," and gave a small nod. Her hand paused on my cheek, her thumb to my jaw and moving there gently, gently.

"Yes," she whispered again. "But only if you go with me."

"This is about you," I said, and felt myself give a smile that carried inside it a pinch of sadness, a moment of saying *No.* "This is about the two of you," I said, still with my hand to hers.

"You are my family," she said. "I told you before. I didn't come here with you because I had nothing else. I came here because I have you." She paused again, said, "If you feel up to it. If you feel like you can do it. I'm not going without you. And Doctor Brookes said—"

"You don't need me," I said, and slowly shook my head. "You don't need—"

"That's where you're wrong," she said, and she lost a piece of her smile.

She lowered her hand from my cheek, my hand still with hers, and then we were holding hands between us.

And I wondered yet again, Who was Naomi?

Who was she to be so blessed as to have a daughter such as this?

"Your family is my family," Ruth whispered, "just like I told you that night. When I told you I was coming with you. And I came here with you." She paused, took in a breath, the matter of her going to a fire station early of a

Christmas morning sealed just that easily, and my accompanying her sealed just as well.

"Then I'll go," I said, and I put my arms up to her, drew her in to me, and held her.

While I held tight to her wedding ring in my hand, still no pain in my fingers for how tight I held it, and how tight I held on to Ruth.

My daughter, my blessing.

Chapter 26

I PUT ON a pair of slacks and a blouse, fished off my hairnet, put on a pair of wool socks. Just clothing, something to wear, no picking it out, so that we might get there sooner, to whatever might happen when we found our kinsman. There'd been a quiet rush to it all, too, this gathering together of me to accompany my Ruth to meet Beau, to see him, to begin with him the beginning of whatever path they might share between them, a path made clear in love by Ruth giving back to me her ring.

I still held it in my hand, right where she'd placed it. I'd held it while I slipped out of my robe and nightgown, while I'd put on my clothes, shrugged on my coat.

Of course I was slower now, had taken my time with the all of this. But now the heaviness in my heart had lifted, the breaths I took in full and clear and cool, the beat of my heart nowhere near the odd and out-of-step dance it'd been.

It was peace in me as I'd dressed, I'd known, all of it in the dark, all of it in my home.

All of it in this place I'd believed meant something because of the light I'd remembered. But all of it truer now, made more real because, even in the darkness of this night, of this early morning, the world had been made over in love.

Then, once I'd gotten dressed, my coat on and me ready to go, I went to my closet, because there was one further gift had to be bestowed. One last gift on this night of gifts one to another.

I saw it there on the floor of the closet, in the darkness even deeper: a white plastic sack in the corner, precisely where I'd left it when we moved in here, never meaning to open it, never meaning to visit it again for the sorrow and guilt and lack of love I'd let fester in me all these many months we'd been here. When love had been here with me, and joy, and forgiveness. They'd all been here with me, all this while, and now, only now did it seem this gift I myself had gotten from those I loved could be put to good use.

To be given away, like all good gifts received.

I picked it up from the corner of the closet, held the bundle under my arm as I made my way back out to the front room. The room was even darker now, the tree lights off for our leaving. But I could see Ruth at the front door, her only a soft silhouette against the white door.

"What if they're gone?" she said, and I heard on her words the fear in her, the anticipation and worry of what might happen next. "What if they're out on a call? Or just getting back? Or if one comes in while we're there?" They were words of worry not over the possibility of what she'd uttered, I knew, but words rushed and fearful of what this morning might hold: the beginning of her own next song.

I thought of Eli, of the two of us walking an oyster-shell road, the evening sky and the growing edge of dark that made the silence between us all the quieter, the small crunch of our steps lonely and pointless, a half-hour walk and whatever talk we could come up with as wide and empty as Charleston Harbor.

But we'd spoken. We'd begun, that evening.

And so I said, "He prayed for you. The morning when I heard him talking to you. When he told you you were blessed. And if he's not there, or he has to go, then we'll wait."

I touched the bundle beneath my arm, said, "That's why I brought this. A quilt," I said, and tapped at it again.

She was still, there in the darkness, and I could hear her breathe, careful and careful and careful. She said, "You have a plan, don't you."

And I said right back to my daughter, "Sometimes I do," then, "I'm praying for you right now." I paused. "That's my plan right now, mine and Beau's both. Just like Tess did for me. Just like she told me that night."

I heard her take in another breath, and another. Then she said, "Thank you," and though I believed I might could still hear that fear, that trembling on her, still she opened the door, in on us the cold air from outside, and the night.

And we left.

ROADS LED one to another in the darkness, not a single car anywhere. This was Christmas morning, not even four o'clock yet, and we made turn and turn and turn, passed through green lights, waited at reds, us moving quick through this town on streets that hadn't been imagined when I was a girl growing up, and there came to me the memory of all the traffic that'd snagged us the day we'd moved here, when rain had banged down on us the whole day long, until at the last moment sunlight had suddenly broken in to give me a mockingbird on a concrete step.

To give me the emptiness of seeking after that which had already passed.

And now, now, we turned off of Longpoint Road onto a side street, this one at the Exxon station a little ways down from the Harris Teeter where I'd met this Beau in the first place, and where I'd seen the goodness in him even if I hadn't wanted to find it there.

Good evening, ma'am, he'd said, and, *Merry Christmas.*

And now we passed an entrance to a Food Lion on the left, next to it a low flat building, out front of it a sign for the preschool it was, and then we turned left onto yet one more little street, to my right and a few yards off across grass a big white warehouse of a building, and I asked, "Where are we?"

"That's the rec center," Ruth said, quiet, like it was some secret, and I turned to her, wondered at why she'd point out a town's rec center in a voice pitched that soft, and I saw she was looking ahead of us, off to my side, her mouth a thin line.

I turned, looked ahead of us, out my window, just as Ruth slowed down, us at a crawl now, and here stood the fire station.

A white brick building, I could see even in the dark. One half, the right, was the truck bays wide and tall, the bays themselves lit up from inside like midday, a fire truck backed into each; the other half was the firehouse itself, a one-story ranch. A flagpole stood out front with no flag up for the night upon us all, a concrete drive out front nearly as wide as the building itself. Woods to the left of it, a row of palmetto trees to the right.

There, leaned against the front bumper of the truck in the left bay, closest to the firehouse, stood a man, alone, and as Ruth edged the car to a stop out here on the road, my side of the car in the grass, I saw the man bring a cigarette to his lips, saw the ember burn bright there at his face.

He was watching us, pushed himself off the bumper, crossed his arms now.

Bill Dupree. The redhead flirt it seemed Jocelyn had eyes for.

But he was a man, I saw. Only that. Working, here on Christmas Day. There was a history to him, too. A heart that had to endure.

Ruth cut off the engine, and the lights. But she didn't move, and I heard her tap the steering wheel with the fingertips of both hands.

I turned to her. She was looking straight ahead, her mouth that same thin line, her fingers still tapping. I could see her chestnut hair down about her shoulders, saw the shadows of her eyes.

She was beautiful, even in this darkness.

She turned to me, quick worked up a smile. "You don't think I should have baked some biscuits?" she said, and I laughed, shook my head, the moment between us of all the fear and worry and sorrow gone for just that instant, and I leaned to her, she to me, and we held each other, held each other, one long last touch before this next story began.

Then we let go, and I said, "There'll be plenty of time for biscuits," and I smiled at her.

It was me to open my door first, to let in light down on us so that I could see into her eyes, catch one more instant of the blue-green so clear and crystalline you could see in them her good heart, constant and certain.

Here she was: Ruth.

"What can I do for you ladies this morn-

ing?" Bill Dupree said then, and I turned, saw
him just a few feet away out my side, his arms
still crossed. He'd lost the cigarette, and had on
his blue T-shirt, and his slacks, boots, him
rocking forward and back on the heels, sizing
us up. I could tell he was smiling, his eyes going from me to whoever it was driving this car:
two women pulling up to a fire station long
before daylight on Christmas morning.

"You're going to catch a cold," I said, and
put both feet to the grass. Here he was beside
me, holding an elbow and helping me up once
he'd seen I was after getting out, and now here
was Ruth beside me already out her door
and around the hood, the three of us out on
the lawn and standing suddenly together, as
though this were what happened all the time.

"We need to see Beau Stackhouse," Ruth
said, and I looked at her. Her arms were
crossed, her purse over her shoulder, her coat
buttoned all the way up.

"Is this an emergency?" he said, and I turned
to him. He'd let go my elbow, had taken a step
back from us, still trying to figure out what
was up in all this, and I said, "Not the kind of
emergency you're thinking of," and I smiled at
him.

He looked to me, then to Ruth, back to me,
then to Ruth once more. "Oh," he said, and

he stood taller, let his arms drop to his sides. "I know you," he said, then, "Sorry," and he took a step to me, put his hand to my shoulder, said, "Are you all right? Are you here for your heart? I mean, Beau told us you were getting home today and that—"

"We're right where we're supposed to be," I said. "Ruth's here to see Beau," I said, and I reached to his hand at my shoulder, patted it. "And don't you worry about me," I said. "I'm fine. And even better than that."

I looked back to Ruth, still with her arms crossed. My car door stood open behind me, and I turned from Bill, leaned into the car, picked up from where I'd laid it on the floorboard between my feet the white plastic sack, this gift I still had to give.

"Beau talked to me," Bill was saying behind me, "and Miss Ruth, if I said anything out of line I apologize for it. I apologize."

Then there came to me the sudden small sound of Ruth laughing, a sweet sound true and bright even in the quiet of it, and I turned from the car, the quilt in its bag in both my hands. Here was Ruth, her arms down now, her purse off her shoulder, a hand out to Bill and touching his arm.

"Beau might worry too much," she said to him, and Bill put his hands to his back pockets,

looked at the ground, and let out a low whistle. "You got that right," he said, and slowly
shook his head.

Then they both were looking at me, there
with the quilt.

"We won't need that," Ruth said. "We'll be
inside," she said.

But I only shook my head slowly, smiled up
at her. "I have a plan, remember?" I said, and
Ruth leaned her head one way, glanced at Bill.

"Now can Ruth get to talk to this man
Beau, or do we have to wait until you get a call
for him to come out?"

Bill smiled, shook his head again. He put a
hand to the back of his neck, rubbed it.
"Well," he said, and let the word drag out a little long. "He's asleep. Been a long night already. Two grease fires, clowns deep-frying
turkeys the night before Christmas, and leaving the rigs unattended in their garages. Both
of them." He shook his head again. "He's
asleep. And there's this saying about letting
sleeping firemen lie."

"But this is an emergency," I said, smiling.
"Only of a different sort." I looked at Ruth,
saw she was biting down on her bottom lip and
smiling just the same.

Bill stopped his hand on his neck, glanced at
us both, shrugged. He crossed his arms again,

said, "Can't argue with an emergency," then, "Let's go on in," and he turned, started up the lawn.

We followed him across the grass, Ruth looking at me and at the quilt as we went. I could see even in the night out here the puzzlement in her, the wonder at what I could mean in carrying a quilt in here.

Then we were on the concrete drive, and inside the bay closest to the house. The truck beside us was big, and seemed new as any fire truck I'd ever seen, the huge number 2 on its door. It was warmer in here, though I could not say why other than we were out of the night air. To my left was a desk of sorts, on it two telephones, another attached to the wall; next to that was a white door into the house itself, past that a row of five or six beige metal lockers. A lawnmower sat down past it all, pushed against the rear wall of the garage.

"I got to let you know this is so against regulations," Bill said, and turned to us, Ruth and I just inside the bay. He smiled at Ruth, then me, winked. "But I got a feeling this is some kind of emergency, if you two are showing up on Christmas Day this early." He paused, shook his head. "Or maybe the two of you are just playing a little Santa Claus."

I looked at him. He was older than I

remembered from that first time in the Harris Teeter, seemed weary somehow, and it came to me: work. This was Christmas Day, and they'd already had two fires to put out.

"Maybe that's all we're up to," I said, and smiled at him, looked to Ruth. "Playing Santa Claus."

She'd crossed her arms again, was biting down on her lip again, and I thought of the fear I'd heard in her words.

But here she was, ready to embark.

Here was Ruth, and it was now that I needed, I saw, to give her what I needed to give, this gift given to me in love surrendered to her in this love too.

Now.

I took the quilt out from under my arm, held it out to her with both hands like the of-fering it had been to me. Ruth looked at me, seemed lost, and lost, and I saw her eyebrows quiver, her chin tremble.

"This is for you," I said.

Still she didn't move.

She'd never laid eyes on it before. I'd left it in the bag I'd gotten it in to this day, the last time I'd seen it myself there in the Friendly's parking lot, even though I'd told them all—Phyllis, and Carolyn, and Hilda, Mary Margaret the only one not there—that it was a gift I would treasure.

"Let me help you with that," Bill said, and here he was beside us, and now without word, without signal between any of us, he was lifting it out of the plastic bag, then stuffed the empty bag into his back pocket, him all motion and meaning and goodwill in helping us here. Ruth swallowed, blinked once, twice, her eyebrows up in whatever it was I was doing in bringing a quilt here, and at the bustle of all this.

And now we were all holding an edge, stepping back and away from each other in the space between a fire truck and the doorway into the house itself, Bill bumping into the row of lockers behind him, me right beside the tire taller than me of the fire truck behind me, Ruth edging close to the desk.

Here it was: a Star pattern, big and sharp right at the center. Around it a ring of handprints, a single circle of them, cut out of all kinds of fabric. Eight of them, left and right alternating, the fingers pointing away from the center.

A halo of hands around the Star.

It was the first time I'd seen it in light, and I began to weep for the beauty of it, and the joy of these hands, and the friendship it meant: hands held out.

And I knew that despite the fact I'd left it in that bag, left it hidden away on the floor of my closet, this was what it meant to treasure it: to give it to my daughter, and to Beau, at this beginning.

I looked up at Ruth, saw her shimmer in my eyes.

"Where did you—" she began, and I shook my head no, smiling as best I could at her, and now she was coming to me, folding the quilt up on an arm and folding it up, and I saw beside me Bill Dupree let go his corner as Ruth picked it all up, saw him step back against the locker altogether, his hands gone to his pockets, his head down at these two women crying.

Then Ruth was holding me, holding me, and I said, "Go to him. Now." I took in a breath, cool and clear and full, and whispered, "Sit beside him, and lay this over you both. Tell him it's an old woman's wish. Because it is a treasure." I paused, let in another cool and abiding breath. "Tell him it's because he's your family, and you're his."

She took in a breath, held it, and then nodded, slowly took a step away from me, her eyes on mine one moment longer, one instant more.

And then she turned, looked to Bill Dupree, who sniffed, rubbed the back of his hand to his eye as though there were something there to irritate him no end.

I smiled, said, "If you would, could you show Miss Ruth to—"

But he was already at the door into the house, nodding without word, and pushing it open. He leaned his head in, no light falling from inside to the concrete floor out here, and then he came back out. His eyebrows were up, and he sniffed again, as though surprised at what could only be the surprise of us here, and carrying on so.

At the surprise, I knew, of seeing the start of this next song.

He nodded to Ruth, pushed the door open a little farther. I could see nothing from where I stood, only the dark wedge of room.

And I watched as Ruth took a step toward him, and another, the quilt draped over her arms, her coat still on, her purse over her shoulder. She was beside him, and she leaned in too, glanced back to Bill, who pointed inside, nodded again.

She turned to me one last time, looked at me.

Here were her eyes, the truth in them, and beauty. It was no wonder my Mahlon had fallen in love with her, and been blessed and blessed and blessed.

Then she turned, went inside, and she was gone.

OUTSIDE THE NIGHT SKY still reigned over this much of Christmas. Outside, the same stars that had been fixed there since before the any of us had ever taken in our first breath still held firm.

Bill Dupree had rounded up two lawn chairs from somewhere once we'd stood there a minute or so, had set them up a few feet out on the driveway. But I hadn't sat down quite yet, instead wanted out here, in this dark, and in this sky I saw was a home all its own.

In a minute I'd take a seat with him, maybe let go the fact Jocelyn was interested in him, if he were good enough for her. But I wouldn't let him know, too, that by every indication I'd seen this night he was a man good enough, good enough.

But for now I stood out in the air, and looked at those stars, thought on a moment to try and see, in my old woman's way, which one up there might be sorrow, and which one joy.

Only then, in looking and looking, seeing stars and stars and stars, did I see that it didn't matter which was which. They were both up there, fixed somewhere in the same night sky of us all.

The both of them a gift from the same God who'd made them both.

And then I looked at my hand, the gnarled fingers of mine that'd been company through this all, the pain there a part of me, and who I was.

Slowly I let them unfurl before me, reveal to me in the darkness the slight and perfect glimmer of a wedding band, held tight in my hand through this all.

A gift back to me so perfect I had no choice but to hold it so tight.

But no choice, too, but to give it back to where it belonged.

I reached to the lapel of my coat, the move so practiced and ready it was no move at all, but this time I reached behind, unfastened the pin that held the locket in place, placed beneath it the hand that held the ring palm up, and I let the locket fall.

Here it was: gold, simple. No filigree to it at all.

I opened it, saw there two photos, each no bigger than a quarter.

Two faces, I could see even in this starlight. Two faces I could see with my eyes closed.

Two faces I knew by heart: Eli, from his Navy portrait, and Mahlon, a baby with his eyes closed in sleep.

I looked at them, looked at them, and then with my fingers I picked up the ring there beside them in my hand, and let this gift from my daughter drop inside the locket, a perfect circle that fit inside a plain gold locket.

I closed it, brought my fingers to my palm until I felt the locket fasten upon itself.

It was warm in my hand.

I closed my eyes, heard whispered so quiet and so deep and so warm in my ear, whispered from somewhere close, somewhere inside me and just beyond touch, *Nice to meet you.*

And I whispered back, *Nice to meet you.*

I opened my eyes, saw again these stars.

Why call me Naomi? I asked one last time, and knew now the answer.

My name is Naomi.

And I am filled.

ACKNOWLEDGMENTS

I want to thank those friends in whose homes much of this book was written: Thomas Lynch, who was so kind as to allow our family a stay in his cottage in Moveen, County Clare, Ireland; Mady Smets and the Peyresq Foundation, who provided for our family an apartment in Annot, les Alpes de Haute-Provence, while I taught at the Campus Europeén, Université de Charleston; and Jeff and Hart Deal, who allowed me untold hours of quiet in their home on Dewees Island. This book could not have been written without your generosity. Nor could it have been written without the prayers and encouragement of my brothers and sisters in Christ at East Cooper Baptist Church, especially the members of the Joint Heirs class, and the Wednesday Night Supper Gang. Finally, I want to thank Eleanor Johnson, a true prayer warrior and woman of Christ, for her prayers, her insight, her faith, and her friendship.

About the Author

Bret Lott is the author of the novels *Jewel,
Reed's Beach, A Stranger's House, The Man Who
Owned Vermont,* and *The Hunt Club;* the story
collections *How to Get Home* and *A Dream of
Old Leaves;* and the memoir *Fathers, Sons, and
Brothers.* He lives with his wife and two sons in
Mount Pleasant, South Carolina.